Praise for *Compulsion*

"Boone's Southern Gothic certainly delivers a compelling mystery about feuding families and buried secrets, not to mention a steamy romance."
—*Booklist*

"Mixes dark spirits, romance, feuding families, and ancient curses into the perfect potion."
—*Justine Magazine*

"A paranormal Southern Gothic with decadent settings, mysterious magic, and family histories rife with debauchery."
—*Kirkus Reviews*

"Skillfully blends rich magic and folklore with adventure, sweeping romance, and hidden treasure . . . An impressive start to the Heirs of Watson Island series."
—*Publishers Weekly*

"Eight Beaufort is so swoon-worthy that it's ridiculous. Move over, Four, Eight is here to stay!"
—*RT Book Reviews,* RT Editors Best Books of 2014

"A little bit *Gone with the Wind*, a little bit *Romeo and Juliet*. . . ."
—*School Library Journal*

"Even the villains and not-likable characters were just so engrossing. I have to say I've already put the sequel on my TBR shelf."
—*USA Today Online*

"Darkly romantic and steeped in Southern Gothic charm, you'll be *compelled* to get lost in the Heirs of Watson Island series."
—Jennifer L. Armentrout, #1 *New York Times* bestselling author

Also by Martina Boone

Compulsion
Persuasion

illusion

HEIRS OF WATSON ISLAND

MARTINA BOONE

Simon Pulse

NEW YORK LONDON TORONTO SYDNEY NEW DELHI

SIMON PULSE

An imprint of Simon & Schuster Children's Publishing Division
1230 Avenue of the Americas, New York, New York 10020
First Simon Pulse hardcover edition October 2016
Text copyright © 2016 by Martina Boone
Jacket photographs copyright © 2016 by Arcangel Images (bridge)
and Getty Images (couple)

For information about special discounts for bulk purchases, please contact
Simon & Schuster Special Sales at 1-866-506-1949 or business@simonandschuster.com.
The Simon & Schuster Speakers Bureau can bring authors to your live event. For more information or to book an event, contact the Simon & Schuster Speakers Bureau at 1-866-248-3049 or visit our website at www.simonspeakers.com.
Jacket designed by Regina Flath
Interior designed by Hilary Zarycky
The text of this book was set in Granjon LT std.
Manufactured in the United States of America
2 4 6 8 10 9 7 5 3 1
Library of Congress Cataloging-in-Publication Data
Names: Boone, Martina, author.
Title: Illusion / Martina Boone.
Description: First Simon Pulse hardcover edition. | New York : Simon Pulse, 2016. |
Series: Heirs of Watson Island | Summary: "Barrie must rescue her beloved
and her family from evil spirits that cursed Watson Island centuries ago"
—Provided by publisher.
Identifiers: LCCN 2016005937 (print) | LCCN 2016031709 (eBook) |
ISBN 9781481411288 (Jacketed Hardcover) | ISBN 9781481411301 (eBook)
Subjects: | CYAC: Families—Fiction. | Love—Fiction. | Spirits—Fiction. |
Supernatural—Fiction. | Blessing and cursing—Fiction. | Orphans—Fiction.
| Islands—Fiction. | South Carolina—Fiction. | BISAC: JUVENILE FICTION /
Legends, Myths, Fables / General. | JUVENILE FICTION / Family / General (see also
headings under Social Issues). | JUVENILE FICTION / Love & Romance.
Classification: LCC PZ7.1.B667 Il 2016 (print) | LCC PZ7.1.B667 (eBook) |
DDC [Fic]—dc23
LC record available at https://lccn.loc.gov/2016005937

To Erin and Susan for their unerring eyes and generous hearts

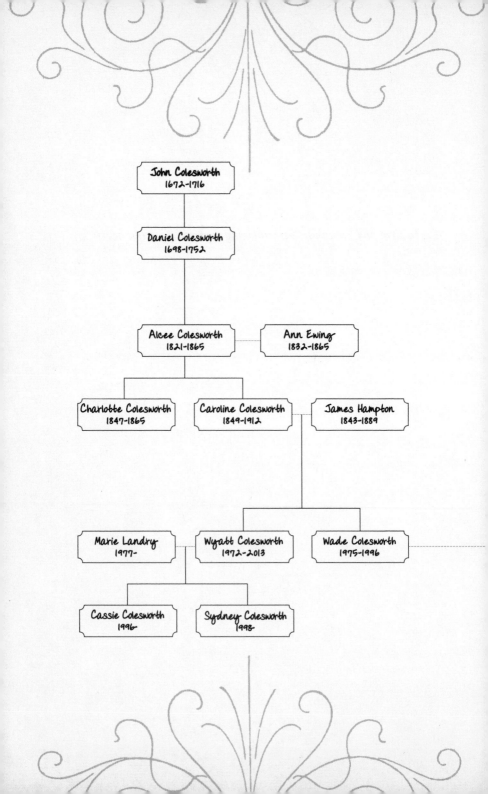

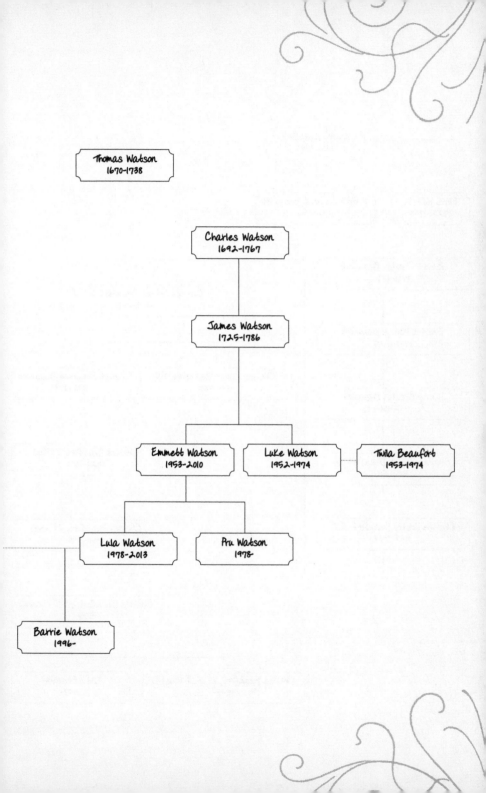

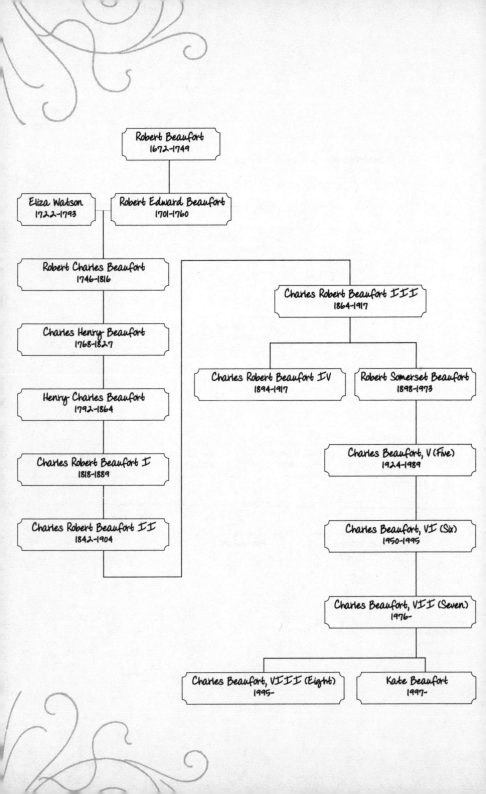

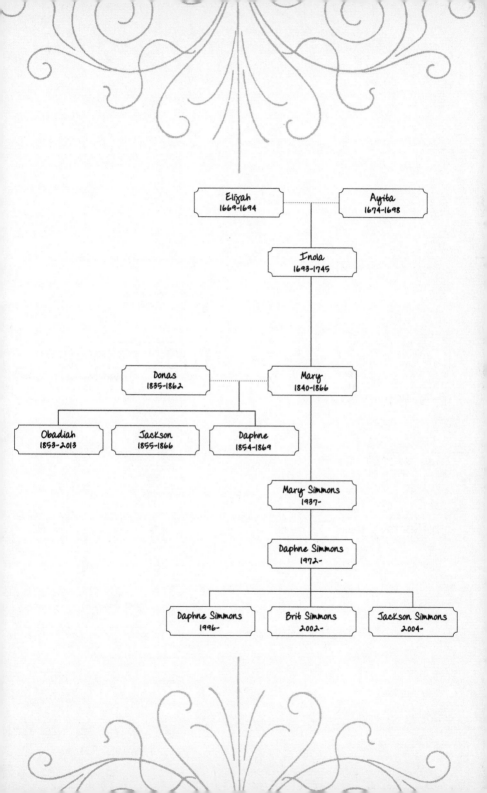

illusion

CHAPTER ONE

Bravery isn't born. It's forged in the nightmare places where fear tears the mind apart. For Barrie Watson, her cousin Cassie's plantation across the river from Watson's Landing had become such a place. There, it was all too easy to see how shards of past events could turn into weapons, until one bad choice led to another, and memories became prisons that trapped people as surely as any door.

Between the memories and the migraine that always formed when she was away from Watson's Landing, Barrie fidgeted in the passenger seat of her aunt Pru's old, black boat of a Mercedes. The sun-pinked skin exposed by her sleeveless top stuck to the leather in the sodden Southern heat and plastered her long, pale curls to the nape of her neck. Her traitorous fingers itched to grab the steering wheel and tell her aunt to turn around. Even the sun slanting low through the oaks that lined the winding drive seemed to whisper a warning, transforming the veils of Spanish moss into something ghostly and macabre.

But Barrie couldn't change her mind. No matter how excruciatingly hard she had tried to make the right choices recently, she had kept hurting other people. She had to set that right, and the first step began here at Colesworth Place.

Pru eased the Mercedes to a stop at the edge of the visitor lot closest to where the lane continued on toward the ruins of the old plantation mansion and the smaller, modern house where Cassie and her family lived. Barrie adjusted the foil over the chicken casserole that Pru had hastily assembled and pushed the door open. Pru didn't move. Sitting there with her hands gripped tightly at the top of the steering wheel, her fine, blond curls haloed around her in the fading light, Barrie's aunt resembled a lovely and slightly demented angel.

Barrie hated what all this was doing to her. "Are you all right, Aunt Pru?"

Pru's lips lifted wryly. "Look at us. We're a fine pair, aren't we? I'm trying to talk myself into getting out of this car, and for all your determination, you look like you'd rather turn around and run." She reached out and touched Barrie's wrist. "Let's just go on home, sugar. At least for tonight. You don't owe it to your cousin to break the Colesworth curse, and you certainly don't owe a thing to this Obadiah, or whatever that magician of yours calls himself."

"I'm not sure 'magician' is the right word, exactly. More like a shaman," Barrie said, avoiding the question.

"You know I ought to have my head examined for even considering letting you come over to look for him, don't you? Not that I seem to be able to prevent you from doing anything. I wish you'd just forget all this."

"We can't forget. This isn't about owing Cassie or Obadiah. We can't walk away when the curse is hurting Mary and her family, too. And Obadiah promised he would break the Beaufort binding if I found the Colesworth treasure. If we don't break that, Eight will be stuck at Beaufort Hall when Seven dies, and I'll be across at Watson's Landing, and we'll have no chance of ever being together. Too many things all center on Obadiah being able to help us. At the very least, I have to know whether he's still alive."

"Can you call it living when someone is more than a hundred and fifty years old? I'm still not sure I believe that, but it's one more reason why I ought to be grounding you for a month instead of bringing you over here and letting you get involved with that man again."

Switching off the ignition with an emphatic motion and a jingle of keys, Pru sat there a moment looking so small and defenseless that it made Barrie's heart swell with guilt. But

Pru was stronger than she looked. The more Barrie had come to know her aunt, the more she had seen the quiet core of steel that Pru didn't even know she possessed.

Strength was a bit like courage, Barrie thought. She herself had found both only when she couldn't live without them, and they had come to her when she had needed them the most. But fighting to protect the people you cared for was one thing. Trusting someone you loved to fight for themselves took a different kind of strength and bravery.

Leaning over from the passenger seat, she dropped a kiss on Pru's smooth-skinned cheek. "Thank you, Aunt Pru."

"For what?" Pru looked over, startled.

"For not grounding me. For coming over here to help distract Cassie's mother. For believing in me and not telling me that letting Obadiah take away the Watson gift like he threatened would have been the obvious solution."

Pru's smile was misty-eyed and ephemeral, and she pushed the door open with fresh determination. Barrie, too, got out, and they stood on the brittle and cracking asphalt looking at each other across the top of the car. "I'm sorry I yelled at you when you told me everything. The fact that I did that makes it harder for you to be honest with me in the future, I know that, and I promise you, I'm through with ignoring problems and hoping they'll go away on their own. I'm done with letting life happen to me instead of living it. Obadiah's already had plenty of opportunities to hurt you, if that was what he wanted, and anyway, if he can change himself into a raven and make himself invisible, there's not much you and I are going to do to stop him coming to Watson's Landing. I'm already having enough nightmares about—"

Barrie looked over as Pru cut herself off. "About what?"

"Never you mind." Pru pushed her old-fashioned white patent purse up to the crook of her elbow and slammed the door. "My point is that you were right. As much as I wish we could, we can't leave things the way they are."

They set off shoulder to shoulder through the trees that cut the visitor parking area off from the cemetery where Cassie's father had so recently been interred. Pru's expression was unreadable, but the kitten heels of her shoes clicked on the asphalt in a decisive rhythm. Barrie juggled the casserole, and as they rounded the corner, the shoebox house where the Colesworth family lived came into sight at the edge of the woods between the Colesworth property and Beaufort Hall. Farther on, toward the river, the ruined columns and crumbling chimneys of the old mansion cast long shadows over the kitchen, slave cabins, and other outbuildings that Wyatt Colesworth had been obsessed with restoring. Watched over by a dozen ravens perched at the top of the columns, the archaeological dig area that had recently been torn up by violence was surrounded by yellow police tape, and on the far side of it, two sheriff's deputies sat in their cruiser beneath a thick-trunked oak.

A sickening wave of lostness pulled at Barrie from the dig site, a physical reminder that, regardless of what she wanted, her gift wouldn't let her walk away. Along with the lodestone that anchored the Colesworth curse and the angry spirits who had cast the evil magic—not to mention eight million dollars, give or take, of stolen Union gold—Charlotte Colesworth's skeleton was still buried down there. Somebody had to get her out, and the archaeologists had already made it clear they were going to continue the excavation.

That was the problem with Watson Island. There were too many secrets and dangers lurking beneath the surface, waiting for someone to stumble over them.

All three of the pirates who had founded the plantations— Watson's Landing, Beaufort Hall, and Colesworth Place—had built secret tunnels and rooms so well hidden that they'd long been forgotten, the way unpleasant things in a family's past were easier to forget when you shut them away. Their descendants had locked the doors, sealed the rooms, moved to the other side of oversize mansions, or let the grass soften the ashes and crumbled bricks of the families' mistakes. They'd put statues of angels with fists raised against the sky over empty graves.

Hiding things was easier than repairing the damage that

they had all left behind them. Barrie had learned the hard way that when it came to emotions, you couldn't heal until you acknowledged what was lost. And thanks to the bindings that came with the magic in all three families, none of the eldest heirs could leave the plantations without suffering migraines that in the past had driven people crazy or moved them to suicide. There was no way to escape.

Thinking of the bindings made Barrie stop abruptly. "Would you mind going ahead without me for a minute, Aunt Pru? I want to try Eight again before I talk to Cassie. I'm worried that he still hasn't called me back."

"Of course." Pru adjusted her purse and took the casserole dish Barrie handed her. Then she patted Barrie on the cheek. "Don't worry too much if he won't talk yet, though. He's got a good streak of the Beaufort stubbornness, but as mad as he may be that you didn't tell him about the binding, you'd only known about it a couple of days. His father kept it from him his entire life. Those two have a lot of ground to cover, and I've no doubt that's keeping Eight distracted."

Barrie wished she were as certain of that as Pru. She dialed Eight's number while her aunt walked on toward the small brick house with its too-bright shutters and overly ornate front door.

The phone rang and rang. Then abruptly Eight's voice

was there, that soft drawl with a sultry hint of gravel. "Stop calling me, Bear. I'll call you when I can talk."

Eleven little words, that was all, but his voice was raw. Barrie wondered if she'd ever stop seeing him the way he had looked that morning at the dig site when she'd finally told him about the Beaufort binding. A salt-edged breeze from the Atlantic had swept up the Santisto River to stir his hair, and his lips had still been reddened from kissing her. But he'd hunched in on himself as if she'd hit him when he'd realized she had known he was going to inherit the binding that would confine him to the place he'd been wanting to escape from all his life.

Barrie's breath hitched, and she felt stupid and lost all over again. In the time that she had known him, Eight had shown her weaknesses inside herself she would never have explored without him, shown her possibilities she had never even considered. Holding the phone to her ear, she looked out across the excavation area, where the evening sunlight glinted on the plastic sheeting that covered the hole that Ryder's and Junior's pickaxes had made in the arched ceiling of the hidden room that morning. The sight was a reminder of what happened when you tried to keep secrets buried.

"Tell me we can fix this, Eight. Tell me what I can do," she said. "At least tell me you're all right."

"How can I be all right? My entire life has been a lie, and

the future I wanted isn't going to be a possibility. You knew that, and you didn't tell me. You made choices for me because you didn't think I could handle the truth—"

"I never intended to make decisions for you. I was only going to help Obadiah break the curse before I told you—I wanted to be sure it was possible and safe before I got your hopes up about him breaking the Beaufort binding—" Barrie cut herself off and sighed. "It sounds like I'm making excuses for myself, and I don't mean to do that. I was wrong. I know I was wrong. I should have told you. At first Obadiah's magic was messing with my ability to tell you anything, and then I thought that if you and your father were ever going to have any kind of a relationship again, he needed to be the one to tell you, but that wasn't fair to you."

"You're still making excuses. I don't need you to protect me. You chose your gift over me, and you didn't trust me to understand the choices you were making. You lied to me. Over and over again, and I always forgave you. This time, I'm not sure I can. All along, you've been worried about my gift making me want what you want and about whether I want you for yourself. I never cared about that, but I don't want someone who can't be honest with me. I don't want to be with anyone who manipulates me. I get enough of that at home. And since my gift makes it harder for me to separate what I want from what you want, at least for now, I can't be with you."

Barrie stared at the ground. There wasn't anything she could say to counter that. All she could do was tell him how she felt. "I should have explained. You're right. I was afraid of losing my gift, and I should have trusted you to understand. I should have known you would. I don't want to lose you, Eight. Don't shut me out. I get that you need some space, but give me a chance to show you that I can do better. I swear I can. I want you to be involved in all the decisions from now on. I'm over here at Colesworth Place, and the archaeologists are coming back to start digging again tomorrow. We still have to get rid of the curse—"

"*We* don't have to do anything. I'm done caring about Cassie, her curse, or her stupid treasure. I have my father to deal with, and I have to go to Columbia tomorrow to meet with the baseball coach again and finalize things at the university for next semester." He paused, and his voice grew softer. "I'm not sure I'm going to come back."

"What do you mean?" Barrie's chest clenched, and for the first time since Eight had walked away from her that afternoon, she let herself consider the possibility that she couldn't fix what she had broken between them. That he was really done. But she couldn't—wouldn't—consider that. "Don't leave," she said. "Running away doesn't solve any problems. You're the one who taught me that. We have to talk—"

"No," Eight said. "We don't. My whole life is up in the air, and I need to figure it out myself."

He hung up before Barrie could say anything else, and she stood with tears burning her eyes and the phone digging into her hand, listening to the silence, as if by some miracle Eight would pick up again and assure her that he'd eventually forgive her. That they could find a way to work things out. But miracles didn't happen, and no form of magic would let her rewind her mistakes. She couldn't make him get over the way she'd hurt him or forget that she hadn't trusted him with the truth.

She had to find a way to fix things. Hurting Eight was the very last thing she had ever meant to do. Losing him had shown her that she couldn't bear to lose him.

She looked up as a bird fluttered out of the lower branches of an oak to perch on the upraised arm of the angel statue above Charlotte's grave. Feathers ruffled and yellow eyes bright, it cocked its head to peer at her. Barrie's heart filled with outrage and dread and hope in equal measure, because it was Obadiah who had pushed her into all of this with his magic and his threats. She reached out toward the bird with her own magic, but she was still too inexperienced, too uncertain of the way the Watson gift had been growing and changing since her mother's death.

The raven wasn't lost. It didn't need returning. As to

whether it was one of the ravens that often accompanied Obadiah or the man himself, on that subject, her gift was stubbornly unhelpful.

Taking a step toward the bird, Barrie held her hand out. "Obadiah? Is that you?"

CHAPTER TWO

The crunch of a footstep on the asphalt behind her made Barrie turn, and she found Cassie coming up the path alongside the cemetery fence. Like Barrie, she was watching the raven that stood hunched on the branch above Charlotte Colesworth's grave with its head cocked toward them.

"You think the bird is Obadiah?" Cassie asked. "On the phone, you said you thought he was down by the excavation area, where Ryder and Junior shot him."

The raven opened its beak, but no sound came out. He hopped once on the branch, then flew away. Barrie turned to watch him fly over the excavation area and land back on top of one of the columns that overlooked the mansion ruins. "I'm not sure what I think anymore. All I know is that I noticed the police and the archaeologists walking around an empty spot

on the grass where Obadiah was lying the last time we saw
him, the way people walk around Obadiah when he's hanging
around not wanting to be seen. He may still be there soaking
up energy from people and trying to heal, or he may have run
off or flown off somewhere, or he may have crumbled into
dust for all we know. I want to be sure."

A breeze lifted, raising the scent of tannin and pluff mud
from the river and flinging Cassie's tumbled black curls into her
eyes. She wore none of her usual sass and bravado. Her beautiful face was bare of makeup, telling its own story about what
she'd been through, and it felt wrong to Barrie to have even
dragged her back outside after everything that had happened.

She caught her cousin's elbow as Cassie turned back
toward the small house where she lived with her family. "If
you'd rather not help with this, I can do it on my own. And
if you need someone to talk to . . . I know we haven't exactly
been the best of friends, but I'm here if you need anything."

"I don't need your pity," Cassie snapped. She stared at the
angel statue above Charlotte Colesworth's grave long enough
that Barrie began to wonder if Cassie was having another of the
flashbacks that had started after her father's funeral, but then
Cassie turned abruptly and hurried down the path. Her long,
flared jeans swished angrily around the outline of the ankle
monitor the police had replaced after Barrie had smashed the
first one that morning to summon help.

Barrie walked after her with an inward sigh. "You and I need to find a way to get along if we're going to figure out the curse situation. I was only trying to see how you're holding up."

"How do you think I'm holding up? Why do people even ask that question? Am I supposed to lie to make you all feel better? Pretend Ryder didn't rape me? I hate that everyone knows. You. Berg. The police. My family. People in town. Half of them are wondering if I made it up. Even my mother. She keeps asking me why I hid it, as if I betrayed her by not confiding in her. But she and Daddy didn't want to know. That's why they never asked the question. Even with Ryder's threats, I kept waiting for them to ask. I felt so different that—" Her breath snagged on the last sentence, the way people sometimes struggle with a foreign language, as if it were still impossible to admit what had happened to her four years before.

Barrie's eyes stung at the pain in Cassie's voice. She searched for something to say. There were so many words in the world, so many ways to communicate, and somehow, too often none of them were good enough.

Cassie walked faster, her stride longer than Barrie's so that Barrie had to jog to keep up. Beneath the oak tree at the far edge of the excavation site, the passenger door of the sheriff's patrol car opened, and one of the deputies got out. Adjusting the utility belt that hung low on his hips, he ambled bowleggedly toward the area ringed by police tape, looped around once, stopped, and peered at Barrie and Cassie, before sauntering back to the car again.

"Maybe your mother feels guilty," Barrie said when he had gone. "Not only for what you went through, but for not having seen how you were suffering. She has to be thinking of all the ways she failed you."

"I shot the man who raped me. I shot him, and she's worrying about her own guilt," Cassie said.

"Worrying about having failed you is probably normal—"

"And then she asked me why I shot Ryder, whether it was because of that or because he tried to steal the gold."

Barrie herself wasn't sure that was an "or" question where Cassie was concerned. "The police said it was self-defense," she said softly. "They're not pressing charges, after all, are they?"

"Not for now." Cassie reached the front steps of the house, and then she turned with her foot on the bottom stair. Anger crackled out of her every pore, but it was the kind of anger that was a form of armor, a way to hide her brokenness the way that Pru hid hers with quiet acceptance. Maybe everyone in the world was a little broken, pretending to others that they weren't.

"I just want this to be all over with!" Cassie cried suddenly. "Is that too much to ask? The curse, the archaeologists, all of it. If Obadiah's still here waiting to steal the gold, then I want him gone. It's mine. I can't leave, and my family and I need the gold to keep this place. He doesn't get to take it. But if he's here, that means Ryder and Junior didn't manage to kill him when they shot him. So how do we get rid of him? I couldn't even tell the police that he was here. My throat felt stuck whenever I tried to say his name."

Barrie looked out toward the dig site where the police tape fluttered in the breeze that came up from the river. A single raven gathered its wings and took off from a broken column and flew a wide, lazy circle toward the woods.

"I think we just have to take it one step at a time," she said. "Let's see if Obadiah's even here. Most of all, we can't jump to conclusions anymore. We don't know what Obadiah was doing when Ryder and Junior interrupted him," she said. "We don't even know for sure that he was the one who tied us up and put us in the cabin."

"God, how can you still be so naïve?" Cassie's breath was too loud as she climbed the remaining two steps toward the door. "But then you can afford to trust him. It's not your curse or your gold he's after. You've never been poor. You've spent your whole life locked away in your neat little corner of the world where everything's been taken care of for you, and you've never been unsafe or uncertain of anything for a single minute."

Given what Barrie had been through over the past few weeks, what Cassie and her family had put her through, a half-hysterical laugh bubbled up in Barrie's throat. Not that there was any point in arguing. Cassie was never going to see past the preconception of the charmed life she believed the Watsons and the Beauforts led. Maybe that was another symptom of the Colesworth curse, or maybe it was Wyatt filling his daughter's head with poison for too many years.

The door opened behind Cassie, and she stood back out of the way. Pru and Marie Colesworth came out with a pitcher of tea and a tray of sandwiches covered with a blue-checkered dishcloth, and a few minutes later, Barrie accompanied Cassie to the police car with the food. She stopped there only long enough to hold up the earring she had brought and to mumble an explanation about needing to search for its mate.

At the excavation site, the neatly measured squares cleared by the archaeologists had been obliterated by the illegal digging. The soil was a torn mess of dirt and brick chips, and the datum, the piece of iron rebar used to set the measurement standards for the dig's grid layout, lay where it had fallen when the spirits of Ayita and Elijah had thrown it, thirty feet from where they had ripped it from the ground.

Circling around the police tape that cordoned off the circumference of the hidden room, Barrie concentrated on remembering exactly where she had seen the police and archaeologists deviate around a seemingly bare spot of lawn. She searched for a hint—some sign she didn't even know how to look for. There was only the broken soil and the usual headache.

Then something grasped her ankle. Brittle finger bones ground against her skin with a touch so cold that it sank straight to Barrie's marrow. She felt her strength ebb away.

CHAPTER THREE

Icy panic clogged Barrie's veins, demanding that she run. But her body didn't want to cooperate, and she wasn't sure if that was fear or magic. Her heart beat too fast, too uselessly, and her chest clenched, her breath coming in and in and in, until she finally remembered she needed to exhale, too, or she wouldn't actually be breathing.

Bitter cold spread through her limbs. She recognized the draining sensation of Obadiah taking energy, but this was nothing like what he had ever done before. Where he had always taken barely noticeable amounts, like sips through a juice box straw, now he was gulping from an open glass, greedy and insatiable.

She swayed and struggled to break his hold on her ankle. Stumbling, she fought to stay on her feet. Her head spun. Her vision tunneled.

And then nothing.

She woke to find Cassie shaking her and someone still holding her ankle. The sensation of energy draining away was gone, though, and the touch was warmer. She tried to kick free, but her limbs were heavy, as if each arm and every finger weighed five hundred pounds.

"What happened?" Cassie asked, her face pale and her eyes dark with fear. "What are you doing? Did you pass out? Or did Obadiah do something?"

Barrie tried to scream, but opening her mouth was too impossibly hard.

"Hold still, *petite*. You'll have some strength back in a moment." The words came from the seeming emptiness beside her, and then the air shimmered and Obadiah flickered into sight.

He was himself and not. Himself but forty years older: the same dreadlocks that grew past his shoulders; the same dark, shiny silk suit and black silk shirt; but his skin and flesh had shriveled like a sponge wrung out of liquid. For once, his clothes were less than immaculate, and dried blood surrounded a hole in the fabric suspiciously near his heart.

Lying rigidly on the ground, he continued to hold her ankle and made no effort to get up himself. "I'm sorry," he said softly. "I had no right to take so much energy from you—I got carried away before I could control myself. I'm giving some back. Just wait a moment."

Warmth slipped back into Barrie's limbs, and with it came the realization of how cold and weak she had really been. Panting and still light-headed, she lay unmoving until he finally released his hold.

Cassie shook her again. "Talk to me, Barrie. Are you all right?"

Barrie wiggled her fingers, and when that worked, she held her hand out for Cassie to help her up.

"I'm fine." She sat up cautiously and stole a glance in the direction of the sheriff's deputies, who were both climbing out of their car. "Go over there and tell the police that I'm clumsy and stupid, would you? Keep them from coming over here." Raising her voice, she called out herself, relieved when her voice sounded relatively normal: "It's all good! I tripped on a piece of brick."

Cassie straightened and peered down at her. "You should have seen yourself. You looked like a ghost. It was Obadiah, wasn't it? He's still here after all."

"Don't you see him now?" Barrie shook her head. "Never mind. I'll explain later. Just go. Get the deputies back into their car." She waited until Cassie had gone before switching her attention back to Obadiah.

No matter what he'd done to her, seeing him lying there, Barrie couldn't suppress a twinge of sympathy. Which made her six kinds of a fool. Cassie had been right—she kept trusting people she had no business trusting.

With obvious effort, Obadiah rolled to his stomach and climbed to his feet like an old, old man. Despite the energy that he had taken from her—and presumably from Cassie—his blue-black skin appeared gray and sunken. Barrie's own limbs still felt heavy and lethargic as she wobbled several steps away from him. Not that he needed to touch her physically to take energy, but right now she felt like she imagined a battery would feel with its meter running low.

"You owe me an explanation for what you did," she said, her voice sounding weak and thready.

He squinted over to where Cassie was exerting all her charm getting the two deputies back into their vehicle. "I am sorry. It's nearly impossible not to reach for energy when you're desperate. I stopped as soon as I realized what I was doing."

"Not just now!" Barrie made an impatient gesture. "Everything. Tying us up and throwing us inside the cabin. Trying to steal the gold. Did you *ever* think you could break the curse? Or was that just another lie to get me to help you?"

Obadiah hobbled away toward the row of restored brick slave cabins that sat in the shade of the woods. Cabins where he himself must have worked as a slave before he ran away as the Union troops approached in search of the gold that Alcee Colesworth had stolen. Barrie shivered at the thought of going back there, remembering the horror of being tied up in the cabin even briefly, the sense of complete helplessness. She couldn't even imagine the kind of memories the place held for Obadiah.

"Stay here and talk to me," she said. "All of this has gone too far."

"I'll talk, but I don't have the strength to keep us hidden from the police. We'll have to get out of sight. Where's the Beaufort boy? You didn't come over here by yourself, did you?"

"Don't try to change the subject."

"Energy *is* the subject, *chère*. I had no intention of hurting you, and I very nearly killed you. I took as much from the Colesworth girl just now as I dared. But Elijah and Ayita are even more desperate than I was. They have no reason to hold themselves back. There are also two of them, and desperation and powerful spirits are a dangerous combination. The first person who gets close enough to that room is going to die."

Hunched and stumbling, he continued his progress toward the cabin even as he spoke, and Barrie had no choice but to follow him. "So then their spirits are definitely still there?" she asked. "What about the curse?"

"Very much also there, but we have an opportunity now—a small one. Ayita and Elijah spent nearly all their strength bringing me back this morning when those two idiots shot me, so it will be some time before they can reach beyond the room where they're confined again."

Out of sight of the sheriff's deputies and the windows of the Colesworth house, Obadiah stopped by the overseer's cabin at the end of the slave street to catch his breath. Barrie stopped beside him.

"Brought you back from where?" Barrie couldn't help asking.

"Death. The other side." Bracing his hands on his knees, Obadiah looked even more gray than he had before. "For the moment, Ayita and Elijah are spent and too weak to break past the magic that confines them in that underground room. They won't have much strength to fight me if I bind them and then try to break the curse."

"Isn't that a good thing? There's a 'but' coming, though, isn't there?"

Obadiah's dreadlocks swung forward to screen his face. "I'll need more energy than I can get here; I learned that much this morning."

Feeling dizzy and speechless at his audacity, Barrie stared at him. "You don't honestly think I'm stupid enough to fall for that a second time, do you?" she asked at last. "You've been saying all along that you're not strong enough to break the curse. But you certainly tried the second the archaeologists left the property. Why don't you just admit you're after the gold?"

The words fell between them like a gauntlet. Obadiah straightened and looked down at her with his eyes glittering and his expression cold. "I've never lied to you, *petite*, and I never made a secret of what I wanted. That first night, I hoped to bind the spirits, remove the curse, and then take the gold from the Colesworths to give Ayita the revenge she's waited for all these years and leave her in peace. She's going to require a sacrifice, one way or the other."

"No sacrifices." Barrie's eyes flew to the bracelet around his wrist. Human teeth.

He gave a sudden rusty laugh and shook the bracelet at her. "Do these scare you? The teeth represent pain. *My* pain. Magic always requires a payment."

He reached into his mouth. With a wrench of his fingers, he extracted a set of false teeth, several of them gold, and shook them at her. "That's the true difference between good and evil, between light magic and darkness. Good pays the price for others. Evil forces others to pay," he said, with the words slurring wetly. Then he placed the teeth back into his mouth before continuing. "I didn't plan what happened this morning. If I'd had more time, I would have treated you and the Colesworth girl more gently. But Elijah and Ayita had made themselves weak destroying the dig site overnight, and I had energy available from the two of you and the Beaufort boy, and when the archaeologists left to replace their broken equipment, it was the perfect opportunity. I hoped I'd finally be able to bind the spirits and break the curse. Even now, I don't have the luxury of shame. The situation's only grown more dangerous."

Slowly, Barrie unclenched her fingers. "Why?" she asked. "You said Ayita and Elijah are confined and weak."

"And what if one of the archaeologists or the sheriff's deputies step over the police tape to look around? Even if everyone stays where Ayita and Elijah cannot reach them, there are small amounts of energy everywhere: in the air, the trees, the rocks. Since she first cast the curse, Ayita has been content to let that work out her revenge, but now yet another Colesworth has tried to kill a member of her family—for all intents and purposes, Ryder Colesworth did kill me. I *felt* Ayita's fury. She and Elijah have had three centuries to learn to project their influence beyond their prison, and it won't be long before they are able to take energy from whoever is unfortunate enough to pass within ten yards, or twenty or thirty yards instead of a few inches or feet. It's mainly Colesworth blood she and Elijah will be after, but that doesn't mean anyone else is safe."

There was no reason to trust him. None at all. Barrie wanted nothing more than to turn on her heel and walk away, but instinct and her gift still stubbornly pulled her toward him for some reason that eluded her.

"What is it that you want from me?" she asked. "You said yourself that even at your strongest it wasn't enough to break the curse."

Obadiah straightened to his full height and looked down at her. "I do have a possible solution. You won't like it."

"I don't like any of this," Barrie said.

Obadiah's gaze shifted away, somewhere across Barrie's shoulder, and his eyes darkened. "There's a spirit path, a dragon line, that runs through here and splits on Watson Island, leaving a vortex of positive energy in the woods there, and a vortex of negative energy at Beaufort Hall, before coming back together again. Depending on where the Watson and Beaufort lodestones are buried, they may have absorbed enough power to let me break the curse. I need you to bring them both to me here."

Barrie went still. "Why both?"

"If either or both of the stones are too near a vortex, they might have absorbed energy of only one polarity. Magic requires balance." Obadiah looked down at his own lined hands, the nails carefully trimmed and pinkly pale. His expression was impossible to read, as if he'd deliberately emptied it.

Empty was how Barrie felt at that moment, too. Empty of anger or even disappointment. She knew what was coming before she asked the question. "What happens to the magic in the lodestones if you use the energy stored in them? To the gifts and bindings?"

Obadiah shrugged, but regret, or something like it, flashed through his eyes. "I'm sorry, *petite*. I know how much it means to you to keep the Watson magic."

The emptiness inside Barrie expanded until it filled her lungs and made every organ and limb feel numb. She needed to get a grip on herself. Still, what had she expected? She had known from the beginning that Obadiah wouldn't play fair.

Risking her gift, the *yunwi*, and the future of Watson's Landing was exactly what she'd wanted to avoid. That, and she'd been trying to make sure that removing the magic was safe for Eight and Seven.

Every instinct in her rebelled at the thought of giving the lodestones to Obadiah. Maybe even that was the magic protecting itself. "Can you promise me that no one would get hurt if you broke the bindings?" she asked. "What if there's some sort of self-preservation mechanism built in to protect the gifts, the way the migraines try to keep us from being away from the plantations too long?"

"I'd have to examine the lodestones before I could begin to guess if that's true."

A nightjar called its own name somewhere in the woods, and the lonely, haunted sound echoed the way Barrie felt. The sun was setting, painting the sky in smoke, soot, and crimson.

"You're asking me to trust you with the whole future of Watson's Landing—not to mention Beaufort Hall—based on guesses. How do I know you'll ever be strong enough—or skilled enough—to succeed? You let Ryder and Junior shoot you—"

"No one else was around when I started to bind the spirits! No one to see or interfere, and I needed all my energy and concentration for the magic."

"That's my point! You couldn't keep yourself from getting shot when you were at your strongest. How am I supposed to have any confidence in you now?" Shaking her head, Barrie rubbed her arms against a sudden chill. "I'm sorry, but there has to be another way. Perform an exorcism. Never mind binding the spirits or appeasing them!"

Obadiah leaned away from her, and his breath hissed dangerously. "Destroy them, you mean? They deserve rest after everything they've been through. Not more pain. John Colesworth didn't just murder Elijah. He set his bones into the wall of the treasure room as a warning to the other slaves, and he drilled the bricks with iron stakes and mixed the mortar with salt and holy water. Later, when he discovered that Ayita had cursed him, he had her bones seared in lye and ground into dust. He mixed that with salt and scattered it into the floor, then bricked it over again. It takes more strength than you can imagine for a spirit to survive a thing like that. The kind of strength that comes with hate and pain."

Sickened at the image conjured by Obadiah's words, Barrie found it impossible to comprehend the kind of evil that would do something like that—the kind of evil that took the horror of slavery from life and extended it into death. Then again, it was impossible to comprehend how someone could think they had any right to hurt or control another person.

In the deep blue sky above the sunset colors, the moon had appeared, a pale curved shadow in the dusk. Obadiah gently pulled Barrie back to face him. "*Petite*, I need your help. I can keep the police and the archaeologists away from the room for a while, but only as long as the spirits can't reach very far beyond their prison. That's why you need to find the lodestones."

Barrie searched his expression. Although she found nothing that said he was lying, she couldn't accept what he said. Somewhere, somehow, there had to be another way. She needed more information. Not just about the lodestones and the Fire Carrier's magic, but about Obadiah himself.

"I have to think about it," she said. Turning her back on him before he could argue—or use whatever brand of power he had left to talk her into something—she walked away.

"Don't think too long," he called after her. "We don't have time for that."

CHAPTER FOUR

Cassie's longer legs easily kept up with Barrie's stride as she rushed toward the car ahead of Pru. "What do you mean you don't know if you can give the lodestones to Obadiah?" Cassie demanded. "You have to find them for him if Ayita and Elijah are after Colesworth blood."

"I'm not even sure I could find them. And what happened to not trusting Obadiah? Why are you suddenly so willing to accept what he says without questioning it?" Barrie wished she hadn't promised herself she would be honest with everyone. She'd had no choice but to warn the Colesworths about the spirits, but as for the rest? What was the point of giving Cassie hope when Barrie couldn't do what Obadiah wanted?

"What if Ayita and Elijah *kill* someone?" Cassie

demanded, sounding half-hysterical. "My family or the dig crew or the sheriff's deputies. How would we explain what had happened? The police will accuse me of having caused it. You know how everyone likes to blame me for everything. I haven't even had the final pretrial intervention hearing, and the judge will send me back to the detention center. I can't go back there. The migraines will kill me—and then Sydney would inherit them."

"First, we have a lot of things to worry about before that one," Barrie said, hurrying past the cemetery gate. "And second, if worse comes to worst, you're stronger than you think. Strong enough to survive a few years of migraines. People have done it. My mother did it."

"And how'd that work out for her?" Cassie snapped. "You think she would have bothered if she hadn't wanted to protect you?"

The question was tossed out defiantly, the way that Cassie navigated through so much of her life, but it sank in gradually, a brush across Barrie's consciousness that opened more and more barbs of meaning.

Self-sacrifice was the last thing she would ever have associated with her mother, but Pru had said something similar once, that Lula must have loved Barrie very much to keep getting out of bed every morning when it would have been easier to give up. Was it possible Lula had kept going despite the pain she'd lived with every day to keep her daughter from inheriting the binding?

Filing that away for later examination, Barrie grasped the handle on the car's passenger side, but Cassie braced her hip against the door. Barrie gave an exhausted sigh. The day had been too long, and all she wanted to do was crawl into bed and pull the covers up over her eyes.

"Cassie, what do you want from me?" she asked, feeling like she was being pummeled from all sides. "Right now, there's nothing I can do. Even if I could manage to find the Watson lodestone, how am I supposed to get the Beaufort one? Eight won't talk to me, so I can't go wandering over there searching the property for it. In any case, I have to think about what happens to Watson's Landing and to us—the Watsons and the Beauforts—if we break the bindings. Unless I know that, I can't trust Obadiah with the lodestones, so you'll have to help him keep everyone away from that room in the meantime. That's the best solution I can offer." Pushing Cassie aside, she pulled the car door open, and slid down into the passenger seat.

Cassie grabbed the edge of the door so that Barrie couldn't close it. "You're the only one who can fix this. You have to fix it."

"Actually, I don't." Barrie gave up trying to wrench the door away from Cassie and sat miserably with her hands folded in her lap. "Maybe that doesn't seem fair to you, but if it comes down to a choice between my family and yours, I'm going to choose mine. I won't apologize for that. And you don't get to preach to me about my decisions. You can't even decide what you want. Quick—pick one. The gold? Or having the curse removed?"

"If you'd help me, I wouldn't have to choose," Cassie said, holding the car door with white-knuckled fingers.

"Seriously, do you even hear yourself?" Barrie lowered her voice as Pru and Marie Colesworth reached the driver's side of the old Mercedes. "Obadiah may seem helpless now, but he won't be once he has the kind of power he says he needs to remove the curse. What's to stop him from taking the gold at that point? No matter what happens, you don't get what you want without losing something else. Apparently, that's how life works, and nothing I do is going to change that."

Taking advantage of Cassie's momentary shock, Barrie yanked the door free and slammed it closed as Pru dropped into the driver's seat. Cassie stood with her arms hugging her waist and her long hair blowing while Pru pulled the car out of the lot and into the driveway.

Neither Pru nor Barrie spoke again until the Mercedes had turned to the right at the gate and was moving along the shaded road that led past Beaufort Hall. The last orange light strobed through breaks in the canopy of old oaks that lined both sides of the road, leaving the road bathed in gloom.

That was fine. The gloom just made it harder for Barrie to see Pru's worried expression.

"From the little I heard, it seemed like you were pretty hard on Cassie," Pru said. "Not that she doesn't deserve it, and not that you aren't right, but it's not like you. I understand that you're upset and scared. We all are, but if giving Obadiah the lodestones is the only way to stop Ayita and Elijah, we may have no choice. Don't you think in some ways, it might even be a relief to get rid of all the magic, as long as Obadiah can do it safely?"

Barrie stared out the window. This was exactly why she hadn't told anyone about Obadiah's threats before. Because no one understood.

A small creature darted across the road, and Pru braked and swerved. Belatedly she switched the headlights on, as if she'd been too distracted before to notice that night had descended while they hadn't paid attention.

Barrie dropped her head back against the seat. "How do we know what's safe, Aunt Pru? We're still guessing and working on rumor and old stories about what happened between Thomas and the Fire Carrier. We need to know exactly what was in the bargains and how they were sealed into the lodestones, or we're going to be relying on Obadiah to tell us the truth. I told Cassie I wouldn't hesitate to choose my family over hers. Don't you think Obadiah would do the same? He says he's never lied to me before, but he hasn't always told the truth."

"That's a good point," Pru said with a reluctant nod.

"We don't even know why the Fire Carrier is here. Why did he bring the *yunwi* to Watson Island of all places?"

Pru gave her an odd look. "The spirits were causing mischief for his tribe, and this was the last piece of land surrounded by water as he went east. That's what the story says."

"The *yunwi* do more good than harm as long as you treat them well. You figured that out on your own—that's why you started leaving food out for them at night. And they stopped taking the house apart once I started paying attention to them on the night that I was bound to Watson's Landing. They're kind, and they take care of the garden. They do their best to help us. We've seen that ourselves, and all the folklore and information that Eight and I found about the Cherokee Little People says so, too." Pulling the seat belt aside, Barrie turned in her seat to face her aunt. "We need to reexamine everything we think we know, everything you thought you knew growing up. Every story and legend people around here consider truth. Obadiah says he wants to remove the curse to save his family, and I believe him. I just don't know what else he wants—or what he'll do to get it. I think we have to tell Mary about him. Ask her—"

"Ask Mary what, sugar?" Pru asked, though not ungently.

"If she has a Raven Mocker in the family who steals years from his victims to keep himself alive? Mary can barely stomach knowing the *yunwi* are around."

"You know he isn't a Raven Mocker."

"How do we know what he is or isn't?"

"We don't—that's why we have to talk to Mary."

Pru stared back at Barrie so long that the car drifted off the road onto the grassy verge. Face pale, Pru steadied the car and drove with her hands clenched on the cracking leather until she turned onto the bridge that crossed the black-water Santisto River west of Watson Island.

"All right," she said. "We'll ask her. It's a shame, but there's no information left at Watson's Landing that would help us. Lord only knows, Lula looked everywhere trying to find something, so if there was ever anything set down in writing about the binding or the gifts, Daddy—or someone before him—had to have destroyed it." Pru leaned forward and adjusted the vent on the air conditioner, since the heat of the day had finally begun to dwindle. Then she glanced back across the car at Barrie. "I suppose I should be glad that you're finally questioning Obadiah. Your tendency to see the best in people is wonderful, but for all we know, the man came up with the whole idea of a race between him and the spirits to see who can get stronger faster as a way to push you into involving yourself again."

Barrie had to acknowledge the truth of that. "Could you ask Seven, too? He has to know something that was passed down in his family, or maybe they have family documents. Whatever is going on between him and Eight, he would tell you, wouldn't he? He loves you. That's one of the things that makes him such an ass—he gave up on you instead of fighting or even trying to figure out a solution."

Pru's indrawn breath was almost inaudible, but her profile was strained and sharp enough to make Barrie realize what she had blurted out unthinkingly. She would have taken back the words, if she could have, but she doubted that apologizing would make things better.

Beneath the bridge, the river flowing around Watson Island appeared colorless in the flat light of the emerging moon. Around the curve of the river, the tip of the Watson's Landing dock was just visible across from the Beaufort one, the two stretching toward each other with no hope of coming together, much like Seven had believed Pru was out of reach. The way that Eight was out of reach. Farther downriver, beyond Beaufort Hall, the Colesworth dock looked almost intact in the distance, the charred and damaged end visible only as listing boards and a broken piling. Tonight was the first time since she'd arrived back from San Francisco that Barrie felt that the gulf between her family and the others—between her and what Eight and Cassie wanted—was as wide as the water.

She had to find a way to get Eight to forgive her. The last thing she wanted was to have to make decisions without him and risk making things even worse between them.

Pru braked to a stop in the circular driveway at Watson's Landing. The knee-high shadowy figures of the *yunwi* darted around the car, nearly invisible but for the fiery glow of their eyes flickering in the darkness. Their antics unsettled the white peacock who had chosen to roost in the far corner of the portico, and he fluttered down like a ghost himself and strutted away with an affronted air. After getting out of the car, Pru linked her arm with Barrie's, and they climbed the front steps together and then went to the kitchen.

Pru downed a couple of Tylenol and drank a glass of lemonade. A few moments later, she excused herself to go to bed. "It's late, sugar, and I'm not sure I've ever been more tired in my whole life. We ought to both get some sleep. It's going to be a long, hard day tomorrow with Mary and Daphne coming to do the additional menus for the restaurant and the appraiser coming for the furniture in the afternoon." She headed toward the door, but paused beside Barrie and caught Barrie's chin between her thumb and index finger. "Don't go thinking this is all on you, you hear me? We're going to find a solution to this mess together, I promise. That's what families are for, so no one person ever has to carry the weight of a burden by themselves."

Pru kissed Barrie on the forehead and went upstairs, but Barrie stayed awhile in the kitchen before going up herself. Lying in the four-poster bed a half hour later, she kicked aside the quilt and stared up at the underside of the embroidered canopy sleeplessly. Then she plucked up her courage and picked up her phone.

It didn't surprise her when Eight's number rang several times and went to voice mail, as if he'd hit ignore. She dialed again, and this time his voice mail picked up straightaway.

Restlessly, she moved to stand out on the balcony. Across the river, Eight's window still shone gold against the dark lawn of Beaufort Hall. The light-sticks and AquaLeds that Barrie had sunk in the water around the Watson dock rippled like liquid fire—beautiful, but a poor imitation of the wild flames of the Fire Carrier's magic. And below, in the Watson garden, the knee-high dark shadows of the *yunwi* darted back and forth across the lawn and wove around the hedges, their eyes winking in and out like fireflies.

Barrie left a message for Eight because she had no choice. She believed what she'd told Pru about fighting—and Eight was worth fighting for.

"I promised you I wouldn't hold anything back anymore, but I can't keep that promise if you won't talk to me," she said, her voice sounding husky and needy enough to make her pause to clear her throat. "Obadiah may have a way to break the curse, but it would probably break the Beaufort and Watson gifts as well. I can't make a decision like that without you. I feel lost, Eight. You're the one who always knows how to figure things out. If that doesn't prove that I don't think you're stupid, I don't know what would. Also, I miss you. I miss talking to you. I miss being with you. Please call me back."

Opening her heart was risky and painful, but risk was part of fighting harder.

She hung up and leaned out across the railing, watching the river and hoping the phone would ring. When it didn't, she retrieved her sketchbook and found herself sketching his face, and Obadiah's, Cassie's, Pru's. When she'd first come to Watson's Landing, it had been the place that fascinated her, but now that it was the people who gripped her, all of them. The people and the spirits and the magic. She tried to imagine the island without the *yunwi* or the Fire Carrier, and she couldn't. Her gift was more than merely an ability to find lost things, or whatever her abilities would eventually settle into when she had figured out how to use them. The guardianship of Watson's Landing, of the magic that lived here and nowhere else that Barrie had ever heard of, that was the true gift the Fire Carrier had given the Watsons all those years ago. How could she let that go?

She wished she had told Eight everything from the

beginning, that she had trusted him with the truth. But she didn't regret that she had fought to keep the Watson gift when Obadiah had threatened it. Her choices weren't any easier now, and Eight wouldn't necessarily agree with her priorities, but she had to let Eight know what was going on and give him an opportunity to weigh in.

A half hour later, she had to admit that he wasn't going to call.

She needed to do something to get his attention, and of all the problems she was facing now, getting him to forgive her seemed the least impossible. It was time to fight even harder. She had to send him a message he couldn't ignore.

CHAPTER FIVE

The secret tunnel that led beneath the river to the Beaufort woods had been daunting every time Barrie had set foot inside it, and crossing to the other side had never ended well. At least the first time, Eight had been with her for most of the trip. The second time, it had still been daylight when she emerged.

Yet what choice did she have except to take the tunnel? She couldn't wake Pru, not for this. She didn't have a boat, and she couldn't swim, and without a driver's license, there was no other way across to Beaufort Hall.

Unable to find a backpack anywhere in the house, she filled two pillowcases with more of the LED light-sticks, then tied the sacks together and draped them across her shoulders. The floorboards groaned in the second-floor corridor of the abandoned wing that contained what had once been her grandfather's bedroom. Heavy furniture mottled with a fresh coat of dust added to the oppressive atmosphere, and Barrie hurried through, looking neither left nor right. She climbed onto the bed. Flipping aside the bearded face in the carving that hid the keyhole, she unlocked the sliding panel, then she climbed over the headboard into the hidden room. Another hidden panel opened onto the musty, narrow steps that descended three floors down to the tunnel entrance. The *yunwi* scampered down with her but hovered on the steps to avoid the iron in the heavy door at the bottom.

Beyond the door when Barrie had unlocked it, the walls of the underground passage curved into a sturdy arch and disappeared into the distance far beyond her flashlight beam. Darkness pressed in, closing around the light. Grit scratched on the bricks beneath her feet, and she kept her eyes averted from the memories that lay in wait. They flew at her anyway: the clang of the door her cousin Cassie had slammed to seal her and Eight inside the tunnel, the ghost that had hovered above the skeletons of Luke and Twila—the brother and ex-fiancée that Barrie's own grandfather had murdered and kept hidden for forty years.

As if they knew she needed them, more *yunwi* than usual had darted inside with her. Instead of milling around, they pressed in close as she followed the tunnel slightly downward toward the river, their insubstantial forms radiating the strange cold-warmth that she was finally getting used to feeling. The floor leveled off, signaling the invisible boundary that marked the water's edge far overhead. Caged there by the spell the Fire Carrier renewed every night, the *yunwi* stopped with a howl of protest that was more a vibration in Barrie's head than a sound in her ears.

She wondered what they thought—whether they knew what had happened at Colesworth Place that morning. It wouldn't surprise her. They'd hated Obadiah from the first moment he'd set foot at Watson's Landing. That should have told her everything she needed to know, but at the same time that they'd told her to beware, her gift had pulled her toward him. It still did.

"I wish you guys would tell me what's going on," she said. "Or tell me what to do. *Why* do you hate Obadiah? Is it because of his magic? Or because he's going to take this place away from you? Because you're afraid he's going to hurt me? Please. Tell me something."

They circled her, pressing in and trying to hold her back with insistent, spectral fingers.

Stay, they said, their soundless voices coming in near unison, little more than vibrations in the air around her.

As information, that didn't help, but something about the word held centuries of aloneness within it. Barrie recognized loneliness when she felt it. She'd spent most of her childhood feeling isolated from people her own age, from her mother. Really, from anyone except her godfather, Mark. Fighting a fresh wave of grief so strong that it bowed her shoulders, she rubbed Mark's watch as she hurried beneath the river. She wondered if you ever got over losing someone you loved, whether it really did get better the way people said. Maybe you just got used to the ache, the same way she coped with the migraines when she was away from Watson's Landing, by never letting her thoughts dwell on any one thing too long.

She reached the opposite end of the tunnel at last, and turned the key to open the thick wooden door as quietly as she could. The *snick* of the lock still seemed too loud in her ears, and she stood on the threshold listening for anything that seemed out of place among the hum of insects, the chorus of the frogs, and the low and constant *kwok, kwok, kwok, kwok* calls of the night herons in the woods around her. The fact that the herons stopped as she pulled herself up through the grate in the stairwell suggested that she was there alone.

Keeping the dome of the flashlight pressed against her palm so that the beam didn't travel far beyond her feet, she kicked some leaves back over the grating as a hurried form of camouflage, then picked her way through the woods to the lightly sloping lawn. Beaufort Hall was lit up like a jewel box at the top of the rise, light spilling from Eight's window and a dozen others, but there was no sign of movement. Barrie didn't let that dissuade her. She had made up her mind to fight for Eight, and even if he wasn't in his room right then, he would have to go there at some point.

She worked fast, breaking each light-stick as she went so that they all glowed softly before she laid them on the grass. It was impossible to see the scale or proportion from where she stood, but the writing didn't have to be perfect. Just legible.

I'M SORRY

Stepping back when she was done, she rubbed her aching head and glanced up at the window. Eight stood there, inches from the paned glass, everything about him clear and so familiar that the finding clicked in her again, puzzle pieces of his faults and strengths, hopes and fears, aligning in just the right way with her own.

What she loved about Eight had little to do with the broad shoulders and strong arms that had wrapped themselves around her to offer comfort, the chest that had cradled her cheek, the stubborn jaw that had softened as he'd rested it against the top of her head. She loved the way he thought his way through problems while she leaped to conclusions. The way he was confident with people when she had no clue, and the way he had recognized long before she had that she too often wanted what others wanted instead of deciding what she wanted herself. She loved the way he argued with her and made her sharpen her wits. The way he made her laugh in the middle of an argument.

Why hadn't she seen that sooner? Why hadn't she had faith in what she felt?

When she'd first found out about his gift, she'd been afraid he was using it to make her like him—afraid that she liked him more than she wanted to like him, simply because he knew what she wanted him to say and what she wanted him to do. That had shifted to the bigger fear that once she'd wanted him to like her, to love her, he'd had no choice. The Beaufort gift had made her reluctant to trust anything between them. Now, though, she wasn't the one retreating from what they had.

He was still standing there, unmoving, so she tapped her heart and then pointed to the words she had spelled out in lights. She waited for a gesture of forgiveness or understanding. Instead he stepped back and walked away. A moment later, the bedroom lights went out.

And why not? The realization that she was waiting for a *gesture* slid through her coldly. Gestures were easy to make and hard to live up to. Of course Eight needed more.

How had she not realized how empty this apology must seem to him? She'd been looking for something to show him what she felt, the way he had shown her so often. Only the things he had done had always stemmed from knowing her and understanding what she needed. He'd found a turtle's nest for her as an example of courage. Built her a tire swing as a reminder of the living they still had to do together. He'd danced with her in the rain beneath a red umbrella to show her that there was no point in being the same as everyone else when you could be something different.

What had she shown him? Words that had no meaning most of the time when people said them.

Barrie's breath hitched and left a slow, rhythmic emptiness in her chest. She set to work slowly gathering up the light-sticks and taking her time putting them back inside the pillowcases, not even realizing until she was finished that some dim corner of her had been harboring hope that Eight had only switched off the light to come downstairs. He wasn't coming.

She couldn't stand there like an idiot any longer. She needed to go home and do what he'd asked of her, to leave him alone. Since the first day she'd met him, he'd barely asked anything of her. She could do this much.

Turning back downhill, she caught her first full glimpse of Watson's Landing across the water. The garden glittered with the fairy lights strung through the trees, and the fountain at the center of the maze was lit with a glow that turned the water into liquid moonlight. On the dock that crossed the marsh grass along the river's edge, small shadows stood waiting for her, their eyes no more than orange pinpricks in the distance and the darkness.

As quickly as her heart had emptied, it swelled again. Not

wholly. She suspected it would never be whole without the missing piece that belonged to Eight. Still, seeing the *yunwi* was enough to remind her that there were other things to fight for, too.

She was halfway down the hill when her phone buzzed in her pocket. Fumbling to retrieve it, she let herself hope again.

"Thank God," she said. "I've been so worried—"

"I'm not your responsibility to worry about. I meant what I told you. Stop calling me, Bear. Don't come over here. Don't think you can fix us when I'm still trying to fix myself. There isn't an *us* anymore, and I can't think when I'm finding you around every corner."

The pain rasping his voice dug into Barrie's chest and clawed it open. She was sure there was something she could say, some perfect combination of words that Eight would have used if the shoe were on the other foot, but she couldn't think what they were.

Refusing to cry and make him feel worse, she focused on being practical. "There's stuff you need to know. Obadiah wants me to bring him both the Beaufort and the Watson lodestones. He says that Elijah and Ayita are so weak that they could drain—"

"God, stop!" Eight shouted into the phone. "Bear, please. I can't care about that right now. Just stay away from Obadiah. And stay away from Kate."

"I haven't even talked to your sister."

"Well, she's pestering me to talk to you, and I know what she's like. She'll be over there whispering into your ear and wanting you to keep me from—"

"From what?"

"Just keep her out of this. All of it. She's prone to getting into enough trouble on her own without you making her even crazier."

"That isn't fair."

"If life was fair, we wouldn't have to deal with the gifts or the bindings or any of this crap."

He hung up before Barrie could say another word.

CHAPTER SIX

Barrie slept badly, and in the morning, her head felt like it was filled with sawdust as she followed the dark aroma of coffee to the kitchen. Still dressed in her sleep shorts and the *There's no way you woke up looking like that* T-shirt that Mark had given her for Christmas, she pushed through the swinging door from the dim corridor and stood blinking against the sunlight. Pru, Mary, and Daphne stopped mid-argument when they saw her.

Already feeling guilty about Eight and Cassie, and scared for everyone at the dig, Barrie was nowhere near ready to deal with the undercurrents that vibrated through Pru's too-chipper "Hello, sugar," Mary's mumbled "Mornin'," and Daphne's "Well, don't *you* look like something the cat dragged in?"

Hoping that Pru hadn't brought up Obadiah without her,

she held up a couple of fingers to ward off any more conversation. "Two minutes," she said, shuffling toward the coffeepot. "Give me two minutes to start a caffeine IV drip, and then maybe I'll feel human enough to figure out what you're all mad about."

"No one's mad, honey." Mary flashed an unconvincing smile, and the elegant bones of her cheeks and jaw stood out tensely beneath her smooth brown skin. "Your aunt's tryin' to get rid of us, and she won't listen when I tell her we're fine."

"I never said I wanted to get rid of you, you stubborn woman," Pru said, getting up from her chair. "I'm just trying to tell you that you don't need to be here when Brit and Jackson need you."

Barrie paused with her cup half-filled. "What's going on with Brit and Jackson?"

For the first time, every one of her fifty-odd years showed on Mary's face and in her posture. Daphne, too, was drawn and fidgety. The red ribbon wound around her braided hair seemed out of place, too aggressively bright and cheerful for her expression.

"Brit gets muscle spasms from her cerebral palsy," Mary said, "and the injections wear out after a while. The spasms were bad last night, and on top of that Jackson broke a tooth—"

"Got into a fight," Daphne said.

"Couldn't get himself *out* of a fight." Mary tapped her pen against a stack of restaurant supply invoices. "Your brother doesn't start things."

"I know he doesn't." Daphne's mouth twisted up. "But he knows better than to hang out anywhere he's liable to run into Crunch."

"Is Jackson okay? Was he hurt apart from the tooth? And what's a Crunch?" Barrie asked.

"An asshole named after the sound his fist makes breaking someone's nose. That about tells you all you've gotta know."

"You watch your language," Mary said. "And Jackson's fine. Just mad, mostly, and not quite as pretty as he was before it happened, is all."

Barrie finished pouring her coffee and stood inhaling the steam as she held the mug between her palms while she tried to understand how Mary could be calm about that. Outside, a sheriff's patrol boat passed on its way upriver, its motor churning milky foam onto the dark surface of the water.

Pru removed a platter of homemade biscuits she'd left warming in the oven and set them on the counter. Pausing beside Barrie, she leaned in close. "Tell Mary she doesn't need to be here today, would you? Tell her you and I can handle the rest of the restaurant preparations on our own."

Snagging a biscuit from the platter, Barrie turned back

toward the table. "Pru's right. And honestly, there's not that much left to do. Everything's ordered, the ads are in, and the reservations are filling up—"

"We're already full for the first couple nights—I've been thinking we could auction off some of the seats and give the proceeds to charity," Mary said.

Barrie nodded. "That's a great idea, but that can wait. The furniture appraisers are coming later today anyway, so it's not like we're going to get much done. Brit and Jackson are far more important—"

"They're more important every other day too, but that doesn't mean I don't have to work. I can't take time off whenever Brit has a bad turn or Jackson does some stupid thing."

"If it's about the money," Barrie began, "we can help—"

"How many times do I have to tell you both that I'm not takin' money I can't pay back?" Mary said, cutting her off.

Daphne hit the enter key on the keyboard of her laptop with an emphatic click. "It would be a loan, Gramma. *I* can pay it back. Eventually. It's for Brit, so if they're offering, we should take it."

"That's enough, child." Mary shot her a quelling look.

"No! It isn't. You know Brit's getting worse," Daphne said, turning to Pru and Barrie and hurrying on in spite of Mary's disapproval. "There's an experimental stem cell treatment I've been reading about. The trial itself wouldn't cost anything, but if she gets in, there'd be flights and hotels, and Gramma and I would have to go with her. Our neighbor's getting too old to keep up with Jackson after school. She sure can't help him with his homework, so whatever happens with the trial, I'm going to have to ask if the university can defer my scholarship until he's older."

"No you aren't," Mary said.

"Yes I am." Daphne looked back at Pru and Barrie. "If I work here and at the SeaCow, and I do some website work and graphics from home, I could start paying you back right away."

Mary bowed her head, appearing as close to defeated as Mary was ever likely to come. "You're supposed to be the first person in the family to go to college," she said softly. "And you're supposed to set an example for Jackson. Give him something to work toward. You let me worry about the money. I'll find it and figure out all the rest. The Lord doesn't give anybody more than they can handle."

The last sentence came from Mary defiantly, as if she could make it true simply through her own insistence. Barrie lost whatever appetite she had left. Because what if Brit's bad night and Jackson's tooth didn't have anything to do with God? Obadiah had explained that as a result of casting the Colesworth curse, there'd been some sort of karmic blowback that had fallen back onto his family. What if Brit never got into the stem cell trial because of that? Or if the curse was the source of Jackson's problems? Who even had a name like Crunch? Who was proud of hitting people and scaring them?

For the first time, it struck Barrie that she was the kind of person who found it easier to accept a world that had curses and magic, spirit paths, and vortexes of energy than it was to think of having to protect someone she loved from a guy named after the sound of a breaking nose. How did Mary send Jackson off to school every day not knowing if he'd be safe? How did she accept it when the doctors said there was nothing they could do for Brit? Or that Daphne would have to beg to postpone her merit scholarship while baseball and the Beaufort name had made it relatively easy for Eight to switch schools to stay in South Carolina instead of going away to school in California?

Pru was still leaning against the counter by the sink, and she gave a scant, helpless lift of her shoulders and shook her head when Barrie caught her eye. Crumbling her biscuit, Barrie studied the swirl of unreadable thoughts and emotions that chased each other across Daphne's narrow face. There was always something hard to grasp about Daphne, as if she kept herself hidden away, and the quiet she wore was like a cloak—or armor against the world.

Barrie pushed her plate aside. "Mary, have you ever heard of someone named Obadiah? Someone related to you."

Mary nearly dropped the newly printed menu she was inserting into one of the empty plastic cases that Pru had ordered. "Where'd you come across that name?"

"He showed up here—"

"*Here?* When?" Mary's breath hissed between her teeth. "Never mind. Doesn't matter. You stay clear of him if he ever comes again. You stay far away."

Daphne's forearms thudded onto the table, and she leaned forward with interest, glancing from Mary to Barrie and back again as if she didn't know where to look. "Who is he?" she asked. "And what did he want? What did he *do?*"

"He's a shaman, or a magician—or something between the two," Barrie replied. "His magic is real, though. I've seen it. Felt it. At least some of it. And he's a descendent of Elijah and Ayita, but he says he's also related to you."

"People can say whatever they like," Mary said tartly. "A boo hag can call itself a king, but that's not going to make it one."

Barrie suppressed a sigh. "Obadiah isn't a boo hag. Or a Raven Mocker or a vampire. He's a person, and whatever he does to keep himself alive doesn't hurt anyone else. He knows your history. *Our* history. He's told me more about the Colesworth curse and the gifts than anyone else ever has, and he's here because he's desperately trying to help you."

She explained how she had met Obadiah, and everything that had happened since, including how she had used the names in Caroline Colesworth's diary to figure out that Mary's family was the one Obadiah had come back to save from the blowback of the curse—because they were his family, too.

Daphne grew more rigid as Barrie talked, and Mary grew more jittery. The shadows beneath Mary's eyes had grown pronounced enough to remind Barrie of when she had first arrived at Watson's Landing and found Pru crying on the steps outside, too paralyzed by emotion and fear to bring herself to leave Watson's Landing long enough to pick Barrie up at the airport. Helplessness was a more desolate kind of pain than any physical ailment could inflict.

"Are you trying to say that this Obadiah is the same Obadiah who was a slave before the Civil War?" Daphne asked when Barrie had fallen silent.

"That's what I suspect," Barrie said.

"He could be." Mary picked up Barrie's plate and took it to the sink. The fork clattered on the porcelain as she scraped off the biscuit crumbs. Then she turned back around, holding the plate in front of her like a shield. "My gramma used to tell stories about the family. Back in the war, when the Federals took Port Royal and the islands, the Colesworths threatened to send any slave who didn't stay and work across to Cuba. Your"—she waved a finger in Daphne's direction—"seven-times-great-grandfather or thereabouts, Donas, had already died by then, and his wife thought the children were too young to risk tryin' to run away. Obadiah, the oldest, was the only one who went, and he got himself shot in the fightin' up north. By the time he made it back here, the whole family was dead except for Daphne, the youngest girl. She had a baby to take care of, and both of them were sick.

"Obadiah refused to let them die. There wasn't any money for doctors, but the family'd always made root medicine as far back as anyone could remember. Obadiah went from one conjure man to another, learnin' whatever he didn't already know about healin'. The way my gramma told it, the magic took hold of him. He went off to study in New Orleans, then Haiti, Africa, Tibet, China. Anywhere and everywhere, and when he came back, the magic had done somethin' to him so that he *didn't* change. Didn't age. Eventually, he stopped tryin' to come back, but he sent packages of money and all sorts of strange odds and ends, each with foreign stamps and no return address—"

"Packages like the ones you hide when you think we aren't looking?" Daphne asked.

Mary's lips went flat. "Packages we don't need or want. All that money has ever brought is misery—"

"How much money?" Daphne's forearms thudded on the table. "And where is it?"

"Never you mind. I've given it away ever since your mama came back and handed me Jackson to raise. Didn't matter how much I ever sent her, it wasn't enough. I hoped she would stay with you—with us—if I told her it wasn't comin' anymore. But that's the problem. Found money is never free, so you tell Obadiah that the Colesworths can keep their gold—we don't want any part of it. Look at all the folks who win the lottery! Or actors. Basketball players. Musicians." Spots of color stained Mary's cheeks as her gaze locked with Daphne's. "Not one of them ends up *happy*. The money makes them lose their way."

"We could be using it to make Brit better—to get help for Jackson. Or for school." Jaw tight with shock, Daphne stared back at grandmother, and she shook her head as Mary nodded. "Didn't it ever occur to you to tell me before you gave the money away? I'm the one who's got to take care of Brit for the rest of her life."

"She's your sister—"

"I'm not saying I mind! I'm saying that it's going to take money. A lot of it. And if the curse is making Brit the way she is, or making her worse, or taking away good luck that could maybe make her better . . . It doesn't matter if *this* Obadiah is *that* Obadiah. Or if he's a boo hag or a Raven Mocker or whatever else. I want to meet him." Daphne turned back to Barrie. "Will you take me over to see him?"

"Of course," Barrie said, ignoring the looks cast at her by both Pru and Mary. "But he's going to ask me about the lodestone, if I do, so I'd better figure out whether finding it is even an option first."

"Are you going out to the Scalping Tree?" Daphne asked. "I'll go with you."

Mary folded her arms across her chest. "The hell you will, child. You stay right here in this kitchen or I'll tan your hide with a wooden spoon. You're not too old for me to put you across my knee."

CHAPTER SEVEN

Pru brought along her shotgun. The pocket of her coral sundress bulged with a load of extra red-cased shells, making the hem hang askew against her thin knees and her stiff rubber Wellingtons. She led the way across the lawn like a woman on a mission, but she deflated when she and Barrie reached the first rank of mingled oak and cypress surrounded by bristling, low palmettos. At the same spot, and right on schedule, the *yunwi* refused to go any farther, either.

Barrie pushed on ahead into the shadowed woods, watching the ground for snakes and alligators and pits of squishy ground. Partly as a distraction, but mostly because it was long overdue, she promised herself that she was going to make time to go online and order her own pair of rubber boots. Borrowing Pru's spare pair was getting to be a regular occurrence, and somewhere there had to be a website that had them in something other than ugly green. A nice flower print, or stripes, or cute little polka dots. Did Louboutin make rain boots? Maybe she'd buy two pairs and give one to Pru.

"You be careful, sugar. Don't charge on ahead of me," Pru called out.

Glancing back, Barrie found Pru was lagging behind, her footsteps slowing and her head turning this way and that as if she expected something to jump out at her from behind every tree. For the first time, Barrie remembered that Pru had never actually been *in* the woods before. Emmett had beaten both his daughters the night Lula had defied him and followed her finding gift inside. He'd been afraid they would find the key to the tunnel where he'd hidden it at the Scalping Tree, so he'd convinced them both that the Fire Carrier was evil and the woods were dangerous.

Barrie stopped and waited for her aunt. "The Fire Carrier isn't going to hurt us, Aunt Pru. What your father told you was a lie."

"I know that now, but knowing something in your head and knowing it deep down where fear lives are two different things." There was no bitterness in Pru's voice, only a wistful note that made Barrie wish Emmett Watson were still alive so she could string him up by the thumbs. Or better yet, lock him in the tunnel and see how *he* liked dying in there with the ghosts of his crimes.

She opened her mouth to tell Pru to go back, to tell her that she didn't have to come, but she suspected Pru had something to prove to herself. Pushing through fear was what eventually set you free.

Brushing aside a clump of Spanish moss, Barrie took Pru's hand and stepped deeper into the woods, winding through the trees and gnarled, low-hanging branches. Sparse light filtered through the canopy overhead, playing tricks on her eyes as the shadows shifted. Even in the gloom, though, she knew the way to the Scalping Tree. The Fire Carrier himself tugged on her senses. It was the same odd connection that let her know whenever he began his nightly walk to the river to renew the island's protective magic, but the pull was more elemental than a simple sense of loss. It was another of those pieces of the expanding magic that she didn't understand well enough. As with Obadiah, it was impossible to say whether the Fire Carrier was a question or an answer.

The underbrush grew sparse, and a short while later, there was a dappled clearing surrounding an enormous oak. The tree's limbs stretched out for hundreds of feet, some of them so heavy that they sagged onto the ground. Outlined in sunlight, strands of moss dripped from the tree's twisted branches like the scalps that legend—probably incorrectly—said had once been left there in tribute for the Fire Carrier.

Blotched spots of color appeared high on Pru's pale cheeks.

"I can't believe it. People come from all over the world to see the Devil's Oak in town, and this is right here. It's been here all my life, and I've never seen it."

Barrie pushed back a fresh surge of fury at Emmett Watson and a wave of pity for the girls and young women his daughters had been. Lula had tried to escape, and maybe if Emmett had told her the truth about the magic and the Fire Carrier, she might have had the information she'd needed to survive and be happy. But Pru had believed what she was programmed to believe. She hadn't known any better.

Well, it was time to break the cycle.

Letting go of Pru's hand, Barrie focused on her gift, except that instead of looking for something lost, she concentrated on anything that fell outside the ordinary sounds and scents and smells of Watson's Landing. Nothing felt out of place among the natural rhythms—the wind creaked in the branches, a dove muttered somewhere to her right, the creek bubbled across the rocks. Then, burrowing deeper, she connected to a steady hum of energy.

Too much energy. It jolted through her. Barrie tried to pull away and close herself off again, fighting as the current sucked her down. But she might as well have grabbed hold of an electric fence.

"Feel something?" Pru watched her with a pulse tapping in her throat.

Barrie felt *everything*.

Sensation filled her past overflowing, beyond her own boundaries, as if she had disintegrated into a million fragments and was being swept down and around and around and around, then flung out again in a fresh burst of energy. The temperature, likewise, had gone from lukewarm to searing hot, then freezing cold, and back to hot again, but she felt it all simultaneously, as if a part of her stayed in each spot and she bounced between them so that she had only to reach out and become aware of one thing or another to feel it, to be there, to *go* anywhere. Places were visible in a stream that hurtled by yet remained curiously still: a warm lake with stands of cypress and a town drowned beneath the water; ranks of wind-bent pines on rows of meandering hills; two boulders stacked on top of each other on a wooded slope; a tree-topped granite dome rising out of the surrounding forest as if pushed out of the earth by a giant thumb.

She fell deeper. Faster. Less and less anchored to herself, less certain not just of where she was but *when*. There was ground below her, and fire, and earth, and sky, and space, darkness, then more light, blinding light. Above her, blue turned to black, and stars and universes spun past. Effervescent, soaring life flowed all around her, and voices . . . There were voices, indistinct and out of range, but she wanted to hear them, needed to get closer. Opening herself more, she strained for clarity, following the energy and gulping it down as if she had been dying of thirst her entire life.

"Barrie! What are you doing? Are you all right?"

Pru's voice floated down to her from far, far away. An unwelcome interruption. Barrie brushed it aside and concentrated on the sense of hurtling through time and space, searching . . . searching for what, she wasn't certain. Then she remembered.

The voices.

Like the *yunwi*, they called to her in vibrations and resonance instead of words. She couldn't understand them but felt she should be able to. If she could simply get past some unseen barrier, get a little closer, or if she could tune to the right frequency, then they would at last be clear.

Something crashed into her. Knocked her sideways. Barrie stumbled and came back to herself with her cheek stinging and her body half-fallen into a brush clump that had torn the skin on her palm and wrist.

"Ow." She shook her head, feeling flushed and breathless and bereft, as if she'd lost something deeply important. At the same time, every part of her still throbbed with energy and awareness, leaving her oversensitized.

"Thank God." Pru eyes were drawn and dark. "I've been shaking you for ten minutes, and you haven't even looked at me. Didn't you hear me calling you?

It couldn't possibly have been that long.

Could it?

Barrie released a shuddering breath. "I think I found the energy Obadiah was talking about."

Pru's back went stiff. "The vortex? What did it do to you? You scared me."

"I'm not sure. Maybe I should try again—"

"No! Barrie, for heaven's sake. What if I hadn't been able to snap you out of it? You don't understand—you weren't *here*."

Barrie struggled to find a way to explain what she couldn't begin to understand, all that sensation, all that power, the whirlpool of energy that had drawn her down and down and then spun her out into a world both smaller and larger than anything she had ever imagined. Would she have been able to swim back to the surface if Pru hadn't been there to help her?

Her hand came up before she even realized it, her fingers reaching toward the trunk of the oak. Reaching . . . then she stopped.

Fingers clenched into tight little balls of self-control, she shook with the temptation to go back, to let go of herself. But she felt good. Full and more awake than she had felt, certainly since Obadiah had taken energy from her. More awake than she'd felt in days or maybe ever.

"Did you find the lodestone?" Pru took Barrie's hands and gently uncurled the fingers. "Lord, your skin's burning up!

Do you see how dangerous all this is? That man sent you out here and never even warned you what would happen."

"To be fair, I didn't tell Obadiah that I was going to look for it."

"It seems to me there's an awful lot he doesn't know and too much he doesn't share." Rubbing Barrie's hands between her own, Pru herded her out of the clearing and back toward the edge of the woods.

Barrie thought of the voices, of the similarities between what she'd heard just then and the way the *yunwi* spoke to her on the rare occasions when they communicated at all. Were the two related in some way?

The *yunwi* hated Obadiah. They hadn't wanted him at Watson's Landing, so maybe the energy wasn't something he was supposed to touch. In which case, did it matter whether she ever found the lodestone?

If the stone held even a small portion of the energy that had swept her away with it, how could she give that to someone she wasn't positive she could trust?

CHAPTER EIGHT

Emerging from the dimness of the woods with Pru, Barrie found the *yunwi* waiting for her in a solemn row, their upturned faces content and beaming as she approached. They darted away again, but they seemed more distinct than usual, more solid and readable. At least they were clearer to Barrie—Pru still didn't seem to see them.

"Sugar, are you sure you're all right?" Pru gave Barrie another concerned glance as they crossed the lawn. "I need to bring the horses in before it gets too hot, but maybe you should go on back to the house."

Barrie shook her head. "I feel wonderful, actually. Like I drank a few pots of coffee but without the caffeine jitters. If only we could bottle that stuff."

"I didn't feel a thing."

"Maybe it's something to do with the binding?"

"Just promise me you won't check out on me like that again," Pru said, rounding the corner to the front of the house. "Don't go back into the woods. Maybe my father wasn't as wrong as you've been thinking he was."

"He couldn't have been more wrong," Barrie said, promising nothing.

Around the front of the house, the white peacock had his tail fanned out, displaying it for the three peahens who waddled in front of him as he half-turned and moved out of Barrie's path. Pru set the shotgun down on the front steps leading up to the portico, then crossed to the pasture beyond the oak-lined lane. Accompanied by *yunwi*, the horses galloped toward them along the fence, with Miranda in the lead. Despite her heavier build, the mare's long black mane, tail, and feathered Friesian legs gave her the appearance of floating on air, while the gelding bucked and kicked up his heels. They came to the gate, and Miranda arched her neck as she blew against Barrie's palm.

Barrie laughed. "Sorry, sweet girl. I didn't bring you anything."

"Here. Try this." Pru dug into the pocket that didn't contain gun-shell casings and pulled out a couple of crumbling lumps of sugar.

Barrie took one. She stood beside Pru, their shoulders

touching while Miranda gently lipped the sugar from her palm. The tickle of Miranda's whiskers, the *yunwi* milling underfoot, Pru's acceptance—all of it was humbling. It was Barrie's responsibility to protect the quiet peace of Watson's Landing. She was supposed to have answers, but all she managed to find were more questions and confusion.

She snapped the lead rope onto Miranda's halter and followed as Pru led Batch away.

"On the bright side," Pru called back over the softened thuds of the horses' hooves, "maybe Obadiah was wrong about the lodestone being buried in the woods, if you didn't find it. At least that makes his original threat to dig it up less worrisome."

"I'm not so sure. There was something. . . . It was hard to isolate with all that energy, but that wouldn't matter if Obadiah resorted to using a shovel."

"Then what's to stop him from coming over here and taking the lodestone for himself if you refuse to give it to him?"

"The *yunwi* didn't seem able to do much when he was here before, but the Fire Carrier killed Wyatt and Ernesto to protect me. If Obadiah isn't meant to have it, the stone is safe enough."

Pru stopped abruptly at the corner of the stable building. Batch kept walking until the slack in the lead rope ran out, and then he turned over his shoulder and gave Pru a look of resentful resignation.

"Barrie, there's something I need to tell you," Pru said, "and I don't suppose there's ever going to be a good time to say it. We didn't want to worry you any more that night after you'd already been through so much, but the police aren't certain that Ernesto died in the explosion."

Dry-mouthed, Barrie patted Miranda distractedly as the mare suddenly tossed her head. "He did. He must have—his body washed out to sea or got eaten by alligators. That's what everyone said."

Or had they?

Barrie replayed the conversations—the various times when *she* had said Ernesto was dead. Had Eight or even Pru and Seven ever definitively said it? She thought of the way Pru went white at the mention of his name. The odd silences.

Barrie's internal elevator lurched again, knocking her off-kilter, and she had to start walking to let her body catch up with a rush of memories and adrenaline—Wyatt and Ernesto unloading drugs from the speedboat at the Colesworth dock as she came stumbling out of the woods, Ernesto's face behind the gun, Ernesto kicking her, he and her uncle, Wyatt, dragging her out onto the boat to take her out to sea and kill her. The boat exploding as she jumped into the river.

Leading Miranda around Batch, Barrie walked into the duller heat of the stable building with its sweet smells of horse and hay, but even that wasn't as comforting as usual. The scrolled mahogany door of Miranda's stall was open, and a trickle of pinewood shavings lay in curls along the wide concrete aisle, rocking lightly in the breeze from an overhead fan.

Barrie turned Miranda loose in the stall and came back out to stand in the aisle. "Did you ever really believe he was dead?" she asked, carefully watching Pru. "Or did you and Seven and Eight all know from the beginning? I can't believe that Eight was keeping this secret even when he accused me of betraying him."

"We weren't positive. We still aren't. Eight spotted him swimming right after the explosion, but by the time Eight had swum across to make sure you were safe, Ernesto was gone. He probably drowned after Eight saw him. He had to have been badly injured, and the police searched and didn't see any evidence that he'd gone ashore anywhere."

Beside Barrie, Miranda scraped her steel shoe impatiently on the ground, but Barrie's stomach had seized into a knot, and she closed her eyes against another cluster of images: the explosion, the smell of burning fuel, the debris raining onto the water, and the fear . . . so much fear.

"You'd been through too much already," Pru said. "You understand, don't you? None of us knew how strong you were. You didn't know that yourself. It seemed pointless to worry you until the police had done a thorough search."

"Should I be worried? Did the police find anything?"

Barrie held her hand out to the *yunwi* who had gathered around her to offer comfort.

Batch's hooves gave a final scrape on the concrete as Pru led him into his stall, and then her voice was muffled by the dividing partition. "Nothing definitive. There've been a few rental properties broken into at the edge of town and out on Saint Helena Island, but that could be anyone. The sheriff's convinced that even if Ernesto did survive, he'd be long gone down to some Quintero Cartel safe house far away from here."

Trying, and failing miserably, not to be angry, Barrie stood and watched Miranda snuffle at the flake of hay laid down in the corner. Pru came to stand in the doorway of the stall.

"Seems to me we're all trying too hard to take care of one another, and what we ought to be doing is spending more time talking," Pru said. "It's like these stalls. There was no need for you to get up so early. I would have come to help if you'd told me you were going to do them."

Barrie scanned the stall and took in the clean bedding, the full water bucket, and the grain waiting in the feed bin. The flake of hay Miranda was eating was only just starting to lose its rectangular shape. Everything she and Pru had come out to do for the horses was already done, and a couple of *yunwi* looked up at her from where they stood pressed against her legs, while others peeked out from both sides of the door behind Pru, their body language mischievous, shy, and proud of themselves all at once. A soundless giggle vibrated in her ears.

"Thank you," she said, but then she shook her head because it felt wrong for them to do so much when she was doing so little. "But don't do this again without me, all right?"

"Who are you talking to?" Pru asked.

"It was the *yunwi* who cleaned the stalls for us, which proves my point from last night. They help without even being asked. The Fire Carrier wouldn't need to protect his tribe from them, so there has to be another reason why they're here."

Leaning against her or with their hands touching hers, the *yunwi* were clearer than ever, their faces less shadowy. But they were still too shapeless for Barrie to distinguish one from another by features alone. There were expressions that she recognized, though. Individuals that she was coming to know, and she had the impression they were allowing her to come to know them.

Her heart swelled all over again with the certainty that she had to protect them. They trusted her, and if the Fire Carrier had brought them to Watson Island to keep them safe, then the bargain had to, at least in part, be about keeping them from harm. The world was full of ugly things and dangerous people.

No matter what else happened, she couldn't risk having

Obadiah break the binding until she knew what would happen to the *yunwi*, not just in her lifetime but in the future. Who would watch over them and Watson's Landing in the generations to come?

Maybe that was another component of the binding. Being able to see the *yunwi* and feel the land the way she did since being bound, she had come to understand how special this place and the *yunwi* were, but not everyone would react that way. Without the binding, how many Watson heirs would choose to stay here? Giving someone a choice was always a leap of faith. Barrie had realized that yesterday when Eight had walked away from her.

She gave Miranda a final pat and closed the stall door with a *snick*. "Last night, I asked you to question Seven about the Beaufort lodestone, but if you haven't done it yet, please don't. I don't want Eight feeling like I'm feeling now, at least any more than he does already. If Seven told you anything he hasn't told Eight yet, it would make Eight feel more betrayed."

"What about Obadiah?" Pru coiled Batch's lead rope into three neat loops across her palm.

"At this point, I'm more convinced than ever that we can't risk breaking the bindings, so Obadiah will have to find another solution. For all we know, he may already have one, but he'll never admit it as long as he thinks he can get the lodestones from me. Hopefully, meeting Daphne will give him extra incentive to be forthcoming," Barrie said, smiling with more certainty than she felt.

Her confidence had dipped even lower by the time she and Daphne had entered the tunnel some forty minutes later. The lemony beam of Daphne's flashlight played along the brick walls and long, arched ceiling and swept the niches built to house the oil lanterns that had lit the tunnel back when it had been built as a means of escape off the island. As usual, the darkness of the tunnel and the ghosts of the past closed in around Barrie, along with the sheer volume of earth above her that seemed to press down onto her shoulders. Daphne was silent, and her posture was stiff as they crossed beneath the river. Her expression was impossible to read. She always kept herself so contained that it was as though she had stuffed herself into a box that was too small and she was simultaneously trying to keep herself in and struggling to escape.

"What do you think of all this? Obadiah and the curse?" Barrie's voice echoed hollowly off the bricks as they reached the Beaufort side of the tunnel, where the floor began to slope gently upward again.

"I'm not sure how much I ever believed in all Gramma's superstitions before. I mean, I knew about the Fire Carrier and the *yunwi* and the gifts in principle, the way everyone around here knows it. But now that I know that the curse could affect our family, too, I'm worried that I'll blame it any time something goes wrong. What if I can't postpone the scholarship, or if Brit doesn't get into the trial, or if Jackson gets hurt again? I'll always wonder if that was the curse, and I don't want to be tempted to use it as an excuse or a justification the way the Colesworths do. I don't want to become like them."

"The fact that you're asking the question probably means you wouldn't become like them," Barrie said, "but I guess we never know the truth of ourselves until we're tested."

The key turned smoothly in the new lock, and Barrie used her shoulder to push open the heavy door, emerging in the small stairwell in the woods between the Beaufort and Colesworth properties. Overhead, through the metal grating camouflaged by leaves and branches, bits of sky hurried past carrying the promise of potential rain.

After she and Daphne had climbed from the stairwell, Barrie locked the grating and covered it with leaves again before leading Daphne out through the woods to the Colesworth beach. Together, they climbed the path above the fire-scarred dock. Around them, kudzu and wisteria blanketed the hillside, engulfing trees, shrubs, and entire structures. At the top of the rise, Colesworth Place suddenly stretched out, the lawn and outbuildings still dominated by the mansion ruins.

Near the trees that screened the slave cabins from where the house had been, a row of domed tents had sprung up again overnight like mushrooms, signaling that the archaeologists were back. The brightly colored nylon surfaces strained against the wind that blew off the river, and like the police tape and the sheriff's car, the tents looked anachronistic against the backdrop that seemed too deeply rooted in the past.

Arms wrapped around her waist in a self-protective gesture, Daphne stared past the tents to the tiny cabins where entire families had lived, where her own ancestors had lived. "It's strange to be here," she said. "To see all this. I've never wanted to. A lot of folks were mad about Wyatt restoring these old buildings and charging people to come and look. Others were upset because Cassie and her drama club were putting on *Gone with the Wind* at night in front of the ruins. I guess everyone's got opinions, but I always figured it was all about how much power you wanted to give something. I just wasn't about to help the Colesworths make money from something that never should have happened in the first place."

Barrie looked around, trying to see the place through Daphne's eyes, or Obadiah's. She couldn't, but it was all too easy to remember the outrage she had felt the night when the spirits of Alcee and Ann Colesworth had brought the Civil War back to life. The fact that their ghosts seemed to have been laid to rest with the discovery of their daughter's body down in the hidden room seemed an even more cruel twist of fate, when the spirits of Ayita and Elijah were still chained to the same room where John Colesworth had confined them.

"Does it bother you that Watson's Landing was open to tourists?" Barrie couldn't help asking. "Or about the restaurant? I never even questioned any of this when I first got here. I should have."

"Watson's Landing is about the house and gardens. It's like any other big house. But this?" Daphne gestured around at the slave cabins, kitchens, and outbuildings that Wyatt had so painstakingly restored. "The Colesworth family is still making money from my family's suffering. Maybe if Wyatt had put in some exhibits when he'd restored the buildings, or if you could see the mansion and how the Colesworth family lived in contrast to the people who gave them the wealth to live that way . . . Even that wouldn't be enough."

Barrie wasn't sure how to answer that, wasn't even sure she had the right to say anything when her own ancestors had owned slaves, too. She held her hand out, and Daphne's fingers closer around her own.

"Tell me what Obadiah is like," Daphne said. "Is he bitter? Or angry? It could have made him both, living through what he did."

Barrie scanned the area for him while she considered what to say. "I think he's tired. Maybe after you've seen that much cruelty, tired is all that's left."

• • •

At the dig site, the archaeologists hadn't wasted any time. Except for Berg, the students were hauling replacement shovels, trowels, and brushes into the overseer's cabin, where the headquarters and cleaning tables had been set up. Stephanie, the second in command, was re-covering the big frames with screens for sifting soil, and Andrew Bey, the grad student in charge of the day-to-day work for Dr. Feldman, had already reburied the iron rebar datum in an even larger bed of concrete. Using it as the measuring point, he and Berg had been marking fresh grid lines with twine and flags of orange tape. The perimeter of the buried chamber was still roped off with yellow tape.

Spotting Barrie and Daphne, Berg broke away and strode toward them, his footsteps silent, his eyes squinting against the sunlight but missing nothing. Even in his cargo shorts and faded plain blue T-shirt, he had the posture of a soldier, and the sharp attention of a former Marine sniper. Barrie wondered how anyone could ever mistake what he was. What he had been.

"I've been trying to figure out how to get ahold of you," he said when Barrie had performed the introductions and trotted out her prepared excuse about looking for an earring she had lost.

"Why?" Barrie asked, more curious than alarmed, until he caught her arm and pulled her aside with a mumbled apology to Daphne.

When they had some semblance of privacy, he pushed a hand through his white-blond hair as if he didn't know where to begin. "I've been thinking through what happened yesterday," he finally said, "and things don't add up. The stolen equipment and the damage at the dig site, that wasn't a coincidence. Someone wanted to make us leave."

"Sure. Ryder and Junior did that."

"No one could pull a chunk of rebar and concrete the size of the datum out of the ground and throw it thirty feet without making any noise. Someone had to have drugged the whole dig crew to keep us from all waking up. Someone who could come close enough to dose the water or the coffee. Cassie's the only person who was out here that night."

Barrie forced herself to look at him. To be convincing. "That's crazy," she said. "You know Cassie wouldn't drug you."

"Then who?" Berg's forehead furrowed. "What's really going on? Cassie called me early last night, asking about finding someone to help her with her flashbacks, and I told her I'd bring some names with me when I came out this morning. Then suddenly, she was out here first thing, trying to convince me to leave and to talk Dr. Feldman and Andrew into postponing the dig. She was barely coherent when I tried to tell her that wasn't going to happen. We're a week away from opening up that room. No one's going to stop now."

"A week? I thought all you had to do was take the roof off."

"Too much risk of collapse, so it's better to dig down and go in from the basement," Berg said distractedly. "Look, I need to know that it's safe. Why does she want us to leave?"

How was Barrie supposed to answer that? She couldn't assure Berg that the dig was safe when it wasn't, but how could she tell him the truth? He would assume she was nuts or protecting Cassie—or both. On the other hand, didn't the dig crew deserve to know the danger?

She did her best to mask her doubt. "We've had this conversation before, haven't we? There's no explaining Cassie. But she didn't drug you. I can promise you that. I'm sure you were all exhausted from working in the sun all day. Maybe you slept more soundly than usual."

Berg's face tightened into stone. "I've had to lie prone for hours in 110-degree heat wearing body armor and then shoot a Taliban fighter from almost a half mile away. You know I like Cassie—more than I probably should—but if she's putting the dig crew in danger, that's a job for the police."

"The police?" Fabric rustled behind Barrie as Daphne stepped up beside them. "What's wrong?"

Barrie shook her head. "Nothing. Berg's delusional."

"You're going to have to convince me about that," Berg said.

"I will. Later." Barrie's head ached, and not just from her usual migraine. Even the thought of coming up with more excuses made her tired. "Daphne and I have that earring to find, and then she has to get home. But I'll come back, and we'll talk. Just don't do anything until I've explained, all right? No police."

Extricating herself before Berg could keep arguing, she hurried toward the cemetery, keeping her head down as if she were searching the ground for her missing earring. Daphne fell into step beside her, also pretending to search.

"What was that about?" Daphne asked.

"More casualties of lies and half-truths," Barrie said, deciding then and there that she didn't care if Berg thought she was crazy. He deserved to know what was going on, and maybe if he knew, he'd be able to get the dig postponed.

They rounded the freestanding kitchen house, and she finally spotted Obadiah. He sat with his back braced against an oak tree, light dappling his skin and picking out the low notes of green and blue and purple, the raven colors, amid the dirt on his black silk suit. He appeared more like himself than he had the night before, as if he'd rolled the clock back a decade overnight. Undoubtedly, that was because the archaeologists had arrived that morning with a fresh supply of energy for him to steal.

He made no move to get up as Barrie and Daphne reached him, and his less than immaculate appearance as much as his stillness spoke of weakness. On the other hand, Barrie had already learned that when it came to Obadiah, appearance had little to do with fact.

CHAPTER NINE

Daphne's red ribbon waved bravely in the breeze, but her footsteps slowed as she approached Obadiah. For his part, while he barely moved, barely breathed, every muscle in his body coiled with anticipation, and his eyes misted.

He knew who Daphne was.

Unlike the dig crew, Daphne clearly saw him. She didn't wait for introductions, either. Finding her courage, or perhaps because necessity had overcome fear, she surged ahead of Barrie and stopped a foot away from him. "How can you be the same Obadiah who was alive in the Civil War? What kind of magic does that?"

His gold incisors flashed as he smiled, and he used the trunk of the oak tree to pull himself to his feet. "I believe it's customary to say hello to your elders before you pepper them with questions. Didn't your grandmother teach you manners?"

"Gramma also taught me to tell the truth."

As if he couldn't help himself, Obadiah reached out to touch Daphne's hair, to cup her face. His expression, his every movement, was so obviously starved to touch her, to connect, that tears stung Barrie's eyes. "Truth is relative," he said, looking pained as Daphne flinched away. "I can't be the same person I was then, but I'm the Obadiah who was alive at that time. There's more in the world than most people are willing to acknowledge. Whether you want to call it magic, or science, or a miracle doesn't change the fact that it exists. All you have to do is make the leap of faith into believing."

Daphne took another step back. "So you really do take energy from people. Boo hags and Raven Mockers and things like that are real?"

"Someone's been doing their homework," Obadiah said with a faint, pained frown. "There's some truth to almost every story, but very few stories are wholly true. I'm not taking anyone's skin or the heart from their bodies, or any other superstitious nonsense that people fear out of ignorance. Simply put, there are different kinds of energy. There's the conscious spirit"—he patted the scalp area at his hairline—"but there's also a more transient energy, the kind that's stored in the heart or liver or bones and flows in and out of the world around us. I've learned to absorb a bit of that from other people to fuel my magic."

Daphne only looked back at him, wide-eyed. "Does it hurt?"

"There's no ill effect." Obadiah smiled wearily. "The person I borrow from may feel a little tired, and for my part, I take in a small imprint from them . . . like a footprint of who they are, what they feel, what they dream and fear. If anything, that makes me value life more instead of less."

He turned back to Barrie. Then he stiffened, and his attention narrowed as if he were only really noticing her for the first time. Leaning closer, he sniffed the air around her. "Speaking of energy, yours is unbalanced," he said, everything about him suddenly alert and eager. "You found the vortex, didn't you? And the Watson lodestone? Did you find that, too?"

Trying her best to look calm, Barrie suspected that she was failing miserably. "It doesn't matter. I'm not going to give it to you. What if the vortex is the reason why the Fire Carrier brought the *yunwi* here? What happens to them in the future if the binding is broken?"

"You're asking me to look into the future and give you guarantees." Obadiah raised his hands in a gesture of surrender. "Magic isn't a recipe for baking cake. There are a hundred variables and complications, and however long I've lived, I'm still only human. I can use my strength to protect the living, or I can try to overcome Ayita and Elijah, or I can try to break the curse. At the moment, I'm trying to do all three. The lodestones are the only way to get the kind of power I need to do that successfully."

Barrie wished he sounded less sincere, but that didn't change her determination. "I know you're trying to protect your family, but I have to protect mine, too."

"She's right," Daphne said as Obadiah's expression darkened. "And you don't even know my family. What *do* you get out of this?"

"What do I get?" Obadiah's eyebrows rose. "I get to finally be free of this life I have had to cling to so stubbornly. I *get* to free my ancestors from the curse that holds them captive. I get to have you"—he pointed a shaking finger at Daphne—"and the rest of my family free to make their own choices and their own mistakes without the past hanging over them. I get to leave those people"—he waved at the archaeologists—"safe so they can keep being ignorant. So that they can keep believing that the scraps they find left behind in the dirt tell more than a fraction of any human story. I'm *here* because this isn't some fairy tale to read about. It's a story about revenge. Ayita was raised to believe a spirit couldn't rest until vengeance was complete, that the living wouldn't be safe until the dead had been appeased. So if the gold is what I need to buy her peace and freedom, I will claim it without a twinge of guilt. But make no mistake, the gold is the path to the end, not the end itself." His voice slowed on the last sentence and dropped in volume, as if emotion had spent what little of his energy remained.

"Then let me talk to Ayita," Daphne said. "If revenge or pride or pain is the only thing keeping everyone caught in this nightmare, let me tell her and Elijah that we don't want it. We don't need them to keep us safe—the curse may be the only reason we *aren't* safe. Maybe if I explain what all this is doing to Brit and Jackson, to my mama and gramma Mary, they'll let it go—"

"You think I haven't tried to convince them to drop the curse? I've come back many times over the years and tried to persuade them—"

"All the more reason to let Daphne try," Barrie said. "You don't know the family well enough to make this personal, and you hate the Colesworths. Maybe deep down you feel a certain satisfaction in Ayita's vengeance. What if she senses that?"

Obadiah made a darting, impatient gesture. "I don't hate the Colesworths, but I can't forgive them, either. No one in that family has ever accepted responsibility for any of their problems."

"Forgiveness isn't about others admitting guilt or you being right. It's about being the bigger person so that everyone can move forward," Barrie said, flushing even as she said it, aware of all the resentments she was still dragging with her. Soon, very soon, she needed to read her mother's letters and lay her own ghosts to rest. "Isn't it possible that Elijah and Ayita are tired of clinging to all this anger, too? What can it hurt to let Daphne try to talk to them?"

Obadiah drew himself to his full height, though his shoulders were still faintly bowed. Then he released a sigh and studied Daphne. "Are you sure you could do it? Communicating with the dead can be dangerous if you're afraid or vulnerable. Once the spirits have a hold on you, there can be residual effects. Dreams—nightmares—visions. You open yourself up to Ayita's hate."

"I'm not afraid," Daphne said, holding herself so stiffly that the lie was obvious.

Obadiah opened his mouth, then shook his head and turned to plod off toward the slave cabins, motioning for them to follow. "You'll have to do exactly what I say. This would work better at night beside the room where their remains are buried, but the cabin where they lived will have to do."

His gait was still slow and faltering. Barrie reached out automatically to steady him, but he winced as if something about her proximity was physically painful. She dropped back to walk with Daphne. They passed the overseer's house, and the dig crew paid them no attention. Barrie was used to that when Obadiah was around, but Daphne stopped to wave a hand in front of Stephanie's face. When that produced no reaction, she picked up a trowel and moved it from one end of the sifting screen to the other. She finally set it down.

"It really is magic, isn't it? This is actually happening, and the stories are true."

Barrie thought what an adjustment that had to be, learning about magic and Obadiah and the spirits all at once. "You're sure you're going to be all right talking to Ayita?"

"I don't want her hurting anyone on my account," Daphne said.

"It wouldn't be your fault."

"Is that how you'd feel if something happened?" Daphne set off after Obadiah again, head down and shoulders forward, and she smiled grimly at Barrie's silence. "See? I didn't think so."

They approached the cabin together. Obadiah had disappeared inside already. Behind the structure and the trees beyond it, a subdivision of minimansions sat on land where Ayita and her family, maybe even Obadiah himself, had worked in the mosquito- and snake-infested water of the old Colesworth rice fields. Barrie was ashamed to realize that before she'd come to Watson's Landing, she had never thought about what that had really been like. Even now, she knew she could never grasp the feeling of impotence and the unfairness of being treated as if you were *less*, and the wounds that had to leave behind. Maybe that was impossible for anyone who hadn't been touched by it, who hadn't felt it, to understand.

Inside the cabin, Obadiah had removed the floorboards that hid the makeshift cellar, and he was lying prone to reach past the assortment of jars, pots, and undefinable objects that Barrie already knew were down there. Eventually, he extracted an earthenware bowl from the far reaches of the cavity. His face was tense and vulnerable as he glanced over to where Daphne had halted in the doorway, but she was staring off into the corner. He pushed himself up to his knees, then flicked up one sleeve of his suit and used his shirt to polish away the dust and grime from the bowl that he'd removed. It was more refined than the others that Barrie had seen in the cellar earlier, beautifully shaped with a lid and a rich brown glaze that shimmered in the light.

Obadiah stood and pried up the lid of the bowl, revealing a white caked substance inside. Daphne moved in closer. "What is that?"

"White clay," he said. "I'll use it to draw a cosmogram as a means of protection and communication, a way to reach from this world to the next so that I can ask the spirits for their attention."

Using his fingernails, he scraped loose enough powder to fill his palm, then placed the bowl on the fireplace mantel and began to sprinkle the clay onto the wooden floorboards, first in the pattern of a cross, then in a large circle to connect the points, and then in a smaller circle inside the outer one. It was the same pattern he had drawn the night he had raised the spirits, when the ghost of the Colesworth mansion had sprung into existence.

Barrie wished she could block out the memories—pale dust sprinkled in a circle on grass faded to purple in the moonlight, a raven and feathers drifting from the sky, Obadiah thrown backward by a blast of power from below his feet. The ghosts of two girls and a woman, an officer and his soldiers, Alcee Colesworth clawing at the ground trying to reach his daughter who was locked in the hidden room as the mansion burned. The echoing death of a house and a cruel way of life. She could still smell the flames and the terror, feel the ground shake, *see* Obadiah lying on the grass withered to nothing but skin and bone.

Having experienced then what happened when one of Obadiah's spells went wrong, Barrie braced herself to pull Daphne away as Obadiah worked. He moved too slowly, as if expending the effort took all his energy, and he seemed unable to keep from looking at Daphne for more than a few moments at a time. His eyes were hungry, needy.

In turn, Daphne seemed determined not to let him know he scared her. She wandered to the fireplace and ran her finger along the lid of the bowl he'd placed on the mantel. "Is this one of Dave the Potter's pieces? It's beautiful."

"Not every pot thrown by a slave was made by David

Drake. My father, Donas, made this one." Obadiah grunted as he straightened, and there was both pain and pride in his voice. "In his spare time, of course, because Alcee Colesworth wasn't about to let a strong back get out of doing work in the fields. And yes, bad eyesight, long days tending rice, then fishing and keeping the corn and hogs that fed his family, and still every piece of pottery he made was beautiful."

For the first time, Daphne turned back to look at Obadiah directly. "What happened to him?"

"Greed. Alcee discovered that my father was making money selling his pottery and decided that meant he wasn't working hard enough." Obadiah rubbed his hands together to remove the last remnants of the clay dust from them. "Everyone had a task at that time, three acres of rice in my father's case, and he was supposed to be free to do what he wanted once that was finished. Alcee gave him four acres to tend, then four and a half, then five, until my father fell over one day, too tired to get up, and the overseer let him drown in a foot and a half of mud and water."

Obadiah's back was turned, making it impossible to read his expression, but the tilt of his head and the stoop of his shoulders said enough. He began a rhythmic chant and started to move around the outer circle. Barrie's eyes were wet and her stomach churned, and Daphne stood gripping the mantel with one hand and staring at the floor.

The ceremony had been quiet the first time Barrie had seen Obadiah conduct it, but now his voice was fervent and loud, as if he were demanding that the spirits pay attention. He traced the circle counterclockwise, his feet shuffling, rotating outward then back in again, clapping his hands at each point of the cross, where he'd left small mounds of chalk. When he'd followed the full circumference, he went around six more times. Finally he stepped into the center and raised his palms.

Barrie hadn't stopped being afraid since the moment when she'd first discovered how badly magic could go awry. She should have been petrified now, but maybe the capacity for fear was finite.

There was no flutter of wings from empty air, no ravens that lived and died and never existed except in the realm of magic. The air stirred as if something unseen had swept into the room.

Obadiah tensed. Arms raised, his fingers contracted into fists, and his muscles bunched as if he were pushing against something heavy. His eyes bulged with effort.

The temperature dropped. The atmosphere throbbed and pulsed, as if it suddenly had weight and mass. Deep in her throat, Daphne made a keening sound, and the fine hair rose on Barrie's arms and the back of her neck.

Obadiah's entire body had gone rigid, and panting open-mouthed, he jerked from one side to the other as if he were being pulled in different directions. Twitching and convulsing, he fought to move his foot.

"What's he doing?" Daphne whispered.

"I don't know," Barrie said. "Maybe he's trying to get out of the circle."

"Should we help him?"

Barrie didn't know that, either. Clearly, something was very wrong. Whatever battle Obadiah was fighting, he wasn't winning.

Taking a deep breath, she ran forward. She plunged her hands into the circle, grabbed Obadiah's shoulders, and yanked him back.

His body was lighter than she'd anticipated. Too light for a man his size, but still too large for her to carry. It was mostly the momentum that brought him back with her, and then he fell on top of her and toppled her to her knees.

Instantly the whispering air went still. The temperature warmed back to normal.

Obadiah lurched to his feet. Flinching in pain, he hobbled back to the circle and stared down at the mess of broken lines where his foot had dragged through the white powder of both the vertical line and the outer circle. He scrubbed at the white powder even more, until he had obliterated the entire vertical section of the cross. Only then did he stop and let his legs buckle. Collapsing to one knee, he held both temples as if his head ached, and his face was twisted and *old* again, leached of blood beneath the dark brown skin. He attempted to get back up but didn't seem to have the strength, and he lowered himself to one hip instead.

"Are you all right?" Barrie asked.

"Never, *ever* step into a cosmogram or any kind of circle," he said without looking at her. "Never interrupt a ceremony. Didn't you learn anything the other night when the Colesworth girl caught the feathers?"

Barrie shuddered at the memory of Cassie grabbing a handful of black feathers as they drifted into the ground itself as if they weren't solid. That was when the explosion had come.

There hadn't been any feathers this time.

"You looked like you were in trouble," she said.

"That's beside the point. I managed to break the connection to the dead as you pulled me out, but you'd have been exposed and vulnerable if I hadn't—and I couldn't have done anything to protect you."

"Protect her from what? What *was* that? What happened?" Daphne demanded.

Obadiah's head dropped to his chest as if he had no strength left to hold it up. "Elijah and Ayita weren't as weak as I expected. Instead of answering me when I tried to communicate with them, they siphoned off the energy I put into the magic, and I wasn't strong enough to break the connection. Help me get back outside. I'll need to take a little more energy from the excavation team—you've already given me too much."

"What about her?" Barrie gestured toward the mantel, where Daphne stood.

Daphne's eyes went wide, and her hand flew to the base of her throat. "Me?"

"Leave her alone. That's why it's better when people don't know—then they can't be afraid." Gathering himself, Obadiah made an effort to get up. His fingers dug into his thighs to support his weight, and his cheeks and eyes were sunken. When Barrie had first met him, he had been so much more alive.

"I am not afraid," Daphne said, looking as if she'd rather bolt out of the cabin. Edging closer, she held out her wrist to Obadiah.

"Are you sure?" He waited until she nodded. Then he raised his fingers cautiously, as though Daphne were a Fabergé egg and could be easily broken.

Instead of grasping her hand, he laid his palm against her cheek, and his eyes closed at the first brush of his skin on hers. Tears leaked from beneath his lids, but that had nothing to do with taking energy. His wistful smile said as much.

Daphne was trembling so hard that Obadiah's arm shook. Then suddenly, she jerked away and backed up until she reached the doorway. "I can't do this. I'm sorry."

She turned and ran out of the cabin.

"Wait, Daphne. Where are you going?" Barrie ran to the threshold. "What's wrong?"

Daphne neither slowed nor looked back, and glancing over her shoulder at Obadiah, Barrie caught her breath. She had never seen Obadiah appear heartbroken, but he looked it now. Lonely and heartbroken, and her heart wrenched at the thought of him wandering for more than a hundred years, watching everyone he loved die around him. Watching everyone leave him, then finding Daphne and having her literally run away because he scared her.

"Will you be all right if I go after her?" she asked him quietly.

"Don't feel sorry for me. Go."

"But the energy—"

"I'm not asking her, or anyone else, to understand the choices I've had to make in my life, but you have to see that it's more important than ever that you bring me the lodestones. I'll take as much energy as I can from anywhere I can find it to keep Ayita and Elijah contained, but they won't stay weak for long. It's not just the chance to break the curse that's at stake anymore. That room is no longer sealed. Once the spirits have the strength to reach beyond it, they won't necessarily stop taking energy when they reach full strength. The feeling can be addictive. The more energy they have, the more they'll crave, and they'll do anything, hurt anyone, to get it."

Barrie bit her lip, remembering the sensation of energy flowing through her, of swimming in energy, of being cracklingly, dazzlingly alive with it. "I'll go after her," she said. "I'm sorry."

"Don't be sorry. Just find the lodestones and bring them here."

CHAPTER TEN

Hurrying after Daphne, Barrie forgot all about her earlier promise to Berg until she heard him calling out to her. She didn't stop. At that moment, explaining the unexplainable was at the bottom of her to-do list.

Daphne had already reached the end of the path and was pacing the beach in front of the dock where the broken boards and charred pylons at the end were the only visible reminder of the explosion that had killed Wyatt and Ernesto—maybe killed Ernesto. Barrie shivered at the thought of him still out in the world somewhere, smuggling drugs again as if nothing had ever happened, as if Wyatt's death were only an inconvenience that had changed where the Quintero Cartel brought the stuff ashore.

She reached Daphne, who stopped pacing as Barrie moved up beside her. "Is Obadiah going to be okay?"

"Probably," Barrie said. "He didn't hurt you, did he?"

"Nothing like that. It's me." Daphne turned to face the water with her arms crossed, her hands gripping her own shoulders as if she didn't know what else to hold on to. "You know what he's been through—all the things he must have lived through and seen, how badly he's been treated. I'm related to him. I shouldn't feel disgusted by what he does, but I can't help it. I grew up hearing Gramma's stories about boo hags, and now I'm realizing that he's what she was talking about all that time. He's got human teeth on his wrist."

"They're his own teeth."

"That's only slightly better than if they were someone else's. Who wears teeth as a bracelet? But the point is, you heard him. He absorbs what people feel when he takes their energy. Their emotions. I think about what he's suffered, and then I imagine how it must feel to know that what he does— what he *is*—makes me want to throw up. What kind of a person does that make me?"

"A normal human one. It's magic. Magic that goes against everything you've ever been taught." Barrie shook her head. "I'm the last person in the world to judge you for running— it's my default response, and I'm not proud of it. But people run out of self-preservation. Fight or flight. Running gets you away from the things you can't beat."

"You can't outrun fear."

"I've damn well tried," Barrie said, smiling in spite of herself. "Plenty of times. If it worked, I'd still be trying. Obadiah's not going to judge you for what you feel. Family is always a mirror. You can hide from other people, you can even hide from yourself, but your family is going to reflect what you're doing right back at you."

She was thinking about her own family as she spoke, about Lula, who for years hadn't been able to look at her own daughter without seeing the burn scars that had destroyed her own beauty. About Pru and Lula's father, Emmett, who, instead of trying to be better and kinder to compete with the brother who overshadowed him, had resorted to brutal murder. Even Seven projected his own hopes and resentments onto his son. It all came down to how people saw themselves, and to what they refused to see.

Daphne's head came up. "Do you think I hurt Obadiah's feelings badly?"

"I think you gave him hope that he hasn't had in a long time. I get the feeling he hasn't been close to anyone in a while."

"So you trust him?"

Barrie stopped to consider that. "I trust him with *you*. The way he looked at you, I trust him to do whatever he feels is going to keep you safe."

"I can't go back there. Not right now. And Gramma is probably worrying herself sick as long as we've been gone."

"So we'll take some time to figure things out logically before we try again—"

"Try what again?" Walking up silently behind her, Berg put a hand heavily on Barrie's shoulder. "I thought we had a deal. You were supposed to find me before you left."

Barrie had forgotten how quietly he moved. She spun to face him, then glanced back at Daphne. "I can't talk right now—I need to get Daphne back to Watson's Landing."

"I can get back on my own. Don't worry about me," Daphne said.

Berg held Barrie's eyes. "I can drive you back in the car later, but I really need that explanation you promised. I don't want to have to bring the police into this . . ."

"Hey. Don't make threats." Daphne's eyes slitted, and she stepped up beside Barrie.

"It's all right." Barrie dug the key to the tunnel out of her pocket and dropped it into Daphne's palm. "Try to pull a branch or something back over the grating as you drop it shut, and make sure you lock both that and the tunnel door. And tell Pru that I'll be back as soon as I can to help with the furniture."

She stood silently watching Daphne walk away, aware of Berg standing grim-faced behind her, waiting for her to begin.

She wished she knew how. Or even how much to say. Finally she turned, headed out onto the dock, and dropped down on the edge facing upriver toward Watson's Landing.

Berg lowered himself beside her. "I take it this is going to be a long explanation. Is Cassie in some kind of trouble? Apart from what I already know about? Was Ryder forcing her to help him steal the gold? Whatever she's done, tell me so I can find a way to help."

His obvious concern made the decision simple. For Berg, the questions all began and ended with Cassie. Even though he suspected she had drugged him and everyone else on the dig crew, he'd waited before calling the police. He hadn't even known what he was waiting *for*—he'd just waited. Which meant he hadn't wanted to make the call. With everything he'd done in the military, Barrie couldn't imagine what it would take to scare him. And the very first time Barrie had met him, he had talked about how much time he had spent in cemeteries growing up. He'd talked about angry angels.

"How do you think Cassie is holding up?" she asked him, slipping off her shoes. "Really holding up?"

His profile hardened. "PTSD-wise, you mean? I'm not a professional. But sometimes, when the flashbacks start, it's a sign that you're starting to process what happened instead of suppressing it. Sometimes. Not always. She needs to see someone."

Beyond the Watson dock, the water of the Santisto swept beneath the overhanging oaks and the tupelos that guarded the edge of the overgrown rice fields. A heron stood motionless, nearly invisible, hunched like an old woman in the grass. Without the ghost hunters and curious lookie-lous who had plagued the area for the past weeks, the river was peaceful again. The patrols the sheriff had set had accomplished at least that much.

"Why don't you tell me what Cassie's done," Berg said. "I can't help her if I don't understand."

"She didn't explain anything to you?"

"Apparently, she doesn't want anyone to disturb Charlotte Colesworth's burial place. That was her excuse for wanting to shut down the dig, but she was spitting out whatever popped into her head: ghosts, curses, psychic energy. That's what's got me worried."

"So you don't believe in ghosts?"

Berg went still, then ran a hand over his close-cropped hair. "Are you saying she was serious? It's always a little hard to tell what the locals are making up around here."

"What if I said that everything you've heard is real? The Fire Carrier, and the gifts, and the curse. You already know about the pirates and the tunnels." She leaned forward so that she could watch Berg's expression as she explained, and in the end, she told him everything—about Obadiah, and Ayita and

Elijah, the gifts and the curse, lodestones, energy, vortexes, magic, and the bindings. Berg interrupted her only a few times to ask questions, and they were sitting close together, deep in conversation, when Cassie's voice from the beach made Barrie give a guilty start.

"What are you doing?" Cassie asked.

Berg's brow was still creased with thought, and he looked up almost absently. Cassie stalked out onto the dock and stopped behind him.

"I thought I saw you two headed down here. You're not talking about me, are you?" She smiled as if she were only joking, but the color in her cheeks nearly matched the bright pink of her hip-length blouse.

"Indirectly." Berg patted the sun-bleached boards beside him. "Barrie was filling me in about ghosts, curses, and spirit paths."

With a resentful look at Barrie, Cassie eased herself down and sat cross-legged on the planks. "Does that mean you're changing your mind about giving Obadiah the lodestones?"

Dunking her feet into the bathtub-temperature water, Barrie pointed and flexed her toes, kicking up small bubbles that drifted down beneath the dock. "Even if I had the stones, which I don't, I couldn't hand them over without understanding what they do and how they work. I need facts. That's where I was hoping Berg could help."

"There are no facts when it comes to magic." Berg's lips tightened.

"But 'lodestone' is another name for magnetite, isn't it? That's fact," Barrie said. "Science, not just magic. Magnetite was used by the ancient Chinese and Olmecs for orientation and navigation, so if magnetite is also a focal point for magic, then—"

"Move!" Cassie gripped Berg's arm and scrambled to her feet. She pointed at a dark, slow-moving shape, pebbled like a log, and a pair of eyes breaking the surface of the water. Vertical pupils seemed to focus on Barrie as the alligator drifted toward the dock.

Berg jumped up and hauled Barrie upright with him. Only as the gator slid beneath the dock did its full length become visible, a good seven or eight feet of teeth, sinew, and tough, ridged hide disappearing just inches from where Barrie'd had her feet. For some reason, that seemed to be the topper on the whole damn day.

But she didn't have time to indulge in panic at the moment.

The alligator must have dived down deep, because there was no sign of it emerging from under the dock downriver. Barrie snatched up her shoes and shuffled to the middle of the dock with a nice, safe expanse of wood between her and the water on either side. That wasn't panic. It was only prudent.

Berg came to stand beside her. "What were you saying about lodestones?"

Cassie sent another resentful glance at Barrie and sank back down to sit on the planks at Berg's feet again in a single graceful motion. Her jeans rode up over the ankle monitor she still had to wear, and she shot a glance up at Berg to see if he'd noticed as she twitched the fabric of her pants back over it.

"What's the point of talking about lodestones if Barrie's not going to give them to us anyway?" she asked.

Berg waved his hand invitingly at the planks beside him and gave Barrie a questioning lift of his brows. She looked around again for the alligator, but it was gone, and the water was quiet. Suppressing a sigh, she sat and pulled her knees to her chest, and Berg settled himself beside her.

"What I was saying," Barrie said, "is that even what I found on the Internet about lodestones as a focal point for magic talks about polarity, attracting negative or positive energies, like a compass."

Berg watched the water absently. "Actually, the Chinese didn't invent the compass for navigation—they invented it for feng shui, which is a metaphysical practice based on the flow of positive and negative energy."

"Magnetic energy?" Barrie asked.

"More than that. *Ch'i, prana, ruah, mana, moyo* . . . or 'the

Force,' if you happen to be a *Star Wars* fan, are all related to life force. Different cultures give it different names and contexts, just like there are various names for the lines that move that energy around the earth: spirit paths, ley lines, dragon lines. I'm not saying these things are real, but based on what you're saying, maybe they're not *not* real, either. Science can't prove this spiritual sort of energy exists, but maybe that's only because we haven't yet figured out how to measure it."

The heron who'd been standing sentry in the marsh grass upriver took flight, blue-tipped wings rowing up in long, slow strokes, legs dripping like a wake behind it. Berg leaned back and watched it pass, but it was clear that he was thinking hard, wrestling with something.

Cassie scooted in closer and leaned across to tap his knee. "If you believe the energy could be real, then help me talk Barrie into being reasonable about the lodestones."

"Could the place be special to the Fire Carrier and the *yunwi*," Barrie asked, ignoring Cassie, "*because* of the vortex or the spirit path?"

Berg leaned forward. "That's interesting. It might depend on when they came. We tend to think of the Cherokee in terms of the culture into which European contact forced them, but earlier they lived in towns and houses of wattle and daub and had complex religious and societal structures centered around a priesthood. Before that, the Mississippian mound builders had pyramids and astrological monuments that may not have been all that different in purpose from Newgrange, or Stonehenge, or the Egyptian or Mayan pyramids, and there are theories about ancient sites around the world being built on areas of high electromagnetic energy. I saw an article just the other day about physicists studying the way crystals in the rocks of Stonehenge might have been used to create an energy field."

Cassie shifted so that she blocked Barrie's view. Barrie peered around her and said, "So we're back to electromagnetic energy?"

Leaning toward her, Berg gave a shrug. "*If* there's a connection, it doesn't mean it's an intentional one. I'd have to research—"

"Oh, for God's sake." Cassie jumped up and glared down at them. "Who cares? Just find the stupid lodestones so that this can all be over."

Beneath the dock, something thrashed in the water and thumped one of the thick wooden pylons hard enough to make it shake. Cassie stepped backward, and Berg jerked Barrie to her feet.

"What was that?" Barrie asked.

"The alligator. Likely it's killing something." Cassie's eyes narrowed on Berg's hand still holding Barrie's arm.

Berg let go as the alligator emerged downriver, struggling

with a four-foot snake of some kind that dangled from its mouth. He moved to the edge of the dock for a closer look.

"That's a cottonmouth," he said.

Barrie backed to the upriver side of the dock. Smiling unpleasantly, Cassie followed her. "Cottonmouths are veeeery poisonous," she drawled, her face close to Barrie's. "You hate snakes don't you, cos? I don't blame you. I hate anything disgusting and slimy that slithers in where it isn't wanted."

With a venomous glare, she whipped around to head back toward the beach, knocking Barrie hard with her shoulder as she turned. Off balance, Barrie staggered but couldn't catch herself, and she plunged sideways into the water upriver from the dock.

The water closed over Barrie's head. Panic came hard and fast, thoughts of drowning because she still hadn't learned to swim, the alligator, the snake, memories of being in the water the night that Wyatt and Ernesto had tried to kill her.

Her heart and lungs clenched into a fist so tight that she couldn't breathe. She swallowed a mouthful of river, and knocked her knee against something hard. Fighting to orient herself in the murky water, she tried to kick her way to the surface.

A splash nearby—the alligator? Arms and legs flailing, Barrie finally got her head above water and sucked in a choking breath. But her lungs spasmed, and she was coughing, taking in more water. Something grabbed her and pulled her backward, and only after her panicked attempt to scream had ended in more water and more coughing did she realize it was Berg.

"Stop struggling. I've got you," he mumbled, his words distorted around a large knife clenched between his teeth.

With long, easy strokes, he towed her toward the shore, and a moment later he had his arm wrapped around her waist to help her walk up onto the beach. They hadn't been more than ten feet out, and Barrie felt stupid and ridiculous, but with her hands to her knees, coughing up water and fighting to breathe, she couldn't even apologize. Berg folded the blade of the knife back inside its black plastic handle, tucked it back into his pocket, then bent beside her and waited while she choked and shivered. A splash behind them made them both turn to where the alligator was just emerging from under the dock at the spot where Barrie had fallen in.

Barrie's legs and hands were numb. Still coughing lightly and feeling sick, she hobbled up the beach toward the path where Cassie had disappeared.

"Where are you going?" Berg followed close behind her.

"I'm going to kill Cassie. And thank you—" Barrie looked over at him and didn't even know how to begin to say what she felt. "Thank you" wasn't enough. "You saved my life."

Berg shook his head. "I'm not even going to pretend that

was an accident. I thought you and Cassie got along okay. But then, I guess she got in trouble with the police in the first place for locking you in the tunnel."

"Yes, and maybe I should have let her go to jail for that," Barrie said. Then she paused and sighed. "I don't know. It's hard to say how much of this is actually Cassie's fault. I wanted your attention—so the curse means she had to want that, too, and she wasn't getting it. Maybe she pushed me because of the curse and not out of spite and jealousy, or maybe the curse was only part of it. It's hard to separate our own feelings from the magic. At the same time, I can't help feeling like Cassie doesn't even try to fight what the curse makes her want."

"I suppose that's why stories about wishes rarely have happy endings," Berg said. "Even in stories, magic can't be pinned down." He sighed, and picked a long piece of marsh grass out of Barrie's hair. "I doubt that yelling at Cassie is going to do anyone any good. Why don't you let me take you home instead?"

Barrie looked behind her. The alligator still drifted in the water. Despite all the splashing Barrie and Berg had done, it hadn't let go of the prey it had already caught, and it still chewed the snake occasionally—torturing it until it died.

Possibly that was an omen.

Probably not a good one.

Barrie wasn't going to let that stop her. If Daphne couldn't talk Ayita and Elijah into dropping the curse, she had to find an alternative solution. Somehow, someway, the Watson Island story needed to have a happy ending.

"What do you know about cosmograms?" she said to Berg. "That's what Obadiah called the symbol he drew on the ground. He used it to try to control the dead and communicate with them."

CHAPTER ELEVEN

Like Barrie, Berg had paused on the beach to watch the alligator. He hurried to catch up as she set off uphill.

"A cosmogram does a lot more than control or communicate with the dead," he said. "It represents a whole belief system. Relationships within a community. Past and future generations. Humanity and nature. Time. Our place in the universe. Life and death. It's funny."

Barrie glanced over at him. "Not that funny."

"I mean, it's strange how a small shift in perspective can have a domino effect on everything you've ever believed was true. Once I accept the idea of spirit paths and ghosts, the realm of the dead represented below the horizontal line of the cosmogram is suddenly real. The underworld could be an *actual* place."

Barrie ran a hand across the back of her neck where the cold was settling in from his words and from her soggy clothes. But, of course, spirits had to go somewhere. Luke and Twila had disappeared once Barrie had found and acknowledged their bodies, and Alcee and Ann Colesworth seemed to have left as well, now that people knew their daughter's skeleton was down in the hidden room. Obadiah had said he'd crossed over into death and that Ayita and Elijah had brought him back.

"When you say 'underworld,' are you talking about heaven and hell?" she asked.

"I was thinking more like the underworld where Hades took Persephone. A place that's here and isn't."

Barrie stopped at the top of the path and looked around until she spotted a smudge of hot pink in the cemetery beneath the statue of the angry angel. She marched off in that direction, trying to ignore the way her wet clothes clung to her as she passed the archaeologists working at the dig site.

"Hey, are you okay?" Stephanie called to her, straightening from where she was pushing a load of soil and debris through the sifting screen.

Barrie flashed a bright and misleading smile. "I fell into the river. Stupid, right?"

A couple of the students stared at her openly as she passed, and Andrew removed his hat and wiped his head, opening his mouth and closing it again. Then he shook his head. "You about ready to get back to work, Berg?"

"Give me half an hour," Berg said. "I need to run Barrie home."

He followed Barrie toward the cemetery, jogging to catch up as she rushed on. "So what are you going to do? After you yell at Cassie, I mean. Unfortunately, I'm serious about not being able to pry Andrew and Dr. Feldman away at this point. And you were right—Cassie and her family would still be here, not to mention the police."

"What if we took Obadiah somewhere crowded?" Barrie voiced the only nebulous idea she'd managed to have so far. "Someplace like a baseball game, where he could take in a lot of energy a little bit at a time. Of course, then he wouldn't be here to protect the crew from Ayita and Elijah, so you'd have to get them away for at least that long."

"You said he mentioned energy stored in the heart, liver, and bones. Let me research that as well as the vortexes and lodestones. I'll also try to look into the early history of the plantations and see if there's anything about the bargains or the bindings. Some of the old records might have been digitized. Even if your grandfather destroyed whatever was at Watson's Landing, someone might have given journals or old documents to the historical society or taken a diary away when they got married. That's common enough."

Barrie reached the cemetery gate and shoved it open hard enough that it banged back against the fence. Beneath the statue at Charlotte Colesworth's empty grave, Cassie's dark jeans and hair blended into the blue shadows of the overhanging trees, and she appeared ghostly, pale, and disembodied as her head whipped around. Berg drew in his breath—a small sound, but a dead giveaway just the same.

Barrie tapped him on the shoulder. "I should slap you for your own good. Are you a masochist? Because you know she's crazy, don't you? With or without the curse."

"Since I didn't run away screaming in the middle of that conversation about Obadiah, I'd say masochism's a given," he said with a reluctant grin. "Cassie does have redeeming qualities, though."

"At the moment, I'll have to take your word for that." Barrie concentrated on navigating the mossy, uneven ground without falling on her face. Roots from the nearby trees had pushed up the surrounding monuments and cracked the tombstones. The air smelled brackish, as if there were standing water somewhere nearby, and mosquitoes hummed in the shade beneath the overhanging trees. She swatted as one buzzed past her face, but Cassie didn't seem to notice the bugs. She sat shivering, her arms around her knees. Tears had left dusty tracks along her cheeks.

From a distance—and as long as Cassie wasn't talking—it

was impossible for Barrie to not feel sorry for her. "Is she having another flashback? I don't want to yell at her if she's having one, but I deserve to be able to yell at her."

Berg gave a half smile and shook his head. "Sorry, flashbacks don't come at your convenience. That's part of what's so hard. You never know what's going to trigger memories, or when, or how bad they're going to be. Being startled by the alligator could have done it, or guilt at pushing you into the river, or who knows. And there probably aren't many places around here that feel completely safe to Cassie anymore after having Ryder walking around."

The idea of not feeling safe in your own house took the last edge off Barrie's anger. Stopping abruptly, she caught the waist of Berg's faded T-shirt as he moved past her.

"Couldn't you find a way to get her away from here for a while? Isn't there some kind of rehab center for PTSD? Maybe one for her and her family? Then the dig would have to shut down and at least everyone would be safe. . . ."

"What about the migraines?" Berg asked. "I'm not sure being in constant pain somewhere else would be any better for her than staying here and dealing with the flashbacks. But I can talk to some friends and see if they have suggestions."

They'd both spoken softly, and they were far enough away that Barrie didn't think Cassie could possibly have heard what they said, but maybe it wasn't the words as much as it was the fact that Barrie and Berg were having a conversation at all. Cassie jumped up and strode toward them with her hands balled into fists. The wind rustled through the leaves overhead, spilling a kaleidoscope of light across her face.

"Can't you just leave me in peace?" she yelled at Barrie. "I came out here to be by myself, but you're everywhere. All the time. And all you ever do is make me feel worse about myself."

The unfairness of that left Barrie speechless.

Berg raised his hands, palms outward, as if he were trying to calm a feral cat. "No one is trying to make you feel bad. Barrie least of all. She's trying to help you." He turned back to Barrie. "Give me a few minutes here, and then I'll come drive you back."

Barrie almost left. She wanted to storm away almost as much as she wanted to scream at Cassie to grow up, to stop being so awful, but what Berg had said about PTSD and the pinched, frightened look in Cassie's face both tore at her. Having the curse directing Cassie's actions, at least in part, had to be frightening and hard enough, but Barrie was starting to recognize the quicksand of the past. The idea of being lost in memories, locked in them with no way of knowing when or if you were going to be able to claw your way back out . . . It was awful to contemplate having to relive the pain and loss of control over and over. That was what it had to be like for

Cassie. Maybe every act of violence was like a stone cast into water, leaving ever-widening ripples.

For the rest of her life, Cassie was going to carry the scars of having been raped. Everyone around her would expect her to "get over it" and "move on" without talking about it, just like no one ever talked to Barrie about the night of the speed-boat explosion. As if by not talking, it would make it easier to forget. On the other hand, not talking meant Barrie never had to tell anyone how many times she relived what had happened, how responsible she felt.

Barrie didn't have flashbacks, not like Cassie's, but the memories and the guilt were always there. Logically she knew the explosion hadn't been her fault. She knew the Fire Carrier had been trying to save her, but she still couldn't escape the guilt.

Guilt didn't need rhyme or reason. It was poison. In a moment of vulnerability, Cassie had admitted that she blamed herself for not fighting back when Ryder had raped her, blamed herself for not being stronger. Barrie had to be strong enough not to abandon Cassie now.

"You didn't manage to drown me or feed me to the alligator," she said, moving up to stand beside Berg. "I guess you can't get rid of me that easily."

"How hard do you want me to try?" Cassie arched an eyebrow, but the venom was gone from her voice, replaced by a hesitant, wobbling hope.

Taking the last two steps to reach her cousin, Barrie held her arms open. Maybe neither she nor Cassie had ever had a genuine friend their own age—their own gender. After all, where were Beth and Gilly, the girls Barrie had met with Cassie at the Resurrection Tavern? Ever since Wyatt's death and Cassie's disgrace, they'd been conspicuously absent.

Not sure whether Cassie would want to be touched, Barrie waited. Cassie leaned forward stiffly, but she didn't pull away, and after a moment, her arms closed around Barrie's back. They both squeezed, just a little, and held on until Barrie's shoulder was even wetter, and she realized that Cassie was crying silently.

"You need to let Berg help you find a therapist, Cassie," she said as gently as she could. "You need to talk to someone honestly. No one deserves to have to pretend they're all right all the time. You don't get better by pretending."

Berg had the air-conditioning in the car turned to maximum cold, which was too cold on Barrie's still-damp clothes. She rested her head against the window, savoring the outside heat against her cheek. The sound of the tires grew echoey and hollow on the bridge that crossed the narrow creek separating Watson's Landing from the rest of Watson Island. Below them, the shallow water bubbled and frothed around a brown pelican perched on a rock near the bank. They passed the historical marker on the other side, and then followed along the length of the brick wall that enclosed the property.

"I remember how confident and put-together Cassie seemed when I first met her," Barrie said as Berg slowed down to turn into the driveway. "Have you ever wondered whether anyone is actually 'normal'? I'm starting to think we all fake it. Maybe the whole idea of 'normal' is propaganda people try to sell each other."

Berg grinned and braked the car in front of the wrought-iron gate. "That's one of the reasons I love the South. Down here, people embrace their crazy a lot more than they do anywhere else. Except maybe Hollywood, but that's a whole different kind of crazy."

"You're talking about eccentricity. I'm talking about desperation and pain. The kind that doesn't leave any physical traces. I always assume everyone else in the world is managing better than I am, but how does anyone know what someone else is going through?"

Barrie dialed the security code for the front gate on her cell phone and leaned back against the seat as the black iron gates opened beneath the overhanging gold *W.* Berg pulled through between the thick brick columns, and the gate closed behind him.

"I think we all put up a wall to keep people out," he said,

squinting into the light that flickered between the double row of overhanging oaks, "but breaking those down, bit by bit, is part of building a friendship. You have to let people in to see the ugly, or you're never going to have the kind of truth that connects people to each other. I guess that's why it's so hard to fathom that Cassie's parents had no idea she'd been raped. Maybe they put it down to the trauma of being kidnapped, but I can't imagine that there weren't clues."

"The word 'clue' implies that someone is searching for a solution to a problem. Cassie said her parents didn't want to ask the question."

"Some people don't. It's easier for them not to know."

Barrie couldn't help thinking of her own mother—and Eight's father. Even herself sometimes. She stared down at the phone she was still holding in her hand. "The problem," she said, "is that the longer you ignore things, the harder they'll eventually hit you."

Two long, white trucks from Edward G. Burnham & Co. Antiques stood parked at the bottom of the front steps with their ramps down. Berg pulled in beside the nearest one, and Barrie unclipped her seat belt and opened the passenger door.

"Thanks for being willing to help with the research, too, and for not having me committed when I told you what was going on. I'm glad you know the truth."

"I'll text or call you if I find something. It may not be until tonight or tomorrow morning—whenever I can get away from the rest of the crew. How long do we have before Ayita and Elijah are dangerous again? Did Obadiah give any kind of timeline?"

"I'm not sure we could count on anything he says. He didn't even know the spirits could hijack his magic."

Barrie climbed out of the car and waited on the steps thinking about what Berg had said as his car billowed dust down the long, gravel-lined drive between the double rows of oak trees. A man in blue overalls came down the steps, carrying the Queen Anne table from the front parlor, and the idea of throwing things away was the last straw. Her thumb pressed Eight's number in her call history before she could change her mind. Of course, the call went to voice mail. She hung up without leaving a message, but then the phone rang almost immediately. It was Eight's sister, though, not him.

"Eight's scared to talk to you," Kate said as soon as Barrie had said hello. "He's not even carrying his phone with him anymore."

"Is he all right?" Barrie let out a breath, not sure if it was relief or pain, and she walked away from the steps, past the trucks, and back up the driveway toward the big tree at the bottom. "Kate, help me out. What I can do? Even if he really doesn't want to see me, I need to be sure he's safe and happy. But I also need to keep Watson's Landing safe, and

I'm starting to suspect that can't happen without Beaufort Hall. I need to know what your father knows—anything he's admitted to Eight—"

"Admitted? You're acting as if Dad's on trial. I know about him not telling us about the Beaufort binding, and you not telling Eight when you found out. I thought that was why Eight is so furious with you both. Is there something else?"

It wasn't that Kate didn't deserve to know what was going on. She did. Barrie had withheld information from Eight in large part because it had seemed as if it would hurt less if his father confessed the lies himself. Even now, despite knowing how badly her silence had hurt Eight, she found that the instinct to protect Kate was still the same. And Eight had asked her not to get Kate involved.

"Come on, Barrie." Kate's voice dropped into a whisper. "Remember how you felt when you first got here? You didn't sit around being the only person who didn't know what was going on. You went looking for answers. So tell me what happened to stir everything up."

Barrie almost laughed at that. "*I* happened. I came here with the finding gift. Then Cassie wanted me to find the treasure for her, and Wyatt was afraid I would find out about his drug smuggling, and the explosion put everything in the news, so Obadiah came and wanted me to find the lodestones—"

"Who's Obadiah? And what lodestones?"

Barrie let out a sigh and picked an old acorn hat up out of the grass, rubbing her finger across the intricately patterned surface. "How about if we trade for information. I'll tell you everything, and you tell me what's going on with Eight."

"You first," Kate said.

Barrie sat down in the grass and picked up another acorn hat as she began to explain. Several *yunwi* who had followed her started to pick up hats as well and brought them to her, until by the time she had finished the explanation, she had a mound of them piled in front of her. She smiled at the *yunwi* and held up her hand for them to stop.

"Now you," she said to Kate. "You promised to tell me about Eight."

"He's packing to go to Columbia to stay with a friend until school starts."

Barrie's heart snagged on the words, and on the idea of not seeing him. Of not having any more chances to fix things between them. "Is that definite? You have to stop him."

"I'm not sure I can. He and Dad screamed at each other nonstop, and now they're barely speaking." Kate's voice was more serious than Barrie had ever heard it.

How had everything become such a mess?

"Please, Kate. I need to talk to him. You have to try to get him to speak to me, at least so I can tell him about the lodestones. Tell him it's important. Tell him anything you have to tell him so that he doesn't leave without talking to me first."

Kate said nothing for several awkward beats. "Don't put this all on yourself. Eight's been broken for a long time. Our family's been broken, and we just didn't know it. That wasn't your fault, but what comes next if you tell either of them about the lodestones, that *will* be your responsibility. They'll both pressure you to give the stones to Obadiah if that's what it takes to break the bindings. Then you'll have everyone pushing you, and you'll cave, even if you don't want to. Not everybody wants what's good for them."

"You sound like Eight." Barrie shook her head, stood up, and headed back to the house. "Like a Beaufort."

"I am a Beaufort. My gift may not be as strong as Dad's or even Eight's, since he's the heir, but that just means I have to be better at the nonmagical part. People are like books. The information's all in there if you know how to read it, and I pay attention. Like, for instance, I know how much you want to give everyone the benefit of the doubt. Everyone but yourself. You don't trust anyone to trust *you*. At the same time, you want to fix everything that's been wrong here for three hundred years. You're too nice."

"Naïve, you mean."

"Potato, po-tah-to," Kate said. Then she hung up.

Barrie reached the front steps and stood aside as two more of the appraiser's staff came down carrying furniture out of the house. Sweat dripped down their faces and darkened the fabric of their blue overalls, and they wrestled the heavy pieces onto the waiting trucks.

Above on the portico, Pru and a balding man with a flat, large-pored nose had emerged from the front door and stood flipping through documents on a clipboard, while a fourth man inched a Searle chest past them.

Pru frowned, then stepped after him. "Hold on, not that one!"

"Again?" The man with the clipboard wiped his forehead as Barrie climbed the last steps to where they stood. "You sure this time?"

"This piece is heavy, Miss Pru. Is it coming or going?" The workman exchanged a look with the appraiser.

Pru pushed her fine, pale curls behind her ear, her expression unexpectedly hesitant, frightened almost, the way that she had looked right after Barrie had first arrived and Seven Beaufort had rung the doorbell. As if the thought of standing up for herself was petrifying.

"Staying," Barrie said. "Definitely staying."

The appraiser waved his fingers back in the direction of the house, and the mover turned to take the chest back inside. Consulting his clipboard, the appraiser flipped through several pages before he found the item and scratched it off. "That's the twelfth time you've changed your mind about a piece we agreed on. At this rate, there won't be anything left, and we're going to go back with an empty truck."

Barrie threaded her arm around Pru's waist. "The list we sent over was just the things Pru wanted you to look at. That's the whole point of an appraisal, isn't it? So you can tell us how much you'll pay or how much you think you can get for it on consignment?"

"People usually stick to the list. My prices are more than fair," the appraiser said in a sullen mutter. He looked as if he intended to keep arguing, but in no mood for anyone else to push Pru around, Barrie gave him a hard stare and squeezed Pru to keep her from apologizing.

When the man had gone, Pru leaned over and kissed Barrie on the cheek. "Thank you for standing up for me. I don't know why I turn into a mess around people like that."

"Bullies, you mean?" Barrie steered Pru into the shade of the portico. "Ignore him. You don't have to give up anything you want to keep."

"I do love you, sugar." Pru gave Barrie a slow and blinding smile. "You're good for me. And you're right. I was letting him walk all over me like my father did, which is the main reason I wanted to get rid of all this furniture and start over with fresh memories in the first place. Now, what happened to you?" She reached over and touched

Barrie's shorts and top. "My goodness, your clothes are wet."

"That's a long, dull story, and I could really use a shower." Barrie forced a smile. "For the record, though, you didn't *let* your father do anything. He did it. That's different."

"True, and I could give away every last stick of furniture he ever touched, and it wouldn't change what happened. That's what I realized when I saw all these pieces going out the door—I'm not only throwing away the bad memories, I'm losing all the good ones. Bits of my mama, and my grandmother, all the Christmases and Sunday suppers, all the shenanigans Lula ever pulled."

"So we'll sell Lula's furniture instead when it gets here."

"You sure you wouldn't mind?" Pru's face pinched into a frown.

"Asking Mark to send Lula's furniture here seemed like a good idea because I thought you couldn't afford to replace what the *yunwi* were taking apart—but that's obviously not true. Anyway, my thinking was all tangled up with grief, and missing home, and wanting to help you because I couldn't do anything to help Mark or my mother. All I really need are a few things, and we can sell the rest."

Pru laid a palm along Barrie's cheek, and in the shade of the fluted columns of the portico, Pru's face appeared a little less pale and drawn. "You and I have both been a bit of a mess, haven't we? But we're like the furniture. All those scars and scratches just prove we can survive whatever's thrown at us."

Barrie hoped that was true, because at the moment, it seemed like there were a lot of knives in the air, and most of them seemed to be pointed in her direction.

CHAPTER TWELVE

After working for several more hours, the appraisers left with only a fifth of the furniture that Pru had originally thought she was going to sell. Barrie, Pru, Mary, and Daphne rearranged the rest to leave room for the pieces from San Francisco that Barrie definitely wanted to keep, and it was only when Barrie finally escaped to the kitchen for lemonade that she had a chance to retrieve her phone from where she'd left it to recharge her battery.

She found a whispered voice mail from Kate. "Why aren't you picking up? You ask me to help you, then you don't even answer when I call."

Barrie bolted up the stairs to her bedroom and paced the Oriental carpet until Kate finally answered. "What's going on?"

"Hold on a second." Kate was whispering again. There

was a long silence, and then her voice came back on the line in a more normal tone. "Man, your timing's bad. Dad confiscated my phone when he found out I had called you earlier, so I had to steal it back. Thank goodness I had it on vibrate, or he would have killed me."

"I don't even know where to begin with that."

"Forget it. I'm calling because I figured you'd want to know that Eight stopped packing. The sheriff called, and Dad went up to talk to Eight, and they started screaming at each other again. Then Dad came out of Eight's room, and Eight stood there with an armload of shirts he was about to put into the suitcase, and he turned around and put them back inside his drawer."

"What did the sheriff want?" Barrie asked, grabbing the bedpost.

"I don't know. They mentioned something about someone being seen in Port Royal. They didn't mention any names that I could hear."

Barrie thought instantly of Ernesto. She dropped down onto the edge of the bed so abruptly that the *yunwi* who had followed her upstairs dove under the armchair in the corner, and a handful of dried purple and yellow blooms of bougainvillea fell with a hiss from the sweetgrass basket on the desk. She told herself she was jumping to conclusions—there was no reason to think the conversation had anything to do with him. Except that Port Royal was just west of Saint Helena Island, where Pru had mentioned there had been break-ins.

"Barrie?" Kate said. "You still there?"

"Did you find out anything else?" Barrie asked.

Kate's voice was softer than usual when she spoke again. "No, but I've been thinking. Remember what I said about not telling Dad about Obadiah wanting the lodestones? Don't let Pru tell him, either. And don't tell Eight anything more than he knows already."

"I'm not keeping any more secrets from Eight."

"What if getting the lodestones kills him? Or Dad? Or even you? You've guilted yourself into helping Cassie and Mary and Daphne and whoever else, but it's too risky to just throw the gifts away. I don't blame you for wanting to keep your magic."

"I never said I was throwing it away." Every part of Barrie recoiled at the idea that her gift was something to be disposed of, like the furniture. Drawing her feet up onto the embroidered quilt, she hugged her knees and stared down at the chipped polish on her rainbow-painted toes. "And what do you mean by 'kill'?"

Kate hesitated briefly. "I did actually overhear something else. Dad told Eight that our grandfather died trying to take apart the wall of a fountain that supposedly has something to do with our gift. A blood vessel burst in his brain, and he *died.*

What if that had something to do with the lodestone being booby-trapped, like you said?"

"I'm working on getting more information," Barrie said, trying to keep her composure. "What else did your dad say? Did he know for certain how the fountain is related to your gift? Did he mention that the lodestone is there, or are you guessing?"

"If I'm guessing, so will Dad. Don't you see? If he finds out that giving the lodestone to Obadiah would break the binding, he'll be tempted to take the fountain apart. That's why you can't tell him what Obadiah said. You haven't seen him since things blew up with Eight. He's so desperate, and how do we know he won't do something crazy and stupid, figuring it would be worth the risk?"

"Your father's not like that—"

"You don't know! Anyway, I'm a Beaufort, too, and I deserve a vote. *I* don't want to throw the gift away." Kate hung up before Barrie could say anything else.

Barrie wasn't even sure what else there was to say. Hunched on the bed, she realized the edge of her thumb was sore from rubbing Mark's watch, and she sat on her hands to keep from doing it again. As if they sensed her despair, the *yunwi* emerged from the corners of the room and crawled up beside her to offer comfort.

"It would be so helpful if you could explain the binding

and all the rest of this to me," Barrie said. "You were here. You know what happened."

They had never had more than a one-word answer for any question she had asked them, so it didn't surprise her when that was all they gave her now in their resonant, silent voices. It was a word she had heard them use before, the first time she had ever encountered Obadiah.

Beware, they said.

"Beware of *what*?"

Was it her imagination, or had the *yunwi* become more shadowy and translucent? Were their bodies colder as they pressed against her?

First one and then the rest vanished out the door and down the hallway. With a growl of frustration, Barrie slid down off the bed. Left alone, she stood staring down at the pattern on the carpet.

What Kate had said scared her as much as everything that had happened with Obadiah. Because what if Eight or his father decided to test whatever was going on with the Beaufort fountain? What if they tried to find the lodestone? What if it *was* booby-trapped?

Even if they didn't touch it, what if the fountain at Beaufort Hall had something like the energy Barrie had felt out by the Scalping Tree? What would that do to someone who reached into that unprepared? The energy had grabbed hold of her and threatened to suck her under, and who knew what would have happened if Pru hadn't brought her back to herself and pulled her away. Obadiah had warned her that energy could get addictive.

She had to warn Eight. Make him listen to her. Explain the danger.

They had to talk. If Eight wouldn't answer her calls, and he wouldn't see her in person, that left only one other option.

She took her laptop out to the balcony and slumped down with her back against the wall. She had never written an actual letter, and she had no idea how to start one. Normal emails and texts were brief, and emojis and pics were shortcuts for feelings and information that were too hard to string together. Maybe it was impossible to say with words what she felt. But defeatist thoughts like that were fireflies trapped in jars; they were already dying by the time she caught them.

Across the river, Eight's window was dark and empty, and she wondered where he was and what he was doing. It felt wrong not to know.

She focused on the laptop with renewed determination.

Dear Eight,

First, no matter what you do, DON'T go to the fountain. The lodestone could be booby-trapped, and you could end up dead like your grandfather. If that's all you read in this letter, that's okay, but I hope you'll keep reading, because I have a lot more to tell you.

I took Daphne to meet Obadiah today, and I ended up telling Berg everything as well. Daphne was pretty shaken up, but Berg took it calmly. Then again, after what he must have seen in Afghanistan, there probably isn't a whole lot that scares him. Not even Cassie. Lately, I feel like I probably wouldn't recognize myself if I weren't afraid.

I'm afraid that having found a place and people I love, I'll wake up to find it was only a dream.

I'm afraid that a brief taste of happiness is all I'll ever have, and that it will have to be enough to last the rest of my life.

I'm afraid that something beautiful and wonderful will be lost forever at Watson's Landing if I don't find the right way to help Obadiah. I'm afraid to trust him too much—or not enough.

I'm afraid to let down Cassie and Mary and Daphne if I don't find a way to break the curse.

I'm afraid that giving Obadiah the lodestones to break the curse will have consequences we wouldn't want to live with.

I'm afraid that something bad will happen to you if we don't understand the consequences before we act.

I'm afraid that you will never understand why I fight

to protect Watson's Landing and the magic, even when it's that same magic that would keep us apart. The magic is part of me. Giving up something you can't give up is not a choice, and any relationship that requires sacrificing yourself is built upon a lie.

The most important thing you should know today is that you were right. About many things, including about the Raven Mocker. Obadiah claims he doesn't actually take life from other people, only the natural energy that everyone absorbs from their environment and stores in their heart, among other places. If that doesn't make him a Raven Mocker, maybe there's more to the story than what we've found so far. Maybe there's an older story that's gotten confused the same way the story of the Fire Carrier has been confused. Stories seem to change every time they're told.

I miss you. I've said many things in this letter, but that's the main thing I need to say. I miss you for a hundred reasons, in a thousand ways, in a million unexpected moments. One of the reasons—only one—is that I need your help to figure this all out.

Love,

Barrie

She hesitated after writing the closing, wondering if she should change it. But it was true, and maybe Eight would take the time to wonder if or how she meant it.

She hesitated before writing the subject line, because unless she got that right, Eight might never read the rest. She finally settled on:

Things you need to know. For starters.

After hitting send, she let her head fall back against the wall. Pouring her doubt, fear, and hope out onto the page had left her emptied. She sat with her eyes closed, losing herself to the river's murmur and the other night sounds, letting the pale gold moon seep in to give her a moment of peace.

She wondered if this sense of catharsis was the reason Lula had continued writing to Pru long after she had to have known that her father was intercepting them. Perhaps words were like energy. If you spilled them out into the universe, did they swirl around, gathering strength until someone else absorbed them? What if no one ever read them? Consequences spilling into one another, cause and effect and complication, all because people didn't communicate, because the words didn't reach their destination.

She thought back to the night when she had found the letters in Emmett's desk. What would have happened if she hadn't run out to see the Fire Carrier and left them lying where her aunt could find them? Barrie wasn't sure she would have ever given them to Pru. Or even read them all herself, for that matter. Possibly, tripping and cutting her hands, washing the blood off in the fountain, and getting herself bound to Watson's Landing by the water spirit had been the only reason that Lula's words had reached anyone.

She sat forward as she had the thought, at the memory of that night and the water spirit, and abruptly the answer seemed so obvious: the fountain.

CHAPTER THIRTEEN

If she wanted to know about the binding, Barrie had to call back the spirit in the fountain. The Fire Carrier had tried to communicate in fire images, and the *yunwi* seemed drained by the energy required to make Barrie hear even a single word, but the water spirit had communicated an entire sentence when she had bound Barrie to Watson's Landing.

Midnight came too slowly. Barrie helped Pru finish up downstairs before supper, while Daphne and Mary went home to Brit and Jackson, and then she and Pru did a bit more work on the restaurant afterward. After finally escaping to her room, she spent the last hour reading and rereading the bundle of Lula's letters.

As Pru had told her, the letters contained no information about the binding or why Lula had run away from Watson's

Landing in the middle of the night. They included only vague references about finding the hidden room behind the panel that led down to the tunnel. But Barrie had already known about that from the images of carvings and the hidden keyhole Lula had drawn in her sketchbook. Really, the only new information the letters provided was a sense of her mother's state of mind, of Lula's inability to get past her scars and her pain. Her certainty that she had nothing left to offer the world if she wasn't beautiful.

She had loved Barrie, though, and Mark. That was clear. She hadn't known how to show it in her day-to-day behavior, but it flooded the pages she had filled with her shaking, painful script. So did her loneliness and longing to come home to Watson's Landing. Lula had never given up hoping that Emmett would someday relent and let her come back if she could prove she'd kept his secret.

Reading the letters ripped the scabs from a million tiny cuts Barrie had gathered over the course of her life and made her reexamine so much of what she thought she knew.

Useless hope clearly ran in the Watson family. Not just her mother, but also the way Pru had kept loving Seven, hoping against hope that circumstances would change. Barrie too often let herself hope against all odds, relying so much on hope that she failed to act—and failed to accept when it was time to let hope die. Maybe she was more like her mother than she had thought. And still, no matter how many times in her own life hope had come back to hurt her, she found herself checking her email every few minutes in case Eight had written back. Even though hours had gone by since she'd sent the email, she couldn't keep herself from hoping.

A palmetto bug landed on the glowing screen of her laptop beside her on the balcony, and the translucent tip of the insect's tail became silvered around the edges by the light. Barrie brushed it off and reread Lula's final letter, but if there was any more meaning hidden in there, she couldn't find it. Maybe that was another similarity she shared with her mother. It had been naïve—even a little arrogant—to think that she could tempt Eight with a puzzle or by tugging on his protective instincts. She had told him the truth. But not all the truth. She had risked her heart, but not all of it. She never came out and said what needed to be stated outright.

Which was worse? Telling a person you loved them when you didn't mean it? Or loving them and never telling them at all? Having read all her mother's letters, she wished she had told Eight more clearly how she felt. She didn't want to end up like Lula, full of what-ifs and regrets she couldn't admit, things she was too afraid to say. Looking back at Lula's life and her own childhood with a new perspective, the wasted years and wasted opportunities made her feel wrung out, as if she'd cried all the tears she had left inside her.

When you loved someone, you couldn't hold back. Love was a leap into the unknown, not a cautious dipping of the toe. That was true for her feelings about Eight, and it was true for her feelings about Watson's Landing.

Careful not to wake her aunt, Barrie eased open the door to the corridor a few minutes before midnight. She tiptoed down the stairs, into the kitchen, and outside to the porch. The *yunwi* found her there and followed her, unusually subdued.

At the center of the maze beside the fountain, she picked up a sharp bit of oyster shell and held it ready until the flickering glow of the Fire Carrier's flames broke through the trees and lit the sky above the river. The Fire Carrier waded out amid the marsh grass in the shallows and stooped to unspool his magic onto the water.

The river turned to fire. Flames roared upstream and around the top of the island by the bridge, and downstream and across the shallow creek that cut the plantation off from the island bridge and the town of Watson's Point. Standing thigh-deep in the water, the Fire Carrier stiffened as if he could sense he was being watched.

He turned slowly. Beneath the mask of black-and-red paint, his eyes met hers, and as always, she felt the connection more than saw it, felt his need to communicate.

The timing was as close as it was possible to get to what had happened the night when the water spirit had bound Barrie. She sliced both her palms with the bit of shell, and her skin slicked with blood.

Her hands stung. A drop of red fell to the white gravel path and glistened, dark in the fire and moonlight, and she half-expected the *yunwi* to dart in and taste it, as they had that first night. Maybe the blood would work its magic on them again as well, and leave her even more connected to them so that they could be clear to her at last. But plunging her hands into the fountain, she was already afraid that the magic wouldn't work more than once. She had already given her heart to Watson's Landing and to the *yunwi*.

Barely visible in the moonlight, threads of blood swirled through the water. Barrie waited, hoping for the dizziness to hit her, for the pipes to gurgle and the water to swell and gather in the uppermost of the three tiered basins.

Nothing happened. The water stayed calm, its susurration no louder than it had been every day since the binding had given her an extra boost of clarity. Flames still crackled on the water, and the Fire Carrier stood in the sea of marsh grass with the war-drum beat of his ancient magic overshadowing the sounds of the night chorus. And that was all.

Barrie tried to swallow her disappointment. After all that

hope, she still had no new information, nothing to help her understand the binding or the gifts, and no way to communicate with the Fire Carrier. That was frustrating in itself. If only she could find a way to speak to him; he had all the answers she needed. For the first time, she wished she had Eight's gift instead of her own.

"Tell me what to do," she said to the *yunwi* pressed around her as the Fire Carrier retreated back to the Scalping Tree. "I don't understand. Why are you here, and what does it have to do with the lodestone or the spirit path? Why don't you want to go into the woods? Why didn't you want Obadiah around here? Were you afraid he would break the binding? What would happen to you if he did?"

The *yunwi* pressed closer but kept their silence.

"Do you know where the lodestone is hidden?" Barrie asked them.

All together, in a single motion, they reoriented themselves and pointed toward the woods, where the wind was bowing the treetops and the cloud-cloaked moon had painted long shadows on the lawn.

"By the Fire Carrier's tree?" Barrie asked.

They continued pointing. Apparently, asking one question at a time worked better, and Barrie bent closer to them excitedly. "Where by the tree?"

Heart, they said.

The word drifted back to Barrie on the night air, as if they were speaking from some great distance beyond a boundary that stripped sound away. The word was fainter than when they had spoken before. Their eyes had dimmed, and since the flames had vanished from the water, their shapes were barely visible at all.

"What would happen to you if Obadiah broke the binding?" Barrie asked, feeling desperate. "Where would you go?"

They backed away and dove beneath nearby bushes, darted behind the trees.

They didn't return. Which, probably, was an answer in itself.

Back in her room and feeling cold despite the heat that seeped into the old house, Barrie lay staring again at the bed canopy above her head. The truth about the binding and the lodestone couldn't be lost forever. She refused to believe that Emmett, through his selfishness and jealousy of Luke and Twila, had destroyed three hundred years of family history. Maybe Berg would find something somewhere, some scrap of information that had been squirreled away. And she would check the library herself, even though Pru insisted that Lula had already looked. Or maybe Barrie could figure out some other way to wake the water spirit. Maybe she should try the fountain again. Maybe she hadn't been faithful enough in repeating what she had done before. Maybe she had missed a step in the procedure she had followed the first time.

Except possibly that was the key right there, that it had been the first time. Maybe because Barrie had been the new heir, adding her blood to the water had woken something that had been dormant since before her grandfather had committed murder and broken the succession.

Barrie sat up in bed. A first time could never be repeated. That was what made a first time special. But hadn't Kate just told her that Watson's Landing didn't have the only fountain? What if it didn't have the only water spirit? Maybe each spirit could be woken only once.

She couldn't reach out to Eight anymore. She hadn't put everything into the letter, but she'd put in enough that his lack of response made it clear that he wanted nothing to do with her. On the other hand, if Barrie involved Kate, she wouldn't need to worry about the fountain giving her an aneurysm. Seven would kill her himself when he found out. Still, what choice did she have? She didn't know where the fountain was at Beaufort Hall. She couldn't just wander around the property, hoping no one would notice her.

She typed out a text message to Berg:

Please find out what you can about the fountain at Beaufort Hall.

Almost instantly she got back an answer:

Okay. Haven't had much luck with anything else.

Then she typed another message to Kate:

Need you to show me your fountain ASAP—I have an idea.

Dear Pru,

My daughter turned six today. Six. Her birthdays have become the measure of my exile. Six years. 2192 days. 312 weeks. 72 months. 6 Christmases. 6 Thanksgivings, Easters, Halloweens.

Of course, it's been longer than that, but the time before the fire seems too much like paradise compared to what it's been like since.

Remember how we used to dress up for Halloween? Mark's determined that he's going to take Barrie trick-or-treating this year. He insists I have to let her be a child.

The world's no place for children. I know what's out there. Monsters. The familiar ones I see in my nightmares, and others I don't know.

I can't bear the idea of Barrie getting hurt because of my mistakes.

I've begged and begged Daddy to send you out here. He says you don't want to come. I don't want to believe him, but I wouldn't blame you after the way I left. If you could see Barrie, you would change your mind. She's sweet, and kind, and generous, and stubborn. She looks like the photos of me when I was her age, but she has your eyes. Your kindness and trusting nature. I dread the day that she outgrows it and realizes that I'm one of the monsters she ought to fear.

Her birthdays are getting harder every year.

As much as I hate Watson's Landing and everything it stands for, every day of my life, I regret that I ever left.

CHAPTER FOURTEEN

The text message from Kate popped in at seven o'clock in the morning.

Meet me outside at the tunnel as soon as possible. Hurry.

Barrie was already dressed, so she slid the keys off her desk and finished throwing her hair into a lopsided ponytail. Followed by a handful of *yunwi*, she ran down the hallway into the abandoned wing of the house.

Emmett's old room seemed even more oppressive this early in the morning. With its massive furniture and dark, ornate paneling, it was the sort of room built by men who deserved their nightmares. Barrie rushed through into the secret room, and then, with a courage-bolstering breath, began the descent down the steep and narrow staircase. She was shivering by the time she reached the bottom. Why didn't she ever remember how cold it was down there?

The *yunwi* waited farther away from the iron door than usual. Although their shapes had grown more substantial overnight, and their eyes burned a little more brightly again, they still seemed weaker, fainter than they had when she had first emerged from the woods after finding the vortex and the spirit path. Only a few of them braved the door once she wrangled it open and followed her to the invisible boundary established by the Fire Carrier's nightly ritual.

By the time Barrie stepped out into the stairwell in the Beaufort woods, Kate was already there, peering down at her through the grating. "Did you take forever getting here to drive me crazy?" Kate asked. "Dad went out for a run, but he won't be gone long, and he's working at home today instead of going to the office. This is going to be our only chance. So what's your idea? You're not going after the lodestone, are you? Because I've decided you don't get to take it."

"I'm not taking anything." Barrie dragged a branch over the top of the grating and bit her lip. "Eight's still here, isn't he?" she couldn't help asking. "He didn't leave last night?"

Kate's smile faded, and she hurriedly started walking. "He's leaving this morning to do more paperwork at the university. He says he's coming back, but he never finished unpacking his suitcase."

"Are you worried?"

"Aren't you?"

Of course Barrie was.

They reached the edge of the Beaufort woods and headed up the lawn that sloped lazily toward the house. Beneath racing clouds, the whitewashed facade of Beaufort Hall lit and darkened, its windows glittering each time the sun emerged. But without the intricate gardens of Watson's Landing, the house appeared bare, like Mark without his drag and makeup. Closer up, it reminded Barrie of the way Watson's Landing had looked when she had first arrived, flakes of paint peeling and the shutters hanging crookedly because the *yunwi* had been trying to get her and Pru to pay attention. Even a single word of communication had been beyond them then.

"So what are we going to do with the fountain?" Kate asked, looking flushed and earnest all at once. "What's your idea?"

"Why doesn't the magic scare you?" Barrie countered, studying Kate's stubborn profile, the tenacious chin and short straight nose, never sure whether to admire Kate or shake her.

"Watson's Landing doesn't scare you."

"I'm bound to it. You aren't."

"Beaufort is still my home. I don't want to lose it, and we don't have *yunwi* like you do at Watson's Landing. That means we need the Beaufort gift more than you do. Do you know how much it costs to keep a place like this running?

And it's not just money. The gift protected us—*and* Watson's Landing—when the Union troops marched through here on their way to Columbia when they burned Colesworth Place. It's why Beaufort Hall is standing now."

"I don't have the answers, Kate, but I think there might be a way to find them. That's why I want to see the fountain." Barrie sighed and briefly explained about the water spirit and the night she had found herself bound to Watson's Landing. "The spirit spoke in a whole sentence. If I can get her to come out, or if there's a different spirit here, maybe she can explain how the binding works."

"I've never heard of a water spirit here," Kate said, disappearing into an opening in the high boxwood hedge beside the house.

Barrie followed her, and something yellow and furry rushed out with a muffled "Woof" and barreled into her.

"Waldo, no!" Kate hauled Eight's yellow Lab back by the collar. "Bad dog. Sorry," she said to Barrie. "Waldo's an escape artist without any manners, and Eight's been so distracted, he hasn't been playing with her the way he usually does. She doesn't know what to do with herself."

Eight had been playing catch with the dog the second time Barrie had ever seen him. She'd hidden behind the curtain in her bedroom to watch him throw, every inch of him perfectly balanced and intent on sending the ball to the exact spot where he meant it to go, demanding perfection of himself the way he demanded perfection of himself in everything.

Barrie had thought he was graceful then, and beautiful. But he'd been unreal, because real attraction shouldn't come five minutes after you meet someone. She'd been fighting what she felt for him ever since, questioning what he felt.

Did it really matter why they had been drawn to each other at first? Whether it had been her gift pushing her to find him, or his gift letting him know the perfect things to say or do, or a more purely Eight kind of magic?

Barrie couldn't doubt anymore. She knew a thousand and one individual things about him now: the way his shoulders curved in apology at even the idea of making someone unhappy; the callused roughness of his hands from gripping a baseball bat; the stubborn way he researched things at night in the privacy of his room, where no one could see him struggling to read; the way his quick, warm smile would slip back into something more vulnerable when he thought no one was watching.

Barrie couldn't bear the thought that she—that anyone—had hurt him.

Emerging through the opening in the tall boxwood, she found herself in an elaborate swirl of paths and rosebushes fully enclosed by the house and three tall walls of hedge. Neatly labeled rows of flowers formed a spiral pattern, their impressionist colors shifting from white to apricot to pink to red and redder still, until the red was so deep that it was very nearly purple.

There was no traditional fountain. Kate pulled her toward a low pool in the center of the garden, where water bubbled over a nearly invisible lip inches from the ground and vanished in a trench cut around the pool's circumference. The effect was like a drop of water gleaming on a table.

"So this is it. Now what?" Kate asked, coming to a halt beside it.

"Nothing, most likely. Maybe there isn't a water spirit here at all. I don't even know what I was thinking, except that I needed something to hope for. That's crazy, right? Did your dad say anything else about how your grandfather died?"

"Just what we already knew. His father dying shook him pretty bad, and Lula had just left. Everyone around here was probably devastated."

Barrie searched the path for something sharp enough to cut her skin, but there were no oyster shells mixed with the smooth, tumbled river gravel. "Run and get me a knife, will you?" she asked. "A sharp one."

Kate sprinted toward the house and up the steps, and Barrie inspected the fountain while she was gone. Smooth marble bricks of the same pale color as the stones in the trench made up the basin. The water bubbled softly, more a hiss than a splash.

Beneath the sound, the hum of energy was nearly as powerful as what Barrie had felt in the Watson woods. Where that had felt warm and pleasant, though, the energy here stung repellently. She didn't dare reach out for it, and her finding sense could not get past it. Stooping beside the fountain, she plunged her hand in the icy water and groped along the bricks.

"What are you doing?" Kate asked, returning with the knife. "You promised you wouldn't take the lodestone."

"I'm not. I won't." Barrie poised the edge of the blade above her hand. Then, scraping it across her palm, she tore off the scabs that had formed there overnight.

Blood pricked sluggishly to the surface. After switching the knife to her other hand, she repeated the process, then returned the knife to Kate. Red warmth slicked her skin, and the scent of iron curled her nose. She dipped her hands back into the fountain.

The water was too cold for the heat of summer, as if it came from deep beneath the ground. Barrie shivered again, waiting, hoping against hope, *willing* it to bubble, to gather and coalesce. Her hands grew numb.

"You going to sit there all day before you give up?" Kate asked. "Maybe it's not working because you're not a Beaufort." Before Barrie could process what she was doing, Kate plunged her own hands into the fountain.

Ribbons of blood swirled out from Kate's palms, and

dimly Barrie registered that Kate must have cut herself. She lunged to pull Kate away, but it was too late already.

The fountain gurgled. Water bubbled and erupted into a column that rose from the center of the pool to form a shape, a woman with legs that were cascades of water, arms and streaming fingers, a face surrounded by waterfalls of hair that held an expression so exquisitely wistful and regretful as she studied Kate that it was clear she wished things could be other than how they were.

Barrie shook her head to dismiss the thought.

This was wrong. *So* wrong. It couldn't be allowed to happen.

"It was me, not Kate. I'm the one who did it," she said, trying desperately to stop what was coming next.

The water spirit looked straight past Barrie, and a voice like a babble of liquid over rock spoke inside her head.

We accept the binding.

"No!" Barrie shoved Kate toward the steps. "Run back to the house, Kate. Right now. Go inside. Go!"

"Stop pushing me!" Kate gazed back at the water spirit in fascination, completely calm. "I know what I'm doing. If Dad or Eight figure out how to break the binding, they will, and we won't be able to stay here. Beaufort Hall will become just another subdivision. This whole place means something to the fabric of the world. Losing one more piece of land might not seem like a big thing, but how many more subdivisions can the river support before it chokes to death? In three hundred years, this is the only home my family has ever known. The fountain is still here because there have always been Beauforts here. I may not know why, but I'm positive that's important, too. I can't save the rest of river, but I can save this place. Me. I can save it."

Barrie was running out of time to argue. She turned back to the spirit to ask the question she had come to ask, but the column was already collapsing back into the fountain. With a final gurgle it subsided, and the pool lay calm and still.

"Dammit," she said. "Dammit, dammit, dammit. Kate, I can't believe you did that."

"Daddy and Eight never wanted to have to stay here," Kate said quietly. "Now they don't have to. They can go anywhere they want."

CHAPTER FIFTEEN

The implications of what Kate had done rang like bells in Barrie's head, a new peal striking before the last had even finished. Not only had Kate bound herself, but neither of them had asked the water spirit a single question. Not about the whereabouts of the lodestone, or who the water spirit was, or why she had appeared. They didn't know what would happen to Beaufort Hall and Watson's Landing if they let the gifts slip through their fingers. They didn't know what the bindings meant.

They knew *nothing* more than they'd known before.

And the binding itself . . . It shouldn't have—*couldn't* have—transferred to Kate. How could it? Not while Seven and Eight were still alive.

Why hadn't it occurred to Barrie that the binding could be

transferred—or that Kate would do what she had done?

She wanted to shake herself. She wanted to shake Kate. Most of all, she wanted to shake up time like an Etch A Sketch, make the lines of her mistakes disappear into dust.

Kate swayed on her feet and stumbled, turning to Barrie with her eyes white-rimmed and her face faded to the color of the marble in the fountain. She pressed her hands to her ears, as if shutting out some sound that Barrie couldn't hear—as if the *more* that Barrie heard through her own binding with Watson's Landing was affecting Kate as well.

"What's happening?" Kate asked.

"It's all right. It's normal—part of the binding." Catching Kate, Barrie steadied her, resisting the urge to scold her again. "Don't be scared. You're all right," she repeated, as though the repetition—and wishing hard enough—could make it true.

"I'm not the least bit scared." Kate pulled one hand away. Holding it three inches from her ear, she tilted her head to the side, and then a smile tugged at the corners of her lips as if she had tumbled across a marvelous secret. "Is this what it's like for you?" She spun around, peering at the roses in the garden and at the house behind her. "Like seeing everything in high definition and hearing it in stereo? I can feel the ground breathing. What is that?"

"Connection," Barrie said, thinking about all the things Kate needed to know.

Kate jumped as a door slammed behind her, and winced when heavy footsteps pounded toward the stairs. Barrie turned with a tremor of dread.

"What the hell did you do?" Seven's expression promised fire and damnation. He glanced from Barrie to Kate and back, as if of course whatever had happened were Barrie's fault.

Which it *was*. If Kate was bound, Seven must have been *un*bound. Pru had felt lighter—freer—once the spirit had accepted Barrie's binding, and Pru'd barely had the gift at all.

Kate's eyes held Barrie's with a silent plea.

But they couldn't deny what they had done. Blood-tinted water still dripped from Kate's hands. The knife lay on the ground.

"What did you do?" Seven repeated. He didn't shout, but he didn't need to—his voice rumbled so deeply that it felt like he was yelling. He towered above Kate, making her seem very small and frail. "Jesus, Katherine Shelby Beaufort. What were you thinking? Tell me exactly what you did."

"I accepted the binding." Kate glared up at him defiantly. "It's the perfect solution. Now you and Eight won't be stuck here, and I've never seen it as being stuck."

"What about college? Having the chance to find out what matters to you? Your dreams?" He shook his head. "Undo it. Whatever you did, reverse it. How does it work?"

"There's nothing to undo." Kate straightened her

shoulders and swallowed, looking around the garden. "I want this. My dreams have always been about this place."

"You're too young to know what matters."

"Only someone who forgot what it means to be young would ever say that." Kate stared at him, neither cowed nor out of words, but it wasn't Kate who deserved his anger, and after glowering at his daughter another moment, Seven realized that. He turned to Barrie, his hand raised as if he wanted to slap her, or shake her. Fighting the urge, he covered his mouth instead, his expression filled with such rage and horror that Barrie couldn't stay silent.

"Kate didn't know what was going to happen. You're right to blame me," she said.

Seven's body clenched up like a spring coiling. "Haven't you done enough to this family?" he thundered. "Every time I turn around, your meddling tears us apart!"

"If you'd only told Eight the truth . . . or told either of them what you knew about the binding . . . We've been begging you—"

"It's not up to you to decide what's best for my children."

"You think bullying them and lying to them is what's best for them? And you asked me to keep the secret from Eight—that hurt him even worse."

"I asked for your *help*! I explained that you couldn't be together anyway, so all you had to do was walk away from him." Seven stepped even closer, and he was near enough, tall enough, enough like Eight, that tears welled in Barrie's eyes. "That's all you had to do," he said, "and Eight wouldn't have been hurt at all."

"Walk away? That's your answer? Because telling him I didn't want to see him, not returning his calls and texts, and never telling him why—none of that would have hurt him *at all*? Walking away is your go-to solution, though, isn't it?" Barrie had jerked back involuntarily, but now rage propped her up, egged her on. "Walking away is exactly what you did to Pru when you thought my mother was dead and Pru was going to be bound to Watson's Landing. You didn't have the courage to tell her the truth then, either! How'd that work out for you? For Pru?"

"You think it takes courage to tell the truth?" Seven's voice was barely leashed. "It takes courage to do the right thing. To deny your children when you know what they want isn't good for them. Sometimes it takes courage to go to bed at night knowing you have to get up in the morning and face your life."

"The life you made for yourself."

"The life," Seven said, "that was chosen for me three hundred years ago."

Barrie gaped at him, and her anger vaporized. Not because Seven didn't deserve it, but because he was pitiable even more than he was infuriating. Because he didn't begin to understand what he had done. She thought of her mother and all the pain that Lula had lived with. But her mother had never blamed the gift.

"We don't get to use the bargain and the gifts as excuses for everything," she said. "Kate getting bound was my mistake—I admit it. I *own* it. This wouldn't have happened if I'd thought things through, and if I hadn't asked her to show me the fountain. At least I'm trying to figure things out! I'm not giving up. You stopped trying to leave, and you gave up on Pru. You talk about not having your own identity, but you never gave Eight a chance to make his own."

"That has nothing to do with the binding. With Kate—"

"It has everything to do with it. This is Kate's home! That's why she did this. And you made Eight want to run away because he hated the idea of being what you tried to make him—another Charles Beaufort. Another number intended to be a carbon copy of yourself. Then you wonder why he's upset when he feels like he can't measure up."

Seven's throat corded as he swallowed, his face combustible and red. "Get out. Christ. Just leave, and don't come back. Leave my children the hell alone."

Barrie glanced at Kate, but she didn't know what to say. Everything she wanted to tell Kate began with "Don't."

Don't let Seven bully you.

Don't let him hurt Eight anymore.

Don't let him convince you that you have to get rid of the binding.

Don't tell him about Obadiah.

There was so much to say that she couldn't say any of it. Then a shoe scuffed on the steps behind them, and Eight rushed down the steps. His eyes locked on hers, and she felt the recognition she always felt when she saw him, the sense of foundness. Of not-lostness. She wanted to run to him and apologize again and have everything somehow be all right—

How long had he been there?

How much had he heard?

His eyes slid past her to Kate, to Kate's hands, and then down to the bloody knife that lay beside her where she had dropped it. "What did you do, Kate?"

"I bound myself. Like Barrie's bound to Watson's Landing." Kate lifted her stubborn chin.

"You're sixteen," Seven said. "Barrie was an accident. But you? You haven't even lived yet. You don't know anything about love or life. What about summer camp, and sleepovers? College? Or Europe? Or Savannah, for Christ's sake?"

Eight flicked Barrie another glance, then looked down, as if he couldn't bear to see her. She hurt worse than if he'd slapped her, and then he was suddenly in motion, running to pick up the knife.

"Eight, don't!" Barrie and Kate both yelled, and Seven shouted, "No!"

Barrie dove to reach him, but he had already sliced his palms and plunged his hands into the water. "Take me instead of Kate," he shouted at the fountain. "Whatever I'm supposed to say, consider it said. I'll accept the binding. I'll take care of Beaufort Hall, and I'll guard whatever I'm supposed to guard. I won't fight it anymore. Just tell me what you want!"

Panic fisted around Barrie's heart, crushing her until her vision went black around the edges. She didn't even know what to hope for—that the water spirit would appear again, releasing Kate, or that she wouldn't appear and Eight would be free of the obligation, free to go anywhere, to be whatever he wanted.

They all watched the fountain. Kate's whole body was rigid, as if she felt what Barrie felt at the thought of losing the binding—that desperate sense of wanting to hold on to something that wasn't definable in words. Water trickled down the nearly invisible groove around the rim and seeped away into hidden drains. Seconds dragged themselves into a minute . . . and nothing happened. Ribbons of blood were still spilling from Eight's palms into the fountain, tumbling over the side and staining the water pink across the pale marble stones. He had cut himself too deeply.

"What do I have to do?" Sounding desperate, he looked at Kate. "Tell me, and I'll do it."

Barrie bent beside him and tried to pull him away. "If it were going to work for you, it would have already. Come back into the house. You need to stop the bleeding."

"It can't be Kate. I won't accept it," Seven said, and he sliced his palms, too—fraught, shallow slashes that trailed wide pink threads in the fountain but left the water still. "No!" he yelled. "You can't do this. Do you hear me? It can't be Kate."

Eight flinched away from Barrie, his hands still bleeding too hard and dripping onto the gravel.

Kate put her arms around her father's shoulders, leaning against his back, holding him the way that Barrie wished she could hold Eight. "Dad, stop. I wanted this. I chose it. The fountain chose—or this isn't how it works. I don't know. But I'm fine. I'm *glad*."

Seven raised his hands, held them up to examine the palms as if he couldn't believe that the cuts were still bleeding and order hadn't been restored. Finally, he shook himself and took one of Eight's elbows to draw his son away.

"Come on, Eight. Barrie's right about one thing. You need bandaging. Or stitches."

"Kate, too. She's cold and probably in shock." Barrie said, nudging Kate toward the house.

"Don't you touch her!" Rage rekindling, Seven pulled Kate out of Barrie's grasp and folded her against him. "Just leave, and I don't want you coming back here or calling. As far as you're concerned, my children don't exist. You understand?"

Barrie had nothing to say in her own defense. Her actions had left both of Seven's children hurt and bleeding.

She turned to go . . . but . . . no. She had to fix things. Seven had to be afraid for Kate. He had to feel responsible, and she hated the thought of adding to his pain right then, but more pain would come unless they found the answers that they needed.

"I'm not leaving until you tell us how this works," she said. "Why didn't you know that the binding couldn't be transferred back once Kate took it? Why didn't you know this was a possibility? If there's a ceremony that passes the binding from one person to another—"

"This wasn't a ceremony," Kate said.

Barrie studied the fountain, which appeared entirely peaceful again. No trace of blood or spirits. "Then what was it?"

"It's none of your concern, that's what it is! It's a Beaufort family matter." Seven reached for her arm as if he wanted to spin her around and physically push her out of the garden.

Eight stepped between them. "You're wrong, Dad. Barrie and Kate are the ones most concerned right now. And if you'd told me what you knew in the first place, this wouldn't have happened. You didn't just lie and withhold information; you asked Barrie to keep secrets from me. How can you not see what kind of damage you're doing? You act like what you want is the only thing that matters, like you know what's best for everyone. You're so busy trying to control everything—"

"I can't control anything about this!" Seven cried. "Don't you understand? None of this is logical, and it's all dangerous." He stood toe-to-toe with his son. Then his shoulders finally loosened, and he looked away. His voice was suddenly flat as he spoke. "The problem isn't what I know. It's what I don't. I never told you this would happen because I had no idea that it could."

They moved to the library inside the house, but Pru refused to come over when Seven called and demanded she come deal with Barrie. Barrie wanted to stand up and applaud. But the decision was practical as much as it was Pru asserting herself. The movers were scheduled to arrive with Lula's furniture in a matter of hours, and Pru didn't want to risk leaving in case they showed up early.

"Put me on the speakerphone and tell me what happened," she told Seven. "Then we can all figure it out together."

Seven mashed the button with his thumb and started the long explanation. On one end of the leather sofa across the room, Eight sat with his head in his bandaged hands, while down on the other end, Kate couldn't stop shivering, despite the hot cocoa she was sipping and the blanket wrapped around her.

Barrie's shivers were all internal.

How was it possible that Seven had never been bound? He had the migraines. Were there different ways of binding? Different degrees? There had to be. Lula had never had the ceremony and yet she'd felt the pull to return to Watson's Landing. Barrie'd had the migraines, too, even before she had given blood and the spirit in the fountain had appeared.

Rubbing her temples, Barrie prowled the room while Seven talked. Hundreds of small pings of loss called out from all around the room, and she filled the time retrieving those things closest to her, long-forgotten notes, bookmarks, letters, and receipts left in books no one had opened in decades or maybe even centuries. None of these types of lost items existed at Watson's Landing, where up until Luke's murder, the family gift had found anything the moment it went missing. Even without the gift, things would have been easier to find on the orderly shelves. Here at Beaufort Hall, shelves crammed with books ran floor to ceiling on three walls of the room, and files of papers, notebooks, and stacks of old yellow legal pads, their pages curled and fading, were stuffed into every cranny. Ancient leather-bound volumes and modern paperbacks were thrown together without obvious connection.

It didn't occur to Barrie at first that "modern" was a misnomer. The newest books were from the 1940s, as if decades before Seven's time someone had decided that they had run out of space for books and didn't need any more.

Glancing over to where he was still pacing beside the desk, Barrie wondered what his childhood must have been like. Maybe in its own way, growing up at Beaufort Hall had been as confining for him as Watson's Landing had been for Pru and Lula.

The gifts hadn't treated anyone well in the recent past.

"Are you saying you never had any idea it was possible to transfer the binding to someone else?" Pru's voice came through the phone's speaker sounding thin and frightened. "Your father didn't warn you?"

"He died before he had a chance to tell me anything. I went to talk to him when it became clear that Lula wasn't coming back," Seven said.

Eight looked up. "What did Lula have to do with it?"

After shoving aside a stack of current law books and legal files, Seven leaned tiredly against the desk, as if all the pacing, or perhaps the question, had worn him out. "I asked my father what would happen if Pru inherited the binding and then came to live at Beaufort Hall. Or what would happen to me if I tried to live somewhere other than at Beaufort."

His voice throbbed with remembered pain, and Barrie felt like an intruder, listening to what should have been a private conversation between him and Pru. A private *confession*, because he was as good as admitting what Barrie had suspected, that he had given Pru up because of the binding.

Hearing him say that now made Barrie wish that she could blink herself across the river to go hug Pru and hold her. Pru shouldn't have had to be alone while she heard what Seven had done and how many years he'd wasted.

"Can you repeat what you just said?" Pru asked in a shaking voice.

Seven glanced self-consciously around the room and leaned closer to the speaker. "I asked my father what would happen to you if you came to live at Beaufort Hall after you inherited the binding—or what would happen to me if I tried to live with you at Watson's Landing. It had never been an issue as long as Lula was going to inherit."

Pru was silent so long that he bent in even closer. "Pru, did you hear me that time?"

"I heard you the first time," Pru said. "I just wanted you to have to say it again."

Seven stiffened. His profile reddened. Then he smiled sheepishly, an unself-conscious smile that transformed him, and for the first time in, well, ever, Barrie could see what drew Pru to him.

"I suppose I deserved that," he said.

"You deserve worse," Pru agreed, "but we can discuss that later. What exactly did your father tell you?"

"He gave me the only example he knew of a Beaufort who had left. His great-uncle—Four, that would have been—who enlisted in World War I with his best friend and was still in France when Three died unexpectedly. Because of the war, Four couldn't get home, and the migraines grew so bad that he couldn't function. He miswrote a message and got his unit shelled by friendly fire in the Argonne Forest. A lot of the men died, including his friend, and he blamed himself. He committed suicide once the battalion was finally rescued."

"That's horrible," Barrie said.

"But that was your great-great-uncle? Not your great-grandfather?" Kate asked.

"I never knew that," Eight said.

"My great-grandfather was his brother, Robert Somerset Beaufort," Seven said, looking at Eight instead of his daughter. "Once he inherited, he named his son after his brother and called him Five to keep up the tradition. But the sudden disruption in the family line meant that most of what Three and Four had known about the binding died with them, and by the time it got to my father, all he knew was that we were meant to protect the fountain in the rose garden, in the same way that the Watsons were meant to protect the tree in the center of the Watson woods, and that it had something to do with a guardian."

"A guardian for what?" Eight asked.

"Or *from* what?" Kate said. "Where's the danger?"

Seven sat down on the edge of the desk, drawing in on himself like a cornered animal, as if the reminder of all the things he didn't know was too hard or painful for him.

"What happened to your father?" Desperate to keep him talking, Barrie asked the question even though she already knew the answer. "How did he die?"

Seven fidgeted with the files on the desk, remaining silent so long that she was afraid she had pushed him into silence instead. But then he raised his head. "When he realized what the binding would mean for me and Pru, he went out and attacked the fountain with an axe. I don't know what he was thinking, but he collapsed as soon as the blade struck, and they said later that an artery had ruptured in his brain. The binding had killed him."

The raw pain in Seven's eyes stole Barrie's ability to breathe.

It was Pru who finally answered him. "Why didn't you tell me? I'll bet you've been scared and guilty about that all this time, haven't you?" Pru's voice sounded like she wanted to crawl through the telephone to reach Seven, and Barrie wished so hard—again—that the two of them could have been together for this conversation instead of having to do it on the phone. Barrie wished they hadn't been apart for twenty years because of a misunderstanding. She wished so many things . . .

Glancing over at the sofa, she found Eight looking back at her. She wondered what he was thinking.

Kate brushed all that aside with an impatient wave. "So what you're telling us is that you never knew about putting blood into the fountain? And your daddy didn't know, either? I just got the binding, but I can already tell you that everything feels different."

"She's right," Barrie said, nodding. "You see and smell and sense the land more intensely. You feel the connection with it as if it flows through your veins. I think you'd understand better if you could experience it. The binding is a trust, not a burden."

Seven and Kate both looked over at her, and Eight hadn't stopped looking. Pru was silent on the phone. Barrie knew she should have been sorry that Kate was bound at sixteen, stuck before she'd been anywhere in the world or discovered who she was. Yet Kate, for all that she seemed more frivolous than Eight on the surface, knew herself. She had depth. Maybe that had been there all along, or maybe the binding was bringing it out the way a stonecutter revealed the facets of a gem.

CHAPTER SIXTEEN

Eight offered to take Barrie home. She tried not to read anything into that, but she couldn't help it. He held the French door to the porch open for her, and she passed beneath his outstretched arm with Waldo bounding along behind her.

"I'm sorry," she said, pausing on the steps outside. She wasn't sure what she regretted most, that he'd been hurt or that she had been the one to hurt him. She regretted that he would never know how the binding felt. But she couldn't regret that Kate had given him back his life. Kate had made that decision knowing and accepting that her whole future was at stake.

Kate had given him a gift. Now Eight could finally choose his future. He could sail the *Away* anywhere he wanted. He could study in California or travel to Rome. He could set his sights on being a major-league pitcher and spend every other day in a different city. The thought poured over Barrie like ice water, the realization that he had the choice to escape Watson Island if he wanted to go, and that she couldn't stop him. All she could do was hope there was a chance he would choose to stay. But every relationship began with nothing except a chance.

Eight adjusted his long stride to hers as they walked down toward the Beaufort dock. Waldo loped on ahead and then bounded back and bowed at them, tail wagging as she invited them to go faster. Eight veered toward the woods and found a stick to throw. Despite his bandaged hands, he sent it spinning through the air.

The familiarity of walking beside him made Barrie's breath catch—the way his hands burrowed into his pockets; the easy grace of his long, lean muscles; the way the sun spun strands of gold through his hair. Her hands ached to touch him, though she wasn't sure whether that was to reassure him or to reassure herself.

"I really am sorry, Eight. For everything." Two-thirds of the way down the hill, Barrie stepped in front of him so he couldn't avoid looking at her.

He edged around her and threw the stick Waldo had brought back to him, sending it hurtling out impossibly far onto the middle of the dock. "Can we just drop it? I heard you the first several times. And I got your email."

"Then let me say just one more thing. I need you to understand that I never meant the 'baseball guy' nickname to be a comment on your intelligence. At first, it was more of a reminder to myself that you were out of reach, and then maybe it was a way to jab at you a little bit for wanting to leave Watson Island. Eventually, it simply suited you—it's who you are."

Eight shifted back to face her. "That's not how it felt the other day. It seemed more like proof that you were agreeing with Dad. That you thought I wasn't smart enough to make my own decisions if you told me about the binding. I know I'm sensitive about the dyslexia, and I guess that's my own insecurity. I projected it onto you, but I've always imagined a relationship would be two people who put each other first. I put you before baseball. I *wanted* to do that. Your binding will never let you do the same for me. That's what happened, isn't it? You didn't tell me the truth because you were afraid you couldn't have both me and the gift, and you didn't want to choose."

Barrie couldn't deny it. "That was only part of it. I knew how much what your father had done was going to hurt you, how betrayed you were going to feel. I wanted him to tell you himself so you could resolve your relationship, but I also wanted to have Obadiah break the curse so I could see what would happen—so I would know whether I could tell you there was a chance of breaking the binding safely. I didn't want you to have to be afraid of the future if I could give you hope, if there was any hope available. I should have trusted you to handle it— What?" Eight's shoulders and expression had stiffened as if she'd hit him. "What is it?" she asked. "What did I say?"

Eight's throat worked as though he were choking on unsaid words. He'd gone pale beneath this tan. "I guess I can understand not wanting to worry someone if you're not positive there's anything to worry about. It seems pointless and hurtful, and you want to protect them."

"Yes, that's it," Barrie said, wondering if they were still talking about the same thing.

"The bindings change things, though. Don't you see that? As long as you have the binding, a relationship between us could never be equal. I would always come in second place, and that's a hard thing to live with."

"It's more of a tie really," Barrie said, feeling helpless.

Waldo brought the stick back, and Eight threw it again, into the river this time so that Waldo bounded through the marsh grass, sending a brace of ducks rushing into the air. "The thing about life," Eight said, speaking very slowly, "is that we all need to lose once in a while. Otherwise we can't grow up. You've changed me since I met you. You've made me think. You've made me want to be better. Not only a better pitcher or better at some*thing*. You make me want to be a better some*one*."

To avoid bursting into tears, Barrie concentrated on Waldo bounding up the slope. Ears flopping, water dripping, and tongue lolling from the side of her mouth, the dog pressed the stick into Eight's hand and wagged her tail hopefully.

Barrie was afraid to hope. "It's the things we've been through together that have made you change. They've changed us both."

"I finally understand why you have such a hard time distinguishing between what you want and what you *think* you should want. You don't see responsibility as a sacrifice, do you?"

"I just accept that sometimes sacrifice is necessary. Do you still feel your gift now that Kate took the binding?"

Eight started walking down the hill again. "I'm not sure yet. Back in the library, there was too much emotion from too many people I care about. Things get muddled. And now? I'm not sure if it's the binding or something else that's changed about you. There's an electric hum that I never noticed before, and everything is muted. I can feel you wanting me not to be upset and wanting Kate to be okay, but it also feels as if what I want is more separate than it was before. More accessible."

"What *do* you want?"

"You." He didn't look at her. "Still. Probably always. I've spent the last couple of days telling myself that you're the last person in the world I should want. Last night, I was so sick of all this that I nearly drove the hour to Columbia to stay with a friend until the dorms opened, and like I told you, I was considering not coming back at all. But then I read your email. It wasn't even that cryptic 'Love, Barrie' that got to me. It was the fact that you still couldn't manage to say 'love' any other way. You're not afraid of anything, but you're afraid of that."

"I'm afraid of everything," Barrie said, her throat clogged with all her insecurities, as if they had congealed into a solid mass, like bacon grease, and gotten caught in a place where she couldn't swallow them away.

They reached the dock, and Eight pushed her curls out of her eyes with his thumb, slowly, as if he was reluctant to touch her but couldn't help himself. "Perfection is a lie, Bear, and we're all born with built-in bullshit detectors. Humans are hardwired to love people because of their flaws, not in spite of them. I think we spend our lives searching for someone who is warped in a way that we can accept, maybe even admire. Someone whose quirks and angles fit our own."

"Are you saying I'm twisted in the same way you are?" Barrie tipped her face to look up at him.

He bent his knees so that their eyes were level. Embarrassed at the intensity that swept between them too suddenly, she turned her head away.

He gave her a soft laugh. "I'm saying people all have layers, and no one wants an unfrosted plain vanilla piece of cake.

189

Don't get me wrong. I'm still furious that you kept secrets from me. I'm still trying to work out how to be second place, and I wish you trusted my intelligence enough to let me help you—"

"I need you to help me. You're the one who's been on the right track about what Obadiah is, and I don't even want to think about how much you must have read to find out about Raven Mockers. But that's my point. You take the time to look for facts and think a situation through. I'm too impulsive, and sometimes, maybe, you're too logical. That's a good balance, though, isn't it? As long as we can be honest with each other."

"*Can* you be honest with me? Can you let me make choices for myself? Part of loving someone is letting them make their own mistakes."

"I don't know. I never had to make those kinds of choices before I came here," Barrie confessed. "Mark was the only person I could really confide in, and I told him everything except the small, hurtful things people said or did—the things he couldn't do anything about. I thought that was kinder, but it never occurred to me to wonder how he would feel if he found out I'd kept secrets from him. Not until I did the same thing to you."

"A mistake stops being a mistake after a certain number of repetitions."

Eight jumped down into the *Away,* and Barrie hesitated

on the dock. Something about Watson's Landing seemed off-kilter, but she couldn't pin it down until she finally realized that the perspective from the Beaufort dock was different from the more familiar view farther down at Colesworth Place. From here, the cemetery and a bit of the chapel were visible. That was the way it was too often—discovering what was missing was harder than seeing what was there.

Trust was like that too. You took it for granted while you had it. But when it disappeared, it left a hole in the fabric of a relationship that was impossible to ignore.

She had been so careless with Eight's trust, and with Pru's. Not because she had meant to deceive them—not all the time, at least, and only for the best of reasons. But when mistakes hurt someone, do the reasons really matter?

"I'm not going to make you promises I can't keep," she said. "I'm not always good at thinking things through before I act, and I can't promise to always put your priorities ahead of the binding. But we both have responsibilities. You didn't think twice before cutting your hand and putting it into the fountain after Kate was bound, even if it meant you would end up bound to Beaufort Hall yourself. Even if it meant you and I couldn't be together."

"I still have to find a way to take the binding back from her."

Barrie should have known that was coming, so it shouldn't

have surprised her. It shouldn't have pulled a lump up into her throat. "She's going to be furious if you do that. Especially now that she knows how it feels."

"I can't let that matter." Holding out his hand, Eight helped Barrie down into the *Away*. His callused fingers were gentle, and dabs of blood showed through here and there on the bandages across his palm. His voice had softened with regret. "She has to go to college. She needs to finish high school without worrying about migraines while she sits in class. She has to have a chance to go out and be normal, and then come back here and choose to be bound—if that's what she wants. It has to be a choice. If that means I have to take the binding from her to make that happen, then I have to find a way."

"But you're taking *away* her choice if you do that. Don't you see? What if you take the binding and can't give it back?"

"That's a risk I have to take."

"She'll hate you for it."

"I know that."

The *Away* swayed, and the dark water lapped the hull and slipped on beneath them. Barrie watched it go.

"You're choosing what you see as your duty over our relationship, which was the same thing you blamed me for doing," she said.

"Yes, but the difference is that I'm telling you openly what I'm going to do, so that we can try to work around it. If you can't accept that, then we really don't have a future."

"And what about Ernesto? Since we're being open, when were you going to tell me that he might still be alive but that you didn't tell me because you wanted to be certain before you worried me? If we're going to be open with each other, then shouldn't we be really open?"

CHAPTER SEVENTEEN

Thanks either to the wind or the *yunwi*, the kitchen door blew shut behind Barrie faster than she had expected. Her aunt wasn't there. The avocado kitchen appeared bare without the old table and chairs, and the crisp linen cloth was folded on the counter beside the crystal bowl of roses. Beach music trickled quietly from the radio on the counter, the Drifters singing "Under the Boardwalk," reminding her of Lula.

Barrie crossed through and pushed through the swinging door out into the mahogany-paneled corridor. "Aunt Pru? Are you here?"

The words echoed in the stairwell, and several *yunwi* peered down at her from the second floor. Barrie stopped to poke her head into the library, unsettled by the empty spaces where her grandfather's desk and chair had been and by the lack of any sense of anything lost or missing. She pushed at her senses, walking up and down in front of the shelves, but she felt no tug of loss, and there were no books helpfully labeled *History of the Watson Family* or *Magical Bindings 101*. Giving up after a few minutes, she let the *yunwi* herd her toward the front door and around toward the stables.

Pru was out in the paddock, trotting Batch in an even circle. She sat tall and quiet, so much a part of the horse that her hands barely moved. Batch's white stockings flashed in a perfect rhythm, his steps seeming to skim the ground instead of trotting over it.

Thinking that Pru didn't realize she was there, Barrie climbed up onto the white-painted fence and hooked her feet through the rungs as she settled in to watch. A row of *yunwi* came to sit around her.

Pru shifted her weight, and Batch's trot melted into an equally elegant walk, remaining on the same circle until Pru finally loosened the reins and his neck and stride both lengthened. Stopping beside Barrie, she dismounted and held out a stirrup. "Hop on," she said. "It's time you had a lesson."

"What happened to the movers? Aren't they coming any minute?"

"The phone's in my pocket. I'll know when they reach the gate—and I was desperate to get out of my head for a while after what Seven told me."

"Are you all right?"

"That's not what I want to talk about. Get on up here," Pru said tightly, and for the first time, Barrie realized how upset she was, and that it wasn't entirely about Seven. Pru gestured and held out the stirrup, her tone brooking no argument.

Barrie mounted awkwardly. She held her hand out for the reins, but Pru picked up a lunge line and a long whip from beside the fence post instead, did something complicated to fasten the rope to Batch's bit on either side, and tied the reins securely out of Barrie's reach.

"Were you and Eight able to get anything resolved between you on the way over here?" Pru asked as she adjusted the length of the stirrups and nudged Barrie's legs and seat into the proper position.

Barrie would have been more optimistic about their relationship if he hadn't been trying to force Kate to give up the binding. Or if he had kissed her when he'd dropped her off at the dock. He had looked like he was going to—looked like he wanted to—but then he hadn't. He had apologized about Ernesto, though, and at least they had cleared the air.

"We need to keep talking," she told Pru, "but he has to go out to Columbia to finish the rest of the paperwork with the baseball coach and the university admissions people. He's coming over later."

"Beaufort men are complicated, aren't they?" Pru smiled

at Barrie sadly. She clucked and, snaking the whip along the ground, scattered the *yunwi* and urged Batch out into the same wide circular pattern he had been following earlier. "Now concentrate. Keep your weight in your heels, keep your back loose, and look forward between Batch's ears. You need a strong foundation, or you're eventually going to fall and hurt yourself. And if you watch the ground, that's where you'll end up."

Sensing Barrie's discomfort, Batch walked cautiously, his neck stretched long and his ears flicking back between Barrie and Pru as if he weren't quite sure who was giving orders.

"What do I do with my hands?" Barrie asked.

"You're going to hold them out at your sides, shoulder level, until the balance is second nature. In the meantime, you're going to have to trust Batch—and me. We're a team, the three of us. If one of us lets the others down, anything could happen. You could fall. Batch could get frightened. I could get trampled. We work best when we communicate. You understand?"

She narrowed her eyes at Barrie in a way that made it clear she wasn't speaking just of riding, and Barrie tensed. The gelding took a couple of shortened steps.

"Relax," Pru said. "You're making Batch nervous. Just like you make me nervous when I expect you to be in your room asleep and instead I get a call telling me you're at Beaufort Hall sacrificing blood into the fountain."

"Oh."

"Yes, 'oh.' This is where that teamwork comes in. You don't have to ask my permission before you go out, but with all that's happened these past weeks, I'd have thought you would let me know before you disappeared—not to mention that if we had talked things through, maybe we could have headed off some problems."

"Kate texted me to hurry, and I didn't stop to think."

"Well, you can't do that anymore. Don't go racing off by yourself, do you hear me? I was going to tell you this morning that the sheriff called last night. There's a chance someone spotted Ernesto down in Port Royal yesterday. It's probably nothing—a bald guy with a face tattooed on the back of his skull. That's unusual, but not definitive. The good news is that if it's Ernesto, he's heading south like we thought. Still, even without Ernesto, Lord only knows what else is going on around here. You don't know who might be sniffing around after the gold and hanging around in the woods by Cassie's house. The sheriff's patrols aren't necessarily going to keep everyone away from there, and we still don't really know what Obadiah is up to."

"I can't argue with any of that," Barrie said. "I'm sorry."

"I realize that you being bound to Watson's Landing when I'm not is an awkward situation. Watson's Landing chose you, and I'll do my best to accept that you have a role to play that I don't have. That's a lot of change and adjustment for both of us. But even if I don't have the magic that you do, I am your guardian. You're my family. My only family. I love you, and I can't bear the thought of you being hurt, not to mention that what affects Watson's Landing concerns me, too. So from now on, you have to at least talk to me before you put yourself in danger, all right?"

She clucked again before Barrie could answer, and Batch picked up an easy trot. Barrie's arms dropped to grip the slight rise in the saddle above the gelding's withers. Her nerves translated to Batch, who jigged sideways, sending the *yunwi* who had been running alongside diving back for the fence. Barrie closed her eyes and made herself relax, and the horse's gait immediately smoothed out.

"You see? Trust is a chain reaction," Pru called as Barrie brought her arms up again. "Now, why don't you try telling me what you're up to. Whatever you're planning. Full disclosure."

Barrie wondered if she was the only one who continuously underestimated Pru. She didn't mean to—Pru had such a quiet demeanor that it was easy to lose track of her competence and intelligence, but Barrie was done making that mistake.

"I wish I were up to something," she said, "but I'm at a standstill and out of ideas. There's nothing in the library, and Seven doesn't know anything, and we can't talk to the water spirits. I guess I can try the Fire Carrier again, though I don't know what good that will do. I'd love to get a better look at the Beaufort library. I'm going to try to talk to Eight about that, but Seven isn't exactly going to be eager to have me poking around there."

"He'll come around eventually."

"Yes," Barrie said, "but is eventually going to be too late?"

Barrie tried to focus on the work at hand while she put the horses away and then supervised alongside Pru and Mary all afternoon while the movers brought in Lula's things. Though Mary managed, as she usually did, to do the lion's share of the effort and keep the rest of them organized, they were all bone tired by the time the empty truck rolled away down the driveway between the oaks. Mary left soon after that. Retreating back into the house with the *yunwi*, Barrie couldn't help looking at Lula's inlaid mahogany table in the center of the foyer and wishing she could bang the edge of the heavy vase down a few times on its mirror-polished surface. There must have been dents in it once, back before it had been restored. Dents and scratches and signs of living that Lula would have considered too ugly to bring into her house in San Francisco. Here at Watson's Landing, its smug perfection made everything else look shabby by comparison.

"Keeping this instead of the old one was a mistake, wasn't

it?" Coming to stand at Barrie's elbow, Pru looked down at the table with a critical eye. "It fits here and it doesn't, and all I can think is how sad it is that Lula was trying to erase all the imperfections from her childhood. But I almost made the same mistake yesterday myself."

"I've been angry with her for so long. I was mad because she locked herself away. Because I thought she didn't want me. Because she died. I suspect I didn't want to stop being angry, because now it hurts more when I think about everything she lost. What I lost by not knowing her well enough."

Pru tipped her head against Barrie's and rested it there. "I've been angry with her too, and she didn't deserve any of what happened to her. Even so, I can't understand the choices she made. Why run off with someone she knew was dealing drugs? Violence—disrespect of any kind—is a cycle that's hard to break, and she had our father's legacy, I know that. Thinking of her makes me examine myself and my relationship with Seven. I have to question the way I tend to look for reasons to excuse his choices and the way I want to overlook his mistakes, not just to forgive them."

"That's what we do when we love people, isn't it?"

"Yes, but each time we do, we lose a piece of ourselves. I did that with my father, and Lula did it with your father, and Seven and I will need to have many long conversations before there's anything except a wide river standing between us. Love makes us want what's best for people, but half the time, it's hard to see what that will be. It's why you need to be careful with Eight." She sighed and pivoted toward the door. "Have you read your mother's letters yet?"

"I did last night. It was like seeing a Lula I didn't know existed. I always thought she hated me a little."

Pru's eyes softened, but her voice was firm. "Learning to love yourself is easier when you have someone to show you how. She should have told you a thousand times how much she loved you. The fact that she didn't left you without a foundation, so count each one of those letters as an 'I love you' and read them a million times over. And never forget that I love you too."

Barrie's vision blurred behind a veil of tears.

"Come with me," Pru said. "There's something I haven't done in much too long."

They walked into the kitchen, where sometime in the course of the day, Mary had managed to make up a pot of fish stew that simmered on the back burner. She had also left a neatly printed note by a pair of blue willow bowls on the counter.

Don't forget to eat! Neither of you have a lick of common sense.

Pru smiled and switched the burner off. "Mary doesn't approve of me lately. Changing my mind about furniture.

Letting you take Daphne to see Obadiah. Feeding the *yunwi*. Bringing the horses back. 'Impulsive' and 'illogical' are both dirty words in Mary's book, and I feel like I'm letting her down if I don't work until eleven o'clock every night. I'm tired to my bones, though. Tired in a different way than I used to be before you came. A wide-awake kind of tired."

"I'm worried about Daphne," Barrie said. "I know Mary said she was fine, but it bothers me that she didn't come back over here today. They all worry me."

"I think it's just what Mary said: more problems with Brit." Pru smiled faintly. "I do wish Mary would let us do something for them."

"What if we offered something that wasn't a loan or charity? Mary's helping us plan the restaurant, which is management, and she's had great ideas. And once I go back to school, you're going to need even more help running things. It's a lot of extra work—"

"Don't feel guilty about that. I love the restaurant, and so does Mary. It's given us both a whole new lease on life."

"Then what if we made her the restaurant manager? Or a partner. In essence, she is one already since she's been with us every step of the way. What do you think?"

Pru regarded Barrie so long that Barrie flushed and shifted from foot to foot. Then Pru laid both hands along Barrie's cheeks and kissed the top of her head. "That's perfect. You're right, and she more than deserves it." She vanished into the butler's pantry and emerged a moment later carrying a pair of scratched sterling silver spoons and a Tupperware tub glazed in frost. "And since we're already doing what Mary would consider frivolous and irresponsible, we'll save her stew for tomorrow and celebrate with dessert for dinner."

"My favorite meal," Barrie said, laughing.

"Tonight it's peach ice cream, and I'm going to teach you the best way to eat it." Leaving Barrie to follow, Pru went down into the garden and out onto the lawn. Halfway between the woods and the house, she lay down on her back, gesturing for Barrie to join her. She wedged the lid off the tub and held out a spoon. "I like to come out here when I need perspective. When things seem too big."

Barrie stretched out beside Pru on the grass. Above them, the sky was enormous, interrupted only by drifting wisps of clouds. Pru waved the Tupperware container at her, and Barrie dug out a bite of ice cream, her thumb leaving an imprint in the misted frost. The silk peach flavor slid down her throat like a minor sin, cold, tangy-sweet, and enticing.

Pru pointed up at the clouds. "Other people go out to the ocean for solace, but up in the sky, there's always something beyond the boundaries of what we know. The solar system is within the galaxy, which is within the universe. Maybe more universes. Who knows what's out there? I've always told myself that tomorrow was like the sky, filled with possibility. That made it easier to stay here and wait for something good to happen. But I've spent my whole life waiting."

"You're not waiting anymore," Barrie said, feeling fiercely proud.

"The hardest part of changing things is knowing how much needs changing," Pru continued as if Barrie hadn't spoken. "I went from not throwing away anything in thirty years to almost throwing away three hundred years of Watson history. We can live without furniture, but we can't throw ourselves away without feeling the damage. I'm going to say this one more time, and then I promise I won't bring it up anymore. You lost everyone and everything you loved when you moved here, and every bit of what you thought you knew about your family was snatched away and replaced with something else. That kind of change makes you want to retreat inward, but I'm realizing that you can't have relationships if you're not willing to open yourself up and lean on people as much as you want them to lean on you. That goes for me, and it goes for Eight as well."

Barrie stared up at the sky, and it felt too close, as if it were falling all around her. Because Pru was right. She didn't want to do what Lula had done, push away the people she loved the most. Refusing more ice cream as Pru offered her the container, she folded her arms behind her head.

"What about you?" she asked. "Do you feel like you can lean on Seven?"

"I can't help loving him, but I'm not ready to forgive him yet."

"I think what matters most about people is what they make us feel about ourselves. You and Eight both make me feel loved and special, like I want to be a better person. . . . Does Seven make you feel like that? If he makes you *happy*, then I'll be happy for you."

The clouds above them shredded in an unseen wind, casting shadows over Pru's face—the thin, aristocratic nose, the high forehead with fine strands of pale curls blowing against her skin. Barrie had an urge to reach out and push the hair away, tuck it safely behind Pru's ear, tuck Pru safely where Seven and life couldn't hurt her anymore. Where Barrie couldn't hurt her anymore.

A surge of love pushed through her, like a tangible rush of energy. She had fought Mark so hard about leaving San Francisco before he was truly gone—she'd been furious, but he had insisted that he needed to know she had someone who loved her before he died. Mark would have adored Pru, and knowing that Barrie was with her would have brought him comfort—maybe it still could. Maybe it did. It was impossible for Barrie not to believe in an afterlife when there were spirits all around her.

If there was a world of the dead, and Ayita and Elijah had brought Obadiah back from it, did that mean there was a way other people could cross over from it?

She would have traded years of her life to see Mark sashay across the lawn in his melon-colored Isaac Mizrahi dress with the bows at the elbows. Traded anything for him to lie here with her and Pru, eating cold, tart ice cream on a sticky Carolina night while she had a few stolen minutes to tell him all the things there had never been time to say.

Across the river, Beaufort Hall crowned its slope above the mud and marsh and water. The sun was setting, painting the clouds in fairy-tale colors that reflected on the dark water separating the mainland from Watson Island.

Barrie had been wrong. You didn't find strength when you couldn't live without it. You found it when you had someone or something you loved so much that it forced you to stretch the edges of yourself further than you thought was possible.

"I don't want a life that's safe," she said to Pru, interrupting their comfortable silence, "not if it means sacrificing other people. And I don't want to look back on roads not taken. I don't want you doing that anymore, either. Promise me something."

"What's that?"

"Take Seven out for a hot dog at Bobby Joe's and talk things through. I want to like him. But not if he's going to turn out to be the kind of person who makes you feel smaller instead of better."

"I'll take your advice if you'll take it yourself," Pru said. "Be careful with Eight, but don't hold back. Don't punish him for making the same kind of choices about the Beaufort binding that you feel you have to make yourself."

"Pinky swear." Barrie held up her little finger and shook it when Pru hooked her own around it. "Also, while I'm thinking about Mary and Daphne and bridges that need building, I have an idea about how we can get Obadiah more energy without having to sacrifice the lodestones. I'd need your help, though. A lot of it."

CHAPTER EIGHTEEN

While she waited for Eight to come back over, Barrie finished setting up the entertainment center in the back parlor beside the kitchen. Crowded with the sofa, chairs, and flatscreen television from the family room in Lula's house, the room looked achingly familiar, yet it was empty of the main thing that had made it feel like home. The oversize chair still smelled of popcorn and Mark's perfume. One breath, and Barrie was back in San Francisco with him, the two of them watching *The Princess Bride* or singing along with *Pitch Perfect* for the forty-fifth time.

Thinking of Mark singing was another reminder that life was too short for could-have-beens and should-have-beens and if-I'd-onlys. Every person was an unfinished puzzle, and if you spent too much time focusing on the missing pieces, you never got to appreciate what you'd already put together. Pru was right. She couldn't fault Eight for making the same choices she had made.

"Barrie?" Pru called from the kitchen. "Are you about done? Eight's here."

Smoothing her shirt as she turned, Barrie found Eight standing in the doorway smiling at her. Her two worlds collided, the past of San Francisco and the present, and Mark's voice sounded in her head so vividly that he could have been standing beside her.

So this is your number boy? he would have said. *Someone's got the math all wrong, baby girl. He's a ten and not an eight. Now, what the heck are you waiting for?*

Barrie ran the last few steps. Standing on her toes, she kissed Eight softly and then pulled back, giving him a chance to escape. The suddenness of it must have surprised him, because his eyes held hers, his pupils dark and wide, his expression faintly puzzled but unguarded enough to give her hope. Then he cupped her face, gently, as if she were fragile. Still watching her, his lips descended, moving over hers, claiming hers. Her eyes closed, and she let herself get lost in the sensation.

He raised his head finally, and watched her before he pulled away. "This doesn't change what I said about looking for a way to take the binding back. Real problems don't get solved with kisses."

"So we'll keep working at the problems until we figure them out," Barrie said.

Eight kissed her again, fiercely this time, and when he pulled back, he grinned. "So tell me this plan you called about."

"There are stages. I want to take a look at your library for information about the binding, but I assume that has to wait until your dad goes back to the office. The main idea, though, would involve Kate meeting Obadiah. I figure you and your dad will both hate that."

"If the plan makes sense, then Kate and I'll either figure out how to get Dad on board or we'll sneak her out of the house when he's not looking."

Barrie raised an eyebrow. "What happened to honesty and disclosure?"

"I'll be the first one to meet Dad partway any time he's ready to roll up his sleeves and help us find a solution," Eight said, "but this involves all of us. He doesn't get to make all the decisions like he's the only one who has a stake in it, and we don't have time to wait for him to understand that, not with Ayita and Elijah putting people in danger. Right?"

"As long as you're sure." Barrie took Eight's hand and led him into the kitchen, where they talked things through with

Pru, ironed out all the details, and made the necessary phone calls. Another hour passed before Pru managed to get Seven over to Watson's Landing on the pretext of discussing a restaurant partnership agreement for Mary.

En route to Colesworth Place, Eight and Barrie collected Kate on the other end of the tunnel, and then they climbed the river path all together. They found Obadiah eating his dinner on the ruined steps of the old mansion. The postsunset sky had yet to bring out the night chorus of frogs and myriad insects, but the dig crew had already stopped work and sat in a half circle of camp chairs beside the overseer's cabin. The dusky hush had an expectant quality, a sense of something coming.

Like the ravens perched above him on the fractured columns, Obadiah had swiveled around to watch Barrie, Eight, and Kate approach. Kate walked nearly sideways, watching the dig crew and the patrol car parked beneath a tree.

"Are you positive they can't see us?" she asked. "The deputies, either? How does Obadiah know we're coming to see him? He might assume we're on our way to visit Cassie, and then he'll have to make us disappear all of a sudden, right? Won't people notice that?"

"There are some kinds of magic he's good at. The kind that would be great for robbing banks, apparently. He's just not so great with curses. Or ghosts," Eight said. His tone was light, but his arms hung stiffly at his sides, fingers clenching and unclenching.

Barrie looped her arm around his. "Relax, would you? You're supposed to be the one with the gift. Ham it up, or Obadiah will realize that it's Kate who's trying to figure out what he wants."

"But don't blame me if I can't," Kate said. "I haven't had a chance to practice on anyone except you two and Dad—and all that told me is that all y'all are dysfunctional. Also, being here is giving me a headache."

Barrie gave Kate's shoulder a little squeeze. "That's the downside to the binding, but you'll get used to it. As for the rest, we don't expect you to be perfect. You may not be able to read Obadiah at all, but like you said, even without the gift, you've gotten good at reading body language and figuring out how people feel. At the very least, see if you can read what he thinks about the idea. Figure out if it makes him scared or nervous. He might downplay the danger to us because he's willing to risk it, but if he's nervous about being able to protect everyone, then it's probably too dangerous for us to try."

Obadiah appeared stronger, or at least less weary and heartsick, than he had the last couple of times Barrie had seen him. As they reached him, he set the half-finished ham-and-cheese sandwich he'd been eating down on a paper plate.

Barrie introduced Kate and settled on the step beside him.

The stone was still warm after absorbing a full day's heat. "I'm glad to see Cassie brought your dinner."

"Not graciously, but at least she didn't forget." Having looked Kate over, Obadiah shifted his focus back to Eight. "You going to sit, or do you plan to stand there glowering at me until I lose my appetite?"

"Glowering has a certain appeal." Eight remained standing, his stance tense and ready, until Barrie crooked her finger and gestured at the step beside her. Then he sat reluctantly.

"How positive are you that Ayita and Elijah can't take energy from someone as long as that person stays outside the police tape?" Barrie asked. "Or hurt them some other way?"

"Am I positive there's no chance?" Obadiah wiped his fingers on a napkin, one at a time, and then folded the napkin over the remains of his sandwich. "There's a chance the sky could fall and the earth could crack open. Anything is possible."

"Then can you do this in stages? Put Ayita and Elijah to sleep temporarily while they're weak, bind them the way you originally planned, but *then* gather the energy you need to remove the curse, instead of trying to remove the curse right away?"

Obadiah shifted his attention across to the dig site, where order had more or less been restored. The dig crew had relaid the stakes in neat rows, scraped away the torn soil from the grid squares, and hauled the soil away so that they could push it through the giant sifting screens. But around the perimeter of the buried room, yellow police tape still flapped in the wind, and plastic sheeting weighted down by sandbags covered the small hole in the arched brick ceiling.

"I could try, but what's the point? At best it would buy only a little time, and without the lodestones, it would take too long to gather the energy I need. Then, even if I managed to remove the curse, Ayita and Elijah would wake eventually, and they'd be even angrier than they are right now. Their vengeance could simply take another form—one even more dangerous than the curse itself."

"How is that different from what you intend with the lodestone?" Eight asked impatiently. "You'd still have to send them back to where they came from. Can't you put them into a spirit bottle or burn the bones or something?"

Obadiah laced his fingers together and leaned forward, elbows on his knees. "I didn't summon them, so I don't control them. They'll fight me if I try to force them to cross over, and that takes power and energy I don't have without the lodestones. But if I can bind them and remove the curse, then convince them that they've had enough vengeance, they might cross over on their own. Or I threaten them and force them to cross over. As long as I have access to their bones, there are ways to release trapped spirits without destroying them. It comes down to how much power I have versus how much they have, which isn't an exact formula—this much energy, versus that much energy. There are two of them, and there is skill involved, and magical aptitude—talent—not to mention that rage and the need for revenge fuels them and makes them stronger. But that's not what you're really asking, is it?"

Barrie stared down at her shoes, which were more brown than pink now, after her dunking in the river. "I—*we*—have an idea, but we need to be sure you can protect people first."

"You're still harboring the delusion that magic is precise, that it can respond to promises." Obadiah's smile was a feral gesture, a baring of teeth gleaming in the darkness. "Magic and spirits . . . what we're engaged in . . . is a battle between opposing forces. Anyone who tells you there's no chance for casualties is a charlatan, a fool, or both."

"Then I think we're done here." Barrie pushed herself to her feet.

He caught her hand and held her in place, which brought Eight surging to stand beside her. Obadiah released Barrie with a sigh. "Tell me exactly what you have in mind, and I'll tell you whether I can make it work. Or at least tell you the risks involved."

A burst of laughter from beside the overseer's cabin carried across the expanse of grass, and several Coleman lanterns switched on. Obadiah was already doing his glowing thing again, making light emanate from his skin, and the area around him was brighter than the surrounding dusk.

"You said that Elijah and Ayita surprised you yesterday when you were going to help Daphne communicate with them," Barrie said, "but you've had some time to recover, and you have more energy now. What if you tried letting Mary talk to them? She's the one who's having to hold the family together. Daphne said she'd convince Mary somehow. Can you make that safe for them?"

"My answer won't change because you asked the question in a different way, *petite*. When it comes to spirits, there's no such thing as completely 'safe.' Elijah and Ayita spent themselves bringing me back because they recognized me as family. That *should* offer Daphne and Mary the same protection, but there are no guarantees. And what happens later—if they won't remove the curse willingly, or if I can't release them?"

"What if we brought a lot of people here? If you can keep Mary and Daphne safe long enough to talk to the spirits, then it would be worth risking an open house, a chance for Cassie and her family to mend fences with people in town now that Wyatt's gone. And we'd be bringing a crowd to you at the same time. Would that give you the energy you need?"

Something hungry slipped into the look Obadiah gave her. "Depends on how many and who they are. But why not do everything at once?"

Barrie held his eyes. "Because if Ayita and Elijah remove the curse on their own and cross over willingly, there's no reason to do any more. Unless removing the curse and releasing the spirits isn't all you're really after. You keep saying the gold is only a means to an end—but Mary doesn't want it."

"How many more times do you need me to explain my motives?" Obadiah's muscles had tensed, and he stretched his neck first one direction and then the other and let out a breath, though whether that was an effort to calm his temper or to gather his thoughts, Barrie couldn't tell. "Is it so hard to understand that I want to leave my family better off before I die?" he asked. "Leave them safer? I'd like to go back to my apartment in Paris and know they are taken care of. In the end, isn't that what most people want?"

"You would think so, wouldn't you? But people seldom want what they're supposed to want," Eight said.

CHAPTER NINETEEN

Supported by Daphne at her elbow, Mary stepped onto the Colesworth property with the air of a cat walking across wet carpet. Kate, Barrie, Pru, and Eight quietly shut the doors of Pru's ancient Mercedes in the parking lot before following Mary and Daphne to the excavation site.

Barrie's head ached more than usual. And not just from the inevitable, unrelenting pressure of being away from Watson's Landing. There were too many moving pieces to track.

It was after eleven. The waning moon left the trees and the overlong grass on either side of the road in darkness, and the gray of Mary's hair and the whites of her eyes were eerie glimmers as she darted looks from one cluster of shadows to another. Nerves had bowed her shoulders and aged her by a decade.

The group passed the small, boxy Colesworth house,

which was shuttered and quiet, and beyond it, the icehouse and kitchen that initially blocked the view of the overseer's cabin. A few steps farther, the dig crew came into view, still laughing and talking in their camp chairs, though Berg was absent. A square bluish glow, like a laptop screen, from inside one of the brightly colored tents behind the cabin suggested he was working or researching as he'd promised.

Having already witnessed Obadiah's magic in action, Daphne ignored the dig crew, but Mary waved and then stopped abruptly when none of the dig crew waved back.

"They can't see you, remember, Gramma?" Daphne gestured over beneath the trees to the sheriff's patrol car. "The police can't see you, either."

"That's not natural. Or right. I still say none of this is right," Mary said. "And if something happens to us, who's going to take care of Brit and Jackson?"

Pru gave Mary's arm a reassuring squeeze. At the same time, she leveled a fierce glance at Barrie, doing her best to seem brave when she was almost as scared as Mary was herself.

The responsibility of what they were doing suddenly engulfed Barrie and made her shiver. It was one thing to trust that Obadiah would keep them safe. It was another to know that if anything went wrong, a big part, the biggest part, of the blame would fall squarely on her own shoulders. How could she bear it if someone—anyone—got hurt?

Up ahead, Obadiah was already standing beside the excavation site, rocking impatiently on his feet. His eyes fastened on Mary and Daphne, drinking them in, but he was tense and his expression was shuttered, as if he was already anticipating their rejection.

"Still can't read him?" Kate jabbed a sharp elbow into her brother's ribs. "Let me help you out. I think he wants Mary and Daphne to like him."

Eight's jaw tightened. "Keep laughing, Frog. Let's hope that you still think it's funny an hour from now."

Not in the least apologetic or afraid, Kate skipped ahead. Barrie slipped her hand into Eight's and squeezed his fingers. He could say what he wanted about being happy that his gift was weaker, but it had to feel strange to have Kate know more about what people wanted while he knew less than he ever had before.

"Kate will get over showing off eventually," Barrie said. "It just hasn't all sunk in yet, so it still seems like an adventure to her."

"That's what worries me. Don't get me wrong. It wasn't a bad idea to get confirmation that Obadiah wants to protect his family more than he wants the gold, but you don't know Kate like I do. She's reckless, Bear. Even more than you are." He brought the back of Barrie's hand up to his lips, and she realized how much she had missed having him call her "Bear" with that softening in his voice. She had missed him, plain and simple.

Near the yellow police tape by the excavation area, Mary stopped six feet from where Obadiah stood. He came forward, his hand outstretched, but she clamped her fists into her armpits, arms crossed over her chest, and he pulled up short with a small, defeated slump to his shoulders.

Barrie wondered, how long had it been since he'd had a real family? Someone who cared about him? How long had he ever been able to stay in one place before people noticed that he wasn't aging? How many wives or children had he put into caskets and lowered into the ground?

"Stand a little closer to the police tape," he said to Mary. "The spirits need to sense who you are. It's important for them to know you're family."

Mary wagged a finger at him, her hand veiny and very brave. "What do you mean 'sense'? I said I'm not goin' to put up with any voodoo."

"This isn't voodoo. I'll draw a cosmogram and stand in the center to control the spirits—"

"See that right there?" Mary clutched at the small silver cross she wore on a chain around her neck. "Fact you need to control them ought to tell you this is a bad idea. The good Lord meant for the dead to stay dead, and you're lookin' for trouble askin' them to come up out of their graves."

Seen side by side, there was a resemblance between her

and Obadiah. The set of the lips, the arch of the eyebrows, the shape of the ears. The stubborn pride.

He moved to a spot just outside the police tape and pointed to the ground. "Just stand here so they can hear you. All you need to do is talk to them. Tell them how the curse has hurt you. Be specific. Talk about your daughter, how your grand-children aren't doing well—"

"My grandchildren are fine," Mary said, staying right where she was. "They're all good children, and I'm takin' care of them the same as I've done every single day of their lives."

"No one's questioning that. You've done a great job with them," Pru said, squeezing Mary's shoulder.

Barrie looked down the row of familiar faces: Pru, Mary, Daphne, Eight, and Kate, and it struck her that not having had close friends growing up, the word "familiar" had taken on a different meaning for her. A literal meaning. Her view of family was binary—family and not family, familiar and not familiar. Growing up, there had been only Mark and Lula. Now she had Pru, and Eight, and somehow without her hav-ing realized it, Mary and Daphne, Kate, and even Cassie had all snuck in. Family wasn't finite. It was a rubber band with a limitless capacity to stretch.

With a quick glance at the police car parked beneath the trees, Obadiah gestured again for them all to come forward. "Stay here within reach," he said, eyeing Barrie with a silent message, "but don't cross over the police tape or interrupt the ceremony. Understood?"

"What kind of a ceremony?" Mary demanded, staying right where she stood.

He sighed deeply. "I told you—it isn't voodoo, and it isn't *wrong*. Our family have been borrowers since back in Ayita's time, using whatever we had and whatever worked. I've studied Cherokee and Native medicines, Bakongo, Buddhism, Taoism, Chinese traditional medicines, Wicca, Obeah, Santeria, and yes, a little voodoo, but—"

"Cherokee?" Eight had been standing with his hands in his pockets, staring at the ground, but now he looked up sharply.

"Of course. Ayita was Cherokee. A good half of the slaves in the Carolinas were Native American back then, most of them women and children. Ayita knew the plants and the countryside—what to plant and when and where to plant it. But mostly she was a healer, a medicine woman, and we passed that down in the family and used it to survive."

Obadiah's face had locked into stillness, all hint of expression wiped away as if he were speaking of a shopping list or of the weather, and somehow that made the meaning of the words stand out as sharply as if each one had fallen into the air like the long note of a bell. He was talking about children and women, people, being bought and sold because of their skills or talents or muscles. Like cattle or sheep. Beside Barrie, Eight squeezed her hand, and she squeezed back, because once again he'd been right. Ayita had been Cherokee, and a slave.

How did they not teach any of these things in school?

But Eight had guessed that either Ayita or Elijah had to have been Cherokee, or they wouldn't have been able to communicate with the Fire Carrier to make the bargains. But in Mary's family, that information had been lost in the fog of time, and everyone else on Watson Island had taken the story of the Fire Carrier at face value and never thought to examine it more closely.

Standing with his back to them, Obadiah was silent, absorbing the strength he needed. Then, softly, he began to chant. Barrie nudged Pru and the others up to stand at the police tape where Obadiah wanted them, making sure that she herself and both the Beauforts stood close enough to give him a source of energy, as they'd earlier discussed.

With a quick glance at the police car parked beneath the trees, Obadiah climbed across the tape. Working quickly and still chanting softly, he drew a cosmogram on the broken ground beside the plastic sheeting that covered the brick roof of the buried chamber. When he had finished, he dusted the white clay powder from his hands. His thick dreadlocks brushed his shoulders as he tipped his head skyward, squinting at the moon. Then he began to chant more loudly, shuffling his feet as he moved counterclockwise around the outer circle of the cosmogram. While the movements were deliberate and small, there was a new spring in his step, a straightness to his back, a different set to his neck, a removal of all the small signs of age that Barrie had never considered before.

Whenever he reached a point of the cross, he stopped and clapped multiple times in rhythm. Pru startled each time, and Daphne didn't watch at all, but Kate kept edging closer, fascinated, until Eight grabbed her by the elbow and pulled her back to stand beside Mary, who stood with the cross she wore around her neck clutched tightly in her fingers.

"It really *isn't* voodoo," Eight said to reassure Mary, "or anything evil. I looked it up. All he's doing is following the movement of the sun and the phases of human life, the past, the present, and the future—"

"Child, don't you think I know a ring-shout when I see one?" Mary tapped Eight on the arm. "I may not have known what it was when he talked about it, and I've never seen whatever he drew on the ground, but the movements and the *sound* are the same. The rhythm and the shuffle and the hope and despair."

Kate sidled closer. "What's a ring-shout?"

"It's a dance." Daphne moved to the very edge of the police tape, watching Obadiah even more sharply. "From church—from the praise houses. It goes back to slavery times."

Eight, looking guilt-ridden, exchanged a helpless look with Barrie, but Obadiah completed the seventh lap around the circle and stepped inside to stand at the center of the cross, bringing the chanting to a crescendo. Slowly he raised his hands.

A thin mist rose through the plastic sheeting that covered the hole in the bricks of the roof, and, gathering itself, the mist coalesced into a dark mass that divided into two individual shapes. Each figure was backlit by the moonlight and tethered by a rope of fog that disappeared down into the chamber. The first was clearly a man, larger than the other, big-framed but with one shoulder held higher as if he'd been injured at some point and hadn't healed properly. Beside him, the smaller shape, a woman, stood only as high as his chest. Her hair fell to her waist, and her eyes were almond-shaped above high cheekbones, but unlike Elijah's, they weren't weary—they were alive with rage. The very mist that formed her was slick and oily, as if it had been dipped in fury.

"Talk fast," Obadiah said to Mary across his shoulder. "They're stronger than they were, and I won't be able to hold them long."

Mary had brought the small silver cross to her lips, and she was mumbling against it, praying or reassuring herself, or both. She didn't seem to hear Obadiah. She didn't answer.

"Talk!" Obadiah insisted.

Shaking her head, Mary backed away. "This isn't right. The good Lord didn't mean us to pull the dead back for conversation."

"The Lord didn't mean for us to be cursed, either," Daphne snapped at her grandmother. "And they're here now, so if you won't talk to them, then they're here for no reason."

"So you say something, Daphne." Eight nodded encouragement.

But as Daphne turned toward Ayita and Elijah, they watched her, and their figures began to writhe above the plastic sheeting, straining at the ropes of mist that held them bound in place. Their faces contorted in pain and fury, they pushed against the boundaries of their own shapes and the constraints of Obadiah's magic.

Obadiah's shoulders trembled visibly.

Daphne was still silent, and Eight looked back at Mary. "If you can't speak to them, then could you pretend you're only talking to me? Tell *me* what it's been like with the curse. You've had to raise Daphne, Brit, and Jackson by yourself. There are always things going wrong. Didn't you ever feel like it was too much? Like you couldn't do it?"

"There's never been a day," Mary said furiously, "that I haven't felt lucky to get the chance to raise them!"

Daphne put her hand on Mary's arm. "That's not help-ing, Gramma. Tell them how the curse *hurts* us. How the only thing their revenge is doing for us is making everything worse!"

Elijah and Ayita surged forward and then rocked back again, straining at the tether that bound them to the grave. Each motion pushed them farther, as if the rope of magic that held them were stretching. Loosening. Obadiah's upraised arms shook, and sweat ran in a rivulet down the side of his face.

Eight clutched Mary's elbow. "Mary, please. What do you want to say about the curse? There has to be something."

"Tell them about Brit and the trial study," Barrie said.

"You're askin' me to say that the curse is at the root of our problems, and how do I know what is and isn't?" Mary snapped. "Don't you think I know a dozen families whose luck is as bad as ours—or worse? This is wrong. I'm sorry, but it is. I thought I could help, but there's no part of what we're doin' here that we've got any business doin'."

The forms of Elijah and Ayita had grown darker and more opaque. Obadiah's chanting grew more desperate and rushed. Daphne started to talk about Brit's condition, and about her mother, and about how hard Mary worked, about needing luck, and airfare, and hotel rooms. She talked about postponing college, and Jackson needing tutoring, and Crunch needing an attitude adjustment. She talked even though few of those things had any place in Ayita and Elijah's world, and Barrie hated hearing it, in large part because she knew how much Mary had to hate hearing Daphne say it.

Elijah and Ayita pressed forward, and Obadiah fought to hold them back. It didn't seem like he was winning. Grinding to a halt, Daphne turned back and looked at Mary. "Say something," she said. "Help me. I don't think they know about college and hotels and airfare. Tell them how things have changed, Gramma. If you can't tell them anything else, tell them about defiance. Tell them about the ring-shout."

"Not defiance. Stories," Mary said. "That's what the ring-shout was. Folks telling tales from the Bible and parents passin' on scraps of memory they'd learned from their parents and singin' them out. Worshipping the God they were told to worship, but in their own way, out in the fields and the praise houses. The only thing defiant about that is the fact that you're clingin' to hope and dignity because it's all you've got." She scowled over at Ayita and Elijah. "You think what was done to you and Elijah was special? Murder is always wrong, doesn't matter who does the killin'. Hurtin' someone else is always wrong. Everyone's got their burdens. The way the world is, we need faith and hope and joyful praise more than ever to get through. And that's what the ring-shout was about. Gettin' by and gettin' through. You ask me, folks don't do the ring-shout enough anymore."

Barrie's eyes stung at the despair of anyone thinking that getting through was the best they could do. She reached for Eight, to take his hand.

Obadiah screamed a warning. Ayita sprang toward him. He shouted words Barrie couldn't understand, brought his hands together and pushed them downward, pushed as though forcing a physical object back into the ground.

Ayita's face contorted, elongated. Her mouth open in shock and fury, she tilted into Elijah, her form spilling into his and his spilling into hers as both were sucked back through the plastic sheeting, into the small hole between the bricks, and back into the buried chamber.

Obadiah fell, landing with a thud in the dirt. The fabric of his suit puddled around him as if the flesh inside had shrunk again. His face was still and ancient.

Eight vaulted over the police tape and ran toward him. Exactly what Obadiah had made them promise not to do.

"No! Stop!" Barrie yelled. "You can't go where they can reach you!"

Eight froze and then sprinted back, vaulting over the police tape with frustration and impotent fury in every bunched muscle. "So what do we do? We can't leave Obadiah there. What if Ayita and Elijah drain his energy?"

"They wouldn't have brought him back if they'd wanted to do that."

"You don't know that," Eight said.

"But if she's right, if family is important to them," Daphne said, "then Gramma and I can go and help. We're family, too." Her eyes were frightened slashes in her moonlit face, and probably because she knew Mary wouldn't agree with her, she didn't wait. Darting forward, she crossed the police tape and ran to where Obadiah lay on the ground, his body half in and half out of one of the partially dug squares of the excavation grid.

Mary ran after her with a muffled cry and barreled through the tape. Pru and Kate darted forward, too, and Barrie, even though she knew better. Eight stepped in front of them, arms held out to keep them from crossing. By the time Mary reached Obadiah, Daphne had his shoulders off the ground and was dragging him away from the cosmogram and the plastic sheeting held down by scattered bricks.

"Get his legs," she said to her grandmother.

Pru's fingers dug into Barrie's arm, and Eight stood bent low, almost like a runner at the beginning of a race. As soon as Daphne and Mary had dragged Obadiah back out of the area confined by the police tape, he took over.

The spotlight on the police car switched on. Swiveling unsteadily over the excavation area, the light bathed the ground, then landed on the cast of shocked, scared, and guilty faces around Barrie. She stood blinking, blinded, as two car doors slammed closed and one of the deputies gave a shout.

"Hey! What are y'all doing there? Put your hands up and freeze!"

Barrie had gotten used to spirits and bindings and even men with guns. Getting caught by the cops was something new and somehow worse. Claws of panic tore her lungs, making it impossible to exhale as she pictured the cosmogram still drawn on the ground in chalk. She could already see the headline: WATSON HEIR DIES OF PANIC ATTACK AFTER PERFORMANCE OF SATANIC RITUAL.

Eight set Obadiah down and raised his hands, the cogs in his head spinning so obviously that it would have been comical if Barrie'd had any ideas of her own to contribute. Pru was the one who strode forward calmly to meet the deputies, as if there were nothing unusual in what she was doing there in the middle of the night.

"Good evening," she called. "Would y'all mind coming and giving us some help here?"

"Shhhh. What are you doing?" Barrie hissed.

"Trust me," Pru said without looking at her.

Behind them, from beside the overseer's cabin, the dig crew members were also calling to one another and standing up, looking in their direction. Berg poked his head out of the tent nearby. Clearly, whatever invisibility or distraction spell Obadiah had woven had dissipated when he'd become unconscious.

"Go pound on Cassie's door and tell her we need her over here," Eight said to Kate. "Right now. Don't argue."

Kate opened her mouth, then closed it silently as Daphne sprinted toward the house, her white shirt streaming behind her. Pru raised her voice again, speaking to the deputies, who were approaching Obadiah with puzzled expressions.

Pru didn't give them time to ask any questions. "I'm so glad you two are here," she said. "This is Mary's cousin Obadiah, and we've got to get him over to a sofa and get him some ice. I think he fainted—low blood sugar, maybe, or the heat."

As excuses went, it was hopeless, but Pru spoke with quiet authority and complete assurance, as if no one could doubt her. The deputies peered at her, and then blinked and gave her a sheepish smile.

"Oh, it's you. Miss Pru, Ms. Mary. How y'all doing?" The deputy who spoke had a narrow head made even narrower by buzz-cut hair bisected by a widow's peak and wide shoulders balanced out by a wide torso encased in a bulletproof vest. He examined Obadiah dubiously. "You sure that's all that's wrong with him? Looks like we ought to maybe call an ambulance. And where'd y'all come from anyway? What are you doing here in the dead of night?"

Obadiah groaned where he lay on the ground, his head resting on the toe of Eight's battered leather boat shoes, and he reached over to clamp a hand around Eight's leg. Eight staggered a bit, and Barrie pushed between them to nudge Eight away, letting her own bare calf rest against Obadiah's skin.

"I know you, don't I?" Pru smiled at the deputy. "My memory these days is not what it was, but you've got the look of a Price about you."

"Yes, ma'am. Jeffrey Price. Ms. Emma's grandson." The deputy grinned at Pru with a dip of his head.

Pru's smile widened coquettishly, and Barrie blinked, because if Pru wasn't channeling Cassie, she was channeling someone else—Lula maybe, someone dazzling and charming and bigger than life. "My goodness," she said, "the last time I saw you was at my father's funeral. Wasn't it?"

"That's right. I'd just finished up training for the sheriff's department. Now, what's going on here? I don't know what happened, but we never even saw you arrive."

"Listen to you." Mary waggled her finger at him. "First you fall asleep on the job, and then you stand around doin' nothin' while my cousin Obadiah's on the ground. You should be ashamed of yourself!" She gestured to Kate. "Child, you pick up his feet, and you"—she pointed at Eight—"stop dawdlin'. We need to get the man up to the house."

Unwilling to risk letting Obadiah take energy from Eight for a third time that night, Barrie shook her head. "Let me help Obadiah. I think Eight might be feeling a little under the weather himself. Maybe we all ate something that didn't agree with us."

She maneuvered herself into position, but one of the deputies came and picked Obadiah up beneath the shoulders while the other deputy took over carrying his legs as Berg, Andrew, and the rest of the archaeology team arrived. Barrie motioned for Berg to help.

"What's going on here? Where'd you all come from?" Andrew's gaze slid past Obadiah to the cross and concentric circles that were still chalked inside the rectangle of police tape. "Is that a Bakongo cosmogram?"

Mary rounded on him, hands propped on her hips. "We're layin' ghosts to rest. What did you think? That fancy equipment of yours broke all on its own the second you found a skeleton down in that room? Open graves need closin'. Now, y'all goin' to stand around here all night or you goin' to do somethin' useful?"

The two deputies exchanged a glance. Jeffrey Price smiled to himself, and his partner, a short, grizzled man with loose jowls and a narrow mustache, shook his head. "No spirit nonsense, now, Ms. Mary. You're all going to have to go on home."

"You believe in the Fire Carrier, but the Colesworths can't have a ghost of their own, is that it?" Mary said. "Or is it because I'm the one tellin' you there's a ghost? Now you listen to me, young man. You take my cousin right inside and stop

meddlin' in what you don't begin to understand." Mary waved
her hand at the deputies, gesturing to where the front door
of the Colesworth house stood open. Cassie and her mother
had emerged, and Daphne was obviously finishing her explanation. Cassie looked up at Barrie, who waved her toward
Obadiah.

The deputies carried Obadiah a few more steps, but he
suddenly raised his head and struggled and tried to kick his
legs free. "You go ahead and put me down," he said. "I can
walk." Suppressing a groan, he sagged a little between the
officers as they set him on his feet. They braced him between
them and guided him in the direction of the house while
Cassie went to meet them.

Andrew, meanwhile, had peeled himself away from the
rest of the crew and wandered to where the fallen police
tape fluttered along the ground. Just before he reached it, he
stopped as if he'd run into an invisible wall. Brow furrowed,
he peered back at Barrie. "I don't understand what you were
doing. And how did we not notice you coming over?"

Gingerly disengaging himself from the two deputies and
leaning on Cassie instead, Obadiah walked back to where
Andrew stood and waved the rest of the dig crew and the deputies closer. Still leaning on Cassie and taking energy from her,
he touched them one by one, speaking in a calm and confident
tone. "There was nothing to see tonight, no cause for alarm.

You're growing tired now, and you want to be back where you started the evening."

The sound of his voice made Barrie think of the way he'd made her forget the first few times she had seen him. Or rather, it made her remember that she'd forgotten. Had he spoken to her like this then, too?

"Hypnotism?" she asked. "Or magic?"

"It's a fine line, isn't it? The difference between persuasion and compulsion," Obadiah said with a shrug. Then he wiped his forehead and briefly closed his eyes.

The deputies returned to their car, and Andrew and everyone on the dig crew returned slowly to their tents. Barrie grasped Berg's elbow and held him there. He shook his head, looking bemused, until Obadiah touched him, and he came back to himself. Then Obadiah's knees buckled. Despite Cassie's help, he crumpled like a rag doll. Eight and Berg swooped in to catch him as he fell.

Together the two of them supported Obadiah the rest of the way to house, the tops of his feet dragging in the gravel and scratching his shoes as he tried to walk. By the time he had reached the stoop, he seemed to have drained away every ounce of strength he had managed to borrow, and he stopped. "I need to rest a minute."

"What went wrong back there?" Eight asked.

"Talking to the spirits took too long, and Mary said the

exact wrong thing. All we accomplished was to give Ayita a taste of freedom. I warned you that she and Elijah didn't have a lot of humanity left in them."

"So what do we do now?" Barrie asked.

"You live up to your end of the bargain. I kept them contained like I promised."

CHAPTER TWENTY

Back in the Watson's Landing kitchen forty minutes later, Eight slumped down at the table. Pru tossed the keys to the Mercedes onto the counter, drank a glass of water, and gave Barrie a stern look.

"Do you think you can please try not to get into any more trouble tonight?" she asked. "I'm not going to have to take the key to the tunnel to bed with me to keep it away from you, am I?"

"No, Aunt Pru. I'll go up to bed as soon as Eight leaves. I promise."

Pru sighed and set her glass down in the sink, then kissed Barrie briefly and pushed her way through the swinging door back into the corridor. Barrie and Eight both listened to the sound of her footsteps retreating against the soft backdrop of beach music from the radio on the counter.

Eight leaned back in the chair and stretched his legs out. They were hard-muscled, long, and tanned. His sun-lightened hair fell across his forehead, rumpled-looking like his yellow shirt.

The air thinned in the room around Barrie, became something forbidden, and she fidgeted with the stacked collection of notebooks, sample restaurant menus, and newspaper ads for the opening that lay beside the roses on the faded countertop. Her fingers felt cold.

"What are you thinking?" Eight asked.

"I'm thinking that hope is possibly the only inexhaustible resource on earth. What are you thinking?"

"I'm thinking that you are like a compass. You veer off course when you hit an obstacle, but I can always be sure you're going to find your way back to the right direction."

"Is this the right direction? I'm not sure this was the result we wanted."

Eight rested his forearms on his knees and shook his head. "I don't want to talk about that anymore. Can we have a few minutes where we're not thinking about bindings and curses and magic? Listening to Mary and Daphne was a good reminder that I don't have nearly as big a stake in all of this as anyone else, and I don't have a right to complain about much of anything. Not when 'getting through' is still the best that a lot of people can hope for."

"We can know we're lucky and still feel a little over-whelmed." Barrie's voice wavered, not quite a crack, but close.

"A little?" Eight asked with a crooked grin.

Moving with the usual grace that made everything he did seem effortless, he shifted to his feet and crossed toward her. "I keep telling myself I'm going to put some distance between us, and the next thing I know, I find myself reaching out to touch you," he said. "I seem to need to touch you."

His touch was gentle as he cupped her face with his palm, then he pulled her close and rested his chin on her hair. He smelled like himself, like root beer, and cloves, and cherries. She didn't know why that surprised her, that his smile and the smell of him hadn't changed.

Slowly, she slipped her hands to his back and slid them up to burrow into the thick cords of muscle that throwing a baseball and swinging a bat had given him, reveling in the solidness and warmth against her fingers. She had seen him without his shirt: the wide planes of his chest, the rippled stomach, the ridges of muscle above his hips. The shift of fabric across his skin was pure temptation, like a present waiting to be unwrapped.

Her breathing had fallen into rhythm with his, both of them breathing harder, their hearts beating faster, the only sound in the room except faint chords of beach music from the radio.

He pulled away.

"We should have music, if we're going to have a reconcilia-tion. It won't matter if Cassie can't give a big speech. Just invit-ing people there will be enough, and we'll get people dancing and laughing. That'll be a start. It's a good idea, Bear. You were right. Hey." He tipped her chin up. "Did your mama ever teach you the Carolina Shag?"

Barrie shook her head, choking on a sudden bittersweet longing, because as much as it hurt for him not to kiss her at that moment, at least he was there with her. She remembered the joy of dancing in his arms in the cemetery beneath a red umbrella while the rain poured down. But she also remem-bered her mother dancing to beach music, moving painfully, shuffling with her odd gait to the beat of the Drifters and the Tams, the Midnighters, the Ravens, the Zodiacs, and the Platters, like her own peculiar form of a ring-shout. Had that been Lula's way of getting through? Of surviving? Thinking of the beach music that had seeped out into the house from beneath her mother's closed bedroom door at odd hours of the day and night, Barrie wanted desperately to understand what that dancing and that music had meant to Lula.

"Whatever you seem to think," she said to Eight, "you haven't lost much of your gift at all. You still know what I want—what I really need."

"Maybe I just know you," he said.

"If that's not magic, it's something even better."

The radio was playing "Drift Away" by Dobie Gray. Eight dialed it louder and held Barrie's hand firmly wrapped in his. "Start with your right foot," he said, "and then it's step-together-back and back-in-place."

He demonstrated and helped her through it, then put it all together.

"There. You've got it. That's the 'basic'—easy, right?"

Barrie frowned up at him, wishing for high heels, confidence, and some of her cousin's sex appeal. "What do I do with my other hand?"

"Just keep it at your waist." He squeezed the hand he was holding lightly and then eased up a little. "You want to feel where I lead with this one, and let me feel where you want to go and how you want to get there. Shag is an improv. You get the foundation and then set off on your own or together into spins and fancy steps. You meet at the turn."

He moved her back and forward—step-together-back, back-in-place, rock-step. Step-together-back, back-in-place, rock-step. When Barrie had the rhythm, he took his place in front of her and kept going, same steps, his left foot to her right, his right to her left, holding her hand and moving apart and back together again. The same push-pull that had always been there between them. But the push all along had been mostly hers, her fear to trust her own feelings as well as his. She let go this time, let herself believe that when they came apart, the rhythm of the dance would bring them right back together, as inevitable as the tide of the Atlantic sweeping up the mouth of the Santisto. As inevitable as the breath that whispered in her lungs and the blood and the binding that sang in her veins when he pushed his thumb against hers, stepped to the side, and pulled her smoothly into a spin, moving around her and bringing her back.

They danced as the songs changed, as the mood changed, their feet moving low and fast, so smooth that it was easy to forget the movement and see only Eight's eyes on hers, always on hers. It was freeing, careless, exhilarating, alive. So alive.

Ultimately, wasn't dance a whispered question? A story told through the position of a foot, the tilt of a head, the touch of a hand, the brush of an eye. A rite of passage. A claiming.

"Too Late to Turn Back Now" by Cornelius Brothers and Sister Rose came on the radio, and Barrie knew it had been much too late for much too long. Eight kept her close as he finished a turn. He pulled her closer, and he kissed her, so slowly and breathlessly that she was dizzy with remembering where they had begun and who she had become because of him. Who she was becoming with him.

The air was charged around them. The avocado kitchen with its years of meals and hopes and fears melted away, and there was only them. Her and him. So alive in that moment that it made her ache.

But just when they were so fused together that she couldn't tell where one of them began and the other ended, he pulled away. Maurice Williams's "Stay" was playing on the radio, and she whispered the word, changing it into a plea.

"I can't," he said. "We have disasters to avert in the morning, remember?"

"We haven't really talked yet."

"If you don't think we've been talking, you haven't been listening, Bear. The dance and that kiss, that was all a conversation. I heard every word you said in here"—he tapped his hand above his heart—"and it reminded me that if you and I had both been listening to our feelings more carefully all along, we wouldn't have had a problem."

"So do we?"

"Do we what?" He lowered his brows in confusion.

"Have a problem?"

He smiled at her so beautifully that it made her want to close her eyes. "Ask me again if I want to stay."

"Do you want to stay?" She caught his shirt in both hands and pulled him closer.

"So much that I have to go."

CHAPTER TWENTY-ONE

Seven o'clock in the morning shouldn't have been allowed to exist when people didn't go to bed until after midnight. Nevertheless, Barrie was resolved to have one day that began without her feeling like she was letting people down. Since Miranda and Batch had arrived, Pru and the *yunwi* had done all the work at the barn, and it was time that she pulled her weight.

Squinting against the infusion of light, she threw on shorts and a tank top, but the pair of muddy hot pink Kate Spade sneakers with the bloodstain on the toe was still the only bit of practical footwear that she owned. Promising herself that she was going to get online and order some new sneakers, some cute flats, and a pair of polka-dotted rubber boots before Eight picked her up and the rest of the day spun beyond her control, she headed down to the kitchen. Then, mindful of her more important promise to Pru, she left a note before heading out to the stable surrounded by a curious huddle of *yunwi*.

Miranda was still lying down in her stall, shavings like daisies dotting her long Friesian mane. She raised her head and whickered softly before rolling to her feet.

Barrie rested her forehead against the wide space between the mare's dark eyes. "Hello, sweet girl. Sorry to wake you up, but it's time for breakfast."

The building smelled of old wood, new shavings, and the oddly pleasant mix of horse and manure. Bedding rustled while Batch scrambled to his feet in the next stall over, and Barrie and the *yunwi* worked together hauling feed and hay and water, and mucking out the stalls and grooming the horses the way that Pru had shown her. She was slowly working the tangles from Miranda's mane when the already humid air went still.

The *yunwi* pressed in close to Barrie and made her shiver.

It wasn't as though the contact were cold . . . exactly. She felt warmth from them. It was more as if *her* body reacted to them by producing a cold sensation, and their touch was strangely electric, amping up her awareness much the way that her senses had sharpened when the water spirit had bound her to Watson's Landing, or when she had connected to the spirit path in the Watson woods.

The *yunwi* tugged her across Miranda's stall toward the

248

open window. Outside, a shadow swept across the ground. The bird circled and passed again. It wasn't a raven. The seven-foot wingspan was too big, and the color wasn't dark enough as it rode the air.

An eagle.

Barrie had never seen one in the wild. It plummeted from the sky in a nearly vertical dive. She held her breath, and when it seemed certain the bird would hit the ground, it stalled its wings and extended its yellow talons to snatch up a luckless rabbit that had been hopping for cover across the grass.

The rabbit screamed as it died.

Its death shivered through Barrie like a draft.

The *yunwi* bowed their heads and stood motionless, but the electric current of their contact increased in volume. Energy hummed through Barrie from them, and then disappeared when their hands dropped away. Once again, their shapes were clearer and their eyes were brighter.

"Is that what you were trying to show me? You absorb energy like Obadiah?"

They looked back at her silently, then returned to work. But Barrie couldn't help noticing how frequently they flitted by and touched her. She was still pondering the significance of that, or wondering whether there was any significance to it, when she let herself back into the kitchen later.

She'd been gone less than an hour, but Daphne was already

at the table working on her laptop, and Pru and Mary were bickering about the open house at Colesworth Place. They had settled on a crab boil and some simple Gullah dishes, and Mary suggested they call Amber at the CopyCat about getting an extra order of the miniature cake boxes with the restaurant logo and website done up.

"At least then we'll get some somethin' out of all this work. I only hope it's not a disaster when everybody gets there," Mary said.

Pru frowned at her, then turned to Barrie. "Mary's still insisting that she isn't coming. I was hoping that Daphne would have convinced her by now. Tell her it's going to look odd if she isn't there—and there will be a lot of people who take their cues from her. If she doesn't go, others will stay away."

"There'll be plenty of folks to steal energy from without me askin' them to go and have it stolen from them," Mary said. "And someone needs to do the regular work, or the restaurant won't open on time. Folks'll expect openin' night to be perfect, and that won't happen by itself."

"It *will* be perfect," Daphne said. "We've all worked hard enough. But, Gramma, how do you know how many people is going to be enough? Obadiah himself said he didn't know. What if he needs just one extra bit of energy to break the curse, and thanks to you, he doesn't have it?"

The two of them tried to outstare each other, neither

willing to back down. Barrie wandered to the coffeepot and poured herself a cup of sultry, dark French roast. She took a sip, letting the heat scald her throat, and returned to the table, intending to work until Eight came to pick her up. Then she realized she needed to change, and dashed upstairs.

Showered and dressed in the red-and-white Louboutin Jeffersons that reminded her of Mark, white capris, and a loose blue-and-white flowered top, Barrie felt both more and less like herself as Eight held the door to the SeaCow open for her a short while later. The shoes reminded her of her first night out with Eight, and they reminded her of Mark, but they felt more like San Francisco than Watson's Landing. She hugged the memory of Mark close to her chest as the hiss of the espresso machines and the murmur of conversation stopped when she entered the bakery and moved with Eight toward the center of the seating area filled with pink-and-brown-striped booths and small, round walnut tables.

You want more confidence? Mark had used to tell her. *A pair of killer heels makes it easier to look fear in the eye.*

Cheeks flushed and hot, Barrie stood beside Eight as he raised his arm to signal for attention and smiled his trademark Beaufort smile. Beauforts had probably been charming the locals with that exact smile for the last three hundred years. A smile and a sword—the way to conquer kingdoms.

"Hey," he said. "How y'all doing? Mind if Barrie and I interrupt your breakfast for a minute?"

The room went quiet. Barrie looked quickly around at the collection of curious faces, searching for Berg, and found him already seated at a booth along the side. He gave her a nod that held more than a hint of amusement.

Eight stood perfectly at ease, his blue oxford just the right degree of rumpled with its tails hanging over the faded red of his shorts. "I wanted to let you know that we're having an open house and cookout at Colesworth Place tomorrow night," he said when the murmur of greetings and a handful of small jokes had settled down. "We'd appreciate it—we'd be grateful—if all y'all would stop by. The whole town. There'll be food and dancing—"

"Why are *you* having a cookout at Colesworth?" someone shouted out.

"The whole town's having a cookout." Eight twitched the rolled-up sleeves of his shirt toward his elbows nonchalantly. "Which, Parker Elliot, includes you, unless you've moved without telling anybody. Right now, with Wyatt dead, we've all got a chance to practice a little forgiving and forgetting. It's past time we buried some hatchets, and punishing Sydney and Cassie—or even Marie—for what Wyatt did makes no sense."

Barrie's palms were slick, but she made herself nod in agreement. "I know I live at Watson's Landing, and I was raised as a Watson, but I'm a Colesworth, too. That's why I hope you'll all come. Pru and I both do. Wyatt hurt a lot of people, but he hurt his own family worse. You've all been generous and more than kind to me ever since I got here. You've never made me feel as though Emmett's mistakes, or Lula's, were my fault, and you've never made me feel like I needed to be ashamed of where I came from. I hope you'll be willing to give Sydney and Cassie the same kind of chance you've given me."

The silence lasted long enough for her throat to begin to close. Then an older man in a red-checkered shirt sitting in the back shouted out, "What time's that going to be?"

"Seven o'clock," Eight said, grinning more widely. "And bring your own chairs."

"They find the gold out there yet?" someone else called.

"Sure. Trainloads of it," Barrie said, then laughed to show she was joking, and was relieved to see the faces around her smile back. Her eyes slid automatically to the booth where Berg was sitting. "Seriously, I wouldn't believe all the rumors. Right now, Charlotte Colesworth's skeleton is the only thing we know for sure is down in the room the archaeologists found. Except possibly some very angry spirits."

That got a smattering of laughter and a few more smiles, but since it was Watson Island, enough people went still that Barrie suspected the rumor of ghosts would spread, and she was glad.

Eight waved to Berg to hold on while they got coffee and

pastries. When they came over to sit down, Eight let Barrie slide first into the booth, and Berg pushed his plate and cup aside to make room for the tray Eight was carrying. Barrie took the tall cup Eight handed her, but her fingers were still trembling slightly as she set it down, and the foam spilled over the side onto the table. "I figured telling people about the ghosts couldn't hurt," she said, wiping the spill with her napkin. "Maybe it will keep a few of them clear of the room, but darn, it made me nervous."

"Good thing you've got coffee to calm you down," Berg said, smiling.

"Says the guy who orders a triple shot." Eight nodded at the note scrawled on the side of Berg's cup.

Berg held Eight's eye, then leaned back in the booth and shifted his focus back to Barrie without altering his calm expression. "I didn't have much luck finding out how to break curses or remove spirits—or how much energy it might take to do that. But this morning, I did get an answer back to an email I sent asking about the fountain. It was mentioned in a letter, along with a description of Eliza Watson Beaufort's garden and that of another local landowner."

Barrie breathed in the caramelized, smoky scent of her coffee. "I didn't think a Watson could marry a Beaufort. Eight, did you know about that? But I guess if she wasn't the oldest child, maybe it didn't affect the binding?"

"I know she had a brother," Eight said.

"Yes, but the brother was younger," Berg interjected, "and Eliza's father was the governor of Antigua while he owned Watson's Landing, so he was off in the West Indies most of the time. Eliza ran all three of the family plantations before she married Robert Beaufort. I've never thought about it before, but Barrie's right. How could that happen, unless the binding didn't exist back then? If her father was governor, he had to function at least fairly well, so he probably didn't have the migraines."

"Who did Eliza marry? Robert the pirate or someone else?" Barrie asked.

"Robert the *privateer*," Eight corrected mildly, and probably incorrectly. He stretched his arm along the bench behind Barrie. "And no. Eliza married his son, who was also Robert."

"So that had to be years after the original bargains, right? What else do you know about Eliza?" Barrie asked, looking from Eight to Berg.

"She was brilliant," Berg said. "Not only did she run the plantations when she was seventeen, but she hired an expert from the West Indies to help her develop the first strain of indigo seed that grew well in the colonies, and she shared it with the other planters. That started the whole American indigo industry."

"Indigo, like the blue color?" Barrie asked, popping a

gooey piece of her maple pecan sticky bun into her mouth and licking her fingers.

Berg grinned—he had a nice grin. "Mostly the dye back then, but yes. It was the third-biggest export before the Revolutionary War. Then Eliza married, and there's not much written about her after that, except for the reference to her rose garden. The fountain was designed to provide irrigation from an underground spring."

Outside the window, a family of beachgoers hurried past the bakery, their faces red and tired. The air had grown thick and syrupy enough to shimmer in the late-morning sun. Barrie licked her sticky fingers again.

"Doesn't it seem like too much of a coincidence to have a Watson build a fountain with the Beaufort lodestone embedded in it?" she asked.

"Sometimes a coincidence is just a coincidence," Berg said.

"I'm starting to believe in those less and less," Barrie said, "but if Eliza married a Beaufort, then I'm even more anxious to have a look in the Beaufort library." She looked at Eight. "Think there might be something there about her or the Roberts?"

"The long, dull line of Beaufort lawyers never met a piece of paper they didn't squirrel away in there." Eight stood up from the table. "Fortunately, I happen to know someone who's good at finding things. We just have to hope Dad went into the office this morning."

They said their good-byes, and weaving back through town toward the harbor, Eight walked beside Barrie, scowling and thinking so furiously that just a few days ago, Barrie would have made a joke about smoke coming out of his ears, or about him hurting himself by thinking too hard. Or maybe something more original. Now she was too afraid of opening wounds, and she hated the distance that self-consciousness created between them.

"What are you thinking about so hard?" she asked. "Eliza, or the open house?"

"Neither." Eight ducked behind a yellow-painted clapboard storefront and cut through a driveway to the next block over. "I was thinking that it's frustrating to have to work so hard to understand what people want."

"Is what they want really so different from what they say?"

"Words are only seven percent of a conversation. I've never had to worry much about that other ninety-three percent before."

Barrie stopped on the sidewalk, earning a glare from a mother pushing a toddler in a complicated stroller who had to swerve to get around them. Curving her lips into a seductive half smile, Barrie looked up at Eight from beneath her lashes.

"What's my body language saying now?" she asked.

"Exactly what I like to hear," Eight said. Taking both her hands, he pulled her toward him, staring pointedly at her mouth. "Want to speak to me some more?"

"Hah. You obviously still see some things with perfect clarity."

"I see right through what you're trying to do now, for example."

Barrie laughed, but she felt very serious. Eight had once compared people to layer cakes, but that was true only for the outer layers. At some point, there was nothing left but the core of a person, and Eight's core was a protective shell formed around a bruised and generous heart.

"You don't need your gift to read people," she said. "Your intuition is good. Trust it, and trust yourself. I worry more about your father. He's relied on the gift even more than you have—imagine how he feels. Maybe you should talk to him about that. At some point, you two are going to have to figure things out. Cassie isn't the only one in this town who needs to build some bridges."

CHAPTER TWENTY-TWO

Barrie pushed the fourteen-foot-high ladder along the specially made groove in the floor of the Beaufort library before climbing it again to continue her systematic search. Behind her, Eight sat perched on the edge of the desk, reading a book report on *The Wizard of Oz* penned by what must have been a very young Seven Beaufort. It was marked with a big fat B-minus in red pencil.

Eight grinned at it delightedly. "This is fantastic."

"It can't be that great if he got a B-minus," Barrie said.

"You should have heard the lectures he gave me when I brought home anything except an A."

"So he wanted you to do better than he did. Also not a surprise."

Eight's expression lost its gleam of humor, and he set

the report aside to continue sifting through the growing pile of lost things that Barrie had been collecting from various shelves, from behind, between, and inside the books throughout the library. Eight had been right about the Beauforts never throwing anything away. There was everything from a thousand-dollar bill to a collection of thirty-eight four-leaf clovers someone had tucked into a book of poetry by William Butler Yeats. Apparently, someone had thought the Beauforts needed all the luck they could get.

The next ping of loss yielded a handwritten note about a long-forgotten legal case, but beyond that, on the upper shelf, the pull was even stronger. Leaning over as far as she could, Barrie still couldn't reach it, and she asked Eight to push the ladder over.

"About three feet to the left. There," she said. "Stop."

She clung to the rungs until the ladder shuddered to a halt, then she ran her hand across a row of untitled spines in dirty jewel tones of reds and greens. Three of them called to her, stronger than anything she had found so far. She tried not to let that get her hopes up as she worked loose the nearest book. The cover was stuck to the one beside it, and separating them tore off a bit of leather. The paper—or possibly parchment—inside the book was yellowed and filled with writing in small, even, and beautifully proportioned letters. The script on the flyleaf read:

Letterbook of Eliza Watson Beaufort, 1739–1743

Barrie climbed down and set the journals on the desk, trying to keep her voice calm. "Look at this."

The yellowed pages of the first volume were filled with a jumble of notes, drafts, jotted memorandums about incoming correspondence, and tucked here and there between the sheets, actual letters from Eliza's father or her friends. Barrie flipped all the way through and handed it to Eight, who'd been looking over her shoulder. She picked up the next.

"I've never heard of a letterbook, but I guess it made sense to copy things out," she said. "There weren't any Xerox machines or computers back then."

Eight plucked two sheets of Kleenex from the box on the desk and took the first volume to the sofa, using a tissue to open the book and turn the cover page. "This includes the dates when Eliza's father inherited from Thomas. Maybe she'll mention the bindings. Here. You read while I turn the pages," he said. "That'll be faster."

"We can both read," Barrie said, hating the faint flush of red that stained his cheeks because of his dyslexia.

The flush deepened, and he shoved the book and the tissues into her lap and bounded off the sofa. "I'll flip through the other two volumes, in case there's anything that jumps out."

Feeling guilty, Barrie skimmed through receipts and correspondence and dinner party menus. Nine pages in, the

Colesworth name jumped out at her near the beginning of a letter, and she went back to read more carefully. After three paragraphs, she raised her head and called to Eight, "Hey, listen to this."

To my dear brother, James,

I flatter myself to think you shall like this part of the world when you arrive in it. I find it more preferable to the West Indias each day.

We have an excellent acquaintance with 6 families nearby, from whom we have received much Civility. The Beauforts who live across the river are most agreeable. The same cannot be said of their neighbors at Colesworth Place, who are disregarded by every body. The Colesworths appear to be intent on revenging themselves upon our family for the strangest circumstance, of which my Father neglected to tell me. No doubt, he expected it should make me afraid. I wonder if he knows me at all!

I shall recount the story to you as I heard it, for I am certain it cannot fail to amuse you. It seems we have a Ghost on our island. He is engaged here in the protection of a number of small Spirits much like our Fairies or Brownies, through the application of a Ceremony which he nightly performs. You will laugh when I promise you 'tis true, but I have seen the fire on the river myself, and the

Servants and Merchants here speak of it all quite openly.
Rest assured that we ourselves have nothing to fear. Our
safety, I'm told, is protected by a Pact that Great-Uncle
Thomas negotiated with the assistance of a Cherokee
woman who lived across the river. This pact is at once
an inconvenience and a blessing. I had hoped to persuade
Papa to let me clear additional acreage to the east of the
house for rice, but the woods there contain some portion
of the Power that protects the magical spirits, and this we
are not allowed to touch.

Why Great-Uncle Thomas would have agreed to this
Limitation, much less to living here on this plantation, I
have not yet discovered. You can be sure I intend to learn
the Truth. Property in this Colony is plentiful. Only today
Papa wrote to set me the task of finding two additional
plantations farther inland for him to purchase, for the rice
here is plagued with disease and uncertain success. I have
written back to him asking for a collection of different
seeds from the West Indias to plant.

This Pact of Uncle Thomas's appears to grant us
the ability to retrieve whatever the Spirits here carry off,
which I can attest myself happens with some frequency.
Only today, I was forced to search for my embroidery hoop,
which I found hidden in the Garden beneath a bush! Now
if only the Gift extended to allow me to find the answers

I need to make this family prosperous and safe, I should indeed be happy.

This Carolina is a strange land, I assure you. I am amused by it, and should think myself very content here if you were only with us.

Your most affectionate and most obliged humble Sister,

Eliza Watson

Eight dropped back onto the sofa beside Barrie. "I thought the Fire Carrier's ceremony was meant to keep the *yunwi* from leaving the island. Not to protect them."

"Does that have to be mutually exclusive? I'm more interested in the fact that she confirms that her father was gone, despite the finding gift. What about the binding?"

"Maybe she talks about that later. Keep reading."

Clearing her throat, Barrie nodded and turned her attention back to several chatty letters Eliza had written to her friends and to a former governess. There were notes about seeds that Eliza's father had sent and about "pitch and Tarr and Lime and other plantation affairs," about various purchases and changes she was making, and then discussions of several naval battles in which her father had been involved. Eliza began to sound increasingly worried.

[To Colonel Watson]
Honored Sir,

I have not the words to tell you of our concern at the absence of news from you. We hear daily of the dangerous situation in which you find yourself! I have had the Deed for the Wappo plantation recorded, and will attempt to plant the Indigo and Cotton &c soonest.

A strange circumstance occurred this week. Finding myself unable to sleep, I ventured into the garden and came across a woman I had never seen before. Her features are more Indian than Negro, and on inquiring of the Servants, I found that she is the daughter of the very woman who helped Great-Uncle Thomas engage upon the Pact with the Ghost who haunts our woods. Her courage in entering that dark grove is great, for none of the Servants will venture there, nor even our own mischievous Sprites. I should very much like to speak with her, but it seems she is more afraid of me.

"Eight?" Seven's voice from the corridor was loud and unexpected, bringing Barrie's head up to collide with the bottom of Eight's chin.

"Dammit!" Eight jumped up. Barrie slammed the book shut. The door creaked open, and Seven pushed his head inside. Seeing Barrie, his eyes narrowed.

His voice was arctic. "What are you two up to now?"

He'd said "two," but his gaze had locked on Barrie, so he clearly meant only "one."

Eight stepped in front of Barrie as Seven crossed over to the sofa. "I asked her to search for information about the bindings and the lodestones."

"You think I haven't already done that? After my father died, I spent the entire summer looking."

"You didn't have the Watson gift working for you—we just found Eliza Watson's letterbooks."

Seven reached for the volume they'd been reading, and although her fingers tightened reflexively, Barrie couldn't refuse to give it to him. He picked up the crumpled Kleenex that Barrie had discarded and used it to turn the pages.

"I can't imagine it will help us. Eliza wasn't here until years after the first Robert was already dead, but I'll have a look this afternoon." He glanced around at the bookshelves. "We probably ought to go through the whole library to catalog and preserve what's in here. I've neglected that for far too long, and books like this could be valuable." He fixed them both with a knife-sharp look. "Not that either one of you understands the first thing about value. Poor Pru just told me about the open house. How could you commit to that kind of an expense without asking me? Who's going to pay for all that food—not to mention who will do the work? What exactly are you two up to now, and don't bother giving me the story about reconciliation. Colesworths have no interest in reconciling anything."

"*I'm* half-Colesworth," Barrie said. "And no one's asking you to pay for anything. Pru can approve the expense for me out of my trust fund."

"Don't try to bully Barrie about this," Eight said, stepping in front of her again. "Or me, either. Pru already said she thinks this is a good idea, and the food's ordered and most of the arrangements are done already. Kate and I will represent the Beauforts at the party. We don't need you to approve or disapprove."

He and Seven faced each other, the same height, the same hard green eyes, but for once, Eight showed no sign of backing down in the face of his father's rage. He stood there, silently demanding the respect Seven owed him. Which was good, Barrie thought. Seven was never going to fix the relationship between them until it was pushed past the breaking point.

Barely daring to breathe, Barrie tried to be inconspicuous while they stared each other down. But instead of answering, Seven moved to the desk, scooped up the other two letter-books, and walked toward the door with all three volumes.

"I'm getting tired of playing games with all of you," he said. "Let me know when you're ready to tell me the truth."

Eight hurried after him. "We're in the middle of reading those."

Only the flare of Seven's nostrils and the slight flush across his cheekbones gave away how spectacularly furious he was, until he spoke and his voice shook. "You and Kate—all three of you—think you can do whatever you please, but this is still *my* house. I may not have the gift anymore, but everything else, including these books, is legally mine. I'll let you know if I find something in them worth sharing. Meanwhile, Barrie, you go home, and Eight . . . I don't know. Go somewhere and consider the fact that information is a two-way street. You accused me of not giving you a say in your own life. What exactly do you think is happening to me right now?"

He strode away, leaving Barrie and Eight in silence. Eight sagged back against the doorjamb, closed his eyes, and thumped his head three times against the wood. "How does he make me feel like a jerk, when he's the one being a jackass? That's a very special kind of skill." He held up his hand up before Barrie could answer. "I know. I know. He isn't totally wrong. It's the same thing you were trying to tell me. But that doesn't make it any easier to swallow."

"Maybe you should go ahead and tell him about Obadiah and the open house. I don't like the idea of making Pru keep it from him."

"We never asked her to do that, and after that speech he

just gave me, you don't think there's a chance he would do something reckless to keep Kate from having the binding? There are still the lodestones to worry about."

Barrie considered that, and the library around her seemed suddenly smaller, as if all the books in it and the cumulative weight of all the things she didn't know might crush her. "Let's just hope the open house works and nothing goes wrong afterward. It would sure help if we could have found something in those letterbooks, though."

Eight studied his empty hands and sighed. "Let me see what I can do."

CHAPTER TWENTY-THREE

Still fuming over the books, about the last thing Barrie wanted to take time out for was another riding lesson, but Pru was adamant that they had other responsibilities that didn't involve the bindings, the curse, or either of the other families. She showed Barrie how to saddle Miranda and then tightened the girth while Barrie held the lead rope.

"Seven will come around in his own time, and for now, all we can do is let him brood," she said. "And as for you? The horses need exercise, and there's nothing better to wrap your mind around a problem than thinking about something else entirely. All this has waited three hundred years to come to a boil. It can wait a few more hours." Placing two fingers inside the mare's mouth, she slipped the bit between Miranda's teeth and eased the crown past her black, twitching ears.

Barrie smoothed Miranda's forelock over the supple brow-band. "Do you think we should tell Seven about Obadiah?"

"Seven is, in general, a kind, responsible, and intelligent man," Pru said cautiously. "He's struggling right now."

"That doesn't answer the question."

Pru dug a lump of sugar from her pocket and let Miranda lip it from her palm, then pulled the reins back over Miranda's head and hung the halter on the hook beside her stall. "It may take Seven a little while longer to figure things out. He's spent his life trying to protect people—feeling like he's failed at pro-tecting people. I can't see him embracing anything that might put his children in danger—" She put up her hand as Barrie opened her mouth to protest. "No, hold on. I understand that Kate and Eight want to be involved, but Seven and I are dif-ferent people."

"That's a good thing." Barrie followed as Pru led the mare outside. "Seven's not so good at two-way conversations."

Pru handed the reins to Barrie in the paddock, and her eyes were clouded and far away. She went around and checked to make sure the girth was tight before cupping her hands to help Barrie mount. "I'm not saying that Seven is perfect, sugar. I know what he is, and I'm not sure he's ever going to be different. But then, you shouldn't ever love someone because you hope they'll change. You have to love them for who they already are."

"Seven would be an idiot not to love you, Aunt Pru. I hope he figures things out soon. I want to be able to root for the two of you."

Taking the reins back from Barrie again, Pru gave a vague and unconvincing smile. Then she tied the reins out of reach, clipped the lunge line to Miranda's bridle, and started Miranda moving at a lumbering walk.

The sway of Miranda's gait jarred through Barrie's legs and hips and waist. "Relax," Pru said. "Let your back absorb the motion. And put your hands out. You don't need to grip the saddle."

No hands again. And no control.

Not that that was anything new. None of them had control anymore. The Watsons, the Beauforts, the Colesworths, Obadiah and his family . . . they were all caught in webs that seemed to wrap them tighter the more they struggled.

"You have to find your own balance," Pru said. "Try closing your eyes; that makes it both harder and easier."

Barrie tried. Unable to see where she was going, she felt sheer panic at first, the kind that knotted her lungs and made her dizzy. But then suddenly, her senses adjusted, opening and widening, sharpening, as if sight had held her back. Or as if she had been so busy relying on what she knew that she hadn't taken the time to see what was possible.

With her eyes closed, she was both as high as the sky and

grounded to the earth, connected by energy that trickled into her along the arch of Miranda's neck and through the reins into her hands, down through her legs and heels to spill back into the grass and soil. She felt like a living channel of energy. On a smaller level, it reminded her of the way the fountain spirit's limbs were made of water. Of the vortex that felt like a whirlpool. As if there was energy everywhere, and she simply hadn't known how to find it.

Her eyes flew open. The sensation vanished.

"Don't stiffen up now," Pru said, and Barrie made herself relax again, let her eyes flutter closed. After a while, the sensation of connection was possible with her eyes either open or closed, and she felt like she was sitting deep in the saddle, her hips fused and moving easily forward and back as Miranda walked.

"You ready to try a little trot?" Pru asked. She urged Miranda into the faster gait.

Barrie clutched the pommel, and despite Pru's patient instructions on how to rise out of the saddle along with Miranda's movements, it was long minutes before she felt comfortable enough to let go again. Longer still before the mechanics had sunk in. The connection she had felt with Miranda and the energy in her surroundings melted away each time she left the saddle, and she couldn't let go with her eyes closed the way that she had before. And she missed the feeling of being connected.

After twenty more minutes, Pru pulled Miranda to a stop. "That's about enough. Why don't you take her a couple of times around the pasture by yourself to cool her off? I'll wash up and start working on the pastries for the open house before Mary and the Beauforts get here to help."

The *yunwi* ran alongside as Barrie walked the mare along the perimeter of the fence. Miranda stretched her neck down to blow at them and sent them scampering away, only to have them return with their hands raised to pat her. Barrie sank back into the calm that was a natural part of Miranda and Watson's Landing. Maybe that was part of the reason her gift had told her the mare belonged with her, the way the gift sometimes gave her answers.

She sighed at the thought, because answers were only useful when you knew the questions that went with them. What was it that Eliza Watson had written in the letter to her brother? That she wished the gift would help her keep the family prosperous and safe. Each in their own way, that was what all the four families were still fighting for.

Barrie was in Miranda's stall, brushing the saddle marks out of the mare's coat, when Eight phoned her a short while later.

"What's wrong?" she asked. "Is everything okay? I thought you were coming over in a little bit."

"I told Kate about the letterbooks, and she helped me

steal them back out of Dad's room. He'll probably kill us both when he finds out, but he's going to have to accept that we have just as much a stake in what happens to the family as he does. Maybe he knows that, too, and he's just holding on tighter before he lets go."

"It sounds like you're getting closer to forgiving him." Barrie dropped the brush back into the grooming tote, gave Miranda a pat, and walked out into the aisle.

"I don't know about that." Eight sighed, and then the tone of his voice changed. "But that's not what I called about. Kate and I found something else in Eliza's letterbook."

There was a scuffle for the phone, during which Barrie heard Eight and his sister arguing, first one voice louder and then the other, and while she waited for them to sort it out, she dropped the grooming tote in the tack room and wandered out toward the cemetery.

She had just reached the fence when Kate's voice came on the line. "Tell my idiot brother that I'm not going to give up the binding. He doesn't need to save me."

"We don't even know that it's possible to transfer the binding, do we?" Barrie asked, but her skin was already starting to itch with panic.

"I think it might be. That's what the letterbook says." Kate's voice held an unmistakable note of triumph.

Barrie clambered over the low surrounding fence into the

cemetery and looked around as Eight struggled to take the phone again. The midafternoon sun left short, deep shadows in front of the tombstones and grave markers, and she headed toward what looked like the section of oldest graves.

"Why don't you two put me on the speaker instead of arguing, and then you can both talk? I'd like to hear what you found," she said.

Kate switched to speaker. "Here, Eight. Hold the phone."

Barrie walked along the row of gravestones, looking for names and dates, waiting for something to pull at her. Most of the markers were worn and nearly illegible. Only one gave a dull tug on her finding sense, and that belonged to Thomas Watson, who was buried beneath a headstone engraved with the relief of a ship at full sail.

"So listen to this," Kate said, and she began to read:

[To Colonel Watson]
Honored Sir,

We rejoice to have news from you at last and to hear of your recovery. We have lost nearly all the Cotton and Ginger planted, due to frost, and frost likewise took most of the Crop of Indigo, but I remain confident that Indigo will be valuable if you can send more seed in time for us to plant in March.

As for the other matter in your letter, I beg your

*continued Indulgence and assure you that your peace and
happiness is my greatest wish. As you asked my opinion,
however, I must beg you to assure Sir Nicholas that all
the riches of the Spanish empire could not entice me to
become his wife.*

"I'm beginning to like Eliza," Kate said, interrupting herself. "I hope Robert was nicer than Sir Nicholas."

"Me too," Barrie said. "Where's the part about the binding?"

"I'm getting to that."

*Similarly, the other gentleman, Mr. Cleland, does not
merit favorable sentiment. Until James is ready to settle
here, I cannot envision leaving Watson's Landing, and
single life is therefore my dearest wish. You must make
James listen to Reason, Papa. What does he need with the
military life? He isn't suited for it. He would find circumstances here vastly more pleasing. We dined again last
night at Beaufort Hall, and I find Mr. Robert Edward
Beaufort most agreeable. But enough of that.*

"You see?" Kate interrupted herself again. "Eliza's already
starting to fall in love with Robert, but her brother doesn't
want to be at Watson's Landing, and her father can't be, so she
feels like she needs to stay."

"I got that from the letter, thanks," Barrie said dryly. "Is there more?"

"Not about that, but listen."

Since last I wrote, I have spoken to Inola, the woman from across the river, on several occasions. It seems that she, like her mother before her, comes to our island to learn medicine and wonder work from our small fey Spirits, whom she calls the Yunwi Tsunsdi. *She assures me that they are great Magicians and wise enough for Cherokee healers to think it worth traveling many miles to study with them in the mountain Caverns where they are customarily found. She is reluctant to trust me fully yet, but I shall continue to assure her that I mean her no harm. I believe there is a great deal more that she can tell me.*

Dear Sir,

Your most dutiful and affectionate Daughter,

E. Watson

The *yunwi* had drawn closer around Barrie as Kate read, and she studied them with an odd sensation of seeing them for the first time, as if the word "magician" had peeled back a transparent layer of fabric from across her eyes.

"Is that it? Was there anything else about Inola and the *yunwi*?" Barrie asked.

"Eight made me call you instead of going on, and on top of that, he keeps insisting on stopping so he can look things up on the Internet."

"What's the point of reading if you don't understand what something means?" Eight asked defensively. "Inola and Ayita were risking a lot, sneaking over to Watson's Landing every night—they could have been punished as runaway slaves. So I looked up Cherokee medicine people and the *yunwi* again, thinking I hadn't paid enough attention to the legends the last time I did that. Eliza was right; it usually took decades for a medicine person to learn all the botany, sacred formulas, dreamwork, and psychology that they studied, and some of the old myths and legends mention that medicine people went to study with the *yunwi* in caverns inside Blood Mountain in Georgia, and Pilot Mountain in North Carolina. Or sort of inside, because according to another legend, there were whole endless villages inside the caves, in layers on top of one another."

"What does that have to do with Watson Island? Or are you saying that's where the *yunwi* came from?" Barrie asked.

"I don't know. Maybe. The point is that Inola and Ayita couldn't get to Blood Mountain or Pilot Mountain to study with the *yunwi*, but they didn't have to. All they had to do was get across the river to Watson's Landing." Eight's voice hummed with excitement, and Barrie could imagine the way he would have glanced away when he said that, the small tightening of accomplishment at the right corner of his lip.

She fell in love with him even a little bit harder.

"Ayita must have discovered that the *yunwi* were here when John Colesworth made her come over and translate for the Fire Carrier," Eight continued. "Doesn't that make you wonder what was so important about what they learned that she and Inola kept coming back? Once they took the risk and left Colesworth Place to come here, why didn't they keep going? Why didn't they escape?"

"Escaping wasn't so easy," Barrie said. "Where were they going to go? The Colesworths would have hunted them down or hurt their families—not to mention there were potential consequences for anyone who gave them shelter. You're right, though. The *yunwi* must have been teaching them something important."

Throughout the conversation, the *yunwi* had been pressing closer and closer to Barrie. Now one of them tapped her knee and pointed to where another stood near the wall of the chapel where Barrie intended to eventually bury Mark, Luke, and Twila. The second *yunwi* stooped to touch a wild rosebush that had taken root near the wall, and as Barrie watched, the bush sprouted new green branches and fresh leaves, and roses climbed the wall and sprang into bloom.

Chest tight and eyes stinging, Barrie sat with the phone

forgotten in her hand. Because she had known the *yunwi* were magic—of course she had—but she hadn't *known*.

Beside her foot, a fox squirrel scampering along the ground sat up to watch the roses growing, exposing its black mask and soft, pale underbelly. Barrie gave a faint shake of her head.

Bringing the phone back to her ear, she spoke into it again. "What happened to Inola? Does it say?"

"Not so far, at least up to where we've gotten in the book. Eliza wrote about being frustrated because she tried to buy Inola and the rest of her family to get them away from the Colesworths, but the more she was interested, the more Daniel Colesworth refused to sell."

Barrie felt nauseous all over again. "Did she mean to free them? Or only move them here?"

"She doesn't mention which," Eight said.

As if they were trying to comfort Barrie, or distract her, more of the *yunwi* went over to the chapel wall, and soon the entire surface was covered with a tangle of wild climbing roses and moonflower vines. Barrie's skin tingled, and her eyes welled with tears.

"Bear?" Eight asked, his voice dropping. "Are you still there?"

"Y-yes," Barrie answered.

"I thought I lost you. Look, I'm not defending Eliza or

any of the slaveholders. But it wasn't that simple back then, at least not for Eliza. Whatever her own feelings were, and whatever apparent power she might have had running Watson's Landing and her father's other plantations, they were her father's plantations. The slaves didn't belong to her. Even her own clothing didn't belong to her. Women didn't have any rights back then."

In so many ways, for so many people, freedom was still an illusion. Barrie thought of the statistics she had read about how many women and children were still enslaved all over the world. *Now*—not three hundred years ago—and she wondered how it was possible that so little could change. Sometimes it seemed like the world was sliding backward and no one was noticing. And she thought of Ayita and Elijah, still chained by John Colesworth's hate—still enslaved.

"Eliza was the one who reinforced the tunnel that Thomas built from Watson's Landing to the Beaufort side of the river. Did you know that?" Kate said. "She did that to make it easier for Inola to come and go. She did do something to help."

Even knowing that didn't make Barrie feel better. She wondered what the *yunwi* had thought of all that they must have seen over the years. How long had they been on Watson Island before Thomas had arrived? Had they come all the way from Georgia, or from Pilot Mountain up north? Or somewhere else entirely? And *why*?

She had known and accepted that the garden here was magical. It was magic that kept the chapel and the buildings protected, and she and Pru had both accepted the *yunwi*'s help taking care of Watson's Landing. But she hadn't really ever wondered exactly how the *yunwi* did all that. She had seen them working, seen the evidence of their theft of screws and nuts and nails when they had wanted her attention, and the restoration of those same objects when she had accepted the binding. They had helped her remove the wheels from a baby carriage to make a chandelier, even though iron clearly bothered them. They had helped her clean the stalls and care for the horses.

And what had she done? She had regarded them as mischievous and helpful children, like Eliza's early description of fairies and brownies. All of that shamed her, when they were clearly so much more.

They were oddly subdued now, standing around her with uncharacteristic stillness. Some of them—those who had grown the roses maybe? Barrie couldn't be certain—had faded out until, even when she looked at them directly, they were barely visible, and their eyes had dimmed to the gray of dying embers.

"Can you and Kate bring the letterbooks when you come over here?" Barrie said into the phone, her voice coming out strange and strangled. "I have something you have to see."

"What's the matter, Bear?"

"I don't think I can begin to explain it," she said, but when she'd hung up, the words of Eliza's letter seemed to twine around her the way the roses climbed and twisted up the chapel wall. Inola had come to the *yunwi* to learn *wonder work*. The perfection of that word struck Barrie mute. Was it possible to have magic without wonder? Without awe? Without respect?

What were the *yunwi*, really? More important, where did their power come from?

CHAPTER TWENTY-FOUR

All three Beauforts arrived at Watson's Landing to help with the open house preparations, and Seven's presence was as awkward as it was unexpected. The tension between him and both his children made Barrie worry about having them together in a room filled with sharp, pointed objects. Within the first fifteen minutes, he had offered so many nuggets of "helpful" advice that Barrie would have cheerfully stabbed him with a chef's knife herself.

Pru dug an apron out of the drawer and threw it at him. Hard. "It doesn't matter how things get done, as long as the desserts look and taste good—and as long as everyone had a good time making them. So, here. Instead of telling the rest of us how to do the jobs we're already doing, why don't you put this on and come and stir the chocolate in the double boiler?"

"But—"

"But nothing." Pru exchanged a look with Mary and Daphne and shook a wooden spoon at him. "If you're not going to let us have fun, then close your mouth and get out of our way." She shoved him toward the stove.

Barrie caught Eight's eye and tried and failed to bite back a smile. While Seven was distracted, shaking out the black-and-white pin-striped apron and wrapping it around his waist, she took the opportunity to pull Eight aside.

"Did you bring the letterbooks?" she asked quietly.

He tipped his head in his father's direction. "I couldn't, since Dad insisted on coming with us. And I guess his being here means you'll have to wait to show us whatever you wanted us to see. We'll sneak back over later, once Dad's gone to bed."

Swallowing her impatience, Barrie glanced at Seven, who was staring bleakly down at the chocolate chips that were just beginning to soften in the boiler. "Tell me again why we're doing this," Seven said to no one in particular. "We should have our heads examined. Do you think for a minute that the Colesworths are up late tonight cooking and working? I'll give you odds they're sitting comfortably in front of a television set with their feet propped up."

"That's it." Pru spun around to face him with her hands on her hips. "I've had enough. No one invited you, Seven Beaufort, so you can leave anytime. You know, I remember when you used to complain less and have a lot more fun!"

She was breathing a little fast, her face tilted up to his and her hair curling in the humid heat. Seven looked down at her with the chocolate-tipped spoon still raised, and the music in the room abruptly seemed to grow too loud. No one had ever turned the volume down after Barrie and Eight had danced, and the song shifted from Marvin Gaye's "How Sweet It Is" to "I Can't Help Myself" by the Four Tops. The shake of the tambourine counted out the moments like a metronome while Seven's bemused expression suggested he wasn't sure whether to shake Pru or storm out of the house. Instead, he gave a sudden grin and held his hand out with his palm turned toward the ceiling.

Pru stared at it and shook her head.

"Come on. You just told me I used to be more fun." Seven moved his feet in the up-two-three, back-two-three, right, left rhythm of a Shag basic pattern. "If we're going to have beach music at this open house, don't you think we'd better practice? It's been a few years since you and I danced together."

Pru's cheeks flushed a pretty pink. She glanced at Barrie, who nodded encouragement, and then slowly she put one hand in his. Seven dropped the spoon into the pot, switched off the stove, and pulled her into the space between the counter and the kitchen table.

At first, Pru mirrored Seven's movements the way Eight

had shown Barrie the night before. But then the movements shifted, easing into a series of intricate steps and turns, each one slightly different. It became a completely different dance, and it struck Barrie that it reflected the two relationships, the breathlessly stumbling one that she and Eight were just beginning, and the tension and the push and pull of the years and baggage between Pru and Seven, all the attraction that drew them toward each other, and the moments of hesitation in between. Step-together-step, step-together-back, and the rock-step of indecision. The way Pru and Seven did it was as smooth as butter, their hands barely moving, and no obvious signals between them.

"It's practice," Eight whispered into Barrie's ear. "You and I just need to keep on dancing." Taking Barrie's hand, he pulled her toward him. The song changed again, and the Embers sang "Hold Back the Night."

Barrie did her best to remember the steps as Kate, laughing, pulled Mary out onto the floor beside them, and Daphne watched, smiling, from beside the avocado refrigerator with a bowl of cake batter held in the crook of her elbow. It was only the *yunwi*, who would normally have been the first to dance and make their shadowy mischief underfoot, who held back. They were all subdued, and several of them were still barely visible, as if whatever energy they had expended growing the roses hadn't all been replenished yet. For Barrie, the realization made the dancing and the laughter lose their luster, and it occurred to her that moments of pure joy were sweeter than a soufflé straight from the oven, all puffed with steam, warmth, and the hope that enough love and faith might keep them from falling. The fact that there was laughter at all despite what hung over them was a miracle, and she wished it could last more than a brief instant at a time.

She couldn't help wondering, once it was finally over, how many of them would be happy by this time tomorrow. Not all of them could have what they wanted, or even needed.

Perfect moments never stayed unchanged. Maybe it was enough that they existed occasionally at all, or maybe they were sweeter because of the awfulness sandwiched in between.

She made herself keep smiling as Eight squeezed her hand. They danced through two more songs, and the third was so slow that she lost the count and Kate lost interest and Pru and Seven got so lost in each other that it seemed they had forgotten there was anyone in the kitchen apart from themselves.

After returning to Beaufort Hall at ten thirty, Eight and his sister were supposed to come back through the tunnel to meet Barrie as soon as they could. Barrie waited inside, pacing and counting her footsteps, and at last the beam of a flashlight bobbled toward her. Instead of going out to meet it, she stayed with the *yunwi* at the invisible demarcation line of the Fire

Carrier's magic. As weak as the *yunwi* were, she didn't have the heart to leave them. Only two had even followed her inside into the tunnel, and they were so faint that Barrie could barely make out their shadowy forms.

For all her impatience as she waited, the tunnel seemed less daunting now that Barrie knew it had been Eliza who had finished and reinforced it. Memories still lurked there among the shadows, coiled to strike at unexpected moments, but maybe at least at some point in its long history, it had been a place of hope or even happiness. Barrie wondered if Inola had felt safe using it to come and go as she met with the *yunwi*. And had the marriage between Eliza and Robert been a good one? It would have been nice to think that at least once in three hundred years, a Beaufort and a Watson had found a way to be happy when they'd fallen in love. Barrie wished that the *yunwi* would, or could, tell her that much at least.

"Do you remember Eliza?" she asked them. "Did she get to know all your secrets? Did she write them down in the letterbooks? Don't try to talk—just nod if she did."

Their eyes flashed in the darkness as they dipped their heads, but Barrie didn't know which question they were answering. Maybe all along, it wasn't that the *yunwi* hadn't been able to communicate with her. She was the one who hadn't known how to listen.

She didn't even know their names. That suddenly seemed

ridiculously wrong. Names held power, but they were more than that. Names were a shorthand for emotion, the shortest form of story. How could Barrie feel so much for the *yunwi* in general, when she didn't know who they were as individuals?

"Can you show me what to call you?"

Their hands brushed hers, and once again, touching them made her senses sharper. Not only were they now easier to see, but the yellow glow of Eight's approaching flashlight grew brighter, and the sound of his footsteps grew louder. That seemed to be a function of energy. Any infusion of energy had done it: the energy from the spirit path, the death of the rabbit. But it had been the binding, too. Obadiah had touched Eight once to allow Eight to see him when he'd been invisible before, and more recently, he had touched Berg to dispel whatever magical hypnotism had sent the dig crew and the sheriff's deputies back to their tents.

What would happen, Barrie wondered abruptly, if *she* touched Eight and wanted him to see the Fire Carrier and the *yunwi*? Did he still have enough of his gift for that to work? Maybe Kate could want to see the Fire Carrier enough for both of them.

Unfortunately, when Eight finally reached Barrie, Kate wasn't with him. She caught him by the arm and towed him up the branch of the tunnel that led to the Watson woods. "Where's your sister?"

"Good to know you're not in a hurry or anything," Eight said after stealing a quick kiss. "Where are we rushing off to?"

She kissed him back with a warm rush of exhilaration. Standing on her toes, she claimed his mouth, claimed him, because she suddenly felt hope hovering in the damp and musty long-still air. The hand holding the flashlight dropped to his side, and the beam pointed down to the ground. Her own flashlight shone at the wall, from where her arm was wound around his waist beneath the backpack he had slung over one shoulder.

Pulling away, she placed a finger against his lips. "That's another bookmark. We can come back to this activity later. I'm a fan of this activity, but I've got an experiment I want to try. A couple of experiments, actually—provided that I can get the first one to work."

"You're not up to anything crazy again, are you, Buffy? Maybe as a favor to me, we could lay off the spirit-slaying until tomorrow night."

"No slaying. But where *is* Kate? Didn't she come with you? Did you bring the books?"

"Yes, I brought them. But Kate's not coming." Eight hurried beside Barrie as she headed toward the shorter tunnel that branched off the main one and led up to the Watson woods. The backpack he had brought tapped against his shoulder blade like a nervous twitch. "Dad discovered that the books were missing when we got back. He found them in Kate's room, along with the cell phone he had confiscated earlier, so he didn't believe me when I said that I was the one who had taken them. Or he didn't care. Short of shimmying down a trellis, Kate's locked up tight for the next few days."

The beam of Barrie's flashlight jiggled erratically. "How did you get the books back to bring them over here?"

"I told Dad that Eliza was both a Watson *and* a Beaufort, which makes you just as entitled to read them as we are. I also pointed out that he'd promised to read them this afternoon and he hadn't even tried. If he had, he would have discovered earlier that they were missing. Also . . ." Eight's brow knitted, and he shot Barrie a searching, sideways look, as if trying to gauge her reaction even before he said whatever was coming next. "Also, I told him about Obadiah and the lodestones and the open house."

"You told him everything?" Barrie stumbled to a stop. "What happened to worrying about him doing something stupid?"

"I never meant to tell him. One minute we were yelling at each other, and then all our feelings erupted and came flying out. For both of us," Eight said, his voice sounding neither worried nor angry.

"Is that good?" Barrie asked dubiously. "Or bad?"

Eight dropped another quick kiss onto her lips. "Good, I think. He and I have both argued—yelled—about the same

293

things many times before, but after what you said to me about Ernesto, I thought about some of them differently. Not telling him about Obadiah wasn't fair or helpful. He swears he's not going to make any decisions without talking them through, and at least now I know how scared he's been. He's afraid of losing me and Kate the way he lost his father, and Pru, and my mother. The people he loves keep leaving him. Or dying."

Barrie knew that feeling. It scared her, too.

Stopping at the thick iron door that led out to the edge of the Watson woods, Eight held the flashlight while she looked at her watch and pulled the keys from her pocket. "It's almost midnight," she said. "We're going to have to hurry."

"Your experiment has something to do with the Fire Carrier?"

"Partially," Barrie said, unlocking first the door and then the padlock on the grating above the stairwell.

Outside, the unnatural hush that preceded the Fire Carrier's coming was already present, the air so still that the sound of Barrie's own pulse was like a tide in her ears. No insects, no frogs, none of the usual night sounds from the small creatures that loved the darkness. Turning toward the trees, she found the first faint glow of fire tinting the trunks in flickering variations of amber and red and saffron. Along the edge of the lawn, the *yunwi* ran more slowly than usual, the firelight reflecting in their eyes.

Barrie walked through the woods and down toward the river, heading for the bank where the Fire Carrier waded in when he emerged from the trees. It was the same place where she had dragged herself out of the river on the night of the explosion, and she couldn't help looking over at the Colesworth dock. Her limbs felt numb and alien all over again. Finding out that Ernesto hadn't died had ripped open all the scars.

"I'm glad that your father knows about the open house," she said. "We've all been keeping too many secrets."

"The more we love someone, the more we try to shelter them," Eight said. "That's normal, but it doesn't make it right. We can all do better."

The two *yunwi* who had gone into the tunnel darted through the open door and grating and sprinted away from the woods—as if it had taken all that time to work up their courage, or maybe their strength, to pass that close to a large amount of iron. Other *yunwi* met them, and they stopped some yards away and stood watching Barrie. Just watching.

The Fire Carrier walked down the bank. The sphere of flames in his arms reflected on the water, as round and full as a second moon, and he waded out amid the trembling marsh grass and spilled fire out onto the river.

Clasping Eight's forearm, Barrie held tight and wished that he could see the Fire Carrier. She *wanted* him to see what she saw. If any bit of his gift remained, his compulsion to do what she wanted, she needed it to apply at this moment, while the river burned. Because he had never felt the Beaufort binding, and now probably never would, the only way he would ever understand her, fully understand why she had kept secrets and why she had to put Watson's Landing first, why she couldn't give up her binding, was to experience the magic through her eyes.

CHAPTER TWENTY-FIVE

The air crackled with electricity. The Fire Carrier turned his head and looked straight at Eight, who was looking straight at the Fire Carrier. Eight went rigid.

Barrie squeezed his arm more tightly. "Can you see him now?"

"What did you do?" Eight asked, sounding both awed and bewildered. Which was an answer in itself.

Relief and an almost giddy joy rushed through Barrie, but then the Fire Carrier shifted his attention back to her, and as always there was a silent plea in the way he watched her, a request and a sadness. A longing. Seeing the spirit up close the first time on the night of the explosion, she had thought he wasn't much older than Eight, but seeing them together now, she had no idea how old he looked. Both youthful and much older. Older in years and not just living.

She needed to stop making assumptions. That seemed to be the lesson she was destined to keep relearning. Every time she assumed something based on what she knew, she discovered she knew too little.

"What do you need us to do?" she asked the Fire Carrier. "We want to help you, but we don't know how."

The Fire Carrier only nodded silently as always. Turning back to the river, he spread his hands and called the flames back to himself, then spooled them in gold and fiery strands until they had balled up tightly again. He climbed out onto the bank and vanished among the trees.

"Well, that was unexpected." Eight pried his hand away from hers, rubbed his eyes, and wiped a bead of sweat from his forehead. "That's my first actual ghost, if I don't count Obadiah. I have to admit, I pictured him differently. I need to go look up that headdress. It's more of a cap with feathers than a war bonnet."

"I never said it was a war bonnet."

"But you said 'feathered headdress,' and that's where my head went. Movies, I guess. Now we have something specific to work with. Maybe what he's wearing will help us figure out who he is and where he came from—or at least *when* he came from."

"Were you able to read what he wants?"

"It's a shame we didn't think of this earlier when my gift wasn't so weak." Eight half-closed his eyes in concentration, and his expression grew distant. "I don't think what I felt was a *want*, exactly. Nothing that specific. It was more like a concept—like peace, or rest, but also duty, as if all three of those had nearly the same meaning. I know that doesn't make sense."

"But you couldn't read Obadiah properly, either, remember. You said that what he wanted had been with him for so long that it had sunk down like bones in a tar pit. The way you described it makes me think of the binding. After a while, the ache becomes enough a part of you that you're able to think about other things."

The stillness that was partly a Beaufort trait and partly Eight's own thoughtfulness settled over him, the narrowing of focus that made Barrie feel like she was the only person in the world who mattered at that moment. He smiled at her. "Damn, it's sexy that you listen to me." But then he glanced back in the direction of the woods. "You're right, though. Whatever the Fire Carrier wants is old and painful, but it's not like Obadiah. It's not buried deep—it's urgent. But if he wants us to understand him, why doesn't he just use magic again? If he was the one who gave the families the gifts in the first place, you'd think he could conjure up some convenient method of communication."

"Like what? A radio? The *yunwi* aren't as strong as they once were, either. Maybe the magic is fading. Maybe that's the problem . . . or maybe it wasn't his magic in the first place."

"What do you mean?" Eight peered at her and rubbed a hand along the back of his neck.

The truth of what Barrie had just said ran through her like an electric charge, as if she'd tapped into a vein of energy herself. Because suddenly, it was as if things were finally making sense. Maybe, at last, they were getting close to the answers.

"That's exactly what I need to show you." She reached for Eight again, laced her fingers with his, and gestured to where the *yunwi* had wandered down to the edge of the water, as far from the woods as they could get while staying close to her. "What about them?" she asked, wishing he could see them, too. "Can you tell what they want?"

Eight went tense again. The *yunwi* stared back at him, their eyes burning more brightly now that the flames had gone from the river. Head tilted and brow furrowed in concentration, Eight drew Barrie closer to where the *yunwi* waited. Then he stopped where he could almost have touched them. They came to him instead, reaching for the same hand that Barrie was holding.

"Can you feel anything?" Barrie asked.

"Nothing at all. It's like they're not there." Eight held tight to Barrie's hand and peered more closely. Then he gave a befuddled shake of his head. "That's not only because they're spirits—even the Fire Carrier still gave me an impression."

"I need to show you something else, too. Something they did today."

After locking up both the tunnel grating and the iron door, Barrie led Eight out to the edge of the woods toward the chapel and the living tapestry of roses and blooming moon-flower trumpets that the *yunwi* had created on the wall. The scent of the flowers was elusive, the promise of sweetness with undertones of something tart and clean.

"This is what the *yunwi* grew while I was talking to you and Kate about the letter," she said. "It was as if they wanted me to know they could still do what Eliza called 'wonder work.' It took all their strength, weakened them, and afterward I could barely see the ones who had performed the magic. But they're clearer again, now that the Fire Carrier has finished his cere-mony, as if whatever he did recharged them."

The brightly burning eyes of the *yunwi* watched Eight from around the garden, peering from behind benches and gravestones and trees as he walked up to the wall of the church. He plucked a moonflower blossom from a vine, and his expression held a mixture of reverence and panic. He'd taken ghosts, skeletons, and exploding speedboats—even Obadiah—in stride, but moonflowers made him falter.

"Whatever the Fire Carrier does, it's not just keeping them

on the island," she said. "It must also give them energy. Or strength or power, or some combination of the three. Maybe it's all the same thing."

Eight twirled the moonflower between his fingers. "That's more in line with the stories I read. If the Cherokee medicine people were the ones who worked magic, and if at least at some point, some of them went to the *yunwi* to learn, it wouldn't make sense to think that the Fire Carrier could keep the *yunwi* here against their will. Hopefully, there's something about that in the letterbooks somewhere."

Pulling Barrie toward the bench, Eight shrugged out of the backpack and unzipped it before he sat down. He handed Barrie the first of the books and took the second for himself.

"Give me a starting point," he said. "What should we be looking for? Just any reference to magic, the *yunw*i, or the Fire Carrier?"

"Or the Scalping Tree and the lodestones, your fountain, the spirit path, vortexes . . . also ravens and energy."

They settled side by side. Barrie held the flashlight under her chin and tried to simultaneously hold the book and turn the pages as she skimmed.

"How about you read while *I* hold the flashlight?" Eight suggested, scooting closer.

Their arms were close enough that current shimmered between them like summer heat on asphalt. The hair on Barrie's skin ruffled each time she flipped a page, and the butter-yellow beam trembled across Eliza's narrow writing as Eight held it. Eight's breathing grew rough, and Barrie's grew shallow.

She told herself to concentrate. She scooted away a tiny shift at a time so that Eight wouldn't notice her leaving. One of the *yunwi* clambered up onto the bench, scrambled over Eight to wedge between them and peer at the writing, then jumped down again and darted behind the chapel.

Eight shivered, as if caught in a sudden draft. "What was that?"

"A *yunwi*. He—or maybe she, I don't know, I can't tell gender—was curious, I think. I wish there were a better gender-neutral pronoun. It's hard to think of the *yunwi* as individuals when I have to think 'they' or 'it' all the time instead of 'he' or 'she.'"

"I wonder what they call themselves," Eight said. "'*Yunwi*' is the Cherokee name for them, but a lot of different Native American tribes believe in some kind of Little People. And not just here; there are stories about them all across the world."

"Maybe it's like energy. If *ch'i*, or *moyo*, or *prana* are all basically a variation on the same concept, and spirit paths are similar to dragon lines and ley lines, then why couldn't *yunwi* be the same as Eliza's English fairies or fey? If the *yunwi* are *real*, what if every culture who encountered them has reshaped the stories about them—seen them through the lens of their own culture and beliefs? It's easy to lose sight of the common denominators, to focus on the differences instead of the more important similarities. It's like pronouns. Once you put a convenient label on something, it's easier not to examine it very deeply. That's human nature."

"Maybe. Partly. But there are Old English documents that used genderless pronouns, and that never kept women from being dismissed as less important."

"When did you look that up?" Barrie forgot the book she was holding, and it began to slide off her lap again.

Eight reached out and steadied it, his face reddening and his eyes avoiding hers. "When I found out you called Mark a 'he' even when he wore dresses. I figured that was what he wanted, but it made me curious."

How could Barrie not love him when he said things—did things—like that? Something must have shown in her expression, on her face, because he tilted the flashlight to look at her more carefully. "What's wrong, Bear?"

"Nothing." She shook her head. "Mark used to have arguments with people about what he should or shouldn't call himself. His theory was that anybody who stuffed themselves into Spanx and learned how to go through life wearing six-inch heels had a right to call himself any damn thing he pleased."

Eight grinned at that, his teeth flashing, white and even. "I wish I could have met him."

"He would have loved you."

"Do *you*?" Eight asked, his eyes searching hers.

She didn't pretend not to know what he was talking about. No more secrets.

"I do," she said.

He kissed her then, long and slow and deep. It was a promise of a kiss, a beginning.

It was perfect.

They sat in silence afterward, reading side by side with the flashlight shining down on the pages and the kiss still shimmering between them. The night, the very air, resonated with all the timelessness, possibilities, truth, and gold dust of a Klimt painting.

Barrie tried to concentrate, but her thoughts were distracted, and with her attention broken, snippets of stories she had heard and read kept creeping in, stories about fairies, and brownies, elves, dwarves, and goblins. Her eyes grew tired from reading the small, ornate script in the dim light, and it was late—past one thirty, according to her watch—but they needed answers, and she didn't want the night to end. Suppressing a yawn, she turned the page.

"Did you find something?" Eight asked as she bent lower to read more carefully.

"Listen," she said. Backing up to the start of the letter she'd been skimming, she read aloud:

[To my Father]

Honored Sir,

    Your recent news of James's illness is met here with much concern. I trust that he will soon find himself on the mend and can return to his Duties, although I would, of course, wish him to return here instead to take up the Responsibilities that he seems determined to avoid. I cannot in honesty understand his Aversion to all the wonders here. Doubting his Bravery is impossible when he does not hesitate in battle with His Majesty's Regiment, and so I must attribute it to some other Failing of his character. You will plead with me to be more charitable toward him, I know. But how can I when his willful disregard for my own happiness causes both me and my dear Robert such great Pain and prevents us from being together? We make do, in the meanwhile, as best we can. I shall not give in, however you entreat me, to consider another suitor. Indeed, even if Robert had not so firmly won my affections with his gentleness and kindness, the very unhappy Mr. Boil whom you addressed to me is such a man as I would wish upon no Body, for he thinks—and speaks!— only of himself.

    To this end, I hope that you will once again entreat with James when next you see him. If you will not, then

I will have no recourse but to consider ways in which to convince him to take up his duty to his Family and to preserve the spirit of the bargain that Great-Uncle Thomas pledged with his blood on the Fire Carrier's Serpent Stone. Inola has assured me that the consequences of risking the felling of the woods and the great Tree would be so dire that they do not bear envisioning. If James will not voluntarily take up his duties here, perhaps there are ways to Compel him to do so! Unlike my brother, I shall not forsake my Honor and my great-uncle's promise.

Honored Sir,

Your most obedient and ever Dutiful Daughter,

E. Watson

"She didn't like her brother much, did she?" Eight commented when Barrie had fallen silent.

"It sounds like she's threatening to force him to come back here, doesn't it? Which means he doesn't think he has to."

"Are you thinking *Eliza* found a way to bind him?"

"Well, it doesn't seem like her father had to be at Watson's Landing," Barrie said, suppressing another yawn. "Unless they had a way to transfer the binding and Eliza had it while he was gone, it could be that the original bargain was a gentleman's agreement. But if Eliza did something that forced one person to be the designated heir, she would have written about it, wouldn't she? It would be good to know before Obadiah does his ceremony tomorrow night."

"Why? You're not thinking of taking the lodestones to him, are you?"

"Not if there's any danger, no. But what if there aren't enough people there tomorrow night? What if—even with everything we're doing—Obadiah isn't able to break the curse?" Barrie yawned again, so tired that her words were slurring.

Eight took the book from her and closed it firmly. "I hate to break it to you, Bear, but you're going to be reading in your sleep here in another minute. We're working as fast as we can, and we can't do any more than that."

What if that's not good enough?

Unsaid, the words hung between them as if both she and Eight had thought them simultaneously. Eight's expression turned worried again, and he gave Barrie his hand to help her to her feet.

A firefly winked by the chapel wall, and she looked up to see a *yunwi* watching her. She wondered how many times a small light flickering in the dark was other than it seemed. How many shadows glimpsed from the corner of an eye were only shadows?

CHAPTER TWENTY-SIX

The text message from Eight came after four o'clock in the morning. Barrie was drifting in the half slumber between exhaustion and too much leftover excitement when she heard the ping. She groped for the phone and peered at the screen.

YOU STILL UP? CALL ME!

Pushing her curls out of her eyes, she dialed him back. The sound of his voice spilled out in the darkened room. "You have to listen to this."

"Are you okay?" she asked. "Is Kate all right? Did your dad do something again?"

"Kate and Dad are both fine, as far as I know. She's asleep, and Dad's still holed up in the library with the door closed. Maybe he fell asleep on the sofa."

"So then what's wrong? It's almost four thirty in the

morning. Don't tell me you've been researching all this time."

"Research is like a rabbit hole. It's hard to claw my way back out once I get started," Eight said. "I just meant to look up the Serpent Stone that Eliza mentioned, and I found a lot of references to ancient Cherokee war priests and medicine men using divining crystals. Sometimes those are referred to as *ulunsuti* stones, but the original *ulunsuti*, the truly powerful ones, at least according to what I found online, were the focus stones taken from the forehead of an *Uktena*, a horned serpent with wings that guarded the entrances to the underworld beneath rivers and lakes and certain springs."

"Berg said Eliza's fountain was fed by an underground spring."

"So it's not just me? I'm not crazy for making that connection?"

Barrie kicked the covers off and swung her legs down from the bed, then wandered to the door that led out to the balcony. "Maybe we're both crazy. We don't have any idea what it means."

"That's definitely true. The one thing I've read over and over is that the Cherokee who know the real stories only pass them along to the people they think are ready to hear them. I can't even tell which stories are purely from modern Cherokee and which came from the ancient ones who lived here before European settlers, or whether some of the stories are remnants from even before that, from the mound people, or the fire priests they mention in the oldest stories. Which means anything I find on the Internet isn't likely to be more than scraps of truth. Maybe that idea of being ready to learn something is also why Obadiah is so closemouthed about information. We aren't ready."

"Or maybe he doesn't know the stories, either. Not completely. But in that case, do you think that Inola would have told Eliza the truth? And if she didn't, how do we ever figure out what the Fire Carrier and the *yunwi* want us to do?"

Eight took a deep breath. "Are you sure we're meant to do anything, Bear?"

Barrie turned to the two *yunwi* who had curled up in the armchair in the corner of the room—the same two who had accompanied her into the tunnel, she was almost sure of it. They opened their eyes and looked back at her.

"I've never been more certain of anything in my whole life," she said. "I feel it. The binding itself has something to do with protecting the *yunwi*, and maybe that's even the reason that my gift is pushing me toward Obadiah, because there's something that I'm supposed to do with him or through him. All I know for certain is that whatever the Fire Carrier wants from me is separate from simply protecting Watson's Landing, and like you said, it's urgent."

Opening the door, she let herself out onto the balcony.

311

Across the river in his bedroom, Eight stood in his window, silhouetted by the light behind him. "If one of the lodestones is Eliza's Serpent Stone, it could be riskier trying to find it than Obadiah said. *Uktena* came and went from the underworld, and the *ulunsuti* were the most powerful things a person could possess. They were fed by blood. Medicine men kept them outside their houses because they were too dangerous to keep inside."

Barrie shook her head. "I still can't believe we're thinking about the underworld as if it's an actual place."

"Why not? You and I are looking at each other from across the river right now, but I can hear you as clearly as if you were standing here beside me. Once you know how, you can cross any boundary. Maybe the *ulunsuti* stones are a key of some kind. There's a reference to an *ulunsuti* being buried with the last priest who knew how to use its power. I also found an article that said the ancient Cherokee called the chief war priest the Fire Carrier, and he carried an *ulunsuti* with him along with the sacred fire—that could have been a plain divining crystal, but what if it wasn't? What if our Fire Carrier had the real thing and brought it here?"

"Then where did the other two lodestones come from?" Barrie asked, leaning her elbows on the balcony railing. The clouds had faded away, and the weak moon glimmered on the river where the Fire Carrier spread his magic. Who was he?

And why was he on Watson Island? Those still seemed to her to be the most important questions, or at least the ones that all the remaining questions branched from.

"If we're saying the underworld is an actual place," she said, "then there are different ways in, and not all of them involve the *ulunsuti*. Obadiah crossed the boundary before Ayita and Elijah brought him back, and Obadiah's intending to send Ayita and Elijah back there."

"Maybe you only need the *ulunsuti* if you aren't dead? I don't know. But we can't postpone the ceremony, if that's what you're going to suggest. Obadiah said it needs to be done when he has the most energy possible—right after the open house—and it's too late to cancel the party now."

"Could we find someone who knows the real stories?" Barrie asked. "An actual Cherokee medicine person or historian?"

"How long do you think it would take to convince someone to come here and help us? And you should see what I've been searching through. Even if we could be sure the person knows the real stories, we can't be sure they'd be willing to share them."

"So what do we do?" Barrie asked, yawning again.

"Unless there's more in the letterbooks, we're going to have to trust Obadiah tomorrow. And right now, we both need sleep. Good night, Bear."

"Good night."

I love you hovered on the tip of Barrie's tongue, but Eight had hung up before she could get it out. She sat a moment thinking, then typed out a text for Berg about *ulunsuti* stones, war priests, and Cherokee history. But she didn't go back to bed. Her head was filled with too many swirling thoughts, and she pulled out her laptop and started searching for the terms herself. In the end, she slept very little.

Barrie rose before seven to go out to the stable. After everything she had learned about the *yunwi*, it seemed even more wrong to let them do anything as mundane as mucking stalls.

As usual, they accompanied her, but their behavior was strange. When she brought Miranda and Batch in from the pasture, where Pru had left them turned out for the night, and returned them to their stalls, the *yunwi* boiled around her. Then suddenly, they dashed away down the aisle and left the stable to disappear in the tangled trees beyond the cemetery. Following the *yunwi* as far as the old chapel out of curiosity, Barrie couldn't find where they had gone, and she couldn't see anything amiss, so she went back to feeding the horses. She had just dumped a flake of hay into Miranda's stall when two of the *yunwi* darted back in after her with a voiceless warning.

Run.

Miranda's ears flattened against the side of her head, and

she stomped her foot. The *yunwi* grabbed at Barrie, pulling her toward the house, but she could barely feel them—barely even see them. Their eyes were cooling embers with scarcely any fire at all.

"What's wrong?" Barrie stepped out into the aisle, unsure whether to stay and try to calm the mare or let the *yunwi* pull her away. Obadiah was the only person the *yunwi* had ever reacted to with such a sense of panic.

The figure who stepped through the open stable doorway wasn't Obadiah.

He was a silhouette at first, backlit by the sun, but even in the split second before her eyes focused, Barrie knew that the shape was wrong. Too short. Too bald. Fear coiled around her heart and squeezed until the blood in her limbs ran cold. Her brain told her feet to move, but there didn't seem to be any functioning nerves available to translate the command.

Yunwi circled all around Ernesto, trying to keep him from coming into the stable, trying to push him out. Their bodies were only hints of shadow, hardly visible—hardly even *there*. Ernesto didn't seem to feel them.

He advanced, dragging the *yunwi* with him along the concrete. Thorny vines, too thin and new for strength, clung to his shoes and pants as if the *yunwi* had used them to try to stop him or slow him down. Leaves had caught in the torn fabric of his shirt, and hundreds of small, bloody cuts covered his arms, crisscrossing older, deeper cuts that had been stitched up, and places where the skin was red and raw as if it had burned. A fresh scar ran from the bald scalp above his forehead, across his eye, and down to the midpoint of his cheek. The face tattoo on the back of his skull wasn't visible, but Barrie remembered it all too well.

Miranda whinnied and knocked the wall as she spooked. The *yunwi* pushed Barrie back into the stall, or maybe she stepped in on her own. They struggled to close the door and didn't have the strength. She slammed it closed, but there was no way to lock it or latch it from inside. Ernesto easily slid it open.

He stood in the doorway, blocking the only exit.

Barrie backed up until she ran into Miranda. Putting her hand out to calm the trembling mare, she tried to think. Escape was impossible. The window in the stall was too high, and the wall was solid. She snatched up the rake she had left by the water bucket.

Ernesto gave a humorless smile, and the raw scar puckered and made him wince. His hand half-rose to touch it, but instead he reached behind him and pulled a handgun, matte black and lethal-looking, from his waistband as a flurry of stall bedding flew at him. The *yunwi* snatched up more to throw.

He waved them away and spat. "What the hell is wrong with this place? Hello, *chica*. Surprised to see me?"

"Should I be?" Barrie croaked. It was a stupid thing to say, but her brain didn't seem to be working right, and she held up the wooden rake handle like a sword in front of her. "Why are you here?" she asked, to keep him talking.

"Because you cost me," he said. "I'd tell you it was nothing personal, but it doesn't get more personal than losing my friends, my customers, and an entire shipment I have to replace myself if I want to stay alive. Picturing the moment when I would get to kill you is the only thing that's made me feel good in weeks."

He advanced into the stall, and Barrie backed up another step. She ran into Miranda again, but the mare was already pressed against the wall with nowhere to go.

Small flames, as thin as matchsticks, burst from the *yunwi*'s upraised palms and landed on Ernesto's shirt. He swatted at them. Miranda squealed and reared back, eyes white-rimmed, hooves churning the air. Her head crashed into the ceiling. Barrie dropped the rake, grabbed her mane, and pulled her downward.

"Shh, honey. It's all right."

It wasn't, though.

The *yunwi* screamed again. No words. Just urgency. Fire burned in their palms. Ernesto's eyes widened, and his mouth fell open, as if he could see the flames, though he hadn't seemed to see the *yunwi*.

Miranda's head hit the ceiling again, hard enough to shake the rafters. Hard enough to crack bone.

Barrie didn't think. Both hands fisted in Miranda's mane, she threw herself up onto the horse's back and kicked her forward. Miranda's forelegs thudded against the floor, her hindquarters bunched, and she surged toward the door.

The *yunwi* dove aside. Ernesto jumped away and fell, scrambling as the mare leaped past him. A shot rang out, but Miranda didn't flinch. Barrie hunkered low over the mare's neck, clinging for balance. Steel shoes struck concrete. Her ears rang. The floor rushed past. The faint acrid scent of burning curled her nose, but whether that was from gunpowder, the sparks cast off by horseshoes, or whatever fire the *yunwi* had thrown, Barrie didn't know. She hoped it wasn't from burning sawdust. She couldn't get to Batch.

Bolting out into the sunlight, Miranda ducked left, throwing Barrie hard to the right. Barely clinging, Barrie pulled herself back up in time to be flung in the opposite direction as the mare rounded the corner of the house.

White shell and gravel blurred beneath Miranda's feet, and the first columns of the portico flashed past. Barrie had time to dimly think that she shouldn't go toward the house because Pru was there and Ernesto would follow her. Because windows were too easily broken and guns were faster than police cars. Then Miranda veered left toward the oak-lined lane. The relief of that was short-lived. The gate on the far end was closed, and they would get there only to have to come back again.

Shifting her weight across Miranda's withers, Barrie yanked the mare's mane toward the right to try to turn her head. Miranda didn't react. Dropping her weight even more, Barrie barely kept her balance, and she wished she'd paid more attention to what Pru had tried to teach her. She wished she had the courage to close her eyes to connect better. Mostly she wished she hadn't switched off the motion detectors at the perimeter of the property when she'd turned off the house alarm to go feed the horses, but she hadn't given it a second thought.

Miranda finally changed direction. Barrie dug her heels in and sent the mare galloping, surging, flying across the grass toward the Watson woods while she clung low over Miranda's neck and prayed and tried to let herself sink into the motion. Snatching a look behind her, she caught a flash of white rounding the corner of the house, and she hunched even lower. Urged Miranda faster.

The woods loomed ahead. That was the only hope. Not for Miranda, though. The trees were too close together, the ground too rough. Mentally, Barrie calculated. She shuddered at the distance to the ground.

She had to risk it.

"All right, sweet girl. You're going to turn when I pull you around. Can you do that? And then you're going to run like hell and leave me—and keep running as far and fast as you can."

Wrapping her arms more tightly around Miranda's neck, she kicked her left leg up over the mare's broad back so she'd be ready to jump off. Unbalanced, she struggled to hold on, her whole body weight shifted to the right to try to swing Miranda around to avoid the trees.

She fell before she was ready. Her shoulder hit the grass. Light flashed and pain splintered in her head.

No breath. Pain filled her up while the thunder of Miranda's hooves shook the ground, and Barrie lay there, useless. For too long.

Inhale. Inhale and exhale.

Get up. *Run.* Barrie forced herself to her knees.

Miranda had run a few more paces, then stopped, blowing hard. Head down, nostrils red and quivering, she was coming back toward Barrie.

She couldn't come back. Scrambling upright, Barrie stumbled and took a few steps. Waving her arms over her head, she shouted: "Yah! Go! Run, Miranda."

The mare shied and reared.

A shot rang out. Miranda squealed in fear and fury, and ducking low to the left, she plunged toward the river. Barrie dove toward the trees. Her feet tangled in the underbrush and she tripped, fought to get her bearings.

There was no place to hide. The fallen logs were too low; the sparse bushes and palmetto wouldn't provide any cover. The trees were too narrow. Nothing was dark enough. Even if she made it to the river, then what? Barrie couldn't swim, and she couldn't get away, and if Pru came out to investigate . . . She couldn't let Ernesto hurt Pru.

Something large thrashed in the brush behind her. Ernesto cursed.

Barrie angled toward the Scalping Tree, navigating purely by the rush of energy from the center of the woods. At the edge of the clearing, a fallen branch caught her shoe. She wrenched free, took two steps, and then went back and picked the branch up to bring it with her. It was as thick as her wrist, rotting at the end, but the core appeared sturdy enough. She broke off the remaining offshoots and took a practice swing.

It would have to do.

Behind her, a stick cracked, as loud as a bullet. Ernesto cursed again.

Barrie sprinted across the clearing. Half-expecting another gunshot, she darted under one of the low, heavy branches of the Scalping Tree and edged around the trunk. Her back pressed to the bark, energy enveloped her. She didn't let herself sink into it. Every drop of her attention focused on the sounds of pursuit behind her.

The birds had fallen quiet. Ernesto had slowed, approaching

more cautiously. Either that or he had reached the clearing.

Barrie tuned into the natural rhythms, the energy of the woods, searching for connection. Abruptly, what didn't belong stood out in stark contrast: the brush of leaves on fabric, the *snick* of a twig snapping, the ground vibrating beneath a heavy foot. Blood sang a warning in her ears, but she sank deeper into the spirit path, her whole body tingling, swirling with the rush of the vortex beneath her feet. She was anchored this time, though, tied to Watson's Landing. Tied to home. And instead of losing herself in the energy, she felt it flowing through her. Every moment made her feel bigger, fuller, less afraid.

Scooping up a small rock from the ground, she waited.

Ernesto's voice was closer than she had expected it to be. "You think you're clever, don't you? You're only making this harder for yourself. That big tree is the only place to hide."

"Yes, but your itty-bitty gun won't shoot all the way through the trunk," Barrie taunted.

"I've got bullets that can run faster than you. They've got your name on them. Every bullet."

Energy roared through Barrie, and she let it ripple through her, let it pull her with it, stretching out into the woods, reaching up to the sky, burrowing deep into the ground. She listened as hard as she could for Ernesto's approach, waiting for the right moment. The timing had to be perfect if she was going to have a chance.

The sound of Ernesto's feet was muffled, but the ground vibrated beneath his shifting weight, sending earthworms and insects burrowing away. Each leaf crushed beneath his boot produced a burst of scent. Barrie could *feel* him approaching.

"You know why I put your name on the bullets?" he called.

"Because your ego doesn't like being beaten by a girl?"

Ernesto's breath hissed. "I'm having to start all over again, thanks to you, clawing my way back up from nothing. And I've got sixty-seven stitches in my back. Every time I look in the mirror and see this"—there was a beat of silence where she suspected he was pointing to the fresh scar on his face—"I'm gonna have to think of you."

The cold in his voice sank like an ache into Barrie's toes and fingers, spread to her hands and feet until she felt like she was going numb from the outside in. The woods changed. The energy changed.

Ernesto had almost reached her.

Barrie threw the rock as hard as she could. It crashed through a bush fifteen feet behind her. She held her breath.

Breaking into a run, Ernesto burst around the trunk where Barrie waited.

Her fingers closed, rough bark digging into her skin. She barely felt it. She stepped out and swung the branch like a baseball bat, allowing herself the brief comfort of imagining

Eight's hands closing over hers, showing her where to hold it, how to grip it, how to swing.

The branch swished through air. She felt the resistance, the disturbance, the wake it left behind.

Then it connected.

The moment occurred in fragments. Her arms vibrating. Ernesto's shock. The sound, the awful sound: *snap* and *slurp* and *spill*.

She had wanted him to stop. To fall. To leave her and Pru alone.

But he fell and he lay at her feet, his eyes fixed, staring. Blood seeping into the ground. Blood trickling down the branch Barrie was still holding. Blood splattered across her fingers.

Barrie found that she was sobbing, taking deep gulps of air that weren't big enough to feed her lungs.

She wanted him to twitch. She wanted him to raise his head. To moan and not be able to pick himself up until she was safe in the house and the police sirens were wailing down the driveway.

But he didn't move. His eyes didn't blink.

She flung the branch as far as she could. Her knees gave out, and she reached for the tree to brace herself.

Something throbbed beneath her bloodied hand. A pulse and then a surge of energy that swelled and swelled and swelled.

Heat seared through her. She jerked her arm away and left a smear of red against a bulge in the gray, moss-edged bark.

A glimmer of light made her whip around. The Fire Carrier's shape was nearly solid as he streamed from the ground beside Ernesto's body. The black of his feather cloak melted into the hair that hung down from where it was gathered under his cap of raven's feathers. His hands were empty, but fire seemed to crackle beneath his skin.

"I k-killed him." Barrie's voice broke on the word, which was appropriate because something inside her felt broken.

The Fire Carrier's eyes shadowed with pain that Barrie felt like a physical thing. He reached his hand out to her, and she took it, forgetting for a moment that he wasn't solid, that the last time she had touched him there had been only a cold resistance. The cold was still there, but briefly there was also skin and sinew and bone beneath her fingers.

He pulled away.

Removing a flint knife from his belt with his right hand, he crouched beside Ernesto's body. Watching Barrie with an expression that held the stillness of regret, he raised Ernesto's shoulders. Lips moving, chanting words Barrie couldn't hear or recognize, he braced Ernesto against his own knee, and laid his left palm on the front of of Ernesto's scalp. Still chanting, he pulled his palm back toward the crown.

A mist percolated through Ernesto's skin where the Fire

Carrier touched, reminding Barrie of the way the spirits of Ayita and Elijah had drifted up through the plastic sheeting covering the buried chamber. Insubstantial and thin at first, the mist was tinged in black, the color of burning oil. As it separated from the flesh, it gathered into a shape—a figure dark with fury that writhed on a tether anchoring it to the body it had once inhabited.

The Fire Carrier spoke again, more silent words quickly uttered. Then he blew at Ernesto's spirit with a force that rustled the leaves and brush around the clearing.

Barrie shivered. The mist lightened, shifting from black to gray to pale. Still tethered to the flesh of Ernesto's scalp, it thinned and stretched toward the river as the Fire Carrier blew.

The Fire Carrier raised his knife. With a final chant, he laid the edge of the blade above the scalp and cut the cord that tethered the soul to Ernesto's flesh and bones. The remaining mist flew like smoke from a rifle, there and gone with another puff of breath. Barrie clutched the tree, the knot beneath her hand a reassuring warmth in a world where nothing seemed familiar.

Spreading his hands in the air above Ernesto's empty body, the Fire Carrier pushed downward. Energy shimmered beneath Barrie's feet, and the body sank into the earth like Obadiah's feathers, without so much as a ripple.

CHAPTER TWENTY-SEVEN

The Fire Carrier straightened to his feet. Warily he stepped toward Barrie, his hands held out in a gesture of openness.

She didn't—couldn't—move. Dimly, in some corner of her mind, she heard someone calling—she heard Pru calling—but the sound was distant, like something heard from underwater, and she couldn't make out the words. She couldn't respond.

Hot energy poured through her from the Scalping Tree, and that was all that was keeping the shivering cold and her sense of brokenness at bay. If she severed that connection, if she let go of the bulge in the wood, she didn't think she would have the strength to stay on her feet.

The Fire Carrier placed his hand over hers where it rested on the tree. The sensation was like plunging cold limbs into a steaming bath. Pressure built beneath Barrie's palm as if something in the oak was pushing her away, burrowing its way out from under the trunk. Heat pressed against her skin, smooth stone instead of uneven bark. Her fingers curled automatically, grasping for what the tree had given her. She found herself holding a diamond the size of her fist.

Only half a diamond. Part of it had been sheared away, leaving a flat surface that formed the base of a pyramid, and there in the center, Barrie's finger caught on a metallic impurity, like a vein of dark silver in the shape of a bare and twisted branch. The entire stone vibrated and heated as Barrie touched it, tickling the back of her ear and making her skin hum, heating to the cusp of pain and pleasure. The energy within it felt so alive that it seemed to breathe.

In response, the vortex changed, shifted from something outside of Barrie to something within her, spinning her into a swirl of particles so small that she saw herself as the most minuscule part of something that was larger than she could fathom. Just when she feared she would shrink to nothing and disappear, she found herself reversing course, expanding, sweeping, exploding out past the leaves and trunks and trees of the Watson woods, past the boundaries of earth and sky and skin and blood.

The heat and vibration in the stone pulled her back to herself. She heard Pru calling to her again, more clearly this time. And she found that the hand that held the crystal, her own hand, had moved without her knowledge or consent. It was raised toward the river, her whole arm extended as if tugged toward the water by an invisible rope, as if Ernesto's spirit were asking the stone to follow it.

Barrie shuddered at the thought, gasping for breath. She jerked her hand back toward herself, fighting the pull, and when she had brought the crystal to her chest, she clasped it there with the force of both her hands.

"Wh-what's it d-doing?" she asked the Fire Carrier, her voice shaking. She tried to remember the name Eight had used. "This is the *ulunsuti* stone, isn't it? The lodestone? Or part of it, at least."

The Fire Carrier's eyes lit with . . . what? Joy? Relief? Smiling, he pointed to the crystal in her hand and made a chopping motion across his palm. Glancing over to make certain she was watching him, he gestured toward the river. She nodded encouragement. Next, he pointed once more at the *ulunsuti* and cupped his right hand as if he held it. Pretending to pick up another object from the ground, he cupped that in his left hand, and when he straightened, he mimed the sort of pull that Barrie had already experienced from the stone herself, as if the objects in his hands were drawn together by some invisible, inescapable force. Joining his hands, he nodded.

"You want me to put the *ulunsuti* stone back together? Is that it? But how?" Barrie touched the rough edge of the stone again, where it had been split. "Is that what's in the Beaufort fountain? Then how do I remove it? And why is it in two pieces? What happens when I put it together? How does it *go* back together?"

The Fire Carrier only looked at her, his eyes and lips and shoulders shifting downward as if, even if he couldn't understand her words, her doubt and bewilderment were clear. His arm fell. He stood still, no breath lifting his chest, no flutter of motion.

Barrie's mouth was dry, her body clenched too tight to take a step. "I'm trying to understand. Help me." She nodded again and held out the stone. "Show me. Please?"

Again he studied her, unmoving. Then he raised both arms and extended the index finger of one hand upriver toward the tip of Watson Island and the old rice fields, while the other hand pointed north toward the gate at the entrance to Watson's Landing and the road that led to town—or to the mainland bridge to Charleston.

"What does that mean? The stone *doesn't* come back together?"

The Fire Carrier's eyes were as haunted as she felt.

"I'm sorry. I'm trying." She sagged back against the tree, her fingernail picking at the nub of the imperfection within the crystal. It gave a shudder in her hand, and her ears rang.

The sound of her name. She heard it again, clearly. And

it took too long—so long that it made her realize she must have been in shock—to process that it wasn't the rock that had called her.

"Here, Aunt Pru!" she shouted back. "I'm here!"

She glanced back toward the house and felt the disturbance of energy as Pru entered the woods. An added warmth, rippling outward. Her fingers tightened around the stone, and when she looked back over, the Fire Carrier had disappeared.

Her legs shook. She peeled herself off the trunk of the Scalping Tree and tried to walk, and the *ulunsuti* fought her as she veered away from the river.

Tearing through the underbrush at the edge of the clearing with her shotgun raised, Pru spotted Barrie, then made a searching examination of the rest of the clearing until she was satisfied that no one else was there. Lowering the gun, she rushed forward.

"Oh, thank goodness, sugar. What happened? I heard something that sounded like a shot and thought you had the television on. Then I came downstairs and found Miranda wandering across the lawn with a gash across her flank, and there was a bullet casing in the stable. The police are on their way—"

"No!" Barrie's heart fluttered like a moth in a jar, and she caught Pru's arm. "No police. Not until I explain everything to you. Call them back. Tell them not to come—"

"Sweetheart, you're not making sense. Calm down. There was a bullet—someone shot Miranda."

"Please, I'm begging you. Call the police back right now, and tell them—I don't know. Tell them it was the television. Then I'll explain." Barrie sipped panicked breaths, until her lungs ached from being stretched.

Pru watched her and then finally—finally—pulled her cell phone from her pocket and spoke first to the sheriff's office and then to Seven. When she hung up, she laid both palms against Barrie's cheeks as if to reassure her, or reason with her, but then her eyes clouded again.

"You're burning up again, even worse than before! And you're going to shake yourself out of your skin. Come on. Let's get you back to the house. You can talk there, and Seven and Eight are already docking the boat. They'll be here in a minute, so you can explain to all of us at the same time." Wrapping her arm around Barrie's waist, she urged her back across the clearing.

"Is Miranda okay?" Barrie asked gratefully. "She's not hurt badly, is she?"

"It's only a graze, thank goodness. A little antibiotic cream, and she'll be fine." Pru stopped. "Just tell me one thing— are you safe—are *we* safe—now? Did the *yunwi* or the Fire Carrier do something to scare someone off? Who was it?"

Barrie shook her head. "The *yunwi* tried, but it was me. I d-did it."

Pru searched Barrie's face long and hard, and then her lips tightened, and she herded Barrie toward the house. Barrie let herself be led. The *ulunsuti* still tried to tow her in the direction of the river, the sharp tip of the pyramid shape digging into her palm. She had to adapt her every step to counter the force of the pull. Even so, her awareness was focused outward, and she seemed to hear everything, see everything, feel everything all at once. Long before the low brush and dwarf palmettos beneath the trees gave way to grass, she sensed the *yunwi* waiting, weak but simultaneously afraid and eager. They backed away in a huddled line when she emerged onto the lawn, retreating an equal distance each time she stepped forward. Their silhouettes were even less visible than before, and their eyes had dimmed to gray.

Barrie thought at first that it was Ernesto's blood they hated, the way they had shied away from Obadiah's. Remembering the red streak she had left on the oak, she examined her fingers, but there was almost no blood visible on her hands. The stone cast a faint glow across her palm as the sunlight plummeting through the trees set the branch within the crystal on fire. The silver inside the stone turned a deep reddish gold as if it had heated with some kind of electric current.

"Wait. Please wait." Pulling out of Pru's grasp, Barrie retreated a step. The *yunwi* moved forward an equal step. They stopped when she stopped, advanced when she retreated, and retreated when she advanced, as if they wanted to keep their distance, the same way they kept their distance from the woods.

"What are you doing?" Pru asked, watching as if Barrie had lost her mind. Maybe she had, but that was part of being a Watson, too. Magic and sanity were not entirely compatible.

"Watching what the *yunwi* do. This is the lodestone," Barrie said, holding it up and opening her fingers enough to let Pru see the way the *ulunsuti* blazed in the sunlight. "Only it's more than a lodestone—it's a stone the Fire Carrier brought here and split into two pieces to bind the bargains to the families. There's something about it that the *yunwi* don't like."

"Then leave it wherever you found it." Pru's face was all sharp angles and bruised eyes. She stood with her back to the lawn, the shotgun drooping in her hand, and Barrie felt a wave of love so enormous that she thought she would burst with it.

"Thank you," she said.

Pru raised her head. "For what?"

"For rushing out here with a shotgun."

Pru came and squeezed her so tightly that it made Barrie's ribs ache. "I honestly need to start grounding you more often. There's probably some rule in the motherhood manual about punishments for nearly getting yourself shot, but since I never got one of those manuals, we'll have to muddle through the best way we can. That's all we can ever do, right? Muddle through together."

Barrie let Pru's love start to fill her back up again where she'd been empty. Then Eight sprinted into her line of vision at the edge of the lawn with Seven not far behind.

Eight stalled midrun. His eyes raked Barrie's face and traveled to the stone in her hand. Narrowed on a faint smear of blood. "Are you okay?"

Ernesto's face flashed through Barrie's memories: the thud of the stick, the vibration as it hit him, the way the sound traveled up her arm. The way his eyes stared sightlessly.

"I k-killed him. I k-killed Ernesto, and the Fire C-Carrier took his body." The words tumbled out without planning or thought or control, and when they had spilled out into the daylight, she couldn't take them back. She wanted to—oh, how she wanted to. She was so afraid to look at any of them.

Pru's hands had flown to her throat, and Eight's muscles bunched, ready for a fight that was long since over. And neither of them—none of them—could *do* anything to change what had happened. Except that now, now that Barrie had told them, they would all have to make choices about what she had done. Truth wasn't merely a knife that could set you free. It could sever relationships and leave you bleeding. Or it could damn you.

Meeting Seven's eyes was hard, but she forced herself to do it. Because he had already hated her, in one way, it was easier to watch for his reaction than to wait for the understanding of what she'd done to descend on Eight or Pru. Then again, Seven was a lawyer. An officer of the court. And Barrie had just confessed to murder.

CHAPTER TWENTY-EIGHT

They all examined the ground where Ernesto had disappeared. Apart from a few drops of blood on a handful of leaves, they found nothing. Where the *ulunsuti* stone had come through the tree, the blood was gone entirely—and so was any sign that the stone, or anything else, had ever pushed its way through the bark.

"I'm not saying that I don't believe you." Seven crouched beside the spot where Ernesto had fallen and looked doubtfully at the stone still clenched in Barrie's hand. "But you have to admit that there should be some sign—churned earth or even just an indentation in the wood. When you add something or subtract something, you have to account for the space it takes up."

"You're seriously arguing physics? It's magic," Eight said.

He stood behind Barrie with his arms wrapped around her. His warmth slowly seeped into her marrow and filled up the hollowness she had been feeling. It made it easier for her to think. It made breathing easier.

Seven stood up and dusted off his hands. "I'm sure that even magic has rules. We may not know what they are, but they can't defy the laws of nature."

Thinking of the moment when she had first touched the stone and felt as if she had been broken down into particles so small that they barely existed, Barrie shook her head. "Magic *is* nature. Maybe the laws of physics are only symptoms of the few bits of magic that humans understand."

"Which doesn't change the fact that we can't explain any of this to the sheriff's department. We can't even be certain what's down there under the soil. Would we find Ernesto's body if we dug for it?" Seven shrugged, and then he set off to walk around the perimeter of the tree, searching the ground as he went, as if something would be different this time than it had been a minute before when he had done the very same thing. When that brought no results, he came back to the spot where Ernesto had fallen. Crouching low, he started to pick up and examine individual leaves.

Pru handed the gun to Barrie. "Hold this." She marched over to Seven and stood over him. "What are you doing now?"

"Getting rid of evidence." Seven held up a leaf with tiny

dots of blood on it and let her examine it before stuffing it into his pocket. "It was self-defense anyway, but it never hurts to be safe. There's not much blood. We'll throw the stick into the river and take any leaves that caught the splatter and shove them down the garbage disposal. The laws of nature and physics can be damned. Without a body or any evidence, we can pretend that none of it ever happened. If we report this to anyone, we'd only be exposing Barrie, Watson's Landing, and the Fire Carrier—the whole town—to more upheaval and danger."

Almost frantically, as if she welcomed the distraction, Pru went to work beside him, checking each leaf and placing a few here and there into the pocket of her sundress. She hadn't bothered to put on shoes before running out of the house, and her faded pink bedroom slippers were speckled with dirt, leaves, and broken bits of dried Spanish moss.

Eight squeezed Barrie's arms, trying unsuccessfully not to grin at the sight of his father with leaves sticking out of his bulging pockets. Barrie closed her eyes and let herself slump against his chest. He gathered her even closer. She buried her eyes in the crook of his elbow, giving herself a moment of relief before pulling away. And she needed to pull away. She needed a minute. She needed to touch Miranda and make sure the mare was okay. She needed to check the *yunwi*. She needed . . . so many things.

339

"Take a minute, Bear." Eight's eyes were dark and as soft as moss. "Everything else can wait. We can cancel the open house if we need to. We'll figure out some other way to get rid of Ayita and Elijah and the curse."

Seven grunted softly in disagreement. "Better not. Until we're positive no one knew Ernesto was coming here, we need to do everything exactly like normal. Especially in front of Mary and Daphne, because we don't want to endanger them or make them accomplices." He gave Barrie an encouraging smile. "You can do that, can't you?"

How could anyone act "normal" when they'd killed someone? Barrie couldn't imagine it. Then again, hadn't they all proven they were good at keeping ugly secrets?

"I'll be fine," she made herself say. She forced herself to stoop and start examining leaves and to look for scuff marks in the dirt. To start putting bricks up over the memories, like Edgar Allan Poe's brick wall, even as she talked Pru and the Beauforts through everything that had happened and what the Fire Carrier had shown her. And through it all, she held the *ulunsuti* that the Fire Carrier and the tree had given her pressed tightly against her side, because she didn't dare to let it go.

Seven didn't say anything until they had finished cleaning up the evidence. Then he walked over to Barrie and held out his hand. "Let me take a look. Where is the stone trying to pull you? Is it the river or Beaufort Hall?"

Barrie started to drop the crystal into his palm, but as she lowered it, he jerked away as if it had burned him before it even touched him. "That's really hot," he said. "And awful, in a way that has nothing to do with temperature. It feels . . . wild . . . elemental? I'm not sure that's the right word, either."

Barrie pulled the stone back, and touched it with her other hand. It *was* hot—and the vibration still sounded in the back of her ears, but it wasn't unbearable, as if she had adjusted to it. Tuned in to it.

It was hard to know what she felt anymore; too much had happened.

"Let me try," Eight said, approaching the *ulunsuti* more cautiously.

Seven caught his arm. "Be careful. It could be that the aneurysm my father had was related to the stone itself and not to the binding."

"I was standing inches behind Barrie and I didn't feel anything except that Barrie's skin felt hot," Eight said.

Pru laid the back of her hand on Barrie's forehead, then drew back. "Put that thing down right this minute. It's doing something dangerous to you."

Barrie shook her head. "I don't feel it—I don't *feel* hot anymore, so maybe whatever it's doing is adjusting to me, or me to it. Seven's right, though. We should see where it wants to lead me."

She relaxed her muscles, and the stone tugged her arm

up and toward the river. With the others trailing behind her, she let her feet follow the pull, picking her way through brush and around trees, until she had reached the edge of the marsh grass near where the Fire Carrier came out of the woods every night. The line of her arm pointed straight to the Beaufort garden and the fountain beside the house.

She shifted position, walking up the bank a stretch. The stone reoriented, still pointing to the garden.

"Well, that's pretty conclusive," Eight said.

"Should I try to take it over to Beaufort Hall and see what happens?" Barrie asked.

Seven checked his watch and stopped pacing the riverbank behind her. "There's no time now. We have to appear normal, and Mary and Daphne will be showing up here any minute. I'm supposed to be meeting Darrel at the hardware store about tables and stoves in half an hour."

"So, what do we do with the stone?" Eight asked. "Barrie can't exactly push it back into the trunk of the Scalping Tree for safekeeping."

"Since apparently no one else can touch it, we don't need to put it back," Barrie said.

Taking a quick look around the area, she spotted a cypress tree with a hollowed knot above a low-hanging branch. She climbed up onto one of the tree's knobbed knees, and she pushed the *ulunsuti* down inside the cavity.

Around them in the woods, there were only the ordinary sounds, the birds and squirrels going about their business, and no suggestion of outsiders anywhere nearby. Barrie pushed her senses out, looking for otherness or something that didn't belong, but all she felt was the energy of the trees and shrubs flowing together like a giant web of life. *She* was the one who felt smaller with her hands empty. As if the stone had amplified her and joined her to the universe more completely than before.

The full weight of having taken a life swept down on her, and she wondered if that had diminished her, too, made her less of a person.

"I'm going to head over to check on Miranda," she said, partly because she needed breathing space and crying space. "I'll meet you all back in the kitchen."

She walked away, steeling herself as she headed out of the woods toward the house, the cold of what she had done seeping deeper. How was she supposed to appear normal and pretend that nothing had happened? She had killed Ernesto. Her hands itched, as if his blood were crawling through her skin from the outside in, and she scrubbed at the heel of her hand long after any trace had disappeared.

Eight stayed behind talking with Pru and Seven a few moments. Then he jogged to catch her at the edge of the lawn. He turned her toward him as if she were a spun sugar construction instead of something lethal and awful, and his carefulness made her eyes well. Softness, thoughtfulness, none of that was what she deserved or needed. Right now, she needed motion. She needed to outrun her feelings and her memories.

"Look at me, Bear," Eight whispered. "Are you listening? You made a decision that saved your life. Probably saved Pru's life. You protected Watson's Landing. If you had died . . ."

She waited for him to continue, but he shook his head. Logically, Barrie knew he was right. Still, in her mind's eye, she could see Ernesto's spirit blowing toward the water, cleansed of the blackness that had gripped it in life. It felt as if he had torn away a small part of her own soul as well.

She went stiff as Eight wrapped his arms around her. "Please don't shut me out," he said. "I don't need to be able to read you as well as I could before to know that you want to run away from what's happened. But running doesn't solve anything. That's why I'm staying, why I'm going to be here beside you as long as you want me to be. I know what I want now, remember? What *I* want—and I know that you are up high on that list."

"Even after this?"

"Especially after this. We've been through too much together to think that that's ever going to change now. What happened with Ernesto can't make any difference to how I feel about you. So tell me what you need. If you need space, I'll give you that, but don't internalize what happened and blame yourself. This, Ernesto—you can't blame yourself for any of it."

"Don't you understand? I killed someone! A person. However bad he was, he was alive, and now he's n-not." Without realizing she was moving, Barrie took the step forward into Eight's arms, and he held her, rocking her back and forth until the motion lulled her back into feeling numb.

"Maybe whatever the Fire Carrier did was meant to help you see that you have to let go, as much as what he did was meant to set Ernesto free," Eight said against her hair. He kissed her forehead, then watched her with a permission-asking expression that made it clear the next move was hers. When she didn't pull away, he dropped his mouth to hers, and it was exactly what she needed. Reassurance, and warmth, and a moment of forgetfulness.

She kissed him as if it were going to be the last chance she ever had to kiss him. When she thought of the ceremony that night and the power of the *ulunsuti* stone and what had happened to Eight's grandfather, kissing him that way seemed to her to be only common sense. As long as you loved somebody, each kiss was hope and wonder, but it was also the potential for good-bye.

CHAPTER TWENTY-NINE

For hours after that, they baked, frosted, and decorated desserts in the hot kitchen, with the radio playing more loudly than usual, the beat of the music accompanied by the tap of knives and swishing whisks and the oven door opening and closing. There was comfort in cooking, beauty in pouring love and care and creativity into what could have been a purely mechanical need to eat. Even more than the food, having everyone working in the kitchen together helped to plug up the holes through which Barrie's memories crept. That and the mingled sweet scents of dough and baking fruit made it almost possible for her to lock away what she had done in a dark corner of her mind for later examination. She thought she was doing all right, but she still found Pru and Eight, and eventually even Mary, watching her with worried expressions.

By three o'clock, every surface of the kitchen, butler's pantry, and dining room overflowed with miniature pecan and strawberry tarts, not to mention bite-size chocolate, hummingbird, Coca-Cola, and candy bar cakes. Barrie and Daphne filled the black-and-silver cake boxes they'd had printed up with the restaurant logo, and Eight stacked them into the crates for transport.

When they were done, Mary wiped her newly washed hands on a dishcloth and lifted one of the boxes to examine the way the moon, the river, and the branches of the silver trees spilled across the four main surfaces. "These did turn out beautifully, I'll admit it," she said. "I hope they'll bring more people in. Of course, when it all goes sideways this afternoon, folks'll associate it with the restaurant, and no one will want to come when we open."

"First, nothing will go wrong." Daphne pushed the final six boxes across the table. "And second, the whole opening week is full already. We've had to turn forty-three people away for Thursday, and almost as many for the other nights this weekend. We have so many people bidding extra in the auction for seats that it looks like we'll have at least five thousand in donations to give to whatever charity we decide on."

"In that case, we'd better finalize what that's going to be," Pru said. "I'll ask Seven to look into it. He's got some other legal work he's already doing for us."

Barrie paused on her way to the sink to wash her hands. "I'd love to donate to someone who provides after-school tutoring," she said, thinking of Jackson. "Or, Mary, what have you been doing with the money that Obadiah sent?"

"I always give it to Pastor Nelson as an anonymous donation and let him pass it on to the folks who needed it the most," Mary said, putting down the cake box she'd been holding. "We probably need to be more formal with this kind of money."

Pru nodded. "But I doubt people will be as generous once the novelty of the seating auctions wears off."

While Barrie went to rinse her hands, Eight set the final crate full of cake boxes on top of the stack of others. "As long as the food is good and we can create a good experience, I think they will," he said distractedly. "It's human nature to want to help others."

"That's not my experience of human nature." Daphne retrieved a cloth to wipe the table. "For the sake of the ceremony tonight, though, I hope you're right. I hate the idea of Obadiah having to destroy Elijah's and Ayita's souls if they can't let go of the curse."

"Let's hope he has enough energy to do any of this when the time comes. We still don't know how many people are coming, or how many would be enough," Eight said, handing Barrie two of the stacked crates of cake boxes to carry and picking up three to take himself.

Daphne shot a dark look over at Mary, who was leaning against the table. "I really wish you'd change your mind about coming, Gramma."

"So do I," Pru said. "I'm worried that a lot of people are going to hear you aren't there and change their minds about coming, too."

"I haven't said a word to anyone one way or the other, but you can tell me up one side and down the other that this is safe, and I still won't like it. I have no intention of sendin' other folks over there to have Obadiah take pieces of them without their permission."

"You keep saying that." Daphne slapped the cloth down against the table. "But what about Elijah and Ayita? Doesn't it feel wrong to have them stuck there? Or to have people getting hurt because of them? To have Brit and Jackson hurting—"

"We don't *know* that's the curse."

"We don't *know* otherwise, do we?"

The two of them glowered at each other until, with a sniff, Mary went off to the pantry. A moment later she emerged carrying a large bushel full of corn on the cob. Eight nudged Barrie with his elbow and nodded toward the door. He pushed through and held it open while Barrie exchanged a rueful smile with Daphne.

They made several trips back and forth from the car to the kitchen, until all the crates and boxes were packed into the trunk of the Range Rover that Eight had borrowed from his father. When they'd finished, Barrie slid into the passenger seat and fidgeted against the searing heat of the leather that seeped through even her mosquito-defying skinny jeans.

"You look beautiful," Eight said as he eased in beneath the steering wheel and gave her a sidelong *You doing okay?* glance he knew better than to put into words.

"I keep thinking what I did should show on the outside, like a scarlet letter, or one of those fleur-de-lis marks in *The Three Musketeers*. Also, what if Mary's right? Is it wrong to bring people over there so Obadiah can steal their energy without giving them the chance to refuse? What if he accidentally kills someone? Or Elijah and Ayita kill someone? That would be more people on my conscience. I picture all that energy swirling around people, and Ayita and Elijah sucking it up and turning into giant Stay Puft marshmallow ghost monsters—"

"You spent your childhood watching too many old movies."

"There's no such thing as too many old movies."

Eight cocked his head in mock consideration. "Possibly." He leaned over and kissed her lightly. *"As you wish."*

She steeled herself to admit what she had never yet managed to say to him—not "As you wish" or "I do" or the other small, safe, and chicken ways she had hinted at it in the past. She steeled herself, not because the words needed to be said, but because Eight deserved to have her be brave enough to say them. How could it possibly be harder to tell someone "I love you" than it was to take a human life?

"I love you, too," she said. "I should have told you that a hundred times before."

"You have. You just didn't know it," he said, laughing when she smacked him lightly on the arm.

It felt impossible and good for Barrie to hear that laughter. Impossibly good. Then Eight sobered and switched on the ignition and threw the Range Rover into gear. She tried to think of something to say to bring the laughter back again. To make him happy.

"We're getting close to figuring things out," he said while she was thinking. "We really are. The open house will be good, and the ceremony after that will be fine."

"Said every movie hero ever right before disaster struck," Barrie said.

Eight reached over and covered her hand with his. "I'll take the hero part, but leave the disasters out of it. I'm choosing to believe that it's all going to go according to plan."

Barrie looked out the window, but as Eight turned onto the road and the sun glinted on the river across the highway, she couldn't help seeing Ernesto's staring eyes and the flash of the Fire Carrier's knife. She shuddered. Then she dug through her purse, pulled out her cell phone, and opened the web browser.

"What are you looking up?" Eight glanced over at her.

"Scalping," she said, typing in the letters. "I always thought it was for taking trophies, but the way the Fire Carrier pulled Ernesto's spirit from the top of his head, I can't help wondering if it meant more than that. And Obadiah patted the top of his head when he talked about the conscious soul."

"Scalping was more complicated than taking trophies." Eight pulled the car out onto the main road shaded by overhanging oaks. "It was meant to keep the soul from haunting the living, or keep it from going to rest, or provide proof of retribution, or transfer masculinity from one warrior to another. European settlers were the ones who made it about bounties— and they took Indian scalps. Not that the practice even began with American Indians. It's been done all over the world since ancient times."

"When did you even have time to look that up this morning?" Barrie asked, swiveling toward him in her seat.

"It wasn't this morning." He shrugged and looked away. "I researched it a while back—after you first questioned the story about the Scalping Tree."

Barrie wanted to reach across the car and grab his face and kiss him. Which wouldn't have been safe, so she grinned like an idiot instead. "And did you ever figure out where the tree got the name?"

"No idea. It's possible that local tribes really did come here to pay tribute to the Fire Carrier, like the story says. Or maybe it was the way the Spanish moss hung on the tree. There's no telling. We've seen how stories change—and how people had different motives for telling them. When you're stealing someone's land and screwing them over, I guess it makes sense to paint them as savages to justify what you're doing."

Barrie thought about that, and about Ernesto, nearly all the way to Colesworth Place. Every time there was a lull in the conversation, she came back to it, wondering how many other things in her life she had accepted as truth without a second thought.

At Colesworth Place, there were a few cars in the parking lot already. Eight pulled into the space beside Darrel from the hardware store. Standing in the back of the truck, Darrel tossed a stack of plastic trashcans over the tailgate, and then pushed a bundle of plywood sheets down to a couple of his minions, before glancing over at Eight and Barrie and dipping his chin.

"How y'all doin'?" he asked, wiping his forehead.

The two boys gave Barrie similar embarrassed grins as she said hello and thanked all three of them for helping. Grabbing the end of the plywood bundle, one of them navigated it backward until the other boy took the opposite end, and they waddled up the path with it like penguins, swaying to and fro. Beyond them in the distance, Seven appeared suddenly and without his usual scowl, coming back toward the parking lot from around the corner of the overseer's cabin. He waved and increased his pace.

"Look at that," Barrie whispered to Eight. "He's looking positively friendly. In fact, he's been nice all day. What did you do, drop some valium into his coffee this morning?"

Eight's smile was wistful enough to suggest that he wished this kinder version of his father would stick around. "He actually apologized to Kate and me this morning before Pru called. Apparently, the argument we had last night sank in, and he spent most of the night thinking about the decisions he's made. Thinking about what all of us have said to him the past few days."

Barrie leaned a hip against the fender while Eight got the crates out of the trunk. "So do you forgive him?"

"We've all made a lot of mistakes. There's a narrow line between trying to protect someone and not trusting them enough to protect themselves."

Barrie nodded. "And what about Kate? How's he handling her having the gift and the binding? Can he accept that?"

"I never said *I* was going to accept it, remember? But Obadiah promised you he'd break the Beaufort binding if you helped him find the lodestone. If we can't figure out how to transfer the binding, I'm going to make him keep that promise. No matter how much Kate will hate me for it."

Barrie stared at him, but if he didn't understand that that was only going to do the same thing to Kate that Seven had done to him, she wasn't going to get through to him. She wondered if there was some overprotective gene in the Beaufort men that made it impossible for them to let others make their own mistakes. Even if the mistake wasn't really a mistake at all, just a different point of view.

"Kate will hate you unless you talk to her first. Ask her for her opinion and really listen to her."

"Trust me, we all know exactly how Kate feels. She's never shy about sharing her opinions."

"And yet you're still not listening."

Eight pressing the trunk closed and turned away. They met Seven a few steps up the path. He clapped Eight on the back and nodded at Barrie almost civilly. "I'm glad you're here," he said to Eight. "I'm going to go get Pru, and you can keep an eye on your sister, since she decided to show up to 'help'—as she put it. You know how helpful she can be." He squeezed back into his Jaguar and drove off with a wave.

Barrie and Eight carried the first load of crates out to the lawn below the mansion ruins, where the open house was going to be held. Kate and her friend Blakely were already there working with Sydney and several others.

Smoldering charcoal was spread out on several four-by-six sheets of stiff metal, and a second row of sheeting balanced on top of concrete pillars made up a giant makeshift stove. Beside it, Marie Colesworth and her mother, Jolene, looking decidedly wilted in the heat, stood stirring cauldron-size vats of potatoes and onions. Chunks of corn on the cob and smoked sausage were nearby, ready to be added later, along with crab legs keeping fresh in vats of ice. Already the scent of Old Bay Seasoning, fragrant with bay leaf, celery salt, mustard, and sweet paprika, drifted on the rising steam. Barrie picked out the scents and sorted them in her head, mentally translating everything into recipes, and the smell brought back memories from the first time she had ever come out to Colesworth Place. Somehow, every time she came, she ended up happy to escape. She hoped today would be the exception.

"It's about time you two showed up." Cassie pivoted on the stepladder where she was fitting tea lights into old jars, bottles, and metal kitchen whisks and stringing them like minichandeliers from the branches of the overhanging oaks. "You're the one who suggested all this stupid decorating, but then you left me to do the work."

Eight set down the crates and exchanged a glance with Berg, who was holding Cassie's ladder, but the eyebrow he raised at Cassie lacked real intensity. "I wonder if they sell any kind of a filter that would keep words from falling out of your mouth before they hit your brain? You might want to look into that. We're doing 'all this' to help *you*, in case you haven't noticed."

"Cassie's too embarrassed to say it, so I will." Sydney looked up from where she and Blakely were spraying soda and beer cans with bronze and silver paint to make vases. "Thank you. Seriously. Mama, Cassie, and I all appreciate it."

"You and your mama are very welcome—" Eight said, breaking off with a wince as the speakers hung up in the trees and placed around the buildings gave a sudden screech.

Behind a makeshift table, the DJ waved his hand in apology and moved the headphones from around his neck to cover up his ears. The speakers settled into the smooth rhythm of the Dells' "Oh, What a Night."

Barrie waved at Andrew and the archaeology students, who stood a short distance down from Marie, snapping the heads off bushels of brown Carolina shrimp. Behind them, on top of the ruined mansion's broken pillars, Obadiah's ravens watched it all with apparent fascination. Obadiah himself was seated ten feet from the police tape around the excavation area, while everyone unconsciously gave him—and the dig site—a nice wide berth. He stood up on seeing Barrie and came to meet her, but stopped a few feet away and winced.

"What have you been doing?" he demanded. "You're bleeding energy, and it's off balance. Completely wrong."

Barrie wondered if sins left scars on your soul. Maybe the blackness that had sloughed off from Ernesto's spirit had spilled back onto her somehow and self-defense didn't matter in the cosmic scheme of things.

Eight took Barrie's hand and squeezed it. "What do you mean 'bleeding'?"

"Radiating. As if she's received an infusion and it's too much for her to hold on to all at once—you have to learn to spool it up, and that's not easy. Also, the footprint of energy in the whole area shifted earlier. So once again"—he studied Barrie—"what did you do?"

"Well," she said, "that's a long explanation."

CHAPTER THIRTY

To conserve Obadiah's strength, they moved to the chapel, so that he didn't have to remain invisible. Barrie brought Cassie and Berg along as well, and she gave a modified account of finding the lodestone, one that didn't mention Ernesto or blood or the Fire Carrier. She didn't mention hiding the lodestone, either.

Not that Obadiah didn't guess. "You moved it, didn't you?" he said, pressing himself against the far wall of the chapel as far from Barrie as he could get inside the building. "And the vortex moved with it. That shouldn't be possible. Lodestones conduct energy; they don't control it—unless the stones are what's creating the vortexes and causing the imbalance in the spirit path."

"That's the second time you've used the word 'imbalance,'" Eight said. "Is that dangerous?"

"Those who know how can tune themselves to a spirit path and use it for communication, or regeneration, or travel . . . but all systems and forces in the universe require balance. Including people. Too much of an incompatible type of energy can make a person sicken or even die—physically, mentally, or spiritually."

"Are you trying to say that *Barrie* could die?" Eight's lips went pale. He stormed across the room as if shaking Obadiah would make him unsay the word, and then he caught himself and stood there looking furiously helpless. "How do we fix it?"

"I didn't mean Barrie specifically. She doesn't seem to be experiencing any adverse effects, but that doesn't mean there aren't any. As I suspected, one stone without the other is problematic. I'm having to work harder to balance myself with her around. That's draining my strength, which is the last thing I can afford right now."

Eight exchanged a look with Barrie, a silent message of worry and warning, but the stone didn't feel dangerous to her. She felt fine. Better than fine. In the back of her head, a small voice cautioned that that could have something to do with what Obadiah had said earlier about energy being addictive, while another voice argued that Obadiah could have his own reasons for wanting to pair the stones together. And what had he meant about spooling up the extra energy? How exactly did one do that, and what did it achieve?

Leaning back against the jamb of the open doorway,

she tried to drown out all the chaos in her mind and think. Unfortunately, just being inside the chapel was a reminder that death could creep up too easily. Someone had carted away the chairs and stripped the drapes of black cloth that had decorated the stark, bare walls of the structure for Wyatt's funeral, but beyond the physical hollowness, there was something additional missing. Something less substantial. She finally realized it was the sense of peace, of comfort, that had been present in the few churches she had ever visited. Even the ruined chapel at Watson's Landing had that.

"You mentioned a footprint," she prompted, trying not to let emotion crack her voice.

Obadiah tilted his head to watch her, the gesture reminding her of one of his ravens. "Every place on earth has a unique combination of energy composed of type, frequency, strength, and polarity. That footprint is as good as a geolocator, if you know what to look for. It's similar to how pigeons use the earth's magnetic field to navigate."

"I've read about that," Berg said, standing beside the wall with his hands clasped behind his back. "They have microscopic bits of iron in their inner ears and beaks, and a special protein in their eyes that makes them magneto receptive. That's how they can tell how high they are, where they're headed in relation to the horizon, and the direction they're going."

Cassie peered through the gloom at him. "You're making that up."

"Not at all. There was a time when humans could do the same thing," Obadiah said. "A percentage of the population still can. It requires the genetic makeup as well as opening oneself, admitting you can feel things without understanding the rational reason for it." His expression turned mildly accusing, and he raised his head to look at Barrie. "Twice today there's been a shift in the energy coming from Watson's Landing strong enough for me to feel it from here. You keep asking me for answers, but I can only help you if you are honest with me. What is it that you're hiding?"

"She told you—" Eight began.

Barrie raised a finger to stop him from trying to misdirect. It was time to stop playing cat and mouse with Obadiah. All in or all out—except about Ernesto. No good could come of admitting that.

"The Watson lodestone isn't magnetite." Closing her eyes, she took a breath before she dared to look straight at Obadiah. "Have you ever heard of an *ulunsuti* stone?"

Obadiah straightened away from the wall and took two steps toward her, which brought him into the light streaming through the window. The bones in his face had all sharpened disconcertingly. "Where did you hear that word?"

Gesturing at Eight, Barrie left him to explain about finding the reference to the Serpent Stone in Eliza's letterbook and the research that he had done afterward. Then Barrie explained about what the Fire Carrier had given her and shown her.

Obadiah went very still. "Describe the stone," he said slowly. "And be exact."

Barrie tried not to be afraid. "It's half of a clear crystal the size of my fist. Like a diamond, except there's a vein of impurity in the middle that looks like a bare, twisted branch. The branch is dull silver in the shade and red gold if the sunlight strikes it right."

Obadiah turned to the window and stood with the sun streaming around him. "All *ulunsuti* are sacred," he said, "but most are only quartz fed with blood. There are older stories, though. Old, old stories about stones that came from the great *Uktena* and opened the spirit paths between the past and the future, and between the land of the living and the dead. It is said that those crystals had an impurity in them, a line that could turn red or milky."

"What if it isn't just for communication with the dead? What if there's an actual entrance to the underworld here somewhere and that's what the bargains were meant to protect?" Barrie asked tentatively.

Cassie drummed her fingers on her folded arms. "You

realize how crazy this sounds? You're all jumping to conclusions. And what would any of this have to do with the curse? That's what we're here for."

"Actually, the bindings and the curse are separate. We already knew that." Still watching Obadiah, Barrie gave Cassie an impatient shrug. "The rest makes sense. What if the *yunwi* came here because there was a passage, and then something happened to the stone and they couldn't open the passage to go home again? Maybe the ceremony the Fire Carrier does every night is meant to keep them alive—or keep their magic alive—until the passage opens again."

"But they aren't alive," Cassie said. "They're spirits, so why couldn't they get to the underworld without the stone—if that's where they need to go?"

"What they need can't be that simple. All I know is that there's something specific that the Fire Carrier wants me to do with the *ulunsuti*, and it has to do with the *yunwi*," Barrie insisted.

Berg's eyes gleamed in the shadow by the wall. "Maybe this isn't as crazy as it sounds. The fey are associated with the underground or otherworld in some way in a lot of different cultures. Or there are stories about them disappearing into the hills or retreating from the world. What if—"

"What if," Cassie snapped, "we go back to the reason we're here in the first place? People are going to be arriving any minute for the open house, and we aren't finished preparing—and don't you *dare* try to postpone tonight's ceremony after everything we've done to get Obadiah the energy he needs. I don't care where your *yunwi* or the Fire Carrier belong, as long as it isn't anywhere I can see them. And the same goes for Ayita and Elijah. We're finally supposed to get rid of them and the curse tonight!"

Barrie pushed away from the doorjamb and spun toward Cassie, all the emotion and rage and *unfairness* of everything bubbling up inside her and finally spilling out. "Can you for once think about someone besides yourself, Cassie? There are bigger things in the world than your curse. Things worth protecting."

"Elijah probably died protecting them, if you think about it," Eight said. "Refusing to trap the Fire Carrier. Maybe he knew that the *yunwi* needed whatever magic the Fire Carrier performed each night." Stepping up behind Barrie, Eight rested his hands lightly on her shoulders. "For whatever reason, Elijah gave up his life protecting the magic on Watson Island. So did Ayita, indirectly."

"What does that matter?" Cassie cried. "The point is that we need them to leave!"

"What does it *matter*?" Forgetting about—or at least ignoring—whatever he didn't like about Barrie's energy, Obadiah stalked across the chapel toward Cassie as if he were going to single-handedly throw her out the chapel door. "Ayita was raised to believe blood revenge was the only way to restore harmony once a wrong was committed," he said. "And if Elijah died protecting something important, then killing him was an even bigger wrong." He stopped in front of Cassie. "John Colesworth didn't simply kill Elijah; he prevented Elijah's spirit from getting peace. Forever. Killing John wouldn't have avenged that, so Ayita gave up not only her life but her own peace, her very soul, to create a curse that would avenge Elijah's murder. If you can't acknowledge that and understand what's at stake, then nothing good will come of the ceremony tonight anyway. I won't risk having to destroy whatever is left of Ayita's and Elijah's spirits simply because you are too greedy, vain, and *stupid* to acknowledge that there is anything in the world more important than you are."

Shaking with anger, he veered off and exited through the chapel door before Cassie seemed to collect herself. She ran after him. "I'm sorry. I am sorry. I'll say whatever you need me to say tonight—and I do understand that what John did was unfair and horrible. What more do you want from me?"

Obadiah straightened the lapels of his jacket and brushed off the sleeves before he answered. His voice was very cold. "*I* don't want anything from you. Unfortunately, you're right. There's too much danger in postponing the ceremony, but you had better hope that I can amass enough energy in the next few hours to break the curse *and* destroy the spirits. I'd hoped that an apology from you along with another plea from Daphne and Mary and the threat of the possibility of destruction would sway them—"

"I said I'll apologize—"

"That's not the point," Barrie said, coming up behind her. "Obadiah's not asking you to say the words, Cassie. You have to mean them. What Obadiah is trying to tell you is that you need to let go of the idea of being cursed so that the curse can be released."

CHAPTER THIRTY-ONE

Steam from the pots of boiling shrimp, crab, corn, sausage, and potatoes mingled with the summer humidity and hung in the air like clouds of gnats. Barrie had served so many people that her face felt like it would melt off her bones and leave her teeth gritted in a skeletal smile. Her hair stuck to her temples, and her shirt clung damply to her chest, and she glanced resentfully down at the end of the row of tables where Cassie was holding court like a queen. Smiling and nodding, Cassie was chatting with a group that included Joe Goldstein from the newspaper and Julia Lyons, who had been Lula's very best friend growing up. She was soaking up the attention, back in her element, shining with the light and charm she was able to switch on and off—the light she hadn't bothered to turn on much since Wyatt's death. And of course, she had managed to avoid any semblance of the grunt work that the rest of them were doing.

Although the lawn around them was crowded with people, many of whom Barrie had never seen before, there wasn't a crowd of hundreds. Maybe seventy-five, all told. They gave every appearance of enjoying themselves, though, and they all stayed clear of the excavation area, wandering away when they got too close, as if they'd suddenly remembered they needed to be somewhere else.

Crackling with energy, arms outstretched, and his dreadlocks pulled back in a rubber band, Obadiah walked among them. He touched everyone he passed, his fingers brushing bare arms and hands while they shivered and stopped speaking as if a cold draft had passed across their skin. Energy buzzed in the air, so much that even Barrie felt it.

She wondered how much would be enough. Straining the liquid out of another serving of the low-country boil against the side of the pot, she watched the plastic sheeting at the excavation site billow up off the roof of the buried chamber, despite the heavy bricks in place to hold it down. And around the perimeter, the police tape flapped and shuddered even though the branches in the nearby trees stayed quite still.

Obadiah's ravens felt the disturbance, too, whatever it was. Perched on the columns above the mansion ruins, they had all turned to peer down at the arched brick roof of the buried chamber and the plastic that stirred and rustled above it.

Obadiah claimed he had it under control. Barrie wasn't sure she believed him.

She wished she could go talk to him again, but the next person in line had already moved up and held out a paper bowl. Half-expecting it to be another person she didn't know, Barrie smiled and looked up.

The person who beamed back at her was an elderly woman in a brown dress and matching brown midcalf socks stuffed into leather sandals. "Hello, Barrie, dear. That steam is making you look nearly as pink as the shrimp you're dishing out."

Barrie's smile grew genuine. "Hello, Mrs. Price. How are you?"

The retired teacher appeared much as she had the first time Barrie had met her at the Riverbank Farm and Market, her faded blue eyes were as round as a china doll's and as sharp as ever. Unfortunately, the sour, impatient expression on her granddaughter's face also hadn't changed.

As soon as Barrie had ladled the boil into Mrs. Price's bowl, Lily Beth prodded her grandmother and shouted into her ear, "Go on, Granny. You're holding up the line."

Ignoring her, Barrie held on to the bowl and very slowly added another serving. "It's good to see you, Mrs. Price. I hope you're enjoying yourself."

"I am. Very much. Never thought I'd see myself out here,

though, but I was glad to come for your sake and Pru's." She leaned in closer. "It's nice what you and the Beauforts are doing. Mind you be careful with that Cassie girl, though. Kindness can hurt you if you don't keep a lookout."

"I'm glad people are trying to be friendly."

"Bless your heart, dear. Folks down here are always going to seem friendly. It's what's simmering underneath that you have to worry about. Small towns have long, long memories, and people don't get fresh starts unless they earn them. So far, none of us have seen anything from Cassie or her mama to show they're even aware they've got ground to make up. I know they've had a hard time. That's not the point, though, is it? Suffering yourself doesn't excuse what you do to anyone else." Adjusting her grip on the bowl Barrie handed her, Mrs. Price threw a disapproving look back at Lily Beth. "Of course, no one sees their own actions clearly until after the fact. Not even then, half the time. Lord knows there'd be dust blowing down the streets if we locked up every idiot on Watson Island."

Barrie coughed to disguise a laugh, which faded as Lily Beth placed a hand on her grandmother's back and nudged her again. "Your food's going to be stone cold," Lily Beth said. "And we're not going to find a table if we don't get going, Granny."

Mrs. Price rolled her eyes. "I'm not the one no one wants to eat with. Truth is, people lose their appetite with you nagging at them all the time."

She waggled her fingers at Barrie and moved on while Barrie ladled out a bowl full of crab boil for Lily Beth. After handing it over with a smile intended to—very politely—convey her hope that Lily Beth choked on it, Barrie turned to the next customer, the ginger-haired boy from the QuickMart, and then found herself pushed aside gently as Mary came up and took the ladle from her.

"Child, at the rate you're going, it'll be breakfast before you're through servin' supper. Why don't you let me take over here? You go find Kate and keep her out of trouble."

Barrie pushed her damp curls out of her eyes and tried not to feel guilty for being happy to have a reprieve. "I thought you weren't coming."

"I can change my mind, can't I?" Deftly, Mary grabbed a bowl with one hand and used the other to dip the ladle into the pot. "I got to thinkin' about human nature—about what Daphne said about people not helpin' others. I hate that that's what she thinks, and you can't see the best in people if you never give yourself a chance to see it. So that's why I'm here. Now, don't just stand here. Get goin'."

Barrie grinned and kissed her cheek. "Thank you."

"Don't thank me yet. Kate's down there by the police tape watching that underground room the way a cat sits and watches a mouse hole. You'd better get her away and go ask Obadiah what he's up to, stirrin' things up like that. Least, I

hope it's Obadiah doin' it, or we'd better see to it that all these folks eat fast and get on home."

The plastic sheeting and the police tape were billowing around the dig site, and toed up right to the edge of the tape, Kate stood watching with wide eyes while she nibbled at the food in her bowl. She wasn't in the least contrite when Barrie physically pulled her back.

"Stay clear of here, Kate," Barrie said. "I mean it. Go help your father if you're bored."

"No one else is keeping an eye on what Elijah and Ayita are doing, so I am," Kate said, yawning.

"Obadiah is watching, and so am I. So is your brother. We're all watching—from a safe distance. Now back away." Barrie pointed Kate in the direction of the table where Seven was passing out drinks.

Kate wasn't wrong about Elijah and Ayita, though. With a worried glance at the plastic sheeting, Barrie set off to find Obadiah. He was still weaving slowly back and forth through the crowd, but he looked more like his old self again—as strong and young as he had been the first time Barrie had seen him, only *more*. Energy pulsed off him, making the air shimmer. She crooked her finger at him and turned her back on the crowd to walk around the back of the old kitchen building.

"Whatever's going on in the room is getting worse," she

said when he caught up. "Are you sure you don't need to do something?"

"I *am* doing something," he said tartly. "I'm gathering energy, and I'm keeping people away, and I'm keeping Elijah and Ayita contained, and I'm fighting to keep them from taking any of the energy I'm expending on all that magic."

"Are you positive they aren't taking in any of the energy that's floating around here?"

Obadiah sighed, and his expression was distant—which wasn't precisely reassuring. "I'm doing the very best that I can, *petite*. They're flexing their muscles because they sense all the people. Possibly they're getting a little—a trickle, not a torrent, and it will stay that way unless I'm distracted."

Barrie tried to look unconcerned as she crossed to where Eight and Berg were frying Mary's Vidalia onion corn cake batter under the careful observation of just about every girl in Watson's Point. Circling around behind them, Barrie sidled next to Eight and pulled him aside.

"Do you think we should find a way to wrap this up?" she asked quietly. They both turned to look at the buried room, standing shoulder to shoulder in silence while the plastic seethed and bubbled as if Ayita and Elijah were pushing it up from underneath.

"That flimsy plastic doesn't seem like much of a barrier, does it?" Eight said too calmly. "And Ayita and Elijah have to know that, since Obadiah already pulled them through it once."

Barrie tried to match his even tone, as if they were simply talking about what was good to eat or the chance of rain instead of a forecast that most probably predicted a 70 percent chance of disaster by ten o'clock. "Obadiah managed to push them back down there—and he's kept them sealed inside ever since. He'd be more worried if there was something to worry about. Wouldn't he?"

"You tell me," Eight said. "What's got you concerned?"

"Energy makes you feel good. It's like a high. What if he can't feel the danger the way he should?"

"So what do we do?" Eight gestured across the lawn toward the driveway and the path that led from the parking area, where a steady stream of people had suddenly begun to arrive. "Unfortunately, the rest of the town just decided to show up. Short of shouting 'Fire,' there's no way that we're going to empty this place out for a few hours yet."

Barrie gave brief consideration to committing arson.

Eight smiled almost indulgently at her. "Don't do it, Bear. I'm not sure if it's the Beaufort gift, or just me knowing the devious workings of your mind too well, but I read you loud and clear."

"I wasn't really going to burn anything, but I don't know what else to do."

Coming up unnoticed behind her, someone tapped her

shoulder, and Pru's voice sounded gratingly cheerful, considering Barrie's mood. "This is a party, you two. Remember? At least pretend that you're having fun. Go dance and mingle. Give the people what they came for. I have to hand it to Cassie and Marie, they're doing at least that much."

Barrie and Eight both swiveled around to look where Pru had gestured. Cassie, Marie, and Sydney Colesworth were all greeting people as they came, giving every appearance of being charming and happy to see everyone. In Sydney's case, at least, the charm was genuine.

Feeling ashamed of herself, Barrie made a point of putting aside her own shyness and more reserved nature and stopped to speak to everyone she and Eight passed on the way to the dance floor on the open section of lawn. About a third of the people were already dancing with varying degrees of competence, but it didn't seem to matter to anyone whether they were experts or fudging the basic steps of the Carolina Shag. The DJ stopped briefly to speak to the crowd before putting a new song on, but the four-four shuffling beat recommenced with a song about "dancin', shaggin' on the boulevard." Eight took Barrie's hand and pulled her onto the floor, where she tried to ignore the curious stares.

"Nothing like a command performance, right?" Eight smiled down at her and squeezed her fingers. "Don't worry. You'll be all right. Just follow my lead."

"I bet you say that to all the girls," Barrie said.

"Dancing is the one thing I can do with you where I actually get to lead."

Barrie's smile slipped. "Do you mind?"

"I think that's how it's supposed to be. Real life isn't dancing. You lead sometimes, I lead sometimes, and most of the time, we make it up as we go along."

"Just don't give up on me, okay?" Barrie said.

"Never." Eight drew her into the dance, and they came together. "Haven't you figured out that I'm even more stubborn than you are?"

They danced several songs, and then as the tempo slowed, he glanced around and pulled Barrie away, back behind the icehouse, out of sight. Deep in the shadows with the old brick building at her back, the twilight didn't allow for much visibility, but Barrie felt unexpectedly apprehensive, as if what she felt for him would shine out of her so that he would see into her heart even more clearly than usual. It made looking at him painful for anything longer than the briefest flashes of lips, and throat, and green, beautiful eyes that tried to hold on to hers.

"I'm going to kiss you now," he said.

"I suspected that might be the case."

"Do you mind?"

"Very rarely. Not today," she said, mindful that tomorrows didn't come with guarantees.

His mouth came down too slowly. Then talk and thought fell away, and Barrie's breath came in sharp, ragged bursts that she told herself explained the pain in her chest and the heat that rushed through her nerves like wind rippling across the surface of the river. She wondered if she would ever grow desensitized to Eight, to this overwhelming sense of being swept up in a tide of want and unexpectedness and possibility.

Needing to be even closer, to feel even more, she worked her hands up under the loosened tails of Eight's shirt and splayed her fingers against his heated skin, following the smooth swells of muscle and the long curve of his spine as he sucked in his breath. She smiled against his mouth, reveling in the sense that the feeling was mutual, in the power that gave her, knowing that even if he made her disoriented and vulnerable, she could do the same to him.

His heart pounded against her ear. He kissed her more deeply, his tongue playing gently against hers, his lips moving smoothly, hungrily. Any space that had been between them vanished. Doubts vanished. Because who could doubt with the way he held her? He was simultaneously fierce and gentle, protective and respectful, strong without being overwhelming. Slipping beneath the elastic of her bra, his thumbs brushed the sides of her breasts, softly, almost reverently, his breathing as ragged as hers. Then he stepped away.

"We have to stop." His voice was rough. "This isn't the place, and we have people counting on us."

"You're so sexy when you're responsible," she said with a sigh, and everything crashed back into place when his warmth wasn't there anymore. "It's a good thing you don't have to want what I want anymore, or else we'd be hiding back here and never coming back out."

He frowned and then raised his head and gazed out into the trees. "We just have to tackle this one problem at a time, Bear. Curse first, and then the rest of it, and eventually there won't be any problems left to solve. Don't you think?"

"Thinking," Barrie said, "seems to be your job. I work better on instinct, and listening. The gift and the *yunwi* keep showing me that over and over, and I haven't been paying enough attention." She shook her head. "So here's what I feel. I *feel* that as long as you and I are talking, as long as we listen to each other, we are going to be all right, whatever comes. At some point, the bindings may break, and our gifts may be lost . . . or you'll get the binding and the gift again, I don't know. I may even lose the magic at Watson's Landing. But whatever happens, you and I will still be magic together."

Eight lifted both hands to her face and then kissed her again. "You're a wise woman, Barrie Watson. And now let's finish mending fences so we can get everyone out of here. The faster they're gone, the sooner Obadiah can try to bind Ayita and Elijah and really get the party started."

Clasping her hand in his, he led her back around the side of the icehouse. Briefly the scene seemed picturesque and almost peaceful, with the music playing and most of the population of Watson Island milling around the lawn dressed in their best Sunday-go-to-the-beach clothes in a bright array of colors.

But when Barrie and Eight were halfway back to where the tables were set up, the plastic sheeting over the buried room yanked itself loose on one side, sending the bricks that held it flying with enough force that one shattered against a tree. Then the other side pulled free and the sheet hurtled away, gaining altitude until it snagged on the lights of the sheriff's patrol car parked nearby.

CHAPTER THIRTY-TWO

The deputies were both standing beside the car when the sheeting flew at them. One of the deputies, an officer with a sunburn and the muscles of a weight lifter, reached over and grabbed the plastic, then stood looking around in consternation. Across the distance and twilight haze, it was impossible to read his lips and tell what he said to the second deputy, but Barrie expected it had something to do with the utter lack of wind anywhere else. No sooner had she had that thought, though, than Obadiah raised both arms and a hurricane-strength wind came out of nowhere, blowing across the entire Colesworth property.

The trees swayed, and branches whipped back and forth. Mary jumped back as the stiff metal from the top portion of the improvised stove upended itself. Folding lawn chairs skittered across the grass and smashed into tables and buildings. The dig crew had packed away their tents and most of the equipment and stored it all in the overseer's cabin, but they'd left out some of the giant sifting screens and buckets. Those blew over and smashed against the wall. People grabbed purses, bags, children, and one another and ran toward the buildings.

But there wasn't any shelter there, either. The wind raced along the walls and pushed them away, then abruptly changed direction and sent debris that had fallen to the ground flying back at the crowd, pushing them in the direction of the parking area. In less than fifteen minutes, the open house was over, and apart from the deputies, who had retreated into their car, and the dig crew, who had all run into the overseer's cabin, Cassie and her family, Pru, Barrie, Mary, Daphne, and the Beauforts were the only people who remained. They huddled together inside the kitchen house.

Obadiah had moved to stand beside the police tape, immune to the wind as if he had fashioned an invisible bubble around himself. Not so much as a single dreadlock lifted off his shoulders.

Barrie ran to join him, with Eight right behind her. The others hesitated briefly. Then, heads down and shoulders braced, they all ran over too. The wind stopped as they reached him, just stopped, while everywhere around them the branches still lashed in the trees and churned the paper plates, bowls, and plastic cups along the ground.

"What is this?" Seven gestured at the branches lashing above the patrol car, where the deputies sat. "Did you raise this wind to stop the party?"

"Better that than something worse. In any case, I had all the energy I could store," Obadiah said. "It doesn't matter—"

"It does," Barrie said. "Of course it does. This wasn't only supposed to be about the magic. We wanted it to be a real chance for people to come together at the same time."

"When magic goes wrong, it has to take precedence. You wouldn't have wanted to see anyone get hurt. Seriously hurt. More than the few cuts, bumps, and bruises they're nursing now. In any case, they'll understand. They'll drive five minutes, the wind will clear, and the Weather Channel will decide it was a microburst. A few people will assume it was the curse, but after a day or two or three, the people at the subdivision will have retrieved their lost window screens and the covers for their backyard grills. They'll forget all about it and move on. Now," he said, "let me concentrate." Climbing over what remained of the police tape, he pulled a bag of the white clay powder from his pocket.

"What are you doing?" Eight asked. "It's not even dark yet. You said it would be easier to bind Ayita and Elijah and break the curse at night."

"We don't have the time to wait for 'easier,' and whatever I lose in strength, I'll make up by conserving the energy it would take to try to keep Ayita and Elijah contained until then. Now, where's the girl?" He looked around and crooked a finger at a visibly reluctant Cassie. "You stand over there." He pointed right behind the police tape. "And you"—he gestured to Eight—"move back and let me work."

As Cassie and Eight took their positions, Barrie glanced back at the two sheriff's deputies who were paying no attention to the activity at the dig site. Obadiah must have worked his magic on them already.

Chanting softly, he dusted the white chalk onto the ground to form the cosmogram. The air rippled with energy. Obadiah glowed again, brighter than Barrie had ever seen him. The sight made her jittery and cold, and the chant and the motions pricked every hair on her body to attention.

"You're shivering again." Eight slid his arm around her shoulders.

"I'm entitled. This wasn't the way things were supposed to go," she whispered back.

She looked down the row of faces beside her, all of them tense, all of them doggedly hiding their fear. Pru, Seven, Kate, Mary, Daphne, Marie, Sydney, and Berg. Seven had one arm around Pru's waist and held Kate firmly in front of him with the other, and Mary and Daphne's hands were clasped. Kate bounced on the balls of her feet, watching every move that Obadiah made, and Berg watched as if he was memorizing everything so that he could run off and jot it in a notebook. Around her own shoulders, Eight's muscles were as tense as steel.

Only Cassie and her family stood apart from the others. Cassie's cheeks shone pale again after her earlier animation, as if being "on" all afternoon had taken its toll.

Obadiah raised his head and lifted his hands. A swell in energy made the air heavy and resonant, as if he had pushed the atmosphere itself with the motion and left the atoms explosively charged. Eight pulled Barrie closer.

She knew it was coming; she should have expected it. Yet her stomach still dropped when Obadiah pulled a raven from the empty sky. She braced herself when he stroked the bird with this thumb, then twisted deftly and threw it, dead, into the air, only to have it evaporate, leaving nothing but soft black feathers curling to the ground to sink into the earth and disappear.

Was the raven real? Or a magical construct, a representation of Obadiah's own pain?

She was too afraid to ask the question.

Like a kettle at full boil, a dark mist streamed through the small hole in the roof of the buried room. Where it was still anchored to the stakes, the police tape curled and snapped, the DO NOT CROSS text blurring into a tangle of illegible letters. Then, faster than before, much faster, Ayita and Elijah formed and hovered a foot above the arched bricks, tethered by the dark threads that tied them to their physical remains inside the room.

The wind stopped. The cups, napkins, and plastic cutlery that had been flying around dropped back onto the grass, and the trees went still. Obadiah rolled his head on his neck, and his dreadlocks spilled across his shoulders.

"Talk," he said to Cassie. "Apologize."

Ayita and Elijah looked at Cassie, then briefly at Marie, Sydney, and Barrie, before swiveling their heads back to where Cassie stood. Their forms swelled, and they surged forward, but instead of catching on the tethers the way they had before, they ran into an invisible barrier that flattened their shapes as if they'd hit a sheet of glass. That only made them more furious. Ayita's eyes slitted, and she bared her teeth.

Cassie recoiled, then stiffened her back and stepped forward. "I'm sorry," she said. "On behalf of the whole Colesworth family, I'm sorry for what John did to you. It was horrible and awful, and I wish it had never happened."

Barrie thought Eight was going to cut off the circulation to her brain, he was squeezing her shoulders so tightly. Ayita and Elijah grew bigger, more opaque, and rushed at the barrier again, making themselves thin and thinner as they strained.

"Tell them something genuine, girl!" Obadiah's voice cracked like a peal of thunder. "Make an effort. I don't want to have to destroy them because you couldn't bring yourself to care."

"Why *should* I care?" Cassie snarled at him, her eyes white-rimmed with fear. "Mary and Daphne couldn't talk them into giving up the curse. I don't see why you expect that I can say something that will make a difference. Who says they even deserve to have peace in their afterlife? Just do the damned exorcism or whatever it takes to destroy them and be done with it. Remove the curse like you promised."

"Cassie, you don't mean that." Berg moved over to where she stood and turned her to face him. "I know you don't mean it. You're scared and you're lashing out, but that's not you talking."

Tears streamed down Cassie's face. "You don't know who I am. What do you all want from me? Why can't you leave me out of it?"

Disengaging from Eight, Barrie moved over, too. "What you said, Cassie, that's the right question. Think. What do Ayita and Elijah want? They don't seem to care that Mary and her family are suffering as much as they care that your family suffers. That's why Obadiah thinks you need to be the one to try to convince them to give the curse up. So think what they need to hear. When I found the skeletons of my great-uncle Luke and his fiancée, I saw their ghosts repeating the moment of their deaths, over and over again. Once I found them and acknowledged who they were and what happened to them, that was enough to make them stop. And we haven't seen the ghosts of Charlotte's parents since we discovered her skeleton was down there, either."

Reaching out toward Cassie, she found herself wanting to grab her cousin and shake her, and she lowered her hands and clasped them in front of her. Because how could Cassie not feel the pain Ayita and Elijah had suffered, trapped down in that room for all these years? The Fire Carrier had even set Ernesto's spirit free before putting his body underground.

"You have to try to help them," Barrie added, wishing she had some magic words to make Cassie understand. "Acknowledge what they want. Make an effort now, or you won't want to live with yourself. You'll always wonder if there was more that you could have done."

Obadiah was beginning to show signs of strain. Sweat beaded at his temples, and the muscles of his neck corded as he looked back over his shoulder, and Ayita and Elijah looked more solid and clear than ever, as if whatever strength he was expending was going straight to them.

"It's going to take more than acknowledgment," he said. "Ayita and Elijah aren't residual echoes or spirits reaching back from the other side. They're sentient. They may have lost most of their humanity to their anger, but we still have to treat them as human beings. They want to know they've had their vengeance, and that it has been enough. Obviously, that's the problem. It hasn't been, or the girl would care."

"I do care! Of course I care." Cassie turned to Berg, as if he were the one she needed to convince. "But I'm not the one who killed them, and they're the ones who've been hurting *my* family. Why can't any of you understand that? The curse is hurting *us*!"

"It's hurting Mary and her family, too, but you don't see her complaining about it!" Kate said. "Grow up, Cassie."

It was instinct for Barrie to want to defend Cassie, knowing what she had been through—what Ryder had done to her. Had that been the curse? Or simply the product of Wyatt's greed? Or was it possible to separate one from the other at all? Where did the cycle stop? So many people had hurt one another.

"Kate's right." Barrie caught Cassie's hand to get her attention. "'Sorry' isn't a synonym for 'guilty.' It's a way to say you're listening. Think outside your own skin, and take responsibility for what you're doing instead of wallowing in what they—or other people—have done to you. Acknowledge the good things. The rest of us have worked all day, and half the town came out here for the sake of making peace. Eight and I got you out of juvenile detention after you locked us in the tunnel. We've all been here trying to help you, but what have you been doing to help yourself? Obadiah claims magic always requires sacrifice. Maybe he's been right all along about using the gold to appease the spirits. Think of it as giving up something that's important to you for a chance to make something better. For a chance to set Ayita and Elijah free so that you can be free yourself."

She was looking at Ayita and Elijah as she said the words, but in her mind, she saw the image of the Fire Carrier cutting Ernesto loose, the look of regret and concern that the Fire Carrier had given her. She saw his relief as he had blown Ernesto's spirit toward the river.

Maybe letting the spirits go was as much about the dead as it was about those left behind. Ghosts came in all different guises, from specters to echoes to memories. The way Barrie felt at having killed Ernesto. The ghost of Watson's Landing that Lula had re-created for herself in San Francisco. Mark's voice in Barrie's head. The regret she felt about not knowing her mother better, about having been angry at Lula for so long when what Barrie should have felt was pity. The dead could haunt the living in countless ways.

"All right," Cassie said. "Sure. I'll give Mary some of the gold." She turned to face Ayita and Elijah, and she gave a vehement nod.

Her expression closed and furious, Mary put her hands on her hips and shook her head. "We don't want your money!"

"Take it, Mary. It isn't Colesworth money," Obadiah said. "It never was."

Cassie's face went red. "If she doesn't want it, then what

the hell are you nagging at me for? Fine. I'll give it to charity, I don't care. I'll give up half of all of all the gold that's down there. Or all of it. There? Does that make you any happier?"

Silence fell. Obadiah turned toward her, his hands falling and his face slack with surprise.

"She's lying," Kate said. "That's not what she wants."

Seven grabbed Kate's arm, and Obadiah's head whipped toward her. At the same time, Ayita and Elijah pitched forward, bulldozing through Obadiah's invisible barrier with an audible *pop*, until they hit the end of the tethers that tied them to their bones.

The roof of the buried chamber exploded. Bricks, shards of wood, bones, and a burst of gold and silver coins fountained upward and then fell down again in a dangerous rain. Eight grabbed Barrie's hand and started to run. Berg pushed Cassie out of the way, shielding her body with his own and grunting as a brick slammed into the back of his head. He staggered but kept running. Seven herded Mary and Pru and Daphne in front of him to safety, jerking Kate forcibly by the collar as she strained to see what was happening.

Obadiah moved in the opposite direction, stepping in front of Ayita and Elijah with his arms raised and shaking with strain. The glow of his skin had dimmed, where in the descending darkness it should have been brighter. He was using up energy too fast.

Whatever new barrier he had erected against Ayita and Elijah, they hit it and flattened out, pressing against it and trying to force their way through. Obadiah's concentration was intact this time, though. It held.

Berg stumbled and fell to one knee, bleeding heavily from the head. Barrie ran to help, while Eight snatched up several clean napkins that had blown off a stack and landed nearby. He handed them to Cassie. "Hold these on the wound and press down hard," he said to her. Then he and Barrie helped Berg to sit on the ground a safe distance—or at least a safer distance—away from Ayita and Elijah.

"How do you feel?" Eight asked.

"I'll be all right. Is it finished?" Berg swiveled to look behind him, where Obadiah was starting the whole ceremony over again, walking the perimeter of the cosmogram and clapping and chanting.

Barrie felt sick, physically and in her heart. Not just at the blood and the ruins of what Obadiah had been trying to do, but at the sight of Charlotte's bones scattered on the ground, and the dark, gaping hole where the roof of the buried chamber had been. And at the tethers that still anchored Elijah and Ayita and wouldn't let them go.

"Wait," she said suddenly. Turning back to Berg, she asked, "Do you have your knife with you?"

"What do you need it for?" He shifted onto one hip and

removed the knife from his pocket. He opened the blade before handing it to her by the thick, black handle.

Barrie shook her head and ran to Obadiah. "I read somewhere," she lied, "that you could cut a soul free of its body and blow it toward water to set it free. Is that true?"

"I've never heard of the precise practice, but that doesn't mean it isn't true. Going to water is sacred or purifying in some cultures, and the river can be a path for the dead." Shifting his attention to her briefly, Obadiah raised his brows, but then continued walking the outer circle of the cosmogram. "Still, even if it worked, there's nothing to say Ayita and Elijah wouldn't come back, and then they wouldn't have anything restraining them."

Berg raised his eyes. "Unless we destroy the bones and the things that hold them here. That's possible, now that the room is open, isn't it?"

"It's worth trying." Obadiah snapped his fingers at Seven and Kate. "Run and get as much of that lighter fluid and kindling as you can find. And the charcoal."

Cassie straightened, still holding the bloody napkins she'd been pressing against Berg's head. "You can't burn the room! The rest of the gold is still down there—"

"Then that's your sacrifice, isn't it?" Mary moved up beside her and caught Cassie's chin between her thumb and forefinger. "Look around you, child. Look at how everyone else has come together to save a couple of lost souls, and if you can't see that that's worth more than any amount of gold, then money's all you'll ever have. That's a poorer life than anybody deserves to live. Don't you see what the curse is really about? It's easier to hate than it is to forgive when someone has hurt you. For three hundred years, your family has stored up every slight and grievance and used them to justify every bit of harm you do to someone else. You end up hurting yourself more than you harm anyone else that way. You end up hating yourself."

Cassie looked back at Mary expressionlessly. Then her cheeks reddened and she dropped her eyes. Her shoulders trembled as she nodded and turned away.

"I don't want to be like that," she said. "I *am* sorry."

Kate, Daphne, and Sydney each had brought back armloads of wood and supplies, and stopped beside Obadiah. Seven carried three partially opened bags of charcoal. "What now? Just throw everything down there?"

"Not yet. Open the bags and hold them ready. Barrie, hand me that knife." Obadiah took a can of lighter fluid from Seven and poured some onto both sides of the blade. Then he looked around, as if realizing he didn't have a match. Seven held up a long-handled lighter and flicked the button. Holding the blade inside the small orange flame, Obadiah waited until the fire burned itself out. Then he gestured and the wind rose, gusting in bursts that flung Ayita and Elijah to the limit of their restraints, across to the far side of the jagged hole and just beyond the corner closest to the river. After edging around the hole to reach them, Obadiah stooped and sawed at the tether that held Ayita while he chanted.

Ayita gave a wordless shriek, her face contorted with desperation, and stretched back to stop him. But he flicked his wrist and braced himself. Severing the connection, he set her free, whispering words that Barrie couldn't hear or understand. Then the knife flashed again over Elijah's tether. Eyes closed in concentration, Obadiah flung his arms toward the river.

The air howled around him, casting both spirits away. Ayita fought, doubling over as if trying to swim against the current, but the blast of wind pressed against her chest and stomach and carried her farther and farther, the oily darkness of her rage growing lighter. Elijah had stopped fighting. He bowed his head, and his eyes locked on Obadiah with an expression of some indefinable mixture of gratitude and sorrow and fear. Then he raised his head and turned toward Daphne and Mary, and the shapelessness of his face, the intensity in his eyes, reminded Barrie of the *yunwi*. Mary and Daphne nodded, crying quietly, but already Elijah and Ayita were fading into the distance and the dusk and becoming as insubstantial as cirrus clouds, thinning and stretching as they disappeared.

It was too quiet suddenly. Barrie didn't realize at first that the wind had died down. She knew only that there was silence and stillness where before there had been too much of everything. There were no insect or bird sounds, nothing of the usual night noises, only a faint distant vibration, as if the stars that had emerged while she'd been too busy to notice were humming softly. Eight's fingers were wrapped tight around her own, and Obadiah gathered himself in anticipation, as if he needed to be ready to fight in case Ayita and Elijah worked their way back.

But they were gone; Barrie was sure of it. An uneasy itch across her skin had disappeared. The change was no more dramatic than that, a stilling of the air, a thing felt rather than seen. Hate was invisible, anyway.

"Burn it," Obadiah said without taking his eyes from the air above the river.

Seven and the others threw the wood and charcoal down into the room on top of the splintered, rotting chests and the scattered, shining coins, and Pru and Marie Colesworth squeezed lighter fluid down onto the floor and the walls, every surface they could find. Eight retrieved another napkin that had caught on one of the grid stakes at the excavation site, and Barrie, Daphne, and Mary ran to get several more. They crumpled them tightly into balls, then set them alight and threw them down into the buried room.

The lighter fluid caught with a *whoosh*. The wood and charcoal, and whatever had been down in the room, caught, sending up a thick, choking plume of smoke, pushing everyone back, but they stayed, none of them speaking. Watching.

Finally Obadiah turned back, and in the orange glow of the flames, tears shone gold on the dark skin of his cheeks. Chanting, he pushed his hands together and lowered them, crouching down and extending them over the burning hole that had been Charlotte and Elijah and Ayita's grave. He opened his arms in a gesture of supplication, and his chant reached a crescendo.

The room erupted. Obadiah fell back, slapping at embers that landed on his clothes, and everyone else rushed backward from the searing heat.

"What was that?" Mary asked, hurrying to help Obadiah. Mary gestured to Daphne, and they both helped him up and walked him to where the others waited. Barrie rushed forward, but Eight stopped her.

"Let them be. They need healing, too," he said.

"So is the curse gone? Is it finally over?" Cassie asked, pressing the napkins back against Berg's head as he sagged wearily. The napkins were red with blood.

Obadiah held up his hand for silence and hobbled to the edge of the room again. He peered down now that the flames had subsided back to a low and steady fire. He listened while energy beaded off him like sweat.

"Do you feel anything?" Cassie asked.

"A disturbance that sounds suspiciously like *you*," Obadiah hissed. "Be quiet."

Cassie clamped her mouth closed in a huff. Then after a moment, he dropped his hands.

"The curse is gone." Obadiah sounded surprised and, oddly, a little apprehensive. Cassie gave a gasp and dropped the napkins to hug Berg, and Daphne clapped her hands.

But a sudden clutch of panic sent Barrie's heart racing and made it impossible to fill her lungs. Eight took her other hand so that he was holding both of hers, holding her steady.

"Do you still feel anything lost?" he asked. "Don't panic. Tell me what you feel."

She let out a gust of breath, but there was nothing. She felt nothing at first, nothing except the usual headache that came from the binding, and beneath that a faint tug that still pulled her to Obadiah.

CHAPTER THIRTY-THREE

Eight helped Pru off the *Away* as Barrie unclipped her own life vest and threw it onto the seat. The sky was weepy and overcast, and that seemed somehow appropriate after what had happened the night before. Barrie's throat was still hoarse from the choking smoke and the crying. She still wasn't sure what she'd been crying for once she'd climbed into bed. Relief and release, and all the years of pain and hatred that no amount of fire could burn away. Obadiah had removed the spell that had held the archaeologists and the sheriff's deputies, and convinced them all that the mess in the room had come from a freak bolt of lightning from his fictional microburst. Barrie and Pru and the Beauforts had left them all to gather up the gold, bones, and questions, while Mary and Daphne tended to Obadiah.

But they still weren't done.

Stepping off the Beaufort dock, Barrie started up the long, gentle slope of the hill that Pru was already climbing. Across on the Watson side of the river, the *yunwi* had gathered to pace at the end of the pier, as if they were afraid to let Barrie out of their sight. She felt the same fear in reverse. Which was senseless and stupid, but maybe also a sense of premonition that she couldn't shake.

Eight squeezed her hand when he caught up after tying off the boat. He looked rumpled and tired, as if it had been far too many nights since he'd slept, but there was a sense of calm about him that she'd almost forgotten he could wear like a cloak.

"Were you up all night reading Eliza's letterbooks again?" she asked, reaching out to brush two fingers across his cheek.

"No. I slept some, but I was curious about a few things, so I looked them up on the computer, and then Kate came in and wanted to talk."

Barrie wound her fingers through his. "What about?"

He pulled her to him, head dipping down to kiss her with a certainty that left her reeling. Her breathing was thin and shallow—too shallow, maybe, because when he pulled away, she had to fight for the strength to keep from leaning against him. He gathered her into his arms and held her, her head burrowed against his pounding heart.

There was safety tucked in Eight's arms that had nothing to do with him protecting her from physical danger. It was the reassurance of having someone who had chosen to stand beside her. She had never felt that before with anyone but Mark, but now she had Pru and Eight, and despite all that had happened, they had helped her discover a core of strength inside herself. She wondered if that strength had always been there waiting for her to find it. Pulling away, she started walking.

Eight adjusted his steps to keep pace beside her. "Kate's convinced herself that the fact that Beaufort Hall is still here and still belongs to us is only because of the bargain," he said. "She's afraid to lose it if we give the Fire Carrier back our half of the *ulunsuti* stone."

Barrie wondered how you could ever go back to a world without magic.

"I know," she said. "Last night, that first minute after the curse broke, it all came crashing down on me. How much I can't bear the thought of losing the *yunwi* and this place. In theory, I know we could figure out how to make it work. Lula left money, and Pru says there's still a lot in the Watson estate. We could invest better. She has a whole strategy we talked about on the way home last night, but lots of people have tried to keep big places like this going and haven't been able to. Maybe Thomas and Robert were smart enough to foresee that. But if the *yunwi* don't belong here, if they're meant to be somewhere else, then Kate and I have no right to cling to the magic that's keeping them at Watson's Landing."

"I did find out something about that last night," Eight said. "At least, it might be related. I went back to reread the stories about medicine people studying with the *yunwi*, and found a legend about a whole tribe of Cherokee who went to live in a 'country' inside Pilot Mountain and were never seen again. Also, there are references to a vortex of energy at Pilot Mountain *and* a ley line running through it. And there's a sanctuary for nesting ravens at the top."

"Ravens?"

"In ancient times, the high priest of war among the Cherokee was called the Raven when he scouted. I'm not sure what's coincidence anymore, but I was hoping I'd find something about a spirit path or a ley line that connected Pilot Mountain and Blood Mountain to Watson Island. There was nothing like that. The whole concept of ley lines is so nebulous. But then I remembered what Obadiah and Berg had said about electromagnetism."

"What does that have to do with the *yunwi*?" Barrie asked as they slipped through the high hedge and emerged in the Beaufort garden.

"Remember how Obadiah said that the *ulunsuti* crystals were paths to communicating between the past and the future? Pilot Mountain is made of rose quartz, and you said

Berg mentioned experiments about crystals in the Stonehenge standing stones. I looked that up, and there are theories about the crystals creating an electromagnetic field and setting up some kind of harmonic resonance, a frequency of vibration that can move particles at faster than light speed."

Barrie came to a stop beside the French doors that led into a sunny morning room off the garden. She remembered too clearly the feeling of being broken into nothing and everything, feeling small and enormous and part of everything around her. There was also the sound beyond sound—the way the stone and the energy made her feel. The *feeling* of sound whenever the *yunwi* tried to communicate with her.

"I don't pretend to speak science, but are you trying to say that the *ulunsuti* use sound to break things into energy? And *that's* how the living can pass through to the underworld?"

"Or move around within our world, maybe." Eight pulled Barrie up the steps. "Searching for keywords like 'magnetism' and 'electromagnetism' and 'lines' and anything else I could think of, I eventually found a map on the National Oceanic and Atmospheric Administration website that shows how the lines of force that a compass follows have changed over the years. If you go back to 1590, which is the earliest date they have, one of those lines ran almost between here and Blood Mountain. A few years before that, it would probably have run straight through here. And now, that same line goes directly from here to Pilot Mountain. What if that's how the *yunwi* got stuck? They came here, and the line shifted. What if that line is our spirit path?"

"It's a lot of 'ifs.'"

Eight's eyes darkened. "You think it's a stupid idea?"

"No!" Barrie grabbed his hands and held them. "I think it's brilliant. You must have been up all night researching it— I just don't know how we prove any of it, or how it helps us. And why wouldn't anyone have put this together before?"

He gave her hands a squeeze and pulled them to his lips. "We have an advantage, Bear. We know that magic is real, and we know that the Cherokee stories have a foundation of truth. We have the *yunwi* and the Fire Carrier, and we know about Ayita's daughter, not to mention Obadiah bringing in the belief systems from Angola and the Congo, and Berg telling us about feng shui and pigeons and all the other pieces of the puzzle. We can see the common denominators because we're looking for them. Maybe it's a case of forest and trees."

"But even if you're right," Barrie said, trying to wrap her mind around it all, "if the *ulunsuti* stone is broken, it can't produce the same frequency as when it was whole. Can it?"

"Maybe that's why the Fire Carrier wants you to bring it back together."

CHAPTER THIRTY-FOUR

Sunlight through the windows struck the strands of crystals hanging from the Georgian chandelier and cast prisms across every surface of the dining room at Beaufort Hall. In contrast, the table resembled that of a war room, with half a dozen laptops and all three letterbooks, not to mention notebooks and pencils and glasses of sweet tea that stood sweating on coasters.

Seven had donned a pair of glasses that Barrie had never seen him wear, and he looked both scholarly and protective as he and Pru sat beside each other, each with a letterbook in front of them. Barrie stole a look at Eight. She wondered if in twenty-odd years, he would look like Seven. A part of her instantly refused the thought, because Seven was too . . . what? "Narrow-minded" and "unhappy" were the best words that came to mind, but glancing at him now, with his body angled toward Pru's as if he couldn't help but slip closer, the stern-ness and rigidity that usually made him so formidable were softened. Pru, too, seemed content as she concentrated on the computer screen with a pencil tucked behind her ear.

Mary had stayed behind at Watson's Landing, attending to the final touches for the restaurant opening, but Obadiah sat beside Daphne. He still pulsed with leftover energy that seemed to make him fidgety. His fingers drummed, and his toes tapped, and his finger pointed too forcefully to things on Daphne's laptop whenever he saw something of interest.

For the seventh time in the space of an hour, Daphne pulled the laptop out of reach. "Please don't touch the screen that hard."

"Well, click that link, then," he said.

"You want to do the searching?"

"No, you type." Obadiah folded his arms and tried unsuc-cessfully not to look impatient.

To Barrie's right, Berg suppressed a grin. His head was still bandaged, and according to the emergency room doctor, he was mildly concussed, but he had refused point-blank not to be included. Since he wasn't allowed to read, he had logged into the university library on his own laptop, and Cassie was doing the reading for him. They were in charge of searching for crys-tals and magnetism and every scientific aspect they could to try to prove or disprove Eight's idea. So far, they'd come up empty.

Barrie had been skimming the letterbook and quietly reading aloud to Eight anything that Eliza had mentioned about Inola, or the things that the older woman had taught her. In addition to medical knowledge, Inola had given advice on planting and psychology and love and family. She had become a counselor as well as a confidante for Eliza, who had often been lonely and frustrated, especially with her brother, James, who had risen in his regiment and been too fond of the military life to give it up for the sedate life of a Carolina plantation owner. Eight scribbled notes in the shorthand style that he'd developed for himself, and Barrie was waiting for him to catch up, when Kate suddenly drew in a breath.

"Hey," Kate said. "I think I found something." She waited until everyone sat back in their chairs before she picked up the book again and read:

Memorandum.

Fulfilled my promise to Inola, and the tunnel is completed today. I have also left a small boat on the other side of our Island, so that she or the others who belong to Daniel Colesworth can use it to escape, if the need arises. The treatment Inola receives cannot be tolerated, but what am I to do? Along with the beads for her needlework, I have gifted her a pearl necklace, which she can take apart and hide more easily than gold. She fears to keep the necklace with her, so we placed it in a sturdy box, which she hid at the base of the oak where the Fire Carrier resides. I hesitate to say that my brother, James, is such a man, but I cannot trust what he would do if faced with the choice of helping her. It is not his Bravery I question, nor his Compassion, but his sense of the rule of law above all else. Too many men hide behind laws when doing so will inconvenience them a little less.

The Deed is done. I have accepted my dear Robert's proposal of Marriage, for James received the letter this afternoon confirming his release from his Regiment. Having tried three times to board a boat to go back to the West Indias, and having been forced each time by the Headaches to disembark, he had no choice but to resign his Commission. The welfare of our small fey spirits, Inola assures me, depends upon keeping my great-uncle's bargain. This applies equally to the Beauforts, so my own Robert's blood shall bind their half of the Serpent Stone, and my sons, should God be generous to give them to me, and their children, and their children's children, will reside at Beaufort Hall and carry forward the trust that the Fire Carrier has placed in us. I hope, for his sake, and for that of my beloved fey, that the wait shall not be too long before conditions are favorable for their return. Inola's belief in God, whom she calls the Apportioner, assures her that such a time is coming. She emerges from her silent meditations with the yunwi *with renewed strength and faith each time.*

"So it *was* Eliza who added the binding to the bargains. Against her brother's will," Barrie said, not really surprised at all.

"And possibly against Robert's, if you read between the lines. I like her. A lot," Kate said.

"You would. You're just like her," said Seven unhappily.

Barrie rubbed her temple, trying to think. "It sounds like it was the *yunwi* who told Inola—and maybe even the Fire Carrier—what to do about the binding, but the stone was split before Inola did that. Does Eliza write any more about how or why that happened?"

"I doubt Eliza would explain that in later pages, since the stone was already split before she wrote this memo," Kate said. "But I'll keep looking."

Berg had been busy directing Cassie to type something on the computer, but he'd clearly been listening with at least half an ear. Leaning forward, he rested his elbows on the table. "That part about the silent meditations is interesting. Some of the Cherokee legends mention fasting before speaking to the *yunwi* or going into their caverns. That could be a form of meditation. But that part about the open country inside the mountains, and layers of cities above them inside the mountain . . . I can't help wondering if that doesn't sound more like an otherworld or alternate universes than the traditional concept of the underworld. I was never much good at physics, but it sounds consistent with superstring theory, the idea of multiple universes stacked or floating above one another."

"Aren't we getting too literal with other people's stories?" Pru asked, tapping her pencil. "We don't know what they mean."

"Medicine people aren't only doctors among the Cherokee. They're priests and a lot more rolled up together. Maybe the stories are written on many different levels all at once," Eight said.

"Most stories are, if you take the time to consider them," Obadiah said. "We'd all be better off if we did more of that." He took the computer from Daphne, then stared at the keyboard as if it were a more dangerous kind of magic than the one he practiced. In the end he slid it back to her. "Myths and folktales especially aren't always meant to be taken literally. Fasting can be a means of spiritual cleansing. It's possible that what the stories mean is that only those with a clean spirit can speak to the *yunwi*, and only those chosen will travel with them. That could be either a suggestion—or a warning."

"What kind of warning?" Seven asked.

"You keep asking questions as if there are easily digestible answers, something as simplistic as the sound bites you're used to on television. True answers are never simple. I've spent a hundred years gathering knowledge, and I've barely begun to scratch the surface."

Pushing back her chair, Pru stood up and swept a stray curl behind her ear. Her fingers left a smudge of pencil lead across her temple. "Maybe we could all use a little break right about now. And a snack. Does anyone want some sandwiches?"

"I'll help," Cassie said, jumping up.

Pru gave a nod of thanks. "I just wish I knew if we're getting any closer. We find trickles of information, and hints of stories—and they all lead to more questions. We don't even know for certain if the Beaufort half of the binding stone is in the fountain, much less whether it's safe to touch it. Or what to do with the stone even if we manage to get it put back together."

"It has to be possible, or the Fire Carrier wouldn't have asked me to do it," Barrie said.

"You're placing a lot of trust in a spirit. One who, by your own admission, is most likely desperate. You're not always the best judge of character, remember?" Seven cast a meaningful glance at Cassie's retreating back.

"People keep saying that." Barrie's chin came up. "But in the end, I've been right most of the time. I know you all think I'm naïve for believing in the wrong people, but even if that comes back to haunt me now and then, I'd still rather believe the best of human nature. I don't know if that's the gift talking, or—" She had been rubbing her temples, and now her fingers stilled. "Of course. God, I'm an idiot."

Eight stopped scowling at the letterbook and raised his head. "Of course *what*?"

"We keep talking about focus and trances and concentration, and I keep admitting that there are too many questions, but I never put that all together with why my gift sometimes tells me what I need to find. When I came in here looking for Eliza's books, I was still just searching for anything lost, because I didn't know what I was looking *for*. The more I thought about Eliza, the more things got easier to find—and then I reached straight for her letterbooks, because that was where the pull was strongest. It's like when we needed the candles at the hardware store. Or even knowing how to get to the hardware store. Or asking the *yunwi* one question at a time—I can't find an answer until I know the right question to ask."

She snatched up the other two letterbooks, stacked them with her own, and concentrated on a single query: *Why are the* yunwi *here?*

The pull was instant, a hint of pressure so faint that it would have been easy to overlook. Tracing it back to the letterbook Pru had been reading, Barrie opened the cover, held the pages upright, and ran her thumb across the top. She let the pages fall away to the left until a tug of protest made her open the book at that point and pulled her attention to a letter. Then she read aloud:

February 10, 1742

To My Father,

I received the congratulations of all our Acquaintance on the happy news of your being promoted yet again. If indeed it is happy news, for it must mean that you shall come home even less frequently.

We have less news from England these past three months and more. With no shipping, we suppose there must be a new Embargo. We expect the Spaniards to come North from Saint Augustine in a matter of months. Mr. Oglethorpe harries their forts and lately killed two prisoners.

I have continued to search for confirmation of Inola's story about the settlement on Parris Island. Robert and I have traveled to the site of the failed French settlement of Charlesfort and the nearby Spanish capital of Saint Elena. Mr. Oglethorpe writes to assure me that the Spanish did abandon it sometime between 1585 and 1590, retreating back to lower Florida after repeated attacks by Indian tribes that had joined together. The island lies a matter of miles from our own, so as in other things, Inola's story is proven correct.

Knowing that the yunwi *came here to help the Indians protect themselves, I cannot help but hope more fervently that the Beaufort and Watson stones together will continue to aid the Fire Carrier's ceremony. May it keep our fey friends strong until the source of their power returns. I cannot bear the thought of being the one to lose them, or that our family should fail them in any way.*

The others sat in silence when Barrie had finished reading, and she took a moment to process. Almost three hundred years ago, Eliza had written Barrie's own feelings into words.

"I knew it." Eight swung to his feet. "I knew it had to have something to do with the energy shifting—that's the exact timeline. The *yunwi* came here and got stuck when the line between here and Blood Mountain shifted away from the island, and for whatever reason, they couldn't simply walk and look for the energy themselves. They must have hunkered down to wait for the energy to come back again, but now that it has, the stone is split between Watson's Landing and Beaufort Hall, and no one remembers or understands what needs to be done."

"But why split the stone in the first place? Couldn't the Fire Carrier have used just any rock to bind the two families?" Daphne asked.

Obadiah rolled a pencil between his fingers. "Maybe he split it to make sure that the *ulunsuti*—and all that power—didn't fall into the wrong hands. Things that important rarely vanish without leaving rumors that someone will eventually want to chase. Look at Cassie's Civil War treasure. How could the Fire Carrier be certain who had heard of the stone from Ayita or Elijah, or Inola for that matter? Splitting it and using it to bind the gifts was brilliant—the rumors passed down in my family and any energy anyone felt in the area would have been associated with lodestones, not the *ulunsuti*."

"Are we still talking about electromagnetic energy? Or is it magnetic energy?" Kate asked.

"They're closely related," Berg told her.

"Then maybe," Daphne said, "what we need is a compass."

Everyone turned to gape at her. Kate pushed back her chair and ran across the room to the butler's pantry. A moment later, there was a sound of drawers opening and slamming shut. Seven rose and walked toward the door, but Kate's head popped back out again. "Dad, where's that old Boy Scout compass you used to have in here?" she asked.

CHAPTER THIRTY-FIVE

Kate insisted on holding the compass, and they all followed her to the fountain while she watched the needle adjust itself. She stopped when the needle pointed at a spot on the fountain wall.

"It's either right here or on the other side of the fountain," she said. "I can't tell which."

Seven put his hand out and crooked his fingers imperiously. "Let me see."

Kate rolled her eyes but handed the compass over. Seven turned to Obadiah. "Even if she's right," he said, "how do we know the stone is safe to touch? Maybe you ought to be the one who—"

"Even standing here is draining my energy worse than being near Barrie yesterday," Obadiah said.

"I can do it," Daphne and Barrie both said at once.

Barrie jumped in front of Daphne. "We know what happened to Seven's father, but I've proven I can touch the Watson half. Logically, it has to be me. Also, the Fire Carrier asked me to do it."

"I could ask you a question about jumping off of bridges," Eight said with his jaw set, "but you'd only ignore me, wouldn't you? You don't know what the Fire Carrier asked you to do. And maybe our half of the *ulunsuti* needs a Beaufort the same way your half needed a Watson."

"Then why would your great-grandfather have died?" Jerking free of Eight's hold, Barrie dropped to her knees and groped the side of the fountain's belowground basin beneath the froth of water. As before, the swell of energy in the area made it impossible to feel much else. Or maybe that was the chill in the water numbing her hands. Her fingers tingled, and her head was pounding, and she was nearly ready to get up and try the other side of the fountain when she leaned a little bit farther down and felt a bulge. Probing it with her fingertips, she identified the triangular shape, like the base of a pyramid, and she cupped it with her hand as she had when she'd grasped the Watson half.

The warmth she had felt before wasn't there this time; there was no pulse of life or hint of moment. What was different?

Blood. Blood magic. With the Watson stone, she'd had Ernesto's blood on her fingers. Pulling her hand out of the water, Barrie reached for a piece of gravel on the ground.

Eight grasped her shoulder. "What are you doing?"

"I think the stone needs blood to be activated."

"Not *your* blood," he said. "The priests used animal blood."

"Maybe any kind will do, but I don't have a dead deer handy. Mine will work." Barrie had only her gut to go by. How did she separate what was instinct, versus good intentions, versus her gift pointing her in the right direction? All she knew was that she couldn't risk losing Daphne or any of the Beauforts, Eight least of all. She forced herself to fully look at him. "You have to trust me. You do, don't you?"

"Depends on what you're plotting."

"Oh, for the love of Jesus." Daphne stepped over to a rose-bush and broke off a stem, then scratched the thin skin on the back of her wrist repeatedly and deeply against the thorns. Blood welled to the surface slowly and glistened like gems against her skin.

There hadn't been more than a few drops of Ernesto's blood on Barrie's hands, but any blood she took from Daphne was going to wash off the second she dipped her hand into the water. On the pretext of rubbing her own left hand back and forth across Daphne's bloody wrist, she reached down, grabbed the stem of the rose, and let the thorns bite deep into her skin. Then she plunged her hand back into the fountain and felt for the *ulunsuti* once again. It pulsed, but instead of growing warmer, it grew colder the longer that she held it. A painful, throbbing, and ugly cold.

She couldn't replicate whatever the Fire Carrier had done when he'd laid his hand over hers, but she tried to remember the pull of energy she'd felt, the feeling of connection. In the end, she focused on her finding gift, pushing at the question the way that she had when she'd searched the letterbook.

The stone began to move, pressing lightly against her hand, then gaining strength until it was free and firmly in Barrie's grasp. She pulled it out of the fountain and held it up triumphantly.

Obadiah backed away.

"Now what?" Daphne asked.

"Now we take it to Watson's Landing and see what happens," Barrie said.

CHAPTER THIRTY-SIX

Energy swelled with every footstep Barrie took. At first, it was nothing more than a pull similar to what she had felt moving the stone through the Watson woods, but as she walked down the sloping lawn toward the river, it grew strong enough to stretch and squeeze the air around her, raising a wind that shifted like a corkscrew as she walked, first in one direction and then another. She felt alternately heavy and weightless, as if gravity came and went, and the *ulunsuti* pulled her feet faster than she wanted to go, until she was almost running toward the water.

The stone also began to warm and vibrate, digging the sharp edges of itself into her palm and sending pulses like electrical charges up her arm. She was afraid to look down at it, afraid to look back at Pru and Kate and the others, for fear of what she would find written on their faces.

She walked and Eight kept pace beside her. A hundred feet from the river, as she leaned against a sudden, chaotic gust of wind, he slipped his arm around her shoulders. "Stop, Bear! Whatever's happening, it isn't right. You need to go back."

He tried to pull her to a stop, but the draw of the stone toward the river was too much—she couldn't ignore it. Wind whipped in front of her, bending the bushes and flattening the grass, and glancing back at Obadiah and Pru, she expected the same turbulence. But behind the stone, the only disturbance came from Pru and the others as they rushed after her, shouting for her to stop.

Obadiah was the closest. He nodded as their eyes met. "Hold on to it tightly," he shouted, his voice raised to be heard above the wind. "It's the energy trying to balance itself. Negative reaching for positive."

"Is that dangerous?" Eight yelled back.

"Might be even worse if you try to stop it now," Obadiah called.

Barrie concentrated on keeping up with her feet as the stone kept pulling. "Then promise me," she shouted back at him, "whatever happens, don't let anyone stop me. Back when I first agreed to help you, you swore you would break the Beaufort binding. You gave your word!"

"This wasn't what I meant!" he shouted, and behind him, Pru was screaming, too, but she was farther away, and the wind around Barrie whipped her words away so that Barrie couldn't hear them.

The river was approaching too quickly. Barrie threw her whole weight back against the slope of the hill, trying to slow her feet. "Get the boat for me," she yelled to Eight. "Untie it, start the motor, and then get off. Hurry, or I'll end up in the river!"

"Just let go of the stone. Release it." Eight grasped Barrie's shoulders and yanked her back, but they had reached the bottom of the hill, and the stone drew her harder, faster. She struggled against the pull. It *hurt* to fight.

Light and energy and something curved and reflective, as iridescent as a soap bubble, formed in front of the stone, crackling into existence and gleaming beyond the edge of her vision before winking out again, something she felt she would see if she only concentrated a little bit harder. Something that flattened the grass on the ground and sank the earth beneath an enormous, invisible weight, and then vanished as if it had never been. The thought sparked a memory, as if there were a connection Barrie should have been making, some clue that she was missing.

Across the river, the *yunwi* had gathered on the dock, and they all stood oddly still. Their shapes were gathering sub-stance, as if they were becoming not just more visible but solid. And down by the Watson woods, the Fire Carrier had come out in broad daylight and stood at the edge of the marsh grass on the bank. But they weren't telling her to stop.

The stone burrowed into Barrie's hand, sending scalding vibrations of pain up her arm. She didn't want to argue. "Eight, please get the boat. I don't think I can hold on much longer. You have to trust me. The *yunwi* and the Fire Carrier wouldn't let me do this if it weren't necessary. You need to believe in me."

"I do. Of course I do." He studied the water where the displacement effect was more pronounced than on the grass. A trough was forming between the stone in Barrie's hand and the spot on the other bank near where she had hidden the other stone. The depression deepened as Barrie drew closer. The shimmer in the air had became more pronounced.

Eight sprinted forward, and Barrie struggled even harder to slow her footsteps. Behind her, Pru and Seven and the others were frozen in place—Obadiah keeping his word and holding them back. Their faces were anguished, and Barrie felt guilty at their helplessness.

The stone pulled her onto the dock, where waves of the receding tide splashed over both sides, as if the river was flowing both toward the ocean and backward simultaneously, like the water sloshing in a tub. The *Away* swayed wildly at her moorings, her mast creaking and the hull slapping against the pilings.

Fighting to give Eight time, Barrie sat down and dug her heels into the boards of the dock, trying to slow the pull. But she was growing weaker, the stone taking her strength, the way Obadiah had drained her energy. The painful vibration along her body was nothing like the exhilarating feeling of tapping into the spirit path or even holding the Watson stone. The pull dragged her forward an inch at a time, the fabric of her shorts catching on the edges of the boards.

Then suddenly the pressure eased. The air still whipped, the stone still pulled, but Barrie felt an opposing force behind her, holding her back. She labored to turn her head, and found Obadiah close behind her. "What are you doing?"

"I'll hold you until the boy has the boat ready." His words came to her clipped and tight, bitten off by concentration.

"Let the stone go, Barrie." Seven's voice was a roar above the wind.

"Barrie, please let go!" The naked fear on Pru's face broke Barrie's heart.

Seven wore impotent rage like a second skin. Kate, too, looked furious, and Barrie imagined how she must feel. She tried not to think that every inch closer that the stone came to Watson's Landing was one bit closer to having the magic there and at Beaufort Hall stripped away.

She wanted to reassure Kate and Pru, reassure them all, that it was going to be okay, but she couldn't be certain that it would. She knew only that the *yunwi* and the Fire Carrier had been waiting all this time for the energy to come back and for someone to join the stones back together, and she couldn't let them down.

Instead of giving Pru or Kate promises she couldn't keep, she turned to Berg and Obadiah. "Do either of you know what's happening?"

"Something like a wormhole, maybe," Berg yelled. "If there's a universe layered above us, think of it as if someone is pushing the eraser end of a pencil through the top sheet of paper toward the sheet below it. Eventually, the top sheet rips apart and things can move through."

Barrie's body felt like it was tearing open, aching from the vibrations that rattled her teeth, and the pressure had grown worse since Obadiah had stopped her from moving forward. "Let me go," she shouted back to Obadiah. "The stone is getting hotter the longer I sit here. I'm not going to be able to hold on to it if you don't let go."

Eight had reached the *Away* and was hurrying to untie the ropes. Obadiah released Barrie, and she shot forward, dragged by the stone as she struggled to her feet. Her legs moved faster than she wanted them to, and her eyes struggled to focus through air that had grown strangely thick.

Heat scorched her hand and up her arm, and her skin felt like it was being flayed from her in strips. She hurtled toward the churning river, and beneath her the dock creaked and shook, and the *Away* knocked back and forth. Across the water and behind the Fire Carrier, a branch split off a tree and shot skyward, before plummeting suddenly as the wind that had carried it had simply stilled. Then the wind gusted again, more fiercely than ever. An entire cypress tree uprooted, burst up through the air, and eventually splashed back into the water, too.

The *ulunsuti* gave another lurch. Barrie stumbled the last feet to the boat. Eight caught her and lowered her down inside the hull.

"You sure you want to do this?" he asked, searching her face.

"Just tell me quickly how it works before you get out. How do I steer and stop?"

He used his foot to shove off. "You don't," he shouted, running toward the motor. "I'm going with you."

"Both of you get out of there," Seven shouted behind them. "It's not safe out on the water."

Barrie barely had time to register the words before someone launched off the dock and landed in the boat behind her. She turned, expecting Seven, but it was Obadiah. The boat lurched again, and her legs gave out as Eight revved the motor and the boat tore away from the dock, rocking fiercely in the waves and spray.

Obadiah crouched on the bottom of the *Away* a moment, his shiny suit beading with water. Then he pitched himself up onto the seat beside her. "Give me the stone, *petite,* before you hurt yourself."

"You're the one who can't touch it, remember?" Barrie spoke through gritted teeth.

"I'm the only logical one to hold it. I still have energy spooled up from yesterday, and there's no shortage of it swirling all around us. I was being selfish and cautious before. Anyway, you were right. The curse is gone, and this is what Ayita would have wanted."

Barrie hesitated, part of her even now still afraid to trust her instinct. Maybe this, though, was what her gift had been leading her toward all along.

Obadiah's hand shook, and his face twisted in pain as he took the stone. Moving quickly, he went to the bow of the *Away* and lay down so that no part of the boat was between the two halves of the *ulunsuti.* The water immediately beneath the boat went calm.

CHAPTER THIRTY-SEVEN

Barrie crawled to the front of the boat, ignoring Eight's shouts to stop, and sat as close to Obadiah as she dared. He lay flat on top of the hatch, the stone stretched above the water in his right hand, while his left hand clutched the railing. His lips were moving, but the wind ripped away the words.

Behind the Fire Carrier, several more trees tore out of the marshy soil at the edge of the woods, leaving the cypress where Barrie had put the other half of the *ulunsuti* stone in direct line of sight. A limb broke off that tree as she watched, but the Fire Carrier stood anchored in the marsh grass as if his magic or the pluff mud were keeping him glued into the ground. The tree limb swirled up into the air, turning end over end, and then it dropped back into the river as the air suddenly went still again. The waves died, and the Santisto returned to its normal lazy perambulation toward the ocean, except for a deep dip in the water off to Obadiah's right, where it appeared as if a heavy bowl had become solid and was pressing the water down.

Between one bounce of the boat and the next, the transient shimmer of air had snapped into place, and both water and air flowed around a clear sphere that had formed between the two halves of the *ulunsuti* stone. Within the orb, a place was visible, distorted by the curvature, a world with a double crescent moon and a night sky lit with stars so bright that they winked and flickered like gems above a dark surface, and farther away, the vague glow of distant lights.

"Do you see that?" Eight's voice was hushed but audible in the sudden quiet. With his attention focused on the bubble, the boat veered downriver. The image inside the bubble changed, zooming in closer to the dark surface as if it were flying toward them, until Eight caught his navigational lapse and turned the steering wheel back toward the dock. The image grew smaller again.

Barrie jumped up and ran toward Eight, gesturing toward the woods. "Never mind the dock. Go toward the woods as if you're going to land where the trees flew away."

He didn't ask for an explanation, simply turned the boat in the direction she was pointing and throttled back the engine so that the approach was slow and gentle. Obadiah sat up, moving into a cross-legged position on top of the hatch, with the crystal held up, cut surface out.

The sphere above the water grew smaller as they approached, and the image inside changed as if they were in an airplane and were looking through a porthole that bent and distorted the ground beyond the window. And it *was* ground. Grass and trees, a meadow of some kind, with the lights and stars gradually shifting out of sight and the foreground shifting closer until it seemed as if someone could step through it from one place to another.

"Don't you dare," Eight said, and Barrie stopped, becoming aware for the first time that she had drifted to the side of the boat with her hand stretched out, drawn to the sphere in a way that was probably dangerous.

Obadiah face was gray, and his hand shook with strain, as if the pull between the stones had intensified. Then Barrie felt the energy shift and settle in place, though the wild wind and turbulence didn't seem to diminish. She felt the change more in the connectedness she had with the world around her, the sense of energy flowing to her and through her that she had first felt while sitting with her eyes closed on Miranda's back. On the shore, the *yunwi* were running toward the Fire Carrier, or toward the sphere, Barrie couldn't tell which. It was too far out in the water for them to reach it, but their excitement was obvious. They, too, felt the sense of *rightness*.

"I thought we were supposed to bring the two halves of the stone together," she said, "but we aren't. This is far enough," she said with certainty. "Can you move in toward shore without changing the distance between the two pieces of the stone?"

"That's a good idea," Obadiah said. "I suspect we don't want to change the size of that thing by much, or whatever is supposed to happen isn't going to work."

"You really think it's a portal of some kind, or a wormhole?" Eight asked.

"Other world, another world, underworld. Doesn't much matter what you call it. It's clearly a gateway to someplace else," Obadiah said.

Eight had throttled back the engine even more, inching toward shore with barely enough power to cut across the flow of the current. Barrie shouted directions, left or right, trying to keep the ground within the sphere as level as possible with the ground on the shore at Watson's Landing. Eight cut the motor entirely and steered through the marsh grass until he ran aground in the mud, but the sphere was still too far out in the water.

"I'll take it from here." Obadiah jumped off the boat into the water and waded toward shore, the silk of his dark shirt and pants gleaming like a raven's feathers, but his movement was slow and labored in the water and heavy mud.

Eight dropped the anchor and jumped over the side of the *Away* to help Barrie out. She pushed toward the shore in Obadiah's wake, careful not to touch the sphere, although she could feel it humming, vibrating through her the way the Scalping Tree had pulled her under. The Beaufort stone was still drawing her toward the Watson half.

There were more *yunwi* now. Their shapes were clearer than she had ever seen them, their eyes no longer filled with fire but dark, kind, and slightly wary instead, in a way that reminded Barrie of the way that Miranda had looked at her the first time they had seen each other, as if the mare had hoped Barrie could be trusted but wasn't entirely certain.

Tears had begun to slip down Barrie's face, and she wasn't sure who she was crying for, the *yunwi*, or herself, or Watson's Landing, or the Fire Carrier, or maybe for the world because she had a sense that it would be a poorer place when the *yunwi* left it. And they *were* leaving, because the two crescent moons didn't belong on Pilot Mountain, or Blood Mountain, or anywhere else in Barrie's own universe. Nor did she think the *yunwi* were coming back. The stories never spoke of the fey coming back once they retreated to their worlds in the hollow hills or their islands in the mist, and it seemed to her that was the biggest tragedy, to know that if she could only have learned to listen to them and understand them, maybe they wouldn't have had to leave at all.

Maybe that was the real tragedy of humanity. Understanding, actual communication, happened only when both participants were at the right resonance, and that was rare. People who shouted that they knew the answers incited resentment, and people who spoke too quietly never convinced anyone to listen. Those who were selfless were dismissed as fools, while those who served themselves and knew how to put on a crocodile's smile were the ones who too often spoke with certainty and united their followers through anger. But the good, the deep truth and quiet beauty of the world, that was offered in a whisper.

His back to her, Obadiah had stopped knee-deep in the water. Beyond this, the mud at the bank had bowed around the sphere so that the ground within it was almost at a perfect level with the ground outside. The Fire Carrier had moved back into the trees and was coming around the other side to stand with the *yunwi*, watching Barrie as she splashed past Obadiah.

The *yunwi* reached for her, their high-cheeked, narrow faces and wide, deep-set eyes finally clear. Barrie tried to memorize them, take memory snapshots until she'd be able to sketch them, but they pushed toward her, milling the way they usually did. She searched for the ones she thought she knew, the ones who always came with her, but she couldn't recognize them, and somehow that was one of the worst things of all.

They pressed close, and she wanted to hold them, but she couldn't. Not if they needed to go. They drew back again, and the Fire Carrier came forward. Barrie tried to think what to say to someone who had stood sentinel for more than four hundred years without complaining, without giving up, even after death. Someone who had watched the Watsons forget their promise, and had had the patience to hope that someday someone would remember.

There were no words, so she said the only thing she could: "Thank you."

The Fire Carrier nodded, and he and one of the *yunwi* stepped up to the sphere and dissolved into a shimmer of mist until they stood in the darkness on the other side, whole again and bathed in the glow of the double moons. One by one, the *yunwi* moved through, until only two were left. When they stood in front of her, Barrie knew.

"Thank you," she repeated, wishing that two words could stand in place of a thousand.

"Thank you," they said. Their voices were still soundless, coming from somewhere far away.

One took Barrie's hand and held it, while the other cupped

her palm. A searing sensation, just past the edge of pain, bored into Barrie's skin and burrowed deeper, racing along the nerve endings up her arm and spreading, radiating, sinking into her blood until it felt like her veins ran with fire.

Flames flickered an inch above her skin, a small bloom of fire three inches in diameter that hovered without visible support. One of the *yunwi* pressed Barrie's fingers closed around it, and the fire went out, but they watched her expectantly, waiting for her to—what? Find it again?

Barrie smiled as she had the thought. Because finding it was as simple as thinking and connecting to the energy that flowed through her to the world beyond. She reached inside herself, and the flame sprang forth. She watched it burn, and when she looked up, the *yunwi* had slipped into the mist inside the sphere. They appeared a moment later on the other side.

There was no long good-bye. No good-bye at all. The bubble shuddered and the image corkscrewed, twisting in on itself and then fracturing with an accompanying burst of wind and spray of water.

A splash behind Barrie made her turn in time to see Obadiah collapse. His face caved in, and for an instant he was an old man falling into the shallow river. He sank beneath the waves, and a raven emerged, water spraying from its feathers in a burst of silver droplets that rained back onto the surface. The bird flew to the *Away*, circled once around the mast, and then winged up the Santisto toward the bridge, following the dark river away from the Atlantic. A single black feather floated away, and then the water went glass-still.

CHAPTER THIRTY-EIGHT

It was a long service, but they had decided to do just one memorial for everyone. There were the boxed urns with Mark's ashes and the newly cremated bones of Luke and Twila, and in honor of Obadiah, Barrie had placed the raven's feather she had found in the water inside a wooden box. She had hunted through the woods behind the stables and found an eagle feather, too, which she had included in another box for the Fire Carrier. And last, she and Pru had talked long into the night about what to do for Lula. In the end, as much as Barrie was reluctant to part with any kind of history, Lula's letters had felt so personal and the grief in them had felt so stark that it seemed wrong to leave them for future generations who couldn't possibly understand because they hadn't known Lula Watson.

Barrie and Pru had taken turns rereading each letter aloud to each other and burning them afterward in a bowl to catch the ashes. That final reading had been more about forgiveness and regret, and Barrie felt lighter as each page flared and vanished into smoke. Then she and Pru had gathered the ashes and placed those in a memorial box as well. The boxes were made of a wood called purpleheart, which had struck Barrie as appropriate when she'd ordered them online. Each person they were burying, literally or figuratively, had been in some way a wounded soul.

Pastor Nelson's sermon was about hope and forgiveness, but also about going home. Barrie had taken apart some old necklaces of Lula's and Mark's, and Pru had scavenged the crystal prisms from an old chandelier. Eight contributed a box of shells and pale blue sea glass he'd been collecting from the beach, and then the three of them had strung everything together to make wind chimes that hung in the branches of the oak tree that formed the ruined chapel's living roof. The chimes whispered in the wind while the pastor spoke, and on the walls of the chapel, the *yunwi*'s roses still tangled with moonflower vines, and it was all perfect, except that it was still good-bye.

Along the wall outside the chapel where the graves had been dug, the mourners stood together while Mary sang "Amazing Grace." Then they each poured a handful of soil onto the boxes laid out in their individual deep, small graves.

Barrie went first, her heart as fragile as tissue paper and ready to tear apart. Pru squeezed her hand before taking her own turn, and Seven was next, then Eight, Kate, Daphne, Berg, Cassie, Sydney, Marie Colesworth, and her mother, Jolene Landry. Mrs. Price had come with Lily Beth; and Lula's best friend, Julia Lyons, was there, as well as Alyssa Evans from the barn, Cassie's friend Gilly, Darrel from the hardware store, and Joe Goldstein from the local paper. Ms. Conley had come from Seven's office, and a host of others that Barrie had seen or met at Colesworth Place or various spots in town. Even Andrew Bey had taken a break and left the police and the archaeology students to man the mess at the excavation site on their own while he came over. At some point soon, there would be a funeral for Charlotte Colesworth, too. But that was for the future and in a different chapel.

Barrie stood with Eight, his hand wrapped around hers, his arm steady against her shoulder. The Beaufort gift was gone, and their half of the *ulunsuti* stone was lost somewhere beneath the waters of the Santisto where even Barrie couldn't find it, but he still seemed to know that she didn't need words, or sympathy. Just company.

The mourners stayed for a funeral lunch of buttermilk fried chicken and corn bread dressing, shipwreck casserole, and twice-baked beans. For dessert, there was hummingbird cake and banana pudding, and a whoopie pie cake that Pru had made to sweeten up Seven's disposition. No one seemed in a hurry to leave. Maybe that was the point of a funeral, to spend time celebrating life. Then, finally, Mary's Honda was the last car to disappear down the oak-lined lane, and the Spanish moss swaying in the trees above was hidden, briefly, in a veil of dust. There were no *yunwi* to see her off.

"You know what?" Pru said.

Barrie glanced at her sideways. "What?"

"We have nothing to do this evening. And nothing to do tomorrow until one o'clock, when Mary and Daphne come back over to do the final prep for the restaurant opening. You've talked to all the lottery winners for the weekend already, haven't you?"

"Yes, and Eight and I explained about the charity, and us matching the funds. I made it clear that Daphne's scholarship wasn't coming out of their share of the money, because you and I would cover that, so that their money would go toward tutoring and funding scholarship recipients next semester who had nothing to do with us or the restaurant. Everyone was fine with that."

"Good," Pru said.

Seven headed back up the steps, holding his hand out to help Pru up. "When are you going to tell Mary and Daphne about the partnership? Do you need me to bring the paperwork in the morning?"

"Yes, let's do that when they first get here tomorrow. Then hopefully they'll enjoy the opening even more," Pru said.

Eight's face lit with a sudden grin. "So then we really have nothing planned for tonight?"

"It's wonderful, isn't it?" Pru said.

"In that case, I'm going to steal Barrie away." Eight was already tugging Barrie toward the foyer. "Come on, Bear."

"Care to tell me where we're going?"

He pointed her toward the stairs to the second floor. "Just put your best shoes on."

She dressed hurriedly, and he was in the sitting room when she came back downstairs. Instead of going in right away, she went to the kitchen to tell Pru good-bye. Pushing the door open, she found Pru standing at the back door looking out toward the river, with Seven's arms wrapped around her from behind. They seemed . . . content. Peaceful. Which had never been a word Barrie associated with Seven Beaufort.

Barrie thought of how empty Watson's Landing would feel when Pru moved to Beaufort Hall. That was going to have to happen in the future, Barrie was certain of it. Pru and Seven would work things out. But there would still be the restaurant four nights a week beneath the fairy lights in the Watson garden, and in the off-season, there would be big family dinners around the kitchen table. It wouldn't matter which kitchen table. Without the Beaufort binding, they could make it work.

Pru would make the kitchen at Beaufort equally welcoming.

That sense of home and welcome was one of the things Barrie loved most about Pru and Watson's Landing. That was Pru's gift, and Mark'd had it, too. Maybe anywhere that combined food, love, and conversation wove its own kind of kitchen magic.

Clearing her throat, Barrie pushed the door open the rest of the way and stood on the threshold. "Maybe you two should go out somewhere while Eight and I are gone. I didn't see either of you eat a single thing all day. Not to mention that Pru and I talked about how long it had been since she'd been to Bobby Joe's. You ought to go tonight."

"Thanks for the thought, but I can manage to make my own dates," Seven said, though he softened the words with a smile.

"In that case, carry on. Just don't wait another twenty years." Barrie kissed Pru's cheek briefly before heading back out to where Eight was waiting. The sound of Pru and Seven laughing together softly followed her through the swinging door.

Eight had settled himself on the striped silk sofa and was reading something on his phone. He stood up and grinned as he took in her red Louboutin Jeffersons that looked like high-heeled boat shoes, only cuter. "Nice shoes. You going sailing?"

"I don't know. Am I? I was hoping for more dancing, actually. Maybe somewhere in Columbia?"

"I think we can arrange that." He kissed her and then

pulled back. "You know, moments like this, I kind of miss having you call me 'baseball guy.'"

"In that case, ask me nicely."

He pulled her closer. "If we both promise not to be idiots in the future, would you call me 'baseball guy' again?"

"Kiss me nicely," Barrie said.

"You're awfully bossy."

"And you, baseball guy, are still doing too much talking."

Eight laughed, and then he bent and kissed her with the perfect amount of heat to leave her dizzy and breathless, making her lose herself again in a sense of having been found, of having been seen and heard and known. She pulled back, flushed and warm, not entirely certain whether the feeling was emotional or physical. Flexing her palm, she concentrated on the sensation of heat, of fire, and the small flames gathered beneath her skin and emerged to crackle along her palm.

"I'm not sure I'll ever get used to that," Eight said.

"Good, then I'll always be able to remind you that there are still magical things in the world. Things bigger and more important than we are."

"Kate is heartbroken at the idea of never seeing or hearing things the same way she did before she lost the binding."

"I know, and I'm sorry. I'm relieved that I don't have to. Losing my connection to Watson's Landing would have left me feeling very lonely."

"You don't ever have to feel alone. The world could disintegrate into a swirl of energy, and I'd still find you amid the chaos. I'm always going to find you." Eight pushed her hair back and kissed the tip of her nose.

Barrie's heart swelled until it squeezed her lungs. Since words were impossible, she slid her arms around Eight's waist and tilted her face up to meet him as his mouth descended. He kissed her slowly, and then more feverishly, until she groaned with want and need and skin that was as alive as—more alive than—any magic had ever made her feel.

That was the thing about both people and magic, about love and family—they were all unpredictable and imperfect. They all kept secrets, and both anger and love were more about what you felt about yourself than about what you felt about anyone else. Barrie had healed so much since coming to Watson's Landing, found so many things and lost so many, but as long as she knew who she was, she was never going to lose the way home to the people who loved her.

Eight kissed the skin between her neck and shoulder, tiny kisses like a necklace of promises. His hand knitted with hers, and he led her outside and down the steps to his car, pausing only to shoo the white peacock off the hood before he held the passenger door open so she could slip inside. She glanced back at the house as they drove down the oak-lined alley. The shadows were lengthening, but they were ordinary shadows, still and empty, and that was bittersweet. In Barrie's hand, though, and in her heart, she still felt the quiet pulse of magic that was both a legacy and a promise for the future. Magic still ran through her blood, and magic was all around her.

Author's Note

Perhaps no other part of the country has as much of a possibility to connect history, myth, magic, and real, current concerns as the beautiful Lowcountry near Charleston, South Carolina. That area and its past touches on so much of what makes this country great as well as what we, as a nation, have forgotten, willfully buried, or need to overcome. Its rich history and mix of cultures is a perfect opportunity to explore how stories, legends, historical interpretations, and even historical records change and disappear over time while family, people, and basic human needs, fears, and failures remain the same.

That idea of finding connections forms the core of the Heirs of Watson Island series. I used the legacy and mystery of a fictionalized legend about the Fire Carrier and wove together several real stories about the *Yûñwï Tsunsdi'*, the Cherokee Little People, to create a framework for the conflict among three families who founded rice plantations and an enslaved family with both African and American Indian heritage with whom they have all lived side by side since 1692. All of that is meant to bring in some questions about the forgotten history and the misconceptions that I didn't question nearly enough until I began this series.

In case you are interested in separating fact from fiction, here are a few historical notes, in order of appearance:

Forgotten History and the Fire Carrier

The story of the Fire Carrier is based on the Cherokee stories of the *Atsil'-dihye'gï,* a spirit or witch so dangerous that almost nothing is known about it. But the Fire Carrier is also an ancient term given to a priest who carried coals from the sacred fire in times of war. Exactly when that was is lost along with much of the context for understanding the great history of the Cherokee nation. Prior to the arrival of Europeans, the Cherokee were an agrarian society who lived in towns with streets and public areas. They had a vast trading network, studied and cultivated plants, had extensive medical knowledge, and developed a productive strain of corn similar to that grown today. But they were among the tribes encountered by Spanish captain Pedro de Salaza, who arrived in Beaufort, South Carolina, in 1514; by the French in 1562; and a short time later by Hernando de Soto as he came up from Florida looking for treasure and Native captives to enslave. Shortly thereafter, as with many Native American tribes, their population was decimated by disease, brutal treatment, and displacement from their ancestral homes and sacred places, which devastated their cultures, societies, and the continuity of their historical record.

The *Loyal Jamaica,* Privateering, and the Founding Fathers

The privateer vessel on which Thomas Watson, Robert Beaufort, and John Colesworth arrived in Charles Town (Charleston) in 1692, the *Loyal Jamaica*, was a real ship. Among the actual crew and passengers who were required to provide bail as a guarantee of good behavior on arriving in Charles Town were several men who went on to become prominent merchants and plantation owners in the area. These included Thomas Pinckney, whose son Charles Cotesworth Pinckney was a delegate to the Constitutional Convention and twice ran for president of the new United States. Records differ widely about the *Loyal Jamaica*, about what became of her, and whether the men aboard were privateers or pirates, but at the time, the line between those was very gray. In many ways, the history of the *Loyal Jamaica* is a perfect example of how records disappear, and a study in the possible reasons for the reinterpretation of historical facts.

Borrowing and Sharing among Belief Systems

The Lowcountry area has a unique nexus among European, American Indian, and African American history, belief systems, cultures, and magical systems. African slaves from the Congo and Angola were among the earliest to work the plantations of the Carolinas. Many of them were brought in from the West Indies, where they had already been forced to work for wealthy planters, who then expanded into the new colonies in America. But at the turn of the eighteenth century, 30 to 50 percent of the slaves in the Carolinas were American Indians, and most of those were women and children. Before 1720, more enslaved Native Americans were exported to the West Indies through ports including Boston, Salem, New Orleans, and Charles Town than enslaved Africans were brought into the new Colonies. American Indians built cities and served the households of the northern colonies, and helped scout, lay out, plant, and police the plantations of the South. The botanical and medicinal knowledge of both Native Americans and enslaved African Americans helped save colonists and enslaved populations alike from a variety of diseases.

The tradition of *hoodoo* long practiced in the Lowcountry is based on the concept of borrowing magic and medicine—whatever worked to save body, soul, and spirit—from among the different cultures that shared the area. That tradition, of course, is not unique to *hoodoo*. Cultures have borrowed from each other and evolved from each other for tens of thousands of years.

I've always been fascinated by commonalities in myths and folktales, and stories of Little People all around the world have been one of my most beloved obsessions because they are in so many ways the stories of displacement, the idea of one culture being driven underground by the arrival of another who doesn't value or respect them.

There are stories of Little People in most American Indian traditions, not only among the Cherokee, and because this trilogy is essentially about finding similarities, finding family that is deeper than blood, and building bridges of understanding, I combined physical characteristics from different traditions to bring the *yunwi* to life.

The *Yunwi, Uktena,* and *Ulunsuti* Stones

The stories about the *yunwi* (technically *Yûñwï Tsunsdi'*), the Cherokee Little People, or in some cases tales of other Cherokee immortals, the *Nûñnë'hï* or "People Who Live Anywhere" that I wove together, along with the tales of the *Uktena* and the *ulunsuti* stones that my characters uncover in *Illusion*, including their associations with the sacred places on Pilot Knob in North Carolina or in Blood Mountain, Georgia, are easily found on the Internet and/or recorded in the early twentieth-century collections *Myths of the Cherokee* and *Sacred Formulas of the Cherokee* gathered by James Mooney. How true these versions are to the original stories or how they should be interpreted is known by only a learned few within the Cherokee community. For anyone interested in a great read and a better understanding of how deeply grounded the Cherokee culture is in story, I highly recommend *Cherokee*

Stories of the Turtle Island Liars' Club by Christopher B. Teuton. I am also indebted to and grateful for many conversations, dissertations, documents, and books from Cherokee traditional and academic sources.

Isogenic Lines and Wormholes

The isogenic lines mentioned in *Illusion* are also real. According to the historical magnetic declination viewer on the NOAA website, there was a line that ran roughly from Blood Mountain to the area around Charleston at the time of the French Charlesfort settlement on Paris Island near Beaufort in 1562 and the later Spanish Florida capital there at Santa Elena, which was established under Pedro Menéndez de Avilés in 1566 and abandoned in 1587. Presently, the line runs roughly from Watson Island to Pilot Mountain, North Carolina. There is said to be a large vortex of energy at Pilot Mountain, and another at Stone Mountain, Georgia. Whether magnetic declination or electromagnetic energy has anything to do with vortexes, ley lines, dragon lines, or spirit paths—and how much the reasons why the ancient monuments were built around the world had anything to do with electromagnetic energy at all—is left for readers, believers, skeptics, and scientists to discover and debate.

For the science behind wormholes and such things, Kip Thorne's *The Science of Interstellar* provides a fascinating overview. He was kind enough to specifically recommend Chapters 14 and 15 for my readers who are interested in this, as well as the last chapter of his *Black Holes and Time Warps: Einstein's Outrageous Legacy*. Also, he provided an interesting essay for Stephen and Lucy Hawking's *George and the Big Bang*, which is very easy to understand and well worth reading. I deviated from the (albeit theoretical) physics to suit my story in many ways, but hopefully a few readers may discover that science is far more interesting and far-reaching than anything we can yet imagine.

Eliza Lucas Pinckney, Her Letterbook, and the Forgotten Stories of Women, American Indians, and African Americans

The idea that history is a living thing and a key to the future as well as to the past is the heart of this trilogy. I want readers to be able to see themselves within that history and feel empowered to believe that they are the ones who hold the key to unlock the future. To do that, I wanted to shine more light on the people who are often left out of the historical record of the Lowcountry area, and of the United States in general—women, American Indians, and African Americans. In many ways women had more equal roles in American Indian and African cultures.

The role of women as healers, priests, herbalists, leaders,

and innovators among these cultures in contrast with the erosion of women's rights and the discounting of nonmale accomplishments in European cultures is a fascinating area for further study. The story of Eliza Lucas Pinckney, who at the age of seventeen ran three plantations for her father and founded the American indigo industry—one of the foundations of Colonial wealth—was one of the things that sparked my interest in writing this trilogy. I couldn't help wondering why I had never heard of Eliza when her story was something that might have captured my interest in history class. As I began to delve deeper, I discovered that was only the tip of the iceberg in terms of what I had never heard or learned.

In addition to the legacy of indigo, which not only provided a new cash crop but also got many people out of the deadly rice fields that were rife with mosquitos carrying malaria and yellow fever, Eliza left behind a letterbook that painted one of the most important portraits of a woman in Colonial life. Her writing is a fascinating look at a deeply moral, kind, and thoughtful woman who nevertheless owned slaves. Indeed, her work with indigo, obviously, owed much to the knowledge, guidance, and hard work of the slaves who toiled on her father's plantations. At the same time, for all her accomplishments, Eliza did not technically even own the clothes she wore.

While obviously Eliza Lucas Pinckney did not write

about bindings, Fire Carriers, or *yunwi*, as my Eliza Watson Beaufort does, I have used her letterbook as a pattern piece for the book of letters that helps my characters unravel the mystery at the core of the Watson Island magic. The quirks of capitalization used in my letters are similar to those that were in fashion at the time.

Plantations, Headdresses, and Scalping Trees

Having been raised by an African American ex–drag queen, Barrie believes she is unbiased when she arrives at Watson Island. In fact, she endangers herself by ignoring the warnings of those who know the Colesworth family penchant to break the law simply because she believes people are prejudiced against the family. What she discovers as the series goes on, though, is that bias and prejudice lurk in unexpected places, and that you have to know that bias exists before you can see it. This is not a lesson she can have learned fully in the first book because the entire trilogy takes place in such a relatively short period of time.

Barrie comes to love Watson's Landing and its landscape before she fully understands what slavery meant and the quiet strength and bravery that it took to survive every day under such a brutal system. Even after she understands, she continues to love the plantation because it is her home and the place where her family was raised. As a result of what she has learned, she comes to discover that there are still thirty million slaves in the world today, most of them, like the early Native American slaves in the Carolina colony, women and children.

Similarly, as she works her way through the mystery, she discovers that many of the "facts" accepted by locals and taught to her in her history books are incomplete. Things like blood magic, sacrifice, scalping, paint, and the forms of head-dress and clothing worn by various cultures, not just in the Americas but all around the world, have very specific mean-ings within those cultures, but our views of them are colored by the biased interpretation of those who wrote about them through a conquering and grasping lens. As with scalping, Western culture often adopted and changed what it didn't understand for its own ends and in doing so made it more brutal than it had ever been. I hope that as readers reach the end of the series, they will be surprised at the differences in their own as well as Barrie's perceptions of Watson Island and its inhabitants past and present.

History truly is an illusion. But we each carry within us the magic to cast the future in a better light.

Acknowledgments

Once again, it took more people than I can possibly acknowledge to create *Illusion*. I cannot begin to express my thanks to:

My husband, who continued to be a rock, a foundation, and the best possible partner in life. Thank you for that and for letting me draft you into helping with the coolest part of the research for this book.

My daughter, who made me cry and made me more determined to keep going through the hardest part of the writing by saying that she is proud of me. She continuously makes me proud of her.

My son, who discussed the books with me as if they were written by a regular (real) author. (Which I still can't believe I am.)

Sara Sargent and Jennifer Ung, my utterly lovely editors at Simon Pulse, who answered all my thousands of questions, put up with my incessant revisions, saw the flaws that I didn't see, and helped me make a story out of a collection of semirandom words.

Katherine Devendorf, Bara MacNeill, and Janet Rosenberg for patiently managing the copyediting and proofreading, and making the semirandom words far better and clearer than I could ever make them on my own.

Regina Flath and Hilary Zarycky, for an even better cover and interior book design than any of the already great ones so far.

The entire team at Simon Pulse and Simon & Schuster, who worked so tirelessly to bring this trilogy into the world: Mara Anastas, Mary Marotta, Carolyn Swerdloff, Lucille Rettino, Christina Pecorale, Michelle Leo, Anthony Parisi, Candace Greene, Sara Berko, Jodie Hockensmith, Shifa Kapadwala, Jennifer Romanello, and everyone on the editorial, art, marketing, publicity, sales, and rights teams—I can't begin to offer enough gratitude for all that you have done for me and for these books.

My agent, Jessica Regel at Foundry Media, for her continued support, kindness, smarts, patience, and faith. I count myself lucky to have her in my corner at least once a week.

Erin Cashman, Susan Sipal, and Danielle Ellison, for critiquing no matter how tired or overworked they were. Without their ideas, tireless support, careful reads, patient advice, and enthusiasm I never would have finished this book.

Liza Wiemer and Andye Eppes, for their beautiful souls, friendship, kindness, cheerleading, and the beta reads and smart ideas—not to mention the courage it took to make me go back for another pass.

Andrew Agha, whose patience in explaining cosmograms and their context in plantation archaeology, as well as his help with spiritual and magic systems, ceremonies, archaeology, anthropology, and historical context, and a thousand other plot points, was above and beyond the call. All mistakes and departures are entirely my own fault.

Mikaela Murphy, for helping me make sure that I represented her culture, and for being the best possible kind of careful reader; Steph Sinclair, for helping me look at *Illusion* with eyes beyond my own privileged viewpoint in the hope that it might help build bridges instead of widening gulfs of understanding; and Elizabeth Dobak, for the early and careful read.

The publications of the Cherokee Nation, the Cherokee Heritage Documentation Center, the Lowcountry Digital History Initiative, and the work and/or insight of Susan Marie Abram, Jane Archer, Randy Bancroft, Gretchen M. Bataille, Margaret Bender, John Bierhorst, J. F. Bierlein, Ras Michael Brown, Harold Courlander, R. Duncan, Andrew Denson, S. Barron Frazier, Christopher C. Fennell, Allan Gallay, J. T. Garrett, Michael Tlanusta Garrett, Sharon I. Goad, William Moreau Goins, Sequoyah Guess, Woody Hanson, M. Patrick Hendrix, Alan Kilpatrick, Bobby Lake-Thom, George E. Lankford, Daniel Littlefield, Johannes Loubser, Thomas E. Mails, Susan B. Martinez, Wyatt MacGaffey, Ben Harris McClary, Pedro Mendia-Landa, Gabriel Peoples, Brett Riggs, Hastings Shade, Victoria Smalls, Charles Spencer, Diane Stein, Sammy Still, Christopher B. Teuton, Jonathan B. Thayne, Robert Farris Thompson, Norma Tucker, Michael

J. Wolyniak, Peter Wood, and of course the work of James Mooney and John Howard Payne. I hope that in weaving together this story from the sum of so many parts, I have been able to at least hint at the richness and unique perspective of what each culture brings to universal themes, dreams, and experiences, and that in doing so, I have managed to convey my utmost respect for the history, traditions, and suffering of those upon whose work this great nation was built. Any mistakes are entirely my own.

All the lovely authors who have, once again, patiently taught me so much this year.

Stacey Canova, for being a fabulous assistant and organizing the *Compulsion* paperback tour; Jaime Arnold, for the Heirs of Watson Island Pinterest recipe board, sweet potato mustard, and an amazing blog tour; Hannah McBride, for being generous, lovely, and beyond supportive with a tour that knocked my socks off; and Katie Bartow from Mundie Moms, for once again making me happy cry.

All the librarians, booksellers, bloggers, reviewers, festival organizers, teachers, and readers who have helped spread the word about the trilogy. In addition, I want to offer an enormous thank-you to the teachers and professors who are using the books and learning guides in their classrooms.

My lovely and wonderful street team and inner circle. So many hugs!

The Literary Council of Northern Virginia, for doing amazing and deeply needed work for the people for whom reading will be a life-changing experience, for reminding me that this is the land not only of opportunity but also of kindness, and for your wonderful support for me and these books.

The Virginia Children's Book Festival of 2015, for giving me a weekend to remember why I adore writing a gothic novel, weaving myths and fairy tales, and writing for and about girls and women who are strong in their own ways, even if those aren't necessarily the ways that society in general too often still thinks of strength.

Leila Nebeker and the wonderful staff at One More Page Books, and the incredible NoVa Teen Book Festival staff, for being unfailingly lovely and supportive.

All my marvelous AdventuresInYAPublishing.com and 1st5PagesWritingWorkshop.com partners and mentors past and present. I'm honored to be part of such fantastic resources for writers.

Amber Sweeney, for designing beautiful bookmarks, and Max Kutil, for making them up for readers to enjoy.

And once again, Carol and Cici, for being you and kicking ass.

For book club and curriculum-related bonus material, discussion questions, and additional information on the history and folklore of the Heirs of Watson Island series, please visit the author's website at www.MartinaBoone.com.